Storm Knights

"Greetings, Dr. Hachi, allow me to introduce my-self," the Sim said, bowing from the waist slightly, but never taking his eyes off of Mara. His leering grin revealed yellowed, pointed teeth. Mara looked about her for help, but all of the volunteers were locked in the cybernet and unaware of the happenings in the chamber. She knew that if the Sim had gotten this far, there were no living security guards left behind him.

She was on her own.

"My name is Thratchen. And, I'm afraid, I must ask you to move away from that console."

"Why should I?" asked Mara, stalling for time and hoping to learn something of the Sim's purpose.

"Ah," smiled Thratchen, "because I would like to find out from you, firsthand, how you discovered our plans of invasion. Dr. Kendal was not very cooperative, if you catch my meaning. He actually was able to shut down his mind before I could glean much more than the location of this facility. Remarkable man, really."

"Alec?" Mara screamed in panic. "You hurt Alec, too?"

Thratchen shrugged. "I sorted his mind, my dear. Even if he lives he will be little more than a lump of flesh with no thoughts to speak of. Now, step away from that machine."

Torg
The Possibility Wars

They have come from other cosms, other realities, raiders joined together to accomplish one goal — to steal the awesome energy of Earth's possibilities!

This spectacular epic of adventure, magic, and high technology is set on a reality-torn Earth — an Earth warped into *someplace else*. Don't miss any of the volumes in the Possibility Wars saga!

Book One
Storm Knights
by Bill Slavicsek and C.J. Tramontana

Book Two
The Dark Realm
by Douglas Kaufman

Book Three
The Nightmare Dream
by Jonatha Ariadne Caspian

The Possibility Wars™
created by Greg Gorden and Bill Slavicsek

Book One
Storm Knights
by Bill Slavicsek and C.J. Tramontana

Cover Art by Daniel Horne

Interior Art by Jeff Menges and
Alan Jude Summa

Graphic Design by Bernadette J. Cahill
and Stephen Crane

Series Edited by Bill Slavicsek

STORM KNIGHTS
Book One of the Possibility Wars
A West End Book/May 1990

First Printing: May, 1990.
Printed in the United States of America.

0 9 8 7 6 5 4 3 2 1

Library of Congress Catalog Card Number: 90-70244
ISBN: 0-87431-301-5

West End Games
RD3 Box 2345
Honesdale, PA 18431

To Scott, Denise, and Rich for giving us the chance to create a new world.

And to the rest of the Torg design team — Greg Gorden, Doug Kaufman, Chris Kubasik, Ray Winninger, Jonatha Caspian, Mike Stern and Paul Murphy — because they made it all come together.

Prologue: The Near Now

Later today, early tomorrow,
sometime next week,
the world began to end …

When *they* chased you, you ran. And if you were a step too slow, or if you twisted an ankle and went sprawling in the hot sand, then you were dead.

Correction. If *they* chased you, you were dead already. It was only a matter of time before your heart stopped pumping and your blood ran red to stain the ground where you fell.

The young man with the light brown skin knew none of this. He simply ran. Faster and faster beneath the gathering clouds until his side hurt and his chest pounded. He had no thought as to where he was running to, just as long as it was away. Away from the horror behind him, away from the atrocity that his mind wished it had never seen.

He ran until each stride sent waves of pain through his body. And still he kept moving, although now the run became a trot. Then a fast walk. Then a shuffle. And then the young man had to stop. Only for a moment, he told himself as he collapsed in the sand. Just to catch his breath.

His eyes closed as exhaustion overtook him. After running most of the night and through the early morning, even fear could not keep it at bay. So, in the hot sand, under the hot sun, mere yards from the lapping waves, the young man slept. He didn't notice the passing minutes, didn't stir as the dark clouds moved in and blocked out the sun. He never heard the terrible wings that flapped closer, never felt the foul breeze of their approach.

But he felt the weight that pressed down on his back, and that jarred him back to consciousness. The young man opened his eyes and tried to rise, but the weight held him fast. He could hear heavy breathing above him, could smell a foul stench that burned its way up his nose and into his lungs. He coughed and his eyes watered. As the young man blinked away his tears, he saw a figure approaching from out of the jungle.

The figure was tall, gaunt, skeleton thin. From the young man's angle, looking up from the sand and through watering eyes, the figure appeared exaggerated, as though seen in a fun house mirror. The figure wore a long black coat and a tall black hat, but seemed unaffected by the humid heat. A shoulder cape billowed as he strode forward, casually swinging an ornate walking cane. His crisp steps stopped a few feet from the young man's face, a face which was reflected in the figure's shiny black boots.

The tall figure knelt down, resting his cane across his knees. He smiled at the young man, and his gaunt features stretched even thinner, revealing a skeletal visage beneath the broad rim of his hat.

"You led us on a merry chase, young man," the Gaunt Man said, speaking clearly in the young man's language. At least, the young man heard it as his language. "But like all stormers, you became tired, careless. Never any real challenge at all, you must admit."

"Let me up and I'll show you a challenge, thin man!" the young man said, forgetting his fear for a moment.

The weight on the young man's back pressed down, and something sharp and pointed cut through his shirt and pierced the surface of his skin. He bit back a scream of pain, trying to ignore the hot stickiness spreading across his back.

"No, my pet, not yet," cautioned the Gaunt Man as he rose to his full height.

He turned in place with his arms outstretched, taking in great gulps of air. "Smell the possibilities in the air!" the Gaunt Man exclaimed. "Oh, this world is rich! I have chosen well this time, my pet, very well indeed."

Then he spun again, and his visage changed. Anger filled his cold eyes, and for a moment the young man saw that his finery was ragged and moth eaten. But then the head of his cane was shoved toward the young man's face.

"What should I do with you, stormer?" the Gaunt Man asked. The cane twirled dangerously close, and the young man could see the carved dragon head spinning before his eyes. The dragon held something firmly in its toothy maw, a strange and beautiful gem of some sort, filled with swirls of blue and red. Then the Gaunt Man pulled it away, and his finery was perfect again. "Perhaps the machine would suit you, stormer. Yes, the machine."

"What are you afraid of, thin man?" asked the young man. "Do I scare you?"

The Gaunt Man did not answer. He simply stepped back and smashed his cane into the sand.

Then the weight on the young man's back shifted and he felt the claws. Sharp, tearing, eager claws. His eyes snapped wide when the ripping began, full of fear and pain and light. He noticed, rather detachedly, that a bright splash of red stained the Gaunt Man's polished black boots.

The light in the stormer's eyes faded slowly as the rain began to fall. But the ripping continued for a long, long time.

Gather the Clouds

I watched the dark clouds gather
I saw them fill the sky
I felt the waves of thunder
The lightning didn't lie ...

> — Eddie Paragon

There isn't always a silver lining hiding behind a dark cloud. Sometimes what's back there is much, much worse.

> — Quin Sebastian

1

In his third-floor, walk-up apartment on Flatbush Avenue, Mario Docelli cursed loudly. He looked out the window at the darkening sky. There was a storm coming, no doubt about it. But maybe it would have the common courtesy to wait until the ball game was over. No way, he decided. The storm clouds were so black that it was like night outside. Great! On Opening Day, too!

He flipped on his radio and hunted for the all-news station, hoping for a weather report. He twisted the dial this way and that, fighting to hear through the static. Damn, the static was bad today!

"... around the world ... with Indonesia ..."

That's it, Docelli thought, tuning in the reporter's voice as best he could.

"Repeating our lead story, all communications with Indonesia have ceased," said the calm news voice coming out of Docelli's radio. "An American satellite tracking station noted the occurrence quietly, expecting communications to resume after IndoCon Sat Three was realigned. But now other countries are reporting that the satellite is working perfectly, or it would be if there were any signals for it to relay. As far as radio waves, phone lines, microwaves, and all forms of electronic communication are concerned, Bali has ceased to exist. As have Sumatra, Java, Borneo, Celebes, the Moluccas and all of the islands of the Malay Archipelago. We switch now to Arthur Cross in Australia. Arthur ..."

A new voice spoke from the radio. "No messages blurted from fax machines this morning. No radio or television signals bounced off orbiting satellites. Nothing was transmitted from the part of the world we call

Indonesia except ominous silence ..."

"Who cares," Docelli said angrily as he switched off the radio. "You can't even get a decent weather report in this town anymore. Ah, maybe they'll get in a couple of innings at least."

Docelli opened a can of beer, cradled a bowl of popcorn in his left arm, and sat in his favorite chair. He hunted momentarily for the remote, found it on the chair cushion beneath him, and aimed it at the silent television.

"Let's play ball," he whispered as he pointed and clicked the remote, bringing the television to life.

2

Police Officer Rick Alder would remember Opening Day for the rest of his life. The moment was caught in his mind like some foul taste that couldn't be rinsed away. He was assigned to crowd control duty outside Shea Stadium, on his horse direct from the police stables in New York's Flushing Meadows Park.

Overhead, the sky was growing increasingly darker as it filled with bloated black clouds. Alder was certain that he would be drenched before the day was out, and had even looked forward to a light turn out for the game. But no such luck; the fans were filing in by the thousands, an almost endless line of bodies flowing down from the Number Seven line and out of the filled parking lots. They were all here to watch Walter "The Truth" Jones throw the first pitch of the new baseball season, to witness David "Sky-High" Glass belt his first homerun. And while Officer Alder loved the Mets as much as the next New Yorker, he would much rather be at home with the millions of other fans, watching from the comfort of his home with a cold beer in one hand and a hot dog in the other, than atop a horse in a sea of excited humanity.

Inside the stadium, Alder could hear the grandstands fill to capacity. It was a sound like no other, loud, a constant murmur welling toward an explosion that would accompany the introduction of the home team.

Overhead, a bolt of lightning cut the sky. Beneath him, Alder's horse became skittish, and it took more effort than usual to control the animal. As a matter of fact, the horse had been tense all day, as though it sensed the coming storm. "Hang on, Simone," he whispered soothingly, "those clouds scare me, too."

Alder tried to turn his attention back to the stadium and its familiar noises. He could hear the vendors as they moved through the packed tiers and rows, each hawking his wares in his own special way. Some were showmen, flamboyantly tossing their bags of peanuts and good naturedly rushing the passage of crumpled, sweaty dollar bills as they were passed from hand to hand, from buyer to seller. Some were clowns, dispensing banter and beer with a flip turn of phrase and filled paper cup. Some were priests, solemnly handing out the mustard-splashed hot dog sacraments of this American rite of spring. Some just wanted to do their jobs and go home. Alder smiled. He could identify with that sentiment.

The police officer navigated his mount toward the open portion of the stadium. From there he could look over the fence and see the crowds. He was too far away to see more than a sea of milling, swaying bodies, but he imagined the fans smiling and waving, jostling and joking. He imagined them sweating in the afternoon humidity, just as he was, waiting for the game to start.

The energy was tangible, and even from his spot

outside, Alder felt the almost-religious fervor. He knew by the subtle change in the roar that the guest singer was walking out to perform the National Anthem. It was that young rock star Eddie Paragon, teen idol and music video superstar. The crowd cheered, then momentarily calmed and quieted as Paragon stepped up to the microphone half way between home plate and the pitcher's mound. There was a pause, and Alder imagined the young man scanning the crowd. Then he began to sing. Alder listened as Paragon's rich voice echoed from the stadium loud speakers, proclaiming the virtues of our star-spangled banner. He ended well, perhaps better than most, on those high, awkward notes that are such an integral part of the anthem. Then the roar of the crowd resumed, louder, more frenzied than before. It was crazy, it was exciting, and Alder could feel himself getting caught up in the moment.

A pretzel vendor who Alder knew by sight moved his cart closer. He nodded to Alder as he adjusted the volume on his radio. An announcer's voice emerged from the tiny black box hanging from the cart's umbrella, describing the scene at Shea. "Here they come," the radio announced, "the New York Mets!"

Now the crowd was standing and cheering, welcoming the home team to another great season. But Alder wasn't listening anymore. He was watching the sky. The clouds directly over the stadium were crackling with flashes of lightning, jagged streaks of white slashing through the blackness. "My God," said the pretzel vendor, "what's happening? Come on, man! Tell me what's happening!"

The horse paced nervously, but Alder didn't notice. Suddenly he was seeing two separate events that were occurring simultaneously. His eyes were watching the sky, fixed on the boiling clouds and lightning. His mind was imagining the scene in the stadium, forming pictures from the radio announcer's words.

He saw the clouds swirl as the wind picked up.

He heard the stands rock with thunderous applause as Walter "The Truth" Jones stepped to the mound.

He saw the fear reflected in the pretzel vendor's eyes as a bolt of lightning cracked the sky.

He heard the thunderous hush as The Truth's arm pulled back. He felt every eye turn to watch as The Truth's leg kicked up. The first pitch of the new season was about to be thrown, full of all the promise and anticipation of the new baseball season.

Full of possibility.

Alder watched, in fascination, as something moved behind the clouds. Something *was* coming.

"And here's the pitch," screamed the announcer, "it's a rocket heading on a straight course for Salter's outstretched glove! What a fastball! What a pit ..."

Suddenly the dark clouds erupted, spewing forth a wave of crackling energy that rained down around the stadium for as far as Alder could see. Inside Shea, the ball never reached the plate. Outside, the radio announcer never finished his sentence. The radio abruptly stopped broadcasting, the lights in Shea snapped off, and even Alder's walkie talkie stopped squawking. Alder barely noticed, though, because the clouds were still rumbling. They parted then, and a ... hole opened in the sky. That was the only way the police officer could describe it. A hole! And in that hole, an even more terrible storm whirled.

The horse was trotting away from the stadium, snorting and neighing its protest to the unnatural events. Alder did not try to control her trek. His attention was locked on the events occurring overhead.

With a powerful clap of thunder and a display of lightning, something fell from the sky. It dropped onto Shea Stadium, crushing a huge section of the facility and the crowded parking lot beyond into rubble. It was a twisting, living mass of greens and browns, more than half a mile across, a fairy tale beanstalk formed from a gigantic, impossible jungle. Had it fallen at a different angle, had it missed its mark by a dozen yards, Alder would have been crushed too.

The beanstalk arced broadly upward, a growing, ladder of cable-thick vines, broad, man-sized leaves, and impossibly long, sharp thorns. Massive, it curved upward past the edge of visibility, back into the dark clouds. The horse was picking up speed now, and Alder tightened his grip unawares. He could not look away from the ruins of Shea Stadium.

How many were dead in there, he wondered. But the scene had not really registered in his mind yet, so he only watched.

Next, from the hole in the sky, another wave of swirling energy swept down the beanstalk and exploded over what remained of the stadium. Then it rolled out in all directions, smashing into Alder and his horse and sending them sprawling. Pain wracked the officer, but he was able to raise his head and watch as the spectacle continued.

Down through the thick growth marched, crawled, slithered, hunched, and flapped a terrible assortment of creatures. It took a moment to register, but Alder recognized these beasts. They were dinosaurs and other prehistoric monsters, or at least someone's warped version of such — including those that walked on two legs and carried spears and other weapons. They covered the top of the jungle beanstalk completely, an unending stream of monsters moving down from the storm and into Shea. They walked upon the growing pathway, standing perpendicular to its broad expanse. Unlike the fairy tale beanstalk, this was not a ladder. It was more a bridge, connecting Earth to ... someplace else.

Alder could not see into the stadium, but he heard the screams. Whoever that bridge did not kill when it smashed to the ground, the creatures dispatched — swiftly, and from the dying sounds, with no remorse.

Giant serpents that stretched over thirty feet slithered down the jungle bridge, their green and brown scales rippling as they moved. Small feathered lizards leaped from branch to branch. Four-legged beasts with tentacled snouts pushed through the twisting vines. And an odd assortment of almost-creatures rushed down into Shea. Almost, because while they resembled the dinosaur toys Alder played with as a boy, there were startling differences.

There was an almost-Tyrannosaurous Rex with large Godzilla spikes jutting from its back. There an almost-Paleoscincus with three thorny tails smashed through the overgrowth. And there an almost-Allosaurus flapped its great wings and swooped toward the ground.

Alder struggled to his feet. He had his service revolver, his radio, his nightstick, and for a moment he contemplated some desperate action. But then he saw the stream of monsters part, making way for an almost-Triceratops. The large, one-horned monster reminded the police officer of the three-horned dinosaur with the armor-plated head he had loved as a child. But there were important differences, not the least of which was the large dinosaur man riding its back and the single horn jutting from its head.

That dinosaur man was the leader, Alder knew. He felt it in his gut. And nothing that Police Officer Rick Alder could do against that being would be enough to save the people inside Shea.

Simone had remained nearby when Alder had fallen. The officer assumed that with all the craziness going on around him, the horse had decided to focus on something familiar. Like the guy in blue who took her for a ride every now and then, and gave her sugar cubes. So Alder struggled back into the saddle, trying to ignore the pain in his right knee. Then, without a look back, Alder and his horse rode off.

They only galloped for a few seconds when the sky opened again and the rain fell. Alder noted wryly that the storm was as bad as he imagined it was going to be.

He didn't know that the storm was just beginning.

And it was going to get much worse.

3

Christopher Bryce pulled the collar of his coat tight around his neck. For a spring day, it felt like late fall. The sky was gray and a chill wind whipped down the quiet streets of Queens. All he needed, on top of everything else, was to catch a cold while taking a stroll.

He walked on, no real destination in mind. His physical actions were a reflection of his mental processes; as his mind wandered, so did his feet. He found himself in a shopping area, one of those neighborhoods in the boroughs of New York that were trying to appeal to Manhattanites who didn't want to — or couldn't afford to — live in Manhattan anymore. Bryce stopped at a bookstore window out of habit, glancing to see what was on display.

What he saw was his own reflection.

His bulbous nose and red beard were visible beneath his Totes hat. His coat collar had slipped open again, revealing the white of his priestly collar. Thirty-four years old, Bryce thought, and my face carries a mark for every year. He clasped the collar of his secular outerwear, covering up the evidence of his priestly calling.

Calling, Bryce thought as he gazed at his unimposing reflection. What did "calling" really mean, he wondered, and would he ever get an answer? Wasn't that the crux of his problems?

Bryce turned to go when a book cover caught his eye. It was a book on Arthurian legends, all about King Arthur and his Knights of the Round Table. The illustration on the cover was of a regal Arthur, decked out in his finest armor, his mailed hands resting on Excalibur's mighty pommel. Such a simpler time, when knights battled for chivilry and honor. In those days, you knew the good guys from the bad.

A bolt of lightning illuminated the sky, startling Bryce. The rain was going to begin falling soon, and the priest did not want to get caught in the open. He resumed his walk, hurrying to beat the storm.

He would never make it.

As he hurried through the streets, Bryce continued his private reverie. He was currently on leave, back home visiting his parents, as he awaited his next assignment. His missionary work as a Jesuit priest had taken him to Australia, the Middle East, and Europe over the years. He, like the knights in the bookstore window, followed vows. Only Bryce's were vows of poverty, chastity and obedience. His was the duty to act upon any command the Holy Father put to him, to work for the glory of God and defend the Roman Catholic faith from heresy, to educate the young.

But recently he had begun to doubt certain things, not the least of which was his role in the Great Plan. Recently? No, not recently. Bryce's doubts started back in college, at Loyola, and later at Georgetown. They followed him through every foreign country, forcing him to seek answers to unasked questions. But answers, if there were any, always eluded him.

In a few days he would get called back for a new assignment. He was sure that, instead, he would ask to leave the order. Perhaps on his own he could discover the true meanings behind those areas that most fascinated him — and frightened him.

He was still quite a number of blocks from his parents' house when a wave of energy rippled through the streets. Bryce turned to watch as the glowing wave rolled down the block. As it passed, store lights snapped off, car engines died. The wave hit Bryce and threw him to the ground. Before he could pull himself up, large drops of rain began to splatter the sidewalk.

In a matter of moments, Father Christopher Bryce was soaked to the bone.

4

In his walk-up apartment on Flatbush Avenue, Mario Docelli snarled one last brutal snarl at the television as he kicked in its picture tube. The TV, the lights, the digital clock in the radio — everything had stopped working at once. And the storm had finally broken outside, dropping huge amounts of dark rain onto the Earth.

So much for the ball game, Docelli grunted.

He flung his window up and stuck his head out into the rain. The foul water soaked his head, plastering his hair to his skull. He roared at the elements, not even aware that only minutes before he would never have done such a thing.

Docelli turned to look in the direction of Shea Stadium and saw the jungle bridge. It appeared to drop straight out of the storm itself, one end lost behind houses, buildings and other obstructions, the other end hanging in the sky. He wasn't sure what it was, but it was calling to him, touching some primal place in his soul.

Docelli walked down the three flights of stairs and out into the street. As he made his way past stalled cars and screaming people, Docelli changed. His shoulders hunched, his jaw thrust forward, and his knees bent as his shambling, knuckle-dragging walk carried him toward the ruins of Shea.

5

"... ashes to ashes, dust to dust. Amen."

Andrew Jackson Decker let the rose fall from his hand into the hole. He watched it drift down, a burst of red against the black of the hole, the gray of the day. Then the dirt was shoveled in, and the crowd started to depart. Most paid their final respects, heads bowed as they repeated some words of comfort to Decker, then moved on.

That was the way of the world. Live, die, but life goes on. Decker felt the crumpled paper in his suit pocket and pulled it out. It was a telegram, from President Douglas Kent, expressing his sorrow over the loss of Victoria Decker and regretting that he could not attend the funeral in person. Decker let the telegram go. He didn't notice which way the wind took it.

"Ace?" Decker looked up. Standing beside him was

Jonathan Wells, Speaker of the House. He was one of the few people who remembered Decker's old nickname, and one of the few that still used it. "Come on, congressman," Wells said, "you'll have time to mourn later. Right now we have to go."

"Go?" Decker asked. "I have to go home. There are people waiting and ..."

Wells gripped Decker's arm firmly. "Ace, I know what you must be feeling right now. Vicky was a wonderful woman, I'm not denying that. But we have an incident. There is going to be a special session of both Houses to discuss it in half an hour."

"Incident? John, what are you talking about?"

Wells looked up at the taller, younger congressman from Pennsylvania. "New York has been ... well, we're not sure what. Terrorists, a foreign power, youth gangs, a simple blackout, we just don't know. All communications have ceased over a rather large area of the northeastern United States, including portions of your constituency. Ace, the President and Vice President are in New York. We ... have no word yet on their condition."

A possible attack on the United States? The top elected officials in danger? Decker couldn't focus on the concepts. It was unthinkable, unreal. "I don't understand ..."

"Neither do I, Ace," said Wells. "But they need us to figure it out and decide what to do before someone else makes a terrible mistake."

Decker nodded. "All right, John, all right. Just give me a second, okay?"

John Wells smiled reassuringly. "Take two, Ace. Then we've got to go."

6

Bryce ran through the rain-slick streets, slipping and sliding but never quite losing his balance. He didn't know what was happening, but if this was the end of the world, he wanted to spend the last moments before the Judgment with his parents. He splashed through deep puddles and sped past men and women who were acting more like animals than people. Finally, after an eternity of running, he turned onto the tree-lined street where he grew up.

And Christopher Bryce, ordained priest of the order of the Society of Jesus, went insane. That was the only rational explanation his mind would accept.

The houses on the street were demolished. It reminded the priest of news footage taken after earthquakes or bombings. But no force of nature or man did this. The creatures responsible were certifiably demonic.

The largest of the beasts were the pair of armored lizards, each roughly twice the size of a tank. Their heavy-plated shells were covered with sharp spines, and each had three spiked tails that swung back and forth to smash houses and telephone poles.

Directing the monsters — yes, directing them, Bryce was certain of that — were six demons. They were reminiscent of lizards, but very tall and muscular, much broader than men, and they stood on two legs. One rode on the back of each armored monster, driving them forward with strangely-shaped staves. The others followed after them, dragging their long lizard tails behind them.

As Bryce watched, the first of the great beasts smashed into his parents' home, knocking it apart as though it were made of match sticks. At the same moment, the second armored monster crashed into Saint Ignatius, the church and school across from the house where young Chris Bryce spent so many years learning and growing up. The sight of both memories collapsing beneath the weight of creatures from hell was more than Bryce could take.

"No!" he screamed, raising his voice above the sound of the falling rain. "Nooo!"

The four walking lizard men turned in response. Now Bryce could see the oddly-formed clubs they wielded. He could see their rain-slicked green scales. Worse, he could stare into their yellow eyes. The closest lizard rocked back on its long tail. It pointed its club at Bryce, and the priest saw that the club still had leaves and roots. Did the lizard simply pluck some strange plant from the ground to use as a weapon? Bryce doubted that even the smallest of the lizard men, who stood over six-feet tall, needed any sort of weapon to rip the short priest to pieces.

Then, an amazing thing occurred. The lizard, still resting on its tail and pointing its club, opened its tooth-filled, beaklike jaws wide, and screamed, "Ssstormer!"

If he were mad, Bryce reasoned, he could stand here with no worry. These horrifying figments of his ill imagination would fade away even as they reached out to touch him. If he were mad.

Father Christopher Bryce turned and ran blindly into the storm.

7

Rick Alder watched the dinosaur men set up a crude camp at the base of the tram station, on the Manhattan side of the 59th Street Bridge. They covered the street and stretched back across the bridge, a seemingly un-ending stream of upright lizards. The entire mass of creatures rocked back on their long tails, excitedly gyrating their lizard bodies and chanting a hissing, raspy hymn.

They seemed to be celebrating. The lizards were having a party, for God's sake!

Alder moved away from the window and backed into the darkened room. He was in an office, somewhere on the sixth floor of a building overlooking the tramway. He remembered when they put the tram up. It must have been over ten years ago, when Alder was still in high school. It was such a big deal then, a fancy cable car to connect Manhattan with Roosevelt Island. He even remembered riding it back then, waiting on line with the others just to travel back and forth to a little island between two boroughs. But that was the old world. Alder didn't understand what was happening now, but he was sure that the old world was over, its items put away for another time.

He settled down on the floor, his back against the wall so that he could watch the door. The police officer was lucky to make it into Manhattan ahead of the dinosaurs. They moved fast for big creatures, quickly spreading out from Shea. He would have made it farther if his horse hadn't gone lame on him.

Poor Simone saved his life back in Queens, galloping away from the jungle bridge while Alder merely watched in dread and fascination. But he had to leave her on the 59th Street Bridge after her hoof caught in a broken patch of grating. The horse went down hard, and he was lucky to escape without further injury to his knee.

He unconsciously rubbed it as he remembered, trying to force the pain away with his hand.

It was starting to get dark by that time, and he was wet and miserable from the constant rain. It was either find a place to hole up or try to make it through the dark on foot, with the dinosaurs right behind him.

He decided to hole up.

This building was perfect. It was apparently empty when he arrived, and he had found no evidence of occupation since. Also, it overlooked the bridge. Alder figured it would be prudent to watch the monsters and try to find out all he could about them. His survival might depend on such information.

A quick check revealed that he still had his utility belt and its accouterments, including his service revolver, flashlight and nightstick. His watch, a black Seiko with gold hatch marks, told him it was ten minutes to seven. He tried his walkie talkie again, but all that came over the speaker was static. He let the box drop to the floor and tipped his head back. In moments he was nodding off, sleep finally claiming his tired body and mind.

But a new sound forced his eyes open. He quickly became alert and listened. The chanting outside had changed. It was more excited than before, if possible, more intense.

Alder crawled back to the window and peered outside. It was darker now, and the rain made it even harder to see, but there was light down in the alien camp. Glowing balls of fire hung in the air throughout the camp, providing enough light to see by.

The camp had grown. Now giant starfish floated over the crowd. The creatures were strikingly beautiful, as though made of stained glass, and the light caused them to sparkle as they moved. In addition, humans were now part of the camp, singing and gyrating with the lizards as though they belonged to the alien festivities. What few details he could make out startled the police officer. The people appeared more brutal, more ... primitive, than your average New Yorker. What clothing they still possessed was in tatters, plastered to their bodies by grime and rain. Alder watched, and for a moment he almost wanted to go down there, to throw off the chains of civilization and run naked through the rain. He had to concentrate to push the image out of his brain.

Suddenly the crowd parted to allow a new addition to emerge from the bridge. It was the great one-horned beast Alder had seen earler, and atop it was the huge lizard man who seemed to command these masses. The lizard man raised his clawed hand high into the air and the crowd went wild. Lizard and starfish and human alike responded with frenzied dancing and shouts of raw emotion. It was so … primal.

Alder felt his blood pumping and his heart racing. It was like being at a rock concert, only ten times — no, a thousand times — more intense. Even if you didn't like the music, you couldn't help getting caught up in the emotions. He could feel himself moving with the crowd, bopping to the primitive beat the lizard camp was keeping. He wanted to raise his voice, to join their exhilirating song. The scene was so … real.

The great lizard man reached behind his massive bulk and pulled a young woman to the forefront. Alder realized that she must have been sitting there the whole time. She was as human as any young woman the police officer had ever seen. She wore what remained of a Mets sweatshirt and jeans, but her clothes were in no way comparable to the humans' in the crowd. Hers still resembled clothing. She tried to struggle, but her strength was nothing compared to the lizard man.

Alder could not stop his swaying body, could not draw his eyes away from the scene in the street below. The tension was almost sexual.

Storm Knights

Alan Jude Summa

The lizard man lifted the young woman high above his head, turning her so the crowd could see. Even in such a precarious position, she continued to fight and squirm. This only made the crowd more agitated, and they danced faster in their lizard way. Even the humans among them swished non-existent tails in time with the frenzied beat.

Alder kept time in his darkened window, letting his body respond as it wished. He watched the young woman battle with all her strength, and a part of his mind admired her defiance. But his body simply shook, vibrating while he stood in place. Then the woman's struggle ceased.

With a roar, the great lizard man pulled the woman apart with one mighty snap and raised his snout to catch her raining blood. The crowd went wild, and total pandemonium took the streets.

Alder stopped moving, his mind shocked back to who he was and what was happening. The silent numbness became silent rage, and the officer found that he hated the lizards and their leader. Hated what they were and what they did. Hated what they did to him. He would make them pay for that woman's blood. He swore it there in a darkened sixth floor office on 60th Street.

He watched into the night, until the crowd finally collapsed in exhausted, exhilarated sleep.

8

Purposefully, Christopher Bryce moved from shadow to shadow, carefully avoiding the ruins that littered the darkened street. He had been running since that awful moment this afternoon when the demon spoke to him. He was wet and tired and angry, but his delusions of madness were gone. At least, if he had gone mad, then the world had gone with him.

His running brought him back to his home, the place where he grew up. It was simple enough to lose the demons, as he was faster than they were. Still, they gave him a good chase, not stopping until he finally lost them in the maze of streets and alleys he had once navigated as a child. But they were persistent, and for all the priest knew they were still searching for him.

The house was shattered. The giant, armored lizards had done a thorough job. But before he could move on, Christopher Bryce had to discover the fate of his parents. He owed them that much. He stepped carefully into the wreckage. By habit he had entered by that section which was once the front porch. Now it was timber.

As he dug his way through the debris, a glint of brass caught his eye. He went over to it, and saw that it was his mass kit. His mother had given the mass kit to him as a gift when he completed seminary. It was a black bag, much like a doctor's bag, which held the sacraments of his station. He never had the heart to tell his mother that the course he had chosen didn't call for him to administer mass very often, as he wasn't going to be assigned to a parish. But he had it filled anyway, and carried it with him from missionary post to missionary post. And, to his surprise, he found that he would celebrate the mass more often than he had imagined.

He reached down to pull the kit from the debris. The case was heavy, a familiar weight in an unfamiliar time. He wiped the dirt from the brass name plate. Christopher Bryce, S.J., the plate read. Christopher, he thought. Christ bearer. Perhaps his parents had been prophetic when they gave him the name at his christening. They were perfect parents, his father once told him, whose only imperfection was their children. Bryce never understood exactly what the old man meant, and he never really wanted to. For all of their idiosyncracies, he loved them dearly.

He placed the mass kit on the side and continued his search. He found his parents thirty minutes later, crushed beneath a roof beam. They weren't buried under tons of rubble as he had expected. They were both killed by the same heavy wooden beam, their bodies exposed to the rain.

That would never do.

Bryce spent the next few hours pulling his parents' bodies from the wreckage of the home they loved. He carried them across the street, one at a time, into the ruins of St. Ignatius. Part of the church still stood, one wall and part of the steeple, providing some protection from the unending downpour.

The priest retrieved his mass kit and administered last rites for his parents. He performed the duties of his calling with loving care. Then, with reverence, he buried them in the best tomb available, using the consecrated stones of the ruined church to form their final resting place.

"Goodbye, mom, dad," Bryce whispered to the stones. He placed a kiss atop the cairn, then wiped at his teary eyes. He stood there watching the burial cairn for a long time.

9

"Dr. Hachi Mara-Two reports on her theory of the cosmverse to the General Council of the Academy of Sciences ..."

Mara, she thought as the images started to fill her

mind. Call me Mara.

"Cosm. A dimension where a particular set of laws holds sway. A specific reality that can be quite different from another reality."

Mara listened to her own voice explain the theory she had set forth to the Academy of Sciences two years ago. It was just after her fourteenth birthday, and the General Council dismissed her findings as the rantings of a young girl. A very gifted genius, they admitted, but a young girl nonetheless.

"Our own cosm is just one of a multitude of dimensions that, together, form what I refer to as the cosmverse. As our own universe contains the whole of our reality, the cosmverse contains the whole of all realities. And what is possible here, using our laws of science, might not be possible in another cosm, where a completely different set of laws govern the workings of their world."

Mara adjusted the clarity of the input, reflexively checking the cable that led from her skull jack to the main terminal. Oh, they were impressed when the prodigy graduated from college at age ten. They clapped ceaselessly when she received a Ph.D. in physics at age twelve. And they almost wet themselves with joy when the child genius received her second Ph.D — this one in microengineering — one year later. But when their prodigy, their trained seal, proposed something real, something that shook the status quo, they simply dismissed her.

"My findings also suggest that these cosms can be connected, allowing us to travel to another dimension for exploration, to make contact, whatever we deem appropriate. But there is a flipside to my findings. As we can travel to another cosm, the inhabitants of another cosm can travel here, to our reality."

The young woman unplugged herself from the terminal and took a deep breath. She had examined her research records backwards and forwards, over and over again. Always her conclusion was the same. The invasion had been her fault. She was to blame for all the death and destruction, and it was about to happen again.

10

In the early hours just prior to dawn, Christopher Bryce found himself walking toward the familiar skyline across the water. He had made good progress throughout the night, as most of the monsters were resting. He passed close to their make-shift camps, but few stirred. A few times he heard things shambling around in the dark, just out of sight. He kept walking when such sounds assaulted him, moving forward with hardly a glance back.

But as the dark sky began to brighten toward gray, more and more of the creatures started to become active again. What was worse, the closer he got to the 59th Street Bridge, the more of the lizard men he encountered. They were migrating across the bridge, and he was sure he would never make it to the other side through that unending mass.

There might be another way, however, Bryce thought. He reached into his pocket and pulled out a fist full of change.

"I even have a token," the priest said softly. He chuckled as he stepped down into the darkness of the subway station.

There were no lights in the underground facility, so Bryce had to go slowly. He felt his way along the tiled wall with one hand; the other held fast to his mass kit.

Since there was no electricity, he reasoned, the tracks should be safe to navigate. If he didn't step wrong and twist an ankle. If he didn't meet up with any of the dinosaurs. If he didn't run into a mugger. He laughed again, and immediately regretted the loud outburst.

Bryce paused to listen, but he heard nothing near by. There were far away echoes, but those sounds could be anything, coming from above or below ground. After another moment of rest, Bryce pressed on into the darkness. At least it wasn't raining down here, the priest thought.

He made his way slowly to the token booth and took a few deep breaths. It smelled of decade-old sweat and urine in the confines of the subway station, and the smell made Bryce gag. He suppressed a coughing fit, settled himself, then searched for the turnstile.

"Never let it be said that Christopher Bryce doesn't pay his own way," the priest said as he deposited the token into its slot. "Now, there should be another stair-case around here somewhere."

He found the stairs and descended further into the depths of the subway system. One, two, three, he counted as he carefully placed one foot upon a step, then another. Eight, nine, ten. There should only be a few more, he thought. But as he stepped down, something jutted out and caught his leg. Bryce stumbled, flailing into the darkness.

The priest landed hard, but he fell only a few feet. Before he could get to his feet, however, a cold object was pressed to his neck while a thin, sinewy arm wrapped around his chest.

"What're ya doing down here, man?" a young voice asked him. "Don't you know this is our turf?"

"I'm sorry," Bryce said carefully, "but it isn't safe

above ground right now.

"Ain't that the truth, huh Coyote?" a second voice called out of the dark.

"Be quiet, Rat," answered the first voice. "Let's have some light."

A torch flared to life, illuminating a small section of the platform. Holding a baseball bat with burning rags wrapped around its top was a small teenager. He might have been all of fourteen, dressed in denim and sneakers. The older youth, perhaps sixteen years of age, stepped back from Bryce, but he kept his switchblade drawn. He was dressed in a similar fashion to the younger boy he called Rat, but he wore more leather.

"What's in the bag, man?" Coyote asked as he reached for the fallen mass kit. "You a doctor or something, man?"

"Please, I need that," Bryce protested. He reached for the black bag as well, his coat falling open as he moved.

"Holy shit, Coyote," Rat blurted, "the guy's a priest!"

Coyote's open hand slashed out, slapping Rat across the cheek. "I told you to watch your language, didn't I?"

Bryce stepped forward, but Coyote's blade shot up. The priest stopped, watching the fire light glint off the sharpened steel.

"Are you a priest, man? Are you?

Bryce nodded. "Yes. My name is Christopher Bryce."

"Father Bryce, huh? Tell us, Father Bryce, is this the end of the world? Is this like Apoklips Now?"

"Apocalypse. It's pronounced Apocalypse. And I don't know what's happening."

"Where ya going, Father. Where ya trying to get to?"

"To Penn Station. From there I'll try to get through the Lincoln Tunnel and over into Jersey. Maybe the lizard men haven't gotten that far. Maybe the army has contained them to Manhattan and Queens."

Rat, still rubbing his cheek, looked up at the older teen. "He'll never find his way by himself." He said the words softly, but his eyes never left Coyote.

"What are you looking at?" Coyote asked, shuffling beneath the younger boy's gaze.

"Are we gonna help the Father, Coyote? Are we?"

There was silence, and Bryce could almost see the thought processes playing across Coyote's face. Were they alone and desperate enough to latch on to a troubled man of the cloth? The teen cleared his throat.

"Yeah, Rat, we're gonna help him," Coyote said, tossing the black bag to the priest. He snapped his switchblade shut.

11

As the sky turned from black to gray, Baruk Kaah rose to greet the new day. What sensations he and his people had experienced already, and the conquest was but one day old! Oh, Lanala would be pleased!

The great lizard man stretched to his full height, working out the kinks of sleep. He surveyed the surrounding camp and watched for a moment as his followers did the same. They are all true Jakatts, my people, worshippers of the Goddess Lanala, Baruk Kaah thought. And how the tribes had grown! There were many of this world's children among his numbers this day. They, like so many others his Holy Jihad had encountered, had come out of their dead existence to embrace the Life that he championed as the First Loved of Lanala.

Baruk Kaah watched the stalenger approach from the corner of his large round eye. It was from another world, a convert to the Life that the Jakatts preached. The star-shaped creature glided silently upon five swept-back arms, spinning gently in the morning air. Its translucent membrane was dark in color, a deep blue-black that reflected its mood. Its news must be grim indeed, thought the lizard man, for it to be so dark. He let the stalenger swoop closer, then let it hover anxiously for a few moments more before he turned to address his servant.

"What news do you bring me," the lizard man asked.

The stalenger uncoiled long, thin tentacles from pouches located on its underside. The tentacles snaked out and gently touched Baruk Kaah's scaled head. It used the tentacles to play a combination of vibrations, rubs and taps upon the scales. In this way it communicated to the lizard man, explaining that emissaries of the Torg had arrived.

The lizard man turned away from the stalenger and strained his neck to see over the crowd. He didn't need to. Standing beside him were three tall beings. Each had a small head atop a long neck, a broad, powerful chest, and long, thin legs. Wings folded around each like dark cloaks, and sharp, pointed teeth jutted from long snouts. But Baruk Kaah was struck by their eyes. They had black, intelligent eyes that hinted of cruelty and worse. The lizard man liked those eyes.

"The Torg sends his welcome, Baruk Kaah, High Lord of the Jakatts and Saar of the Edeinos," said the first of the ravagons.

"He is impressed with the power of your reality and extends his wishes for a successful campaign," added the second.

The third simply stood and watched, his black eyes fixed upon the lizard man.

The High Lord's tail twitched nervously, and he fought to control its movements in front of these outsiders. The Torg, they said. These emissaries claimed to represent a being that did not — and could not — exist.

"The Torg ...?," Baruk Kaah began, but the first ravagon silenced him with a glance.

"Do you deny our master's claim? Do you reject the power of Lord Bryon Salisbury, the Gaunt Man?"

His great tail twitched faster as Baruk Kaah tried to think. He was all-powerful in this reality and could dispatch the ravagons with ease. But he needed the Gaunt Man's power and expertise almost as much as he feared him. His own power was nothing beside the Gaunt Man's, his experience as that of a hatchling to a full-grown warrior. Against such might, even the great Baruk Kaah must bend.

The High Lord of the Jakatts bowed his scaled head. "I ... accept the Gaunt Man's claim."

"Very good," sneered the second ravagon. "We have been ordered to attend to your wishes as servants until such time as the Torg calls us back. Until then, our strength is at your disposal."

Baruk Kaah nodded his understanding. If these great demons were his to command, then he no longer needed to keep up the pretext of diplomacy. And besides, he had a realm to conquer. He climbed atop his faithful udatok, settling his bulk behind its one-horned head. He scanned his camp, which extended in all directions and back toward the maelstrom bridge in what was once Flushing Meadows. Yes, all was going as he planned. All was good. With the added power of three ravagons, he could not fail this raid. He let out a mighty roar, which his followers quickly emulated.

Baruk Kaah, Sarr of Takta Ker, leader of the edeinos, one of the seven trusted High Lords, opened his jaws wide and drank of the falling rain. Then he roared again.

"Onward, edeinos! For Lanala! For Baruk Kaah!"

The ravagons spread their wings and followed the frenzied crowd.

12

Mara checked herself in her lighted mirror. Her mane of silver hair was wild and untamed, in keeping with the current style among people her age. A painted black mask of makeup surrounded her eyes, and her black leather jumpsuit was tight and clinging. She might be a genius, but she was also a teenager.

She moved from her living cubicle into her lab area. Sitting at one of the engineering stations, Mara plugged into the ready computer and lowered her modified eye to the microscope. The data plate was in place, waiting to have more information compressed into its memory circuits.

She accessed a separate memory disk and watched as the coded information jumped from the disk to the data plate. As she watched, she remembered.

"I can't believe those disk errors in the General Council dismissed my findings, Alec," Mara said as she stormed around the apartment.

"Calm down, Mara," Dr. Kendal Alec-Four suggested, "with your enhancements you might break something."

"I want to break something. I want to pound into their heads the importance of my findings."

"Be fair, Mara. Right now all you have are calculations and theories. Yes, I've examined your research and I agree with your conclusions, but the Council won't take you seriously until you have some tangible proof."

"If it's proof they need, then I'll just have to prove it, won't I."

The coded entries continued to flow in a stream of magnetic data, writing themselves into the silver plate as Mara guided them with a skillful hand and computer-enhanced reflexes. She checked the flow of electrons, made a slight adjustment, then went back to her memories.

Mara and her team built a special telescope. It was capable of breaking through the boundaries between the cosms to look at other realities. During one of the recording sessions, Mara's "cosmscope" looked upon a world that was similar to her own. It was one of the similarities that her calculations had suggested, two cosms where the laws of reality overlapped. It was these types of dimensions that were closest to each other, where the boundary of the cosmverse was most fragile.

However, Mara's readings suggested that the similarity was looking back. She took her new findings to the General Council, and they, in turn, took them to the World Council.

This time they listened to Dr. Hachi. Cautiously, the planet Kadandra prepared to meet a new reality. While the World Council hoped that the meeting would be friendly, they insisted on also being ready for any hostilities. That saved Kadandra.

The war that followed lasted only three months. The alien reality broke through the boundary and attached strange bridges to Kadandra. Then, from the other side of those bridges, came the stuff of Kadandra's nightmares.

Mara shivered and halted the process. She ran her right hand through her silver mane, taking a moment to let the memories settle. She flexed the fingers of her left hand, listening to the leather gauntlet stretch as she tightened her fist. She held the gloved hand in front of her face, watching her fingers uncurl. Slowly, carefully, she peeled the gauntlet away. The hand beneath was metallic, shot through with wires and printed circuitry. With a thought, claws snapped from each finger, five sharp points that gleamed in the lab's bright lights.

Just one of Dr. Hachi Mara-Two's reminders of the war against the Sims. Reminders of what she did …

"It's almost over Mara," Alec told her excitedly as he burst into the lab. "We destroyed the last bridge. All that's left now is for us to erase the remaining Sims and …"

Mara spun away from her computer screen, turning to face Dr. Kendal. "It might be over here, Alec, but there's something worse booting up. I've found another cosm. And, triple damn, the Sims have found it too."

It did not matter that it was happening an entire universe away. Distance did not diminish the pain she felt with each new death. For, like on Kadandra before it, this impending destruction was her fault.

Tears flowed from Mara's one natural eye, and she wiped them away. But she couldn't wipe away the memories. They continued to flow, along with Mara's tears.

13

Alder watched the strange procession pass by his hiding spot. He was holed up in a Radio Shack on Third and 58th, trying to work his way over to the West Side. He didn't get far, however, when he had to seek refuge.

Now there was a parade of large dinosaurs shambling toward Central Park. Piled high on the back of each giant lizard were bodies. Human bodies. Victims of the lizard men's slaughter.

A crash sounded from further back in the store. Alder pulled his nightstick from its belt loop and moved away from the door. It was dark in the store, the only light was the rainy gray illumination coming through the display window. The officer slipped his flashlight into his other hand and snapped it on. Its strong beam showed him stacks of stereos and televisions, boxes of radio-controlled cars, and racks of cables, wires, and other electronic do-it-yourself paraphernalia. A pile of calculators had fallen across the service counter. Alder slowly swept the area with his light, stopping when glowing eyes met his.

They belonged to a small gray cat with a red collar. It gave Alder a look that said "feed me or take a hike." The officer smiled, relaxing his bunched muscles.

That was when something large smashed into him. Alder went flying into a computer display. His flashlight and nightstick sailed away from him. As the flashlight spun across the floor, it threw odd shadows. Alder saw three forms advancing on him, first as shadows against the window, then as humans in tattered rags when the light spun its beam their way.

There were two men and a woman, and each appeared more brutal than the one before. The larger of the men stepped closer, revealing Cro-Magnon features as the light beam spun around again.

"Cop," the large brute grunted.

"Fun," the woman laughed, flashing crooked, sharp teeth.

Alder decided not to attempt conversation with the

group. Instead, he drove his foot into the brute's mid section, then rolled behind a pile of clock radios and quickly got to his feet. The smaller man and the woman approached cautiously, acutely aware of their moaning companion lying on the store floor.

The woman held her hands like claws, again showing her teeth. She laughed, but there was no humor in the sound. Instead, Alder heard the sound of primitive passion, and it reminded him of the scene by the bridge the night before.

"What happened to you?" he asked, trying to make sense of the situation.

"Lanala," the woman laughed, "Baruk Kaah!"

Then the small man leaped, hurdling a display as he reached for Alder's neck. He never made it. A massive scaled arm caught the man in mid leap, then sent him sailing into the far wall. Alder gaped as the lizard man turned toward him. It held his flashlight in its other hand, playing the beam onto Alder's face.

The woman's roar reminded the officer of the remaining danger, but she was upon him before he could react. Her leap knocked them both to the floor as she attempted to bite and claw him. The officer struggled, but it was all he could do to keep her teeth and nails away from his neck and face. She was strong, he had to admit. Maybe she was on some kind of new drug.

Her left hand broke free of Alder's grip, and she slashed out with dirt-caked fingernails. They dug into his right cheek, drawing deep gashes of red across his face. Then, as quickly as she attacked, she was gone. The officer looked up as the lizard man smashed her with his heavy forearm. She collapsed without so much as a sound of protest.

The first brute appeared to have recovered somewhat, but the fight was out of him. He ran into the street, leaving his companions behind.

Alder and the lizard man regarded each other warily, curiously. The lizard examined the flashlight for a moment, reverently turning it over in its massive claws. Then it extended it to Alder.

The officer tried to get a sense of the creature's intentions, but he had no common experience to judge this by. So he took the light as it was offered, nodding a thank you.

"Tal Tu," the lizard man said. Then it repeated it, thumping its chest.

That must be its name, Alder thought. No, not it. *He*, he guessed.

"Rick Alder," the officer said, thumping his chest just as Tal Tu had. "You saved my life. Thank you."

The gray cat rubbed up against Alder's leg. He bent down and lifted the cat, gently scratching it behind the ears.

"You're not like the others, are you Tal Tu?" Alder asked, not expecting an answer. But Tal Tu provided him with one anyway.

The lizard reached out and petted the cat.

14

The trek through the subway passed for Bryce as a dreamy, detached memory. After leading them down onto the tracks, Coyote had Rat douse the torch. Immediately Bryce missed the fluttering, smoky light. The uniform blackness was unending and quiet. After a failed attempt at small talk by the priest, the three fell silent. So Bryce concentrated on placing one foot in front of the other, on keeping a hand on Coyote's shoulder, on listening to Rat's cracking gum.

Bryce lost track of time. It seemed as though the only reality in the dark tunnels was the pain in his legs and the leather jacket he held to firmly. His mind turned to other things. He listed his experiences of the past two days, the creatures he had seen, reconstructing events as he understood them.

Could these be the Last Days? Certainly there were similarities between what he saw and what John described in the Book of Revelation. But were those lizards some type of demon? Was the Judgment Day at hand?

The priest tried to recall specific passages, tried to form the words in his mind. But for once his memory failed him. The words would not come. He tried to pray, but that, too, failed to calm him.

Coyote halted abruptly. Bryce banged into him, unaware of the boy's intentions. Then the youth was gone.

"Coyote!" Bryce called, suddenly very afraid of being left in the dark by himself.

"Cool it, Father," whispered Rat as he grasped Bryce's hand. "We've reached Lexington Avenue and Coyote just wants to check out the station before we keep going."

Lexington Avenue. The first stop in Manhattan on the E and F lines, Bryce thought. He hefted the familiar weight of his mass kit, then leaned against a pillar to wait.

Moments passed. Then Bryce said, "Why are you down here, Rat?"

"Same reason as you, man," he said quietly, keeping his voice low.

"But what about your parents?"

"Don't got none. I mean, we don't got none no more. We're orphans, man. We got only each other, but we take care of ourselves real good."

"We sure do," Coyote said, his voice reaching out of the darkness. "The station's clear, preacher man. We can go on."

"What were you looking for, Coyote?"

"Gangs, lizards, winos ... you name it man, it might be down here."

"Yeah," Rat said, "if you're asleep, they might bite your ass."

Bryce wasn't sure, but he thought he saw Rat smile in the darkness.

Then they moved on.

15

Sergeant Dykstra couldn't get his radio to work. He also couldn't get his jeep to start or his compass to tell him which way was north. In fact, nothing seemed to be working.

"Damn," he said, throwing the compass in anger. "What do we do now?"

Corporal Wilson slammed the jeep's hood and shrugged. "Beats me. You're in charge of this operation."

Yeah, he thought, what a privilege.

They had been on practice maneuvers when the call came through. The two of them had been given a jeep and a radio, then told to range ahead to reconnoiter the land while Alpha Company waited to hook up with Bravo Company, another National Guard unit from further south. Who were they kidding, anyway? The whole lot of them were nothing but a bunch of weekend warriors from Buffalo and Erie. But until the army could get its act together, it was up to the National Guard to scope out the situation.

"You'd think that they could have found a couple of units closer to New York City," Wilson muttered as he tried the radio again.

"They tried. But they couldn't reach anyone within three hundred miles of the place. No radio, no telephone, no nothing."

"Just like us."

"Yeah. Just like us."

They were going along well, making good time. They wanted to reach Elmira, on the New York-Pennsylvania border, before it got too dark. But just twenty-five miles out or so, everything shut off. They were stuck, and they couldn't even get word back to their unit.

"So what do we do, Sarge?"

"What else can we do? We wait."

16

Kurst was controlled chaos in physical form. Not that he appeared wild — but his eyes hinted of savage sport and his sweat smelled of thick forests. If you watched him long enough, you could detect his primal nature. He wore a compact, powerful body around his wildness. Just under six foot, he was definitely muscular, but not bulky.

He moved with fluid grace, almost lupine in nature. Every silent step appeared to be the one that would set his taunt muscles free, that would send his body springing wildly into the night. But he stayed on track, in control of every movement.

Thick brown hair fell to just above his jaw line. A warm wind blew his hair back, exposing the tapered tips of his ears. His slightly angled eyes glowed in the dim twilight.

He paused briefly, unconcerned with the falling rain.

Bending down, he scooped up a handful of mud and sniffed it. A step. Another scoop of mud. Then he was off, sprinting silently into the gathering gloom.

The trail led to a small cave. The cave mouth was hidden behind overgrowth, barely perceptible to passers by. But Kurst knew it was there. He could see the shadow that was subtly deeper than the shadows around it. He could hear the change in the wind as it blew across the hollow opening. And he could smell the fear of his quarry, drawing him forward.

Pushing past the overgrowth, the hunter filled the cave mouth. He paused for a moment, reaching out with every sense. The stormer within the cave pulled back, trying to shrink from the hunter's dark form. This world was no different than the countless others, the hunter thought. Even those with the power to oppose him and his master were too frightened to fight for their miserable lives. Perhaps that was why the Gaunt Man was destined to succeed in his grand vision.

Was it not the way of every reality that the stronger take what they need from the weaker? Does not the wolf kill the deer for sustenance? Why shouldn't the Gaunt Man take what he needs from these pathetic beings? It was the way of nature — no matter what world you were on.

The hunter entered the small cave. The game was over. He just had to finish his move. Then he could return to the keep.

"Come with me, stormer," Kurst said, using the words of this world that the Gaunt Man had impressed into his mind. "You never had a chance against me. You are the deer, I am the wolf, and the conclusion of our chase was never in doubt."

Perhaps the hunter had grown careless. Perhaps his

confidence had blocked out the messages of his senses. Whatever the reason, he barely reacted in time as the stormer slashed out with a long knife. As it was, the sharp blade had cut through his tunic, leaving a long gash across his chest. He could smell his own blood, feel the heat of it as it oozed from the gash. It wasn't deep, and he had endured worse pain, but it had been a long time since a quarry had drawn any of his blood, let alone first blood. Perhaps there was more to these stormers, after all.

"So," the hunter growled as he stepped back, out of range of the knife, "the stormer has claws."

In the darkness of the cave, the hunter could see the wide whiteness of the stormer's eyes. He could see the glint of the silver blade. But more, he could smell the intense emotions that emanated from the man, a combination of fear and excitement and anger. Suddenly, the hunt had become interesting again.

"I have claws, too, stormer," Kurst explained in a low, menacing voice.

He advanced, ready to end the game.

17

Penn Station was filled with people. Bryce gaped in astonishment as he and the boys climbed up from the subway platform. Flickering torches were everywhere, and groups huddled around fires burning brightly in trash bins. In recent years more and more homeless people had come to sleep in the semi-warmth of this terminal, but never had the priest seen it filled with refugees. There were so many people, but unlike a normal rush hour, no one was hurrying to catch a train or get to work. These people warmed themselves before fires, or paced nervously, or slept upon the tiled floor.

"Coyote, who are all these people?" asked Rat.

"Orphans," Coyote whispered. "Rabbits hiding in this hole until the lizards go away."

Bryce and the boys wandered for a time. The priest looked into frightened faces, confused faces. But he had no words of comfort for these people. He could not think of a thing to say.

The priest recognized the traditional bums easily. This was where they came to escape the streets and the weather. But now they shared their quarters with businessmen in soiled suits, with young mothers and their crying children, with old women and their mewing, barking pets. They shared their benches with teachers, made room in their corners for office workers. Suddenly, because of the dinosaurs, everyone was a little more like everyone else. Bryce wondered why it took disasters to bring the crowds together.

He noticed a young woman walking aimlessly, carrying a little girl in her arms. The priest watched as she stumbled once, then twice. He reached her just as she stumbled a third time and caught her before she or the little girl could fall. He helped them down, leaning the woman against a wall.

"Are you all right, miss?" Bryce asked. Coyote and Rat stood behind him, unsure of whether they should stay or go.

"I just need to rest a bit," the woman said. Then she noticed Bryce's collar. "Thank you, Father."

"No trouble at all."

The little girl reached out and touched the priest's nose, pushing her tiny finger into the bulbous flesh. "Are you a priest?" she asked quietly.

"Yes, I am."

"I don't go to church."

"Honey!" the young woman protested, but Bryce waved her off.

"That's all right. Let me tell you a secret, little girl." Bryce leaned closer, like he was going to share something very important with her. She leaned forward to meet him, resting her tiny head against his bald forehead. "I only go when they make me."

The little girl laughed, and her mother smiled at the sound.

"Do you know what's happening, Father? Do you know when the trains will start running again?"

Bryce shook his head. He had no answer for the young woman, no words of hope he could spare.

Rat produced a pack of gum from one of his many pockets and offered it to the little girl. She looked at it hungrily, then turned a dubious gaze on Rat.

"Sugarless?" she asked.

"Four out of five doctors recommend it," he answered, and she quickly snatched it away.

Coyote, his eyes darting constantly, tapped Bryce on the shoulder. He pointed toward a bench some twenty feet away. Bryce followed his finger and saw the ragged man sitting there. But he was doing more than just sitting. He was shaking uncontrollably. He stood up, a wild look in his eyes. The ragged man started walking toward Bryce. As he came forward, he reached up and buried his fist in his thick, unkept beard. Then he started to pull on it, and Bryce grimaced at just the thought of the pain. But the ragged man seemed to enjoy it, tugging harder as he approached.

"I am surrounded by corpses!" he called out, fixing his gaze on the priest. "I am trapped in the land of the dead!"

Coyote moved to stand in front of Bryce, placing

himself between the others and the ragged man.

"But I have heard Lanala's voice," the ragged man continued as he stopped a few feet from Coyote and Bryce. "I hear the song that the Jakatts sing! They sing of Baruk Kaah! They sing of Life!"

"What do you want?" Bryce asked, trying to move Coyote aside. But the youth would not budge.

"I want everything," the ragged man said, his voice growing wilder, more guttural. Bryce noticed that he still tugged on his beard, and the priest could see blood dripping down the ragged man's fist. "I *want* everything."

Now the man began to hunch forward, his limbs seeming to re-form as Bryce and Coyote watched. His arms elongated and his legs shortened. Then his face changed. The jaw jutted out and the bridge of his eyes grew thicker, more pronounced.

"Everything," he repeated, forcing the word through crooked teeth.

"Run," Coyote ordered without turning his head from the ragged man.

"But ..." Bryce began to argue, but Rat grabbed his arm.

"Coyote said run, you run," Rat explained, handing the little girl to the priest. Bryce looked at the young woman as she lifted his mass kit. They started to run.

They had only gone a little ways when Bryce halted. The young woman looked at him, confusion in her eyes, as he set the little girl down in a deserted corner. He turned to the woman, wanting to lay a comforting hand on her shoulder. He couldn't quite get his hand to do that, however.

"You'll be safe here," he assured her, awkwardly dropping his arms to his sides.

"Where are you going, Father?"

"Take care of my mass kit," he said, avoiding her question. "And watch out for your little girl."

Then he ran back the way they had come, back toward Coyote and Rat.

Bryce arrived to find that a crowd had gathered. Many of them were shouting and carrying on in a way that scared the priest. He pushed through the throng, using more strength than he would have expected to. In the center of the crowd was a small, circular clearing. And within that clearing, the ragged man lunged for Coyote.

The youth kicked out violently, but the blow seemed to actually amuse the ragged man. He laughed out loud as each punch connected, relishing the sensations that wracked his deformed body.

Then, quite suddenly and with a speed that caught Coyote off guard, the ragged man's large, hairy hand shot forward. Thick, knobby fingers wrapped tightly around Coyote's arm, and the larger man lifted the youth off the ground.

"I bring gift, little dead thing," the ragged man said, struggling with the words. He squeezed his fist closed, and Coyote screamed in pain. "I give you feelings." He squeezed again, and some of those in the crowd screamed along with the youth.

Rat leaped upon the ragged man then, beating upon his broad back with small fists. But the ragged man simply flexed his bunched muscles, and Rat was tossed to the hard floor. Before he could regain his breath and move, the ragged man had grabbed him as well.

Bryce, desperately trying to decide what to do, noticed that a man standing near him was leaning on a long metal pipe. The pipe was about three feet long, probably found somewhere back in the subway tunnels. The man was banging the metal onto the floor, beating out an almost-tribal tune in time with the ragged man's violence. Without hesitating, the priest snatched the pipe from the surprised man.

"Yes, this will do nicely," he said lightly, trying to calm his frazzled nerves.

The ragged man held the two boys at arms length, smiling savagely over his double catch. "Maybe I will present you as gifts to Lanala, as a sign of my love for the goddess," the ragged man said as he tightened his grip once more.

"Maybe not," yelled Bryce as he swung the pipe into the ragged man's brutish face. The sound of the impact was awful as bone and flesh gave way to the unyielding metal. The ragged man crashed to the ground, releasing the two teens as he fell.

Bryce dropped the pipe, disgusted at what he had done. He grabbed both boys and shouted, "Now we run!"

They did.

The woman and little girl were gone when Bryce and the boys returned. Only Bryce's black mass kit sat in the otherwise empty corner, alone. He picked it up and held it close.

"She left, man," said Coyote. "We should be going, too."

The priest nodded, following Coyote and Rat toward the exit.

He hesitated a moment, looking back into the empty corner.

"We never even found out their names," Bryce said

quietly.

Rat put his hand on the priest's arm, and gently led him away.

18

Alder carried a small knapsack over one shoulder. The gray cat's head peeked out from the open flap, watching curiously to see where the police officer was taking him. Alder looked back for the twentieth time. The lizard man was still following him, ambling along at a steady pace.

Tal Tu, he had called himself, Alder remembered. He stopped to rest, leaning against a stalled van. He set the knapsack down and took a moment to study the lizard man.

Tal Tu was over six feet tall, and much bulkier than Alder. His head was reminiscent of a bird's, as the snout tapered to form a sharp beak. But the rest of his body was reptilian, ending in a long tail. He carried a knapsack as well, but he filled his with trinkets from the Radio Shack. What the lizard man wanted with wires and calculators and batteries was beyond him, but Alder hadn't been able to make much out of the happenings of the past two days.

Ignoring Tal Tu, Alder decided to check out the van he was resting on. It was a typical two-door model of American make, with a sliding side hatch and a rear door for loading. It was a New York delivery man's transportation through a crowded city. It guzzled gas and didn't worry about scratches or dents. He tried the door and found it unlocked. Now that wasn't a smart thing to do in New York. Just anybody could borrow your vehicle if you left in unlocked and unattended.

He slid into the front seat. Surprisingly, the key was

still in the ignition and the gear stick was left in drive. So why was it stalled here in the middle of the street?

There was a knock on the door window and Alder jumped when he saw the lizard man's face against the glass. Then it held up the knapsack with the cat sticking out and Alder realized it was Tal Tu.

"You scared yesterday's lunch out of me," Alder yelled, and Tal Tu pulled back. He tilted his bird head to one side so that he could regard Alder with one of his lizard eyes.

"Don't give me that innocent look. You shouldn't sneak up on a person like that."

The ground shook then, throwing Alder into the van and tilting Tal Tu back onto his tail.

"What the ..."

"Udatok, Rick Alder, udatok," Tal Tu rasped, motioning down the street. Alder glanced back and saw the huge monster. It was another of the one-horned dinosaurs. Each step it took shook the ground. There were lizard men with it. And the people who had changed. And the flying starfish. The invaders were coming, and Alder could not escape them on foot.

He grabbed the knapsack from Tal Tu and placed it in the back of the van. Then he led Tal Tu around to the sliding hatch. There were no seats in the rear, just empty cargo space.

"Get in," he ordered, helping Tal Tu squeeze his bulk and strange shape into the van. It wouldn't be comfortable, but Alder felt that if he left the lizard man behind the others would kill him.

Then Alder piled into the driver's seat. He shifted to park and grasped the key. There was no reason for the van not to work, he told himself. It had gas, he had the key. That was all you needed to make it start. That was the way the world that Rick Alder knew worked.

He glanced into the rearview mirror and saw the approaching horde. They would be upon them momentarily, and that udatok or whatever Tal Tu had called it would crush them beneath its scaled feet.

Alder turned the key, willing the engine to start.

It sputtered and died.

He pumped the gas pedal and turned the key again. "Come on, baby, you can do it."

This time the van started. Alder silently thanked God as he gunned the engine and drove off, away from the horrors that were chasing him.

19

Sergeant Dykstra stared out the windshield of the jeep, hoping to see some sign of civilization come rumbling down Route 17. All he saw were the sheets of driving rain.

The rain had started shortly after nightfall. He and Wilson had hurriedly put up the canvas top, hoping that the flimsy covering would keep them dry. Now the gray sky was brightening, and still the rain was falling. It swept across the blacktop of the highway in great waves of water, forming small rivers and ponds as far as he could see.

Beside him, Wilson slept. His snores were loud inside the jeep, but Dykstra didn't complain. For all he knew, he sounded the same when he was asleep. Maybe worse. Dykstra clutched the ignition key for the seventh time in the last hour. He rolled the cool metal between thumb and finger absently, his eyes still fixed upon the sweeping rain.

He turned the key, hoping to hear the engine turn over. Or cough. Or sputter.

All he heard was Wilson's insistent snoring, and the hammering rain.

Dykstra sighed and leaned back in the seat. He let his eyes close, let the sound of the rain lull him to sleep. Time passed, and the sounds changed. Dykstra's eyes blinked open. The rain had stopped, but the day was still dark and gray. Wilson was still asleep beside him, snoring away.

But outside, something was happening in the clouds. Dykstra watched as the clouds roiled. Then they split open and something fell from the sky. It was a plant of some sort. It grew out of the clouds, its vines and tendrils twisting, intertwining, snaking their way toward the ground. Finally the roots struck home, shattering the pavement of the highway to seek the soft dirt beneath.

The sergeant wasn't aware that this plant bridge was much smaller than the one that landed in Queens. He didn't know that others just like it had sprouted from the sky throughout a three hundred mile triangle that stretched east and north from New York City. He didn't understand that huge numbers of lizard men and dinosaurs were even now pouring down those many bridges, spreading their forces, taking control.

Dykstra and Wilson were sent to find out what their units would have to face in the silent zone. Now Dykstra knew, even if he couldn't warn his unit. He was trapped in the silent zone, cut off from communications.

The dinosaurs swept down the plant bridge, an unending force of armored lizards and winged reptiles. One of the larger beasts noticed the tiny jeep. The creature was tall and stood on its hind legs. It flailed a spiked tail behind it and snapped its powerful jaws. Then it moved, more quickly than Dykstra expected, and closed the distance between the bridge and the jeep with great, powerful strides.

"Wilson," the sergeant said, shaking the sleeping corporal. "Wake up, Wilson."

"What? What's the ... my God!" Wilson started screaming then, and Dykstra immediately regretted his action. Perhaps he should have left the corporal asleep.

Then the great beast ripped through the canvas roof. Dykstra raised his pistol toward the snapping maw. He pulled the trigger once, twice, three times. But, like the jeep and the radio, the pistol didn't work.

A wave of disappointment rushed through the sergeant. Not that he expected the pistol to stop the monster, but he did want the satisfaction of shooting it before it killed him. Then the jaws snapped over him, plucking him from the jeep. His screams joined Wilson's, but the screams didn't last long.

Bravo and Charlie Companies joined up where 415 and 17 met, just outside of Kanona. They had not heard from the reconnaissance units, so they proceeded cautiously. But they did proceed.

When the soldiers had gone another fifteen miles, they spotted the enemy. Through binoculars and with naked eyes, the National Guard units studied the shapes on the horizon. There were giant lizards and reptiles of all descriptions. The creatures were ranged in a deep line that stretched to each side and as far back as the soldiers could see. They shook in place, excitedly swaying back and forth. But they made no sounds.

The radio man called in their position, describing the scene before him. He could hear the skepticism on the other end, but he proceeded with his report anyway. He told them about the dinosaurs.

The National Guardsmen checked their weapons. On

command, they started forward. Then the storm began.

The rain swept from behind the dinosaurs, soaking the soldiers with pelting drops of dark water. Behind the rain, following in its wake, was a wave of glowing energy. It rolled over the soldiers, knocking them to the ground as it passed on.

In the first moments after the reality storm, a number of the soldiers began to change. They became brutal, bestial, more Neanderthal than homo sapiens. They tore at their uniforms and howled out their savage passions. The lizard men roared out an answer, letting their hissing voices join those of the transformed soldiers. Then the lizards slithered forward, and the attack began.

The soldiers who didn't succumb to the reality storm were confused. But they composed themselves as best they could and readied their weapons. They pulled triggers and tossed grenades. Except for an occasional gun burst, the modern weapons did not respond.

Some of the men hefted their useless weapons as clubs. Some continued to pull on triggers that did not respond. Others turned and ran.

None of them escaped the lizard men.

20

The world called Kadandra never ceased to amaze Thratchen. He walked its neon streets beneath its neon signs, just another face in the crowd. As long as he kept his hat pulled low and his rain coat closed tight, they took no notice of him. They called him and his kind Sims, beings who were similar to the people of Kadandra. Beings who operated under a similar reality.

But the Sims were from another dimension. And they wanted this world and its energy for themselves.

Thratchen paused in a dark alley, cloaking himself in deep shadows. He rolled the right sleeve of his coat up to his elbow, exposing a metallic arm. Two taps on his right wrist, and a small flap of thin metal snapped open, revealing a tiny screen and input port. He connected his left pinky jack into the port and the screen came to life, displaying alien markings on its luminated face.

Time was passing faster than he anticipated. He had so much to do, and he was among the last of the Sims still on Kadandra. These people were fighters, he had to admit. They were ready for Thratchen's master. When the maelstrom bridges crashed across the dimensions, they found warriors prepared to fight off the raiders, not sheep ripe for conquest as was the usual case. The Gaunt Man would not be pleased by the master's failure here. For it meant that the master would be delayed from rendezvousing with the other High Lords on the world called Earth.

But Thratchen decided he would win at least a small victory for his master. If he had to be trapped upon this world, he would make the most of it. He would find the little brat that warned of the raiders' coming. He would find her, and have his revenge.

He checked his screen once more and read the name that appeared there.

"Dr. Hachi Mara-Two."

He would make her death a slow one, that he promised his far-away master.

21

Coyote led Bryce to the entrance of the Lincoln Tunnel. Stalled vehicles were here and there, but because of the time of day when the storm hit, there were far less than there could have been. There were no people around, but Bryce felt as though he were being watched. He shook the notion and examined the tunnel's entrance. The dark, lightless maw was uninviting, and it only added to his unease.

"Kind of like walking into a lion's mouth," commented Rat.

Coyote turned to the priest. "You saved me back there. And you saved Rat. I owe you, Father."

Bryce shook his head. "No, Coyote, you don't owe me a thing. You have done more for me than I would have expected. If you don't want to go any further, I will not try to talk you into it."

The priest sat down heavily upon a concrete curb. His sigh was loud, pained.

"What's the matter, Father," Rat asked as he sat beside the priest.

"I never hit a man before," Bryce said in a quavering voice, "especially not with such violent intent. My God, I may have killed him!" He buried his face in his hands and wept.

"But Father Bryce, you saved Coyote and me. If you didn't hit that spaced out dude, we'd both be pretty dead right now."

"That doesn't excuse my actions, Rat. It only makes them necessary."

"Father Bryce, we got company," Coyote whispered, trying not to move suddenly or give on that he had noticed anything out of the ordinary.

The priest looked up and let his eyes follow the tilt of the teen's head. There, perched upon the tunnel's arch, was a winged reptile. It observed them warily, its yellow eyes upon them. Bryce stood slowly, and the reptile spread feathered wings. It squawked once, twice. Its call was answered by a cacophony of similar squawks and the beating of dozens of pairs of wings. More of the reptiles appeared in the sky, swooping down to land upon the retaining walls that surrounded the tunnel entrances.

"Come on, boys," Bryce urged, "we have to get out of here."

"What are they, Father?" Rat asked. Coyote could hear the fear in his voice.

"It doesn't matter. All that matters is we reach the tunnel. Then we'll be safe."

"Will we, Father Bryce?" Coyote questioned as more of the reptile birds landed around them. "Will we?"

Bryce had no answer for the young man. He only had a goal. "Run for the tunnel. Now."

22

She was calm, peaceful. The pain was gone. She had left it behind her, along with the fear, back in a place that was nothing more than a fading memory.

She tried to focus on where she was now, but nothing was familiar. She was floating, alone, in a featureless area. But it was warm, serene. The danger was past, she knew that, but she could not remember what the danger was.

There was sound, music of some sort. Majestic, she thought, the music was majestic. And beautiful, so beautiful. She could float here forever, she decided. It was so different from the fading place, so comfortable.

But the comfort was short lived. Another sound began, drowning out the music with its awful buzzing. She tried to block it out, but the buzzing was insistent, penetrating. Suddenly it became the worst pain she had ever experienced, even worse than what she had left behind.

She became aware of something else then, a dark space nearby. It drifted closer, touching her, pawing her with coldness that brushed away the warmth. The darkness smelled of carrion, and she tried to push it off. Tendrils of darkness brushed lingeringly across her eyes, blinding her. Wisps of the stuff entered her nose and mouth, choking her, gagging her with their cloying, foul sweetness.

The dark space flowed in front of her, around her, tripping her, slowing her aimless travel. A breeze blew gently from within the dark space, filling her senses with images of deep, damp earth strongly spiced with bits and pieces of decomposing vegetation.

The dark space became a tunnel, and she felt herself drifting through it, into it, falling. She screamed, but the sound was lost among other echoes. These were the vibrations of memory, echoes of a life that was and was no more. Then the descent began. She was dropping, faster and faster, rushing through the dark tunnel toward a destination she could not fathom.

As she whipped through the darkness, she felt clinging cobwebs tear away. She caught glimpses of dark figures, shadowy forms that she thought she recognized. But they seemed angry, vengeful, reaching for her as she flew past. Still she fell, moving at a speed she never experienced before. It was exhilirating and frightening at the same time.

Then she saw a light. It seemed out of place in the dark space, dim. But it quickly grew ineffably clear. It was brilliant, compelling. It was the source of warmth and peace, and as she drew closer the coldness of the dark space receded and was gone. Then the falling stopped.

Ahead of her was the light. Beyond the light, as compelling in its own way, the dark space loomed, continuing on toward its deep source. The light sparkled, and she imagined a gentle smile. But the dark space reached out with its spidery wisps, and she started to drift again, caught in its unrelenting pull.

"No," she said, but wondered why not as the pull weakened.

"Not yet," she said, and the light increased its brilliance and she knew that this was so.

For the moment, the pull had ceased.

23

Alder drove the van as fast as he could while still being able to navigate around the semi-blocked streets. The two unlikely companions rode in silence; Alder had long since stopped trying to make conversation with the lizard man, and not even static could be coaxed out of the van's radio.

The police officer ignored the sights beyond the van's windows. He focused all of his concentration on the task at hand. It was like driving on an obscene obstacle course. Not only did Alder have to deal with the stalled cars, he had to avoid transformed pedestrians and the occasional dinosaur that ran into the road — or stood over it. But at least he had a goal now, and a method for achieving that goal.

"Hang on, Tal Tu," he said, more just to hear a voice than to inform the lizard. "I think you'll like New Jersey. It's probably a lot like wherever it is you're from."

They finally reached the turn off. Alder slowed even more. The turn onto the Lincoln Tunnel approach was tricky under normal conditions; with unmoving cars hidden around the blind curve, it was downright hazardous.

"Deliksss, Rick Alder," Tal Tu rasped as they completed the turn. Alder pressed down on the brake and brought the van to a halt.

Winged reptiles covered the approach all the way to the tunnel entrances. Each creature was about four feet tall, with snakelike bodies and large, feathered wings. Each had long, skinny legs which ended in sharp talons. They had no arms, but two venomous fangs dripped from their small snake heads.

Alder turned to look at Tal Tu, who was curled up in the back of the van. The gray cat was resting in the lizard man's lap.

"Deliks?" he asked.

"Deliksss," Tal Tu answered.

"If it's not one thing, it's another."

Alder gunned the engine and the van rolled forward. The deliks that did not fly off were crushed beneath the van's wheels. Progress was messy, and Alder could feel bile rising at the back of his throat as each delik crunched under the van's weight, but at least they were moving in the right direction.

A bang sounded on the right side of the van. Then another. Some of the deliks were attacking the vehicle, smashing at it with their clawed feet. Alder simply stepped on the gas, ignoring the creatures. A flock of the winged beasts flew into the windshield with a dull thud. They attacked the glass with claw and fang, trying to reach Alder with an unrelenting fury. There was a crack, and the police officer saw lines form in one corner of the windshield.

He swerved the vehicle violently to the left, then turned it sharply to the right. A number of the deliks fell away, but there were still enough that he could not see. He clicked the windshield wipers on, and the sudden motion caused a few more to fly off. But the most persistent ones were still blocking his view.

"Damn stubborn lizards," Alder cursed, "let's see if you like this!" He hit the horn, and the loud blare scattered the remaining creatures. Now Alder could see again. And, standing directly in his path, were three figures. He quickly hit the brake, and the van skidded to a stop within feet of the trio. One was a priest, or at least he was dressed that way. The other two were kids, decked out in gang colors.

"Somehow, Tal Tu, I think I'm going to regret this." Tal Tu said nothing. He simply stroked the cat, trying to ease the terror it felt due to the deliks.

Alder glanced to each side. He saw that the deliks were regaining their courage. They would attack again soon. He reached over and opened the passenger side door for the trio.

"Move it, we don't have all day."

24

Andrew Jackson Decker sat in the hallway. The session was still going strong, but he needed to get away for a few minutes. So much had happened in three short days, and there was so much that they still didn't know. What was going on in New York? Where was the President? Was he alive? And behind these immediate questions were the unspoken questions that gnawed at his heart. Why did Vicky have to die?

Why, why, why? There were too many blasted whys and not enough becauses in Decker's life these days. He didn't like mysteries or puzzles that refused to yield solutions. They just didn't fit into his game plan.

The door to the meeting chamber opened and a woman stepped out. Decker looked up. It was Senator Ellen Conners, the middle-aged matron of the Senate who did not look matronly at all. She had been in the Senate for as long as Decker could remember, and she had to be in her fifties, but she was still a fine figure of a woman. Decker could only imagine what she must have been like in her younger days. Her raven-black hair was styled short and had only a hint of gray, and her clothes were nothing but conservative, but on Conners the effect was striking.

She sat beside him, resting her head against the wall. She suddenly looked as tired as Decker felt, and he wondered why everyone on the Hill called her Old Lady Medusa. He had little cause to interact with her since he had come to Washington, but he had met her a few times at various functions. Her reputation, however, made Decker cautious. Ellen Conners, everyone said, was no one to take lightly.

"So, Congressman," she said at last, "what are your opinions on all of this?"

"Opinions?" Decker started, he hadn't formed any yet, but the Senator obviously wanted to hear something. "What can I base an opinion on, Senator? New York and much of the northeast have been cut off from the rest of the country. The President and Vice President are somewhere within that area of silence. Rumors of invaders are starting to trickle in. My opinion is that we need more information to base an opinion on."

She turned to look at Decker, a slight smile upon her lips. "You don't understand, do you? My dear young man, we must make the opinions so that the rest of the country knows what to think. That is our duty as elected representatives."

"Even if we don't have any solid information?"

"That, Mr. Decker, is precisely the time when our opinions are needed the most."

The door to the meeting chamber opened again, and a clerk stuck his head out. "Congressman, Senator, I think you might want to see this."

Decker rose to his full height of six-foot-two. "What's going on?"

"The Speaker of the House has called for quiet so that he can address the assembly."

Decker and Conners entered the chamber, each going their separate ways. He found his seat as Jonathan Wells stepped to the podium. The Speaker of the House waited until the last murmurs died down, then he tested the microphone and spoke.

"Distinguished members of Congress. We need more information before we can come to any firm policies regarding this crisis. But I have decided on one thing. I will not be named President at this time. There is not enough evidence in either direction to allow me to take such a definite and final action. We all owe President Douglas Kent and Vice President Gregory Farrel too much to write them off this soon."

Wells paused to sip from a glass beside the podium. He replaced the glass, scanned the crowd, then continued.

"I will, however, take over the duties of the Executive office in President Kent's absence. The country needs firm direction at this time, and it is my duty and obligation to provide that direction. In this regard, I have placed our armed forces on DefCon Two. That's all I have to say. If we could hear from the Defense Committee at this time ..."

Decker leaned back in his chair and let the voices fade out around him. There was so much to do, so much to decide, and here was Congress doing what it did best — talking up a storm. At least Wells wasn't ready to write off the President and Vice President just yet. But what was going on in New York?

He wished he knew.

25

Dr. Kendal Alec-Four input his finger jack into the port at his apartment door. His personal computer recognized the command signal, and the front door slid open. Alec entered the apartment, but paused in the vestibule. For some reason, the lights had not brightened the room like they should have.

"If this computer has crashed again, I'm going to ..."

A strong, probably cyber-enhanced hand shot out of the darkness and closed around Alec's throat. The scientist found himself held fast against the wall, his feet dangling a good half a meter off the ground.

"Don't struggle, Dr. Kendal," warned a calm, composed voice. It was the voice of someone accustomed to causing pain as a matter-of-fact routine. "I require a small amount of data that I know you're going to provide me with."

Alec tried to speak, but he couldn't draw any breath.

"Ah, let me make you more comfortable, Dr. Kendal," said the formless voice as the hand loosened its grip ever so slightly. "Or may I call you Alec?"

"Who ... who are you? What do you want?"

"You are the Dr. Kendal Alec-Four that was involved in the Cosmverse Project, are you not? Of course you are. Now I understand that the leader of that project was a child prodigy of some sort. A regular genius, I am told. But the closest I could come to finding her in the computer net was you. Where is she, Alec?"

"Mara? What do you want with Mara?"

"Mara," the voice rolled her name in its mouth as though it were a fine wine. "I want to meet this Mara. I want to introduce myself to the genius that figured out we were coming to this pitiful cosm."

Alec gasped and his heart grew cold. "You're a Sim!"

"I am Thratchen, you virus!" the voice exclaimed threateningly. "I want to reward this Mara for her brilliant work. And then I want to rip her beating heart from her pretty little chest."

Alec heard the snap of an I/O jack extending from a recessed cavity. "What are you doing?" he asked as he saw the jack extend toward his head. "That's illegal!"

"Illegal?" Thratchen laughed evilly. "You have data I need filed somewhere in your pathetic system. I will simply search through your memories until I find it. Of course, it won't be very pleasant for you, and I do imagine that what's left of your mind after I sort it won't be worth very much. But then, that's life."

Thratchen jacked into the port under Alec's right ear. Then he again tightened his grip on Alec's throat so that no screams would escape the scientist's lips.

And Alec very badly wanted to scream.

26

Bryce sat in the passenger seat, next to the driver who wore remnants of a police officer's uniform. Behind him, in the van's cargo port, Coyote and Rat sat across from a lizard man. The lizard man eyed the two boys curiously, while he absently petted a large, gray cat wearing a red collar. The boys, fighting over whether to be scared or curious themselves, sat with their backs against the van wall, as far from the lizard as possible.

There had been little discussion since they piled into the vehicle. For one thing, the priest and the teens had been glad to get away from the winged reptiles, and they had been totally surprised to see a van that actually worked. For another thing, the cop was too busy navigating through the Lincoln Tunnel to answer any questions. Every so often they reached an impasse, and the van had to squeeze through a narrow opening or push another vehicle out of the way.

The winged reptiles followed them as far as the daylight penetrated the tunnel, but refused to venture further into the darkness. That suited Bryce and the others just fine.

The priest wiped rain water from his beard. "Thank you for your timely assistance, officer. I am Father Christopher Bryce. And these two young men are Coyote and Rat. We are in your debt."

The police officer examined the priest with quick glances, never letting his eyes leave the road ahead for more than an instant. "I'm Rick Alder, and I'm not sure if the NYPD still exists for me to be a member of. But I guess once a cop always a cop, huh? The big guy in the back is Tal Tu. He helped me out of a jam so I decided to keep him."

Alder swerved to avoid a stalled Honda, straightened the van out, and continued on an even path.

"Do you have any idea what this is all about, Father?" Alder asked.

"If only I knew the answer to that question," Bryce sighed. "I've heard it quite a few times since this all began."

"What about you hoodlums? What are you two doing wandering around in the rain with a priest?"

Rat started to say something, but Coyote silenced him with a pat of his hand.

"We don't talk to cops, man," Coyote spat.

"Suit yourself. But if you give me any lip, I'll let Tal Tu eat your face off."

Coyote paled visibly and Rat huddled behind him. "You are kidding, aren't you?" asked Bryce quietly. Alder smiled nastily. "What do you think?"

Tal Tu, apparently pleased by all of the attention, opened his jaws wide and exposed a mean set of teeth.

An hour later, Alder had the van running smoothly along I-95 South. Rain was still falling, but it was much less intense than it had been. They were approaching the Newark exit when Bryce noticed a warm glow off to the right. He sat up in his seat and peered out at the horizon. The glow extended for some distance to each side. It was a natural light, without the coldness of artifical illumination. It took a few seconds, but when it registered, Bryce's mind went into panic mode.

"Officer Alder, there is a fire out there."

Smoke hung in the air, thick clouds of black that darkened an already gray sky. Alder could see the red and orange glow of crackling fire. It had to be a large, intense blaze to create such a display.

"Get off here," the priest ordered. "Maybe we can help."

The police officer maneuvered the van onto the exit ramp. The Newark skyline came into view, and it was burning brightly.

"My God, Bryce," Alder said, "the city is on fire."

At the edge of the ramp he had to stop the van, for the road was filled with people. They were everywhere, spilling out of the city to escape the intense heat. And, worst of all, they were all dead.

"Look at the soot and burns," Bryce's voice cracked as he spoke, "but fire didn't kill these people. Their chests ... my God, look at their chests."

Indeed, each man, woman and child, had empty,

bloody holes where their chests once were. Alder remembered the scene at the 59th Street Bridge, and he had to visibly force his stomach to stay down.

"Edeinos do this," Tal Tu said, startling both Alder and Bryce with the words. "Edeinos Jakatts."

Bryce grabbed his mass kit from the floor by his feet and opened the van door.

"Where are you going, Father?" Alder asked.

"To do my job," he said, and he stepped out into the mass of dead bodies.

Alder, Tal Tu, and the two boys watched the priest go from body to body. They listened to the prayer of last rites over and over again, until the priest's voice grew raw and only the light of the nearby fire illuminated the night.

27

Captain Nicolai Ondarev made his way through the polished hallways of an unmarked building in a rundown section of Moscow. He entered a small, sparingly furnished office and flashed his ID to a portly woman sitting behind the only desk. She studied the identification briefly, then nodded toward a nondescript door.

The Soviet officer pushed through the door and found himself at the top of a stairwell. It appeared to lead down several stories below the ground. He glanced back at the woman, but her back was to him. She had done her job, he realized. Now he must do his. He started down the steps.

After he had traveled down more flights of stairs than he ever cared to travel again, Ondarev reached the bottom landing. There he found a heavy metal door. It, too, was unmarked. Before he could knock, the door swung open. A middle-aged woman in a nurse's uniform met him, nodded, and motioned for him to follow. He did not disappoint her.

The nurse showed the captain into a small room that smelled of hospitals and circulated air. There was a child's desk and chair in one corner. A globe of the world sat atop the desk. A small bed rested against the far wall, and beside it was a hard-backed chair. The nurse left the room, closing the door behind her so that the captain could be alone with the room's two occupants. The first, a man in a white smock, rose from his chair to greet the officer. But the captain ignored the man. His attention was clearly focused upon the young woman lying in the bed.

She was young — perhaps twenty, perhaps less — and she was stunning. But her beauty had nothing to do with makeup or fashion, for she wore no makeup and her clothing was but a simple hospital gown. Her hair was the color of radiant sunshine, and her eyes were pools of light blue water that stared at nothing, but seemed to see everything.

"Welcome to Project Omen, Captain Ondarev. I am Dr. Kazan," the man in the smock said, trying to get the officer's attention. "And this is Katrina Tovarish, the one you have come to see."

The captain continued to look at the young woman. After all these years, was this slip of a young thing the culmination of all the work and money the government had poured into the Department of Psychic Research? And, even if she was, could she really help them?

He took the globe from the desk and studied it for a moment. It was mounted within a curved arm so that it could spin freely. He placed the globe in the young woman's hands, then bent down beside the bed and whispered into her ear.

"What did you see, Katrina Tovarish?"

"Captain, I'm afraid you do not understand," the doctor told him. "Katrina is quite blind."

The officer fixed Dr. Kazan with a deadly stare, then repeated his question to the young woman. He said the words very gently. "What did you see?"

In a haunting voice that Captain Ondarev would never forget, the young woman said, "I saw the storm clouds gather over Earth. I saw the dark rain fall. There are seven raiders coming — seven invaders to attack Earth, seven different places to be attacked."

"She has been experiencing this vision for several months now," the doctor explained. "I reported it to your superiors each time, and each time I was dismissed."

"I am here now, doctor," said Ondarev. "Please do not interrupt us again. Katrina? May I call you Katrina?"

Again the haunting voice spoke. "You may, captain. And might I add that you have a very nice name. I've always liked the name Nicolai."

Ondarev could not remember using his first name since he entered this room. But he must have, he reasoned, for her to know it. He dismissed the mystery and went back to his questions.

"Where are these invasions going to occur, Katrina?"

She tilted her head to one side, as though she were listening to a far-away voice. Then she began to spin the globe, letting her fingers run across its textured surface.

"Here," she said, pointing to Borneo without looking where her finger struck.

"Here," her finger tapped New York.

"Here, here, here." Great Britain, France, the Soviet Union.

"And here, and here." Her finger pointed to Eygpt

and Japan.

Captain Ondarev stood up and wiped perspiration from his brow. He took the globe from Katrina and held it so he could look at it. The outline of his beloved country stared back at him. She had touched the globe there with her fifth tap. That meant there was still time.

"Captain, the storm has already begun," she added, "and the invaders are falling to our world along with its poisonous rain."

"Prepare her, doctor," Ondarev ordered briskly, "she is to leave with me."

"Why?" the doctor questioned nervously. "I do not understand? What is happening?"

"We have lost all contact with Singapore and its Indonesian neighbors, and the United States has come under the attack of unknown forces. Don't you see? Her storm has begun, and I will need her help if our country is going to survive."

As Ondarev moved to leave the room, Katrina's haunting voice stopped him.

"The storm has a name, Captain Nicolai Ondarev."

He forced himself to look at the young woman, even though his sweat was now running cold.

"It calls itself Torg."

28

"Time To Go, Time To Go, Time To Go," streamed redly, blinking across the inside of her closed left eye. Irritatedly, she opened her eyes. The alarm display continued to flash and stream across her vision as she looked about the room. Faint, ghostlike images, leaking backward from the sensover chip in the first socket behind her right ear, through her brain, optic nerves, and to her retinas, overlay the hard reality of the sleeping portion in her living cubicle. She blinked her left eye once, turning off the alarm display and activating the snooze control. That would let her go back to sensover for ten more minutes before the alarm roused her again.

The cubicle faded from her vision and the translucent images became solid as she closed her eyes and returned to experiencing a recording of the Kios City Philharmonic playing Hartel's Post-Invasion Symphony, with herself playing first piano.

Atonal, bass vibrations trembled in the tips of her fingers where they pressed down upon the polished white plastic of the keys, and the attenuator pedal quivered under her foot as she floated back into the sensover scene. She was just getting to her solo when a voice came through the intercom panel near the door. The voice intruded on the music and spoke her name questioningly.

"Dr. Hachi?" the voice of the security doorman forty-seven floors below asked.

"Triple damn," she muttered to herself as she sat up in bed and pulled out the sensover chip of the symphony. She tossed it onto the counter that ran the length of the room, letting it mix with the jumble of electronic equipment, papers, books, program chips and data disks that littered the surface.

"What?" she asked after she had slid off the bed and pushed the speak button on the intercom. Noting her absence, the bed retreated into its wall slot.

"Your driver is here for you, Dr. Hachi."

"Where?" she asked.

"Garage level five, stall twenty-three."

"Okay. Tell him I'll be down as soon as I can."

"Sure thing ... uh, Dr. Hachi?"

"Yes?"

"Good luck, Mara."

Mentally paralyzed for a moment with the thought of luck and how much of that elusive, randomly indeterminate substance it would take to save a world, she made no answer to the doorman's last remark. Then, thinking that even if she could not calculate nor mathematically define luck, only the probability of it, she was going to need all of it that she could get.

"Thanks, Randin-Six. Randy."

"Nothing of it, Mara. Carry your bags up when you get back?"

Back. The word echoed in the shadowy, fear-filled corners of her mind. Back. Step off into the cosmverse and back again. Just like that. Nothing to it.

"Yeah, sure. See you, Randy," she said, and took her finger off the speak button.

29

In sheer reptilian pleasure, Baruk Kaah hissed his approval. The new tribe members were making excellent progress. They used their hands to dig shallow holes throughout this field they once called Central Park. Into each six-paces-by-three-paces-by-one-arm-length-deep hole was laid a gospog seed. Then one of the dead of this world was placed in each hole, taken from the growing piles that lined the edge of the field.

Off to the High Lord's left, another pile of bodies was carted in atop a dinosaur with a large, flat back. After it deposited its gruesome cargo, it trundled back to reload. Baruk Kaah looked to the field again, eager to watch his hand-picked master planters firmly tamp the loose earth back into the holes, sealing the seeds and bodies in place.

Further along the rows of holes, a new member of Baruk Kaah's tribe dug enthusiastically. He wore dark blue slacks and a light blue shirt that had a New York City Transit Authority patch on the left sleeve, and he moved in a rolling, chimpanzeelike gait. His uniform, his mirror-finish sunglasses, and his clean-shaven face looked out of place as he hunched over to dig another hole.

Baruk Kaah tilted his head upward and inhaled deeply. As he exhaled, he closed a flap in his nasal passages and diverted his exhalation through the hollow, elongated and u-shaped bony structure that ran from his nostrils, passing up the center of his face and arching at the top of his head. The trumpeting sound he made was a salute to the planters and diggers. The workers looked up from where they squatted and roared in response to the High Lord's praise.

"What isss your crop?" Baruk Kaah asked hissingly of the edeinos planter nearest him.

"These are gospogsss of the first-planting, Sssaar," the planter said. At the same time, he kept track of the carelessly swinging, sharply-ridged tail of the High Lord. It had been known to strike swiftly if the Saar was displeased. "In seven suns, you will have an army of gospogsss to march at your back."

"How long before we sssee gospogsss of the fifth-planting?"

The answer came, not from the planter, but from the ravagon that landed nearby. "When you win more land for the planting, Baruk Kaah. Then will the Gaunt Man's gift truly bear fruit."

"Sssoon, ravagon, sssoon." Baruk Kaah turned away from the demon and looked back at the workers in the field. He addressed the planter, "Do you have enough workersss?"

The master planter scanned the field. "Yes," he answered. "More of the nativesss are joining usss all the time."

"The Gaunt Man planned well," said Baruk Kaah so that the ravagon could hear, giving grudging respect to the demon's master who looked like the soft-skinned, easily crushed natives of this cosm, but who truly thought and acted as an edeinos.

"Grow well, planter," the High Lord said as he made his leave, not bothering to say anything to the ravagon.

30

On the island of Borneo, a new reality held sway. Gone were the laws of Earth, replaced by the axioms of Orrorsh. In the island's dark interior, a writhing bridge constructed of tortured bodies spanned an expanse from sky to ground. Beside the bridge, a small town had been constructed hastily, though to look at it one would believe that it had been in place for ages. The town lay clouded under a gray pall of burning coal and wood. Its cobbled streets were made odorous from the droppings of horses that pulled an incessant flow of carriages, delivery wagons, and hansom cabs. At the town's center, rising slightly over the other buildings, was a walled estate.

To the general public of Orrorsh, this was Salisbury Manor. But to the lord of the estate, it was Illmound Keep.

Within the walls of the estate was a four-storied manor house. Pointed, domed, and open-topped towers, which were round, square, oval and slanted, stabbed at the sky. Crenelated walkways arced and connected the towers or ended halfway to nothingness. Gable ends, held in the arms of massive, stone gargoyles who crouched upon the peaks of the slate roofs, jutted outward at every conceivable angle. Windows, dark and lighted, of thin-scraped horn and oiled vellum, of glass that was cut and stained and clear, looked out upon the rolling lawns and black, gnarled forests of the estate. Dormers wept from the eaves and down the sides of the manor house. And here and there, a buttress flew.

In a room on the top floor of the manor house, a room paneled in heavy, dark wood and walled in shelves of leather-bound books, stood the hunter called Kurst. He stood with his back to the darkly green upholstered furniture and the massive, oak desk. The room was lit by the yellow, softly hissing flame of a brass and crystal gas lamp hanging from the tin-paneled ceiling. He stood looking out the leaded-glass, diamond-paned window down into the gardens below, tracing out with his eyes the intricate patterns of the hedge maze that dominated the west lawn of the estate. Carefully, as though he were actually walking on the crushed gravel, his eyes followed the angled and curved path. So as not to mar the challenge, he avoided looking at the center of the maze, the small open square that held the prize for any who could win their way there. Yesterday, when the gardeners had rerouted the maze, they had chained a young woman, one of the dark-skinned maidens native to the island, to the iron bench at the center of the open square.

Kurst calmly drank some of the heavy burgundy from the crystal wine glass he held. He almost had the pattern solved, and soon he would go down to the west lawn, enter the maze, make his way through its winding, deceptive paths, and take the prize that the Gaunt Man had provided for him. He had never failed to take whatever prize was set out for him. He did not know if the Gaunt Man knew of this vantage point in the slanting west tower that allowed an overview of the maze

Storm Knights

Alan Jude Summa

below, nor did he care. He finished the wine and set the empty glass down on the tray, next to a half-filled decanter. He was turning away from the window when a hesitant knock came from the other side of the door.

"Yes?" called Kurst. The high-buttoned, tweed suit that he wore, although of obviously rich cloth and careful tailoring, looked out of place and ill suited on the hunter. His slightly pointed ears and elongated eyes that angled perceptibly upward at their outside corners did little to take away from the wildness of his appearance.

"Sir, it is I, Picard. The master wishes to see you," said the voice from the other side of the door.

"Very well," replied Kurst, letting fall to pieces the pattern he held in his mind. Through the glass of the window at Kurst's back, faintly came the sound of a wolf howling as he hunted somewhere in the black forests of the estate. The hair on the nape of Kurst's neck stood on end, and the fingers of his hands curled tautly. How he longed to join the wolf. But that would have to come later.

He left the room, making his way past the manservant, and padded silently through the shadowy corridors of the manor house. Amazing, Kurst thought, that none of the sheep could see the manor for what it truly was. If they could, he was certain that none of them would ever step into its dark shadow, let alone cross its arched entryways.

He made his way down to the underground levels where the Gaunt Man worked in his laboratory. As he passed the windowed gallery that looked out on the eastern grounds of the estate, he glanced at the maelstrom bridge that stretched into the sky. That bridge led back to his world, back to the cosm of Orrorsh. He pulled his gaze from the writhing bridge and continued on. Why dwell on the past, he decided, for if he read the Gaunt Man's plans correctly, none of them would ever see their homeworld again.

Down in the lowest level of the manor house, where bedrock was the floor and the water of the land wept through the fitted stone blocks of the manor's deep foundations, Kurst pushed open the iron studded door to the chamber that was the workshop of the Gaunt Man. Kurst slid sideways into the room and stood silently, unmoving in the shadows. At the far end of the room, hunched, deformed creatures shoveled coal into a gigantic furnace that filled a significant portion of the chamber. Steam whistled and turbines whined. Generators turned and the harsh, yellow light of incandescent bulbs washed over strange machinery. And over three figures.

Kurst moved further into the shadow of a stone pillar that supported the high ceiling of the chamber. He watched two of the figures as they moved about the third where it lay strapped to an altarlike stone table. From where they cruelly pierced the chest of the man on the table, two short shafts pointed upward at awkward angles. The shafts were about two feet long and one inch in diameter. All the colors that Kurst had ever seen shifted and flowed along the surfaces of the shafts. Words in an ancient, arcane script and bathed in the glowing, flowing colors spiraled around each shaft.

The man was the stormer that Kurst had hunted in the jungle, the sheep that, in the final moment, had found its claws. Kurst knew the ends of the shafts in the stormer's chest were pointed and barbed. The outer ends were knobbed and sheathed in brass. At intervals that grew farther and farther apart, bursts of energy coruscated from the brass knobs and dissipated in the damp air of the chamber.

Into the machine.

Beyond the stone table was an assemblage of spinning flywheels, turning cams, arcing electrical sparks, and gauges with bouncing indicator needles. It spanned a quarter of the room and reached halfway to the shadows near the ceiling. Kurst heard the Gaunt Man speaking to the large man standing with him at the side of the stone table.

"This is the last and the bravest of them, Scythak. And the strongest. Look at him now. Shuddering in his flesh and cringing in his spirit."

"Stormers," rumbled Scythak scornfully as he grabbed one of the rods and twisted. The stormer arched his back and screamed.

"Careful, Scythak," chuckled the Gaunt Man. "You might lose part of yourself."

"I do not fear these runes," said Scythak, indicating the rods protruding from the stormer's chest. "Nor do I fear that machine which makes them work."

"You should. Look what they have done to this stormer," the Gaunt Man said as he pointed to the suffering man, "and to Kurst."

"That weakling! Why do you keep him around? Kill him or send him back to the Moors where he belongs." "He serves me well. Now, let's see what more we can get from this one." The Gaunt Man moved to the machine, adjusted some rheostats and turned some dials.

The raw smell of burnt flesh and ozone reached Kurst where he stood, and his fear of the rods and the machine started his shapeshifting. The fingers of his left hand lengthened. The nails grew into claws, and dense, dark brown fur stiffened on the back of his hand and up his wrist. Kurst feared the rods and the machine, because of what the Gaunt Man had done to him with them, and because of what he might do again. Kurst did not know what that machine had stripped from him, but he promised himself that he would not lose any more to it or to the Gaunt Man. He controlled his fear, willed his left hand back to its human shape, and walked out of the shadows toward the Gaunt Man.

On the world of Orrorsh, the world on which Kurst had been born and recruited into his service, he was known as Lord Bryon Salisbury, Earl of Waterford. But to those in his service, to those who understood the mysteries of the cosms, he was the Gaunt Man. Kurst suspected that Lord Salisbury had not been born on Orrorsh, if the word born could apply to him.

The Gaunt Man was six and a half feet tall, only an inch or so shorter than the massive Scythak standing next to him. His narrow head held his hollow-cheeked face on a long, slender neck that merged into narrow shoulders. His thin, long-armed body in the white laboratory coat that he wore when working in the chamber reminded Kurst of an animated stalk of dried winter hay. His dragon-topped cane rested against a nearby wall.

Kurst silently slipped into place at the stone table beside the Gaunt Man, bowing to his master while pointedly ignoring Scythak.

"Ah, Kurst, how nice of you to join us," the Gaunt Man said with a sneer on his long face. Scythak snickered evilly.

"You sent for me, master," Kurst said. "How might I serve you?"

"I wanted you to witness the final stage of this stormer's existence. This is one of your catches, is it not."

Kurst studied the young man, and his hand unconsciously stroked the rapidly-vanishing scar beneath his shirt.

"Ah, yes, Kurst," laughed the larger Scythak, "for all your vaunted speed this stormer actually wounded you. Perhaps you should be put out to the kennels so you might spend your old age in comfort."

"That's enough," said the Gaunt Man abruptly. Then he turned his attention back to the man on the stone slab and said to Kurst, "I am almost finished here. This stormer is hardly worth permanently connecting to the machine, but I can still make use of his possibilities. Watch."

The Gaunt Man made some minor adjustments to the instruments on the machine, and the flashes of energy bursting from the knobbed ends of the rods in the stormer's chest became more intense in their eruptions.

"Now, I shall strip him clean," said the Gaunt Man, and he threw a gnarled lever.

With that, the stormer screamed and thrashed wildly. The pain, while unbearable, only lasted a moment. Then a crackling cloud of light burst from the tops of the imbedded staves and hovered briefly over the stone slab. Kurst thought he saw the stormer's form within the cloud, but then the energy was sucked into the giant gridwork of brass and glass that made up much of the machine, joining with the rest of the lightning that constantly played across the lattice.

"Now," the Gaunt Man sighed as he readjusted the dials, "his possibilities are mine."

Kurst looked to the stone slab, but all that remained of the stormer, once his possibilities were yanked out, was a dried, lifeless husk.

31

Already dressed and waiting for this moment, Mara walked out of the living cubicle, across the cluttered, chrome and pastel-plastic lab area, and toward the doorway leading to the access hall. Even though her fear of failure, death, maybe never being able to come home again, filled her mind, she willed her feet to take steps. Even though the fluttery feeling deep in her empty belly said, "Don't go!" she opened the door. There was nothing to pack. The cybertechs would check out her circuits, enhancements, and power pack when she got to the Transference Facility. But she stopped just short of leaving her apartment, slid her right hand into the right hip pocket of her black jumpsuit, reached through the slit on the inside of that pocket, and pushed open the concealed cover of the storage pouch in her right thigh.

Inside the storage pouch, her hand briefly fondled the data plate that held her recordings of the world she was about to leave. The recordings were incomplete, as yet. But the plate would be there for her to work on when she needed to think about something besides cosmverse physics and war. It would be there when she needed to plug it in and see Kadandra, if only as images imposed upon her brain.

Reassured that the plate was there, she left the apartment. In the hall, after the door had shut silently behind her, she inserted her right index finger into the round security socket on the door. A small, electric tingling rippled from her elbow, through her arm and finger and into the door that then locked with an audible click.

"It's kinda sexual," she had once mentioned to Kendal Alec-Four when trying to describe this enhancement. He had looked at her with either disgust or amusement. With Alec, she knew, it was often hard to tell the difference between the two. At the grav-shaft at the end of the access hall, she pushed the down button and, when the capsule arrived, stepped in and said, "Garage level five."

"Of course, Dr. Hachi Mara-Two," said the rich, male, synthesized voice of the capsule as its circuits analyzed her voice and gave her clearance to use the grav-shaft.

The driver was leaning against the gleaming, stainless steel side of the air sled when she found stall twenty-three. Quizzically, he raised one eyebrow at her.

"Front seat," she said, moving to the passenger side of the air sled. She opened the door and slid into the soft, leatherlike upholstery of the seat.

The driver closed her door, entered the vehicle on the driver's side, took the control yoke in his hands, and asked, "Vehicle shaft or fast drop?"

"Fast drop," answered Mara as she fastened the safety webbing and grabbed onto the handholds attached to the dashboard.

"You got it," said the driver as he grinned at her and fastened his own webbing. Keypunching in the starter code, he spun the speed rheo to maximum and released fan baffles.

Riding ten inches off the concrete garage floor, with a roaring of drive fans ducted down and back, the vehicle jetted through the floor-to-ceiling opening of the unwalled garage. The sled's speed was sufficient to pierce the weak force barrier that kept weather and flying debris out of the garage. Mara's rump lifted from the seat, her stomach seemed to climb up to her throat, and she trapped a yell of excitement behind clenched teeth as the air sled fell thirty feet before its anti-crash units slowed its fall. The sled hit the ground below with a soft thump and bounced up to its standard ten inches of lift, fluttering like a leaf in the breeze before it steadied.

Laughing, the driver cut back the speed rheo and began to steer the sled through the streets of Cape City, toward the Transference Facility.

"Thanks, Mara. I don't get to do that very often, since I normally do chauffeur duty for Council members," said the driver.

"My pleasure," said Mara, still laughing and chuckling inside the sixteen-year-old body that housed the intellect of a genius.

Five feet and four inches tall, light-skinned with a mane of silver hair that fell softly about ears that were a bit too jutting, Mara was a walking contradiction. Force-educated with RNA injections at an early age because of her remarkably high level of intelligence and indentured to the World Council in exchange for her cybernetic enhancements, she was a child with the weight of the world on her shoulders. No, make that the weight of worlds.

If she clicked her molars together in a beat-beat-pause-beat pattern, her diagnostic implants would perform a system's check on her circuitry. Aside from the security implant and microfilament in her right elbow and arm, the storage pouch in her right, upper thigh, Mara had added to nature's design: diagnostic displays in her right optic nerves and retina; a high-resolution scanner enhancement attachment for her left eye; molybdenum fibers sewn into her incisors for straight cutting power; two standard enhancement-input sockets behind her right ear and with tracer filaments leading to the analytical portions of her brain; slightly reinforced tendons in her neck after a minor skiing accident; two-year, weaponry power pack in her right shoulder; and, channeling power lines, a slim cable leading to the weapons socket in her right hand.

But it was the enhancements added to her left arm and hand that had cost her ten years of her life to come. That left forearm and, now, clawlike hand was shot through with wires and printed circuitry, allowing her to run tests on and provide feedback for the microchips she designed. The small, square groove on the tip of her thumb held the chip. Electric micro-probes in the index finger sought for broken paths in the chips. The gossamer-thin extrusions from the middle finger, being most opposable to the work platform on the thumb, were used for the delicate work of burning new paths in the magnetic bubbles of the chips. With her eye-enhancer attached and with her analytical enhancements at full blast (and, therefore, only for short periods of time) she could manipulate that middle finger in the micromillimeter movements necessary. Her ring finger provided the power to unseal and seal the chips and to erect a static charge that kept chip-destroying dust from her hand. The little finger, least controllable, extended a power lead for running full-up tests.

It was this hand that would allow her to work on the sensover data plate she carried in her thigh pouch, to recreate in magnetic flux the world she loved. Sixteen years old, genius, prodigy, two doctorates in three years, and for two years she had fought in the Invasion War against the Sims. Sixteen years old and, for now, when she could forget her guilt, her laughter over the thrill of falling in an air sled for thirty feet sounded fresh and innocent.

32

Baruk Kaah rocked back on his tail and watched as an optant prayed to Lanala for the balls of sun to light the night sky. The edeinos priestess swayed back and forth, chanting her love for the goddess. Then, when her swaying became more frantic, she raised a clawed hand and a ball of sun appeared in the air.

"Excellent, optant," called the High Lord, "your love is strong this night!"

A stalenger swooped out of the darkness and came to rest in the air before Baruk Kaah. Its membrane was like stained glass this night, reflecting the light from the ball of sun into a multitude of colors. Baruk Kaah nodded, giving the servant permission to speak. With that, tentacles uncoiled from beneath its star-shaped body and snaked out to touch the High Lord.

"We have found the stormer you sought, Saar," said the stalenger with its taps and vibrations. "Two edeinos are bringing him and should arrive shortly."

Without a word, Baruk Kaah wiped away the tentacles, dismissing the servant. He rose to his full height and prepared to hold audience.

"Yes, you will want to look the part of conquerer when the conquered is brought before you."

Baruk Kaah turned angrily, his powerful tail raised to strike. But he stopped its descend immediately when he saw that the speaker was one of the ravagons.

"You speak dangerously, ravagon."

"You behave dangerously, High Lord. Why do you seek out a single stormer?"

"My actions are no concern of yours. But I shall tell you anyway, because it pleases me that you should know. This stormer is an optant of these soft-skinned ones. He chanted to a crowd of thousands, and they returned his chant with cheers and excitement. Such an optant must serve me, or he must die."

Minutes later, two edeinos approached. A soft-skinned male in tattered clothing walked between them. Baruk Kaah called to mind the language of these beings, remembering the words that Rec Pakken had whispered to him back in his cosm, back on Takta Ker.

"You are the optant of the soft-skinned tribe?"

The human appeared dazed. His head was bent and he stared at the ground. When he did not answer, Baruk Kaah motioned to the stalenger. It reached out with its long tentacles and attached them to the human's head. Then, gently, it raised the head so that the human was forced to look at the Saar.

"I ask you again, are you an optant?"

The human shuddered, then tried to compose himself as best he could. When he spoke, his voice sounded weak and frightened.

"I'm Eddie Paragon," he finally managed. "I'm just a rock'n'roll singer. Please don't kill me."

"No, singer Paragon, I will not kill you," Baruk Kaah said as soothingly as he could, "at least not while you serve me."

The two edeinos placed their hands on Paragon's shoulders and forced him to his knees. But they really didn't need to. The singer got the idea. He bowed his head to the Saar of the edeinos and choked on the words that escaped his lips.

"I ... will serve you."

Baruk Kaah smiled his lizard smile at the ravagon, totally pleased with the ease of this conversion. He didn't see the tears that streamed down Paragon's face, though.

But the ravagon did.

33

All the colors of the rainbow played over the grimy-rain-streaked bubble canopy of the air sled as it slid on its anti-grav units through the crowded streets of Cape City. The colors emanated from flashing, glowing, gas-filled tubes and liquid crystal displays of signs and building-sized screens that advertised everything from laxatives to prayer. Mara stared through the streaked colors at the collapsed, ruined section where the maelstrom bridge once arched from the sky. The sled whined along the street that paralleled the miles of tumbled metal that had fallen and crushed a half-mile wide path through the city, making a jumbled trail of cyclopean wreckage all the way to the bay.

"I hear the council wants to leave the bridgehead as a monument," said the driver as the sled passed the one section that still stood at the abutment of the bridge.

Mara turned away from the twisted metal. Even though it was ruined, its surface still seemed to ripple like the surface of a deep pond. And below the surface, she imagined she could still she the tortured souls that gave the metal its shape.

"A monument to my stupidity and all the torture and deaths it caused," she said miserably.

"The council cleared you. They said it was simply coincidence."

"Yeah," she said and remembered her vain, childish pride when her paper hypothesizing the cosmverse model of extradimensional space was published. She had propounded that the universe was but one cosm in a cosmverse composed of infinite reflections of an infinite number of realities. Her mathematics had been without flaw, and her conclusions irrefutable, if undemonstrated. Undemonstrated until the maelstrom bridge had crashed into the city and the Invasion War had begun, a war carried to Mara's world by armies from one of those reflection worlds she had mathematically established as being in existence. Tangible proof of her proudly proposed theory brought her bitter shame and guilt as she began to believe that she had caused the Invasion War by acknowledging the possibility of the worlds from which the invaders came. That they flowed through the hole she opened with her cosmscope.

So, she had plugged in the multi-dimensional physics chip and the cosmverse logic chip into the slots behind her ear and immersed herself in her math. When her conclusions forced her up for air, she wrote another paper, taking full blame for the Invasion War. But curiosity urged her to look into the cosmverse again, and this time she saw another world. And the Sims, her calculations told her, saw it too. If they could not have Kadandra, they would conquer the unsuspecting world called Earth.

Mara proposed that an advisor be sent to this Earth to help it fend off the Sims the way Kadandra had. She had mathematically described a method for traveling through the cosmverse using the power that certain Kadandran's had demonstrated in the wake of the Sim's reality storms.

Using the chips Mara designed and built, Dr. Kendal and the rest of her team created the machine that would send the advisor to Earth cosm.

"Dr. Hachi, do you have a recommended candidate?" the World Council had asked her after clearing her of her self-confessed crime and accepting her proposal.

"Me," she had answered.

34

On a rocky outcropping on the Kimberley coast of Australia, an elderly Aborigine sat and watched the Timor Sea. The waves were rough and black this day, thought Djilangulyip, smashing angrily against the land. The sea was pounding on their door, warning them of the danger. But the people had lost the ability to see.

But Djil saw, and that made him responsible.

Far out to sea, where the islands of Indonesia interrupted the waves, an evil had invaded the world. And the world did not like that, oh no. And the world called to its children for assistance. But the children had lost the ability to hear.

But Djil heard, and it scared him so.

He looked to the horizon, and there, at the very edge of his sight, he could see the storm front where the world rebelled against the invaders. His hands moved over the rope he held of their own accord, tying knot after knot into the coiled fabric. He looked down at the knotted rope and knew what it was telling him. The world, like the rope, needed to be tied back together in the places the invaders had frayed. But how, world? he asked silently. How do you knot reality back together?

He contemplated the knots throughout the long night.

35

The air sled reached the parking garage of the Transference Facility, after having passed through three security checks.

"Go save a world," said the driver as he solemnly shook Mara's hand in farewell.

"With luck," answered Mara, remembering Randin-Six.

"Always pick the fast drop," he grinned, offering the

best advice he could think of for what she was about to do.

Mara smiled back at him and said, "No other way to go."

Then she turned and entered the main lobby of the facility which had been built for the single purpose of sending her to another cosm. Once again dressed in her black jumpsuit after the cybertechs had plugged into her and jolted her, and the medtechs had prodded and poked her, after she had been issued a laser pistol and an assortment of enhancement chips and had stored them in her thigh pouch and in the pockets of her jumpsuit, she was ushered into the main chamber.

Around the periphery of the room, the other cybernetically-enhanced volunteers were plugged into the consoles at which they sat. Their heads were resting in the headrests of their seats. Their eyes were closed, and she knew they were lost in the sparkling, glittering pathways of the cybernet. It was their bio-electronic circuitry and their logic pathways that gave the transference machine its power. But it was something else about these people, some intangible constant that she had been able to measure but not identify, that gave the machine the final boost that allowed it to shove her into another dimension.

She tried not to think about being on the Earth world, stranded without this intricate machinery and the enhanced mentalities to help her make the trip home. She nodded to Dr. Mikkos where he sat at the main console. But Alec — Dr. Kendal — was nowhere to be seen. It hurt that he was not here to see her off, but time was running out.

Mara watched as Dr. Mikkos punched in the final codes of the starting procedure. He didn't like goodbyes, and she didn't force hers on him. During the theory and construction phase of the transference machine project, he had treated her as he would his own daughter, and had also come to think of her in that way. Mara, not having seen her father since her parents' divorce, responded to Dr. Mikkos as she would to her actual father. They had said their farewell over a quiet dinner the night before, and both of them were willing to leave it at that. Perhaps, they were hesitant to add more, fearing he would say, "Don't go," or she would say, "I don't want to go."

Mara walked over to the cyberdrive console and inserted her right index finger into the security socket on the console. The implant in her elbow had nearly finished its job of sending coded pulses along the microfilament in her arm and finger, giving the final clearance to the transference system. The final tingle of electricity was leaving her hand when she heard a noise behind her. Without removing her finger from the socket, she turned to see what had caused the noise.

Dr. Mikkos sat slumped over the keyboard of the main console. Blood from his torn throat spurted over the white keys. Standing next to the dead physicist was one of the creatures that she had spent two years fighting, one of the demons who had come over the maelstrom bridge to wreak havoc upon her world before they were finally beaten back by the technology of Mara's world. A Sim.

The Sim had cruel features and blue-black skin that shone in the glittering, flashing lights of the main console. His hands were clawed and the left one dripped blood from where it had torn through Mikkos' throat. His right arm was as cybernetically enhanced as Mara's own. The military-issue tunic and slacks looked incongruous on his feral form.

"Greetings, Dr. Hachi, allow me to introduce myself," the Sim said, bowing from the waist slightly, but never taking his eyes off of Mara. His leering grin revealed yellowed, pointed teeth. Mara looked about her for help, but all of the volunteers were locked in the cybernet and unaware of the happenings in the chamber. She knew that if the Sim had gotten this far, there were no living security guards left behind him.

She was on her own.

"My name is Thratchen. And, I'm afraid, I must ask you to move away from that console."

"Why should I?" asked Mara, stalling for time and hoping to learn something of the Sim's purpose.

"Ah," smiled Thratchen, "because I would like to find out from you, firsthand, how you discovered our plans of invasion. Dr. Kendal was not very cooperative, if you catch my meaning. He actually was able to shut down his mind before I could glean much more than the location of this facility. Remarkable man, really."

"Alec?" Mara screamed in panic. "You hurt Alec, too?"

Thratchen shrugged. "I sorted his mind, my dear. Even if he lives he will be little more than a lump of flesh with no thoughts to speak of. Now, step away from that machine."

The Sim flexed his claws and moved toward the closest console. He eyed the exposed neck below the thrown back head of the plugged in volunteer.

"So, you have found an interesting use for stormers," Thratchen chuckled. "We never were able to do all that much with them ourselves."

With her mind racing, Mara knew she couldn't get to her laser pistol in time to save the volunteer, maybe not even in time to save herself. She had fought these creatures and knew how fast they were in battle. Maybe she could save a world, though. She flexed her elbow and twisted her finger in the security socket. Lights flashed from every screen at every console; printers began chattering, and warning bells chimed. The access hatch on the transference cylinder popped open. For a spilt second, Thratchen's attention was drawn away from her and the volunteer. In that time, Mara leaped into the cylinder and slammed the hatch.

Thratchen leaped after her, covering the distance to the cylinder in two bounds. He inserted the claws of both hands — one natural, one cybernetic — into the seam surrounding the door. Planting his feet against the side of the cylinder, he strained; the muscles in his back, shoulders, and legs bunched and pushed at the fabric of his clothing. He peeled back the door as if he were peeling the flexible skin off some piece of overripe fruit. But he was too late — the cylinder was empty. Dr. Hachi was gone. Roaring in anger, Thratchen leaped with outstretched claws at the nearest plugged-in volunteer, then at the next, and at the next ...

36

Coyote sat in the passenger seat of the van. Beside him, in the driver's seat, the cop snored. It really did sound like a saw cutting through wood, just like in the cartoons. Once, a childhood ago, Coyote would have smiled at the image. Now he only sighed. In the back of the van, he could hear Rat breathing heavily in sleep. He glanced back and saw the lizard's yellow eyes looking back at him. Frightened, he turned to again watch the burning Newark skyline, consciously looking up so as not to see the mutilated dead.

Of all the bodies surrounding the van, only one was moving. Father Bryce, dead on his feet, shuffled from corpse to corpse, pausing at each to say a short prayer and bestow whatever blessing he still had within him.

The teen opened the van door slowly, trying his best not to disturb his sleeping companions. He stepped gingerly around the prone forms strewn everywhere, forcing himself to look anywhere but at their torn chests, at their glazed eyes. A few cautious steps. Then a few more. Coyote stepped again, and his foot sank into a wet pile that squished under and around his sneaker. He had no desire to know what he stepped in.

Finally, he reached Father Bryce. He stopped some feet away, unsure if he should interrupt the solemn ceremony. The priest was leaning over a young man, whispering because he strained his voice long before.

"... amen," Coyote heard Bryce finish as he closed the young man's eyes. The priest stretched, yawned, then started toward the next body.

Coyote spoke softly. "Enough, Father. You've done enough."

He gently touched the priest's arm and led him to a car that had stalled nearby. When Bryce stumbled, Coyote found that he was not strong enough to keep himself and the priest from falling. But Tal Tu was. The edeinos must have followed him from the van, Coyote thought, as the lizard man steadied them.

"Thank you, Tal Tu," Bryce said in a cracking voice. The priest leaned against the car, and Coyote jumped onto the hood beside him.

"You know," he said as he peered into his mass kit, "I ran out of hosts hours ago." He held up a single wafer so that his two companions could see it by the light of the fire. "I saved this one, though. For an emergency, I guess."

The priest looked to the side, and Coyote followed his gaze. There, beside the car, was the mortal remains of a woman. Bryce took his last host, broke it, and placed it in her mouth. Then he made the sign of the cross, and closed her sightless eyes.

"She needed it more than I did," he said.

Enough of this, Coyote thought. He leaped down from the car and grabbed the priest's arm again.

"Let's go, Father. It's time to get some rest."

The priest looked around once more, but he nodded at Coyote's words.

"Yes, I do need to rest. I am so very tired."

Father Bryce allowed Coyote to lead him back to the van, and Tal Tu followed behind them.

37

Old Man Baker watched the man in the work boots, who, in turn, watched the priest and his companions. Baker was once considered mean and cantankerous, a man you avoided if you could. But when the dinosaurs appeared and the fire started, Old Man Baker became just that — an old man. He ran when the rest of the masses ran, and he hid when the dinosaur men started killing. He lay on the floor of a stalled Honda, his eyes shut tight to block out the awful sights.

But he couldn't block out the sounds.

First there were the frightened sounds of the confused masses, typified by muffled sobs and uncontrolled bawling.

Then there were the dinosaur men's shouts of reptilious joy, accompanied by a ceaseless, hissing chant.

Finally, there were the screams. Hundreds of human

voices filled with pain and raised in terror reached the old man's ears at the same time, and those were followed by wave upon wave of screams. Most frightening of all, remembered Baker, was how each wave of screams abruptly ended, cut off the way a power failure cuts off a TV.

He lay on the floor of the Honda through all of those sounds, praying that the chanters, who were so very close, would not find him. And when the sounds stopped, he stayed on that floor, eyes still shut tight, refusing to move in case even one dinosaur man was at the window watching him, waiting for a sign of life.

Old Man Baker would probably still be there, had not the man in the work boots showed up. He must have been calling for quite some time, Baker thought, before the old man responded. Baker finally opened his eyes and looked up from his spot on the floor of the back seat. The door nearest his head was ajar, and the first thing Baker saw was a work boot resting on the frame just inches from his face. The boot had a metal tip guard, and it was stained with a dark, wet substance. His gaze carried further, and he saw the rest of a large man with blonde hair. On the man's right forearm, which rested across his bent knee, was the tatoo of a cobra. Its jaws were spread wide, revealing dripping fangs that were poised to strike.

The large man helped Baker out of the car, then forced him to walk with him among the bodies. And so Old Man Baker's worst fear came to pass. He was forced to put an image to the sounds he had heard, and the reality of the torn bodies was worse than anything his mind had conjured earlier. Once during the long walk Old Man Baker turned to look at the tatooed man. He saw the man's smile, his longing gaze, his studied examination of the wounds that killed the masses. Then he turned away, knowing full well that the tatooed man was enjoying this terrible stroll through the garden of the dead.

When the van approached, the tatooed man made Baker squat down behind a station wagon. They stayed there for a long time; the tatooed man watching the priest make his rounds, the old man watching the watcher. Finally, the priest returned to his van, and the tatooed man turned to Baker.

"The priest is very much like me," the tatooed man whispered. "He works with the dead, I work with the dead. It's my calling."

The tatooed man produced a large hunting knife from a sheath that was hidden under his pants leg. He held it loosely, letting its serrated edge gleam in the fire light.

"These lizard men are artists," the tatooed man continued, "every death along this road is a masterpiece. I admire their style."

With that, the tatooed man plunged his serrated knife into Old Man Baker's chest. Stunned by the quickness, Baker did not scream. Once the pain registered he tried to call out, but only blood gurgled from his lips. The tatooed man twisted the blade, carving a hole very much like those in the bodies littered across the area. He smiled at his own technique, then wiped the blade clean on Baker's coat sleeve.

The last sight the old man witnessed was the metal-tipped work boots walking away.

38

Running. Very quickly. Fast. As fast as he could. Trying to find Vicky. Trying to stay ahead of them.

Trying to survive.

Running. And others ran with him. Others he could not quite see yet. Others he could not name.

They ran from the sound of beating wings. From the smell of sulfer and fire. From the claws.

Running. And something called from up ahead. Something — wonderful.

It was the color of polished turquoise, and it shone with a light all its own. It was the color of bright crimson, swirling through the turquoise like blood-filled veins.

He needed to reach the wonderful thing. He wanted to hear its song from up close.

But the wings were louder now. Terribly loud. Drowning out the song. Pounding against him with rapid beats.

Then he felt the claws.

Decker sat up bolt straight in his bed, sweat pouring down his face, his chest, his arms. He took a deep breath, calmed himself. Already the nightmare was fading, but he knew that sleep would be a long time returning.

He reached for the remote control on the nightstand, and switched on the bedroom television. He flipped through the channels until he found the cable news network. He adjusted the volume and leaned back to watch.

"It is being called the Day of Disaster, that moment almost 96 hours ago when all communication with New York City ceased, and the President and Vice President of the United States were declared missing," said the practiced newscaster as video of the Opening Day ceremonies at Shea Stadium filled the small screen. Decker recognized the rock singer Eddie Paragon, who sang the National Anthem that day. He watched as the video switched to the beginning of the game. Then, as Walter "The Truth" Jones released the first pitch, the screen dissolved to static.

"The disaster was categorized by a massive disruption of telephone lines and television signals," the newscaster continued. "All major media has since re-routed as much of their communications networks as possible, but some services have been irrevocably lost. The effected area, which is roughly 600 miles across, continues to impede most efforts to gather information."

Decker watched the pictures that continued to flash across the screen, but he did not hear the words. Instead, he re-examined the information he had, which was more complete than what the TV news showed.

He knew that spy plane and satellite fly bys were able to map a 600 mile, diamond-shaped area on the eastern seaboard which showed no patterns of electrical activity. He was on hand when the Speaker of the House, acting in the President's stead, declared a national emergency and ordered all armed forces to go to DefCon Two. Even now, reserve units, National Guard and state-side regular army were on their way to Detroit, Cleveland, Pittsburgh, Philadelphia, and Washington D.C. to defend those cities in case the "dead zone" spread. U.S. troops in foreign lands had been alerted to the possibility that they could be called home at a moment's notice.

Efforts to scan Shea Stadium and the immediate area from above were blocked by an intense and quite localized storm. Decker had studied what pictures they had, but he could rationalize little of what he saw.

He had listened to the final communications with the two National Guard units that had been on armed maneuvers that first day. Since they were available, they were ordered to make their way east in order to determine what was happening in New York. Their last report situated them just west of Elmira. But what they reported was strange. The radio operator claimed that a line of "big lizards" was in stationary position some two clicks distant. Then communication was interrupted, and the units, along with 300 more miles of United States area, fell silent.

Towns and cities along the edge of the dead zone were being inundated by more and more refugees every day. These people all told stories of friends and relatives who behaved savagely, of giant dinosaurs that smashed cars and buildings as they walked, and of lizard men who killed for the sheer joy of it.

But efforts to confirm these reports by low-level fly bys, helicopter reconnaissance, and special forces deployment met with disaster. Planes and helicopters that flew too low lost power and crashed, and contact with soldiers air-dropped into the dead zone was cut off almost immediately.

The Canadian government, too, was being kept abreast of the situation, and there was even talk that some kind of joint committee would be formed in case the dead zone spread across the border.

Of all the theories, Decker wasn't sure which one he believed just yet, but one thing was certain: something terrible was happening within the 600 mile zone of silence. Decker finally drifted off to sleep with a thousand questions on his mind.

But not a single answer.

39

On the morning of the fifth day after Baruk Kaah set

clawed foot upon the Earth, Sergeant Richard Macklin, Royal Canadian Mounted Police, stood on the south bank of the Mackenzie River, holding the reins of his horse as he waited for the ferry that was stolidly making its way across from Fort Providence. Macklin watched the creamy curl of water turned by the bow of the ferry as it plowed against the current flowing northwestward out of Great Slave Lake, a current that would eventually flow into Mackenzie Bay on Beaufort Sea in the Arctic Ocean. Torn fragments of dark clouds scudded high in the clear, blue sky of northern Canada. Macklin shivered involuntarily, and noted that even darker clouds were gathering on the horizon.

Macklin's horse whickered and dug with its right forehoof at the loose gravel of the ferry landing. Macklin turned to the horse and stroked its neck, soothing it with the companionship that had grown between them on their patrols into the fringes of the RCMP post jurisdiction at Fort Providence. He glanced skyward again and saw that the clouds had rolled overhead, turning the day into night.

"We're in for a helluva storm," the officer said aloud.

A thunderous sound of an avalanche rolled quickly and briefly across the river, stopped and faded into silence. Macklin, caught by the sound, by his subconscious identification of it as an avalanche, and by his forebrain's conflicting knowledge that there should not be an avalanche here, jerked his head to look across the river.

The ferry slip on the far side of the river was no longer there. The Mountie post and the restored Hudson Bay Company trading post were no longer there. The small town had been obliterated by a huge, growing stalk, half a mile wide, rising in a gently curving arc, and disappearing high in the dark sky.

The sound of the engines on the ferry stopped, and the boat, caught in the current, began drifting downstream. The ferry was still close enough for Macklin to see the high-cheekboned, Slavey Indian face of the pilot through the glass of the windows in the small wheelhouse, and he could see the faces of the two deckhands, who had been leaning against the bow railing. The pilot, with the quick, head-turning movement of a man confused by his surroundings, dashed from the wheelhouse and to the port rail, staring fixedly at the giant stalk that had smashed into Fort Providence. As the boat spun in the current, the pilot ran from port to starboard and back, trying to keep the mutant plant in sight.

The deckhands joined the pilot in his fixation on the stalk, which they now saw was actually hundreds of stalks and vines and leaves twisted together. As the boat drifted farther downstream, they leaped over the rail and began swimming toward the north shore of the river. The current carried them swiftly away and Macklin soon lost sight of their bobbing heads and splashing arms.

"What in hell is going on?" Macklin asked vainly of the horse beside him. For answer, the horse neighed loudly and shook its head as its ears and nose caught the sounds and smells coming downwind from the people and creatures stepping off the stalk on the far side of the river. The horse reared and tried to bolt. With his left hand, Macklin pulled down on the reins, bringing the horse's flailing forelegs back to earth. He grabbed a handful of mane, pulled himself up and flung his right leg over the back of the horse.

As he seated himself in the saddle and fought his feet into the stirrups, he was better able to control the frightened animal. He brought the horse to a snorting, stiff-legged standstill and stared at the plant bridge — which was what his mind decided it was when he saw the things walking off of it.

What Macklin had assumed were people because of their upright stance turned out to be reptiles of some kind. But there was more than that stepping into the remains of the town. Macklin saw tusked, hairy, elephantlike beasts dragging large travois piled high with leaf-wrapped bundles. At the edges of the mass of lizard people were large, tawny creatures that moved with the sleek grace of hunting lions. Some of the lizards rode on the backs of one-horned beasts that looked to Macklin like the pictures and reconstructions of dinosaurs he had seen.

Macklin's horse began to chomp at the bit and stomp and curvet in its aversion to the alien smell of the beasts on the other side of the river and to the tight rein that Macklin was keeping. To calm the horse, Macklin ran him a short distance back and forth along the river bank, while always focusing his own eyes on the exodus on the site of the smashed town. He watched the creatures walk west and east along the northern bank of the Mackenzie, and he watched them move northward, away from the river.

"Easy, boy," Macklin spoke softly while he made mental note of the numbers and types of creatures coming off the bridge. He knew the officers down at the Hay River post were going to want details, not some panicky story about lizard men, mastodons, sabertooths, and dinosaurs camping along the Mackenzie. It was some time before Macklin noticed that there was someone on the other bank, watching him. That the creature watching him was intelligent Macklin knew just from the intensity of its interest in him. That the creature was not human was also obvious from his saurian face and body. "Uh oh," Macklin muttered to his horse.

Then the saurian waved with one of its clawed fore-limbs, gesturing behind, as if calling someone forward from the mass coming off the bridge. Silent in the distance, what looked like two winged reptiles flapped into the air and headed across the river, toward Macklin.

"Shit," said Macklin. "I think it's time to go make our report."

He reined his horse to the right and spurred him into a gallop, heading southeast along the shore of the river, not following the bottom half of the Yellowknife High-way but taking the shorter way across country to the town of Hay River. Macklin had the horse at full gallop along the grassy bank of the river, and he had his service pistol in his hand, when the first winged lizard reached him. Half turned in the saddle, the Mountie saw that one of the lizard people rode atop the winged creature. The lizard man menacingly held a spear at the ready, pre-paring to throw it at Macklin.

With his arm extended and the pistol aimed just to the left of the protruding breastbone of the lizard man, Macklin squeezed the trigger. The recoil kicked his hand upward. The report echoed off the surface of the river. The lizard man screamed wildly; it fell to the ground, crunched into a boulder, and lay unmoving. Macklin yelled in triumph, spurred his horse and galloped on.

The second winged reptile flew high and ahead of Macklin. Judging its angle of attack, it clapped its leath-ery wings closed and plummeted hawklike at Macklin, with its taloned feet opened and ready to grasp. Macklin aimed his pistol forward over his horses head and fired. He missed. His second shot, close upon the quickly fading sound of the first, blasted off the top of the creature's skull, splattering blood and brains onto the seated lizard man.

Before the dying winged reptile crashed to the ground, the lizard man launched his spear. The spear flew into the chest of the galloping horse, burying itself halfway up the shaft. The forelegs of the horse collapsed and it began to tumble headlong to the ground. Macklin let his pistol drop to the end of its lanyard and used both hands and all the strength in his arms and shoulders to haul back on the reins, trying to keep the horse's head up, trying to keep him from running into the ground.

But the horse went down. Macklin pulled his feet from the stirrups and rolled over the horse's neck and head as the horse crumpled and its kicking legs churned up the grass and soil. Macklin made it to one knee before the pain of broken bones and torn flesh hit him like grating, tearing fire in his left shoulder. He lurched to his feet. Slumping, he retrieved his pistol into his hand and waited.

He could see where the flyer had landed, but there was no sign of the lizard man. He cursed himself for losing sight of it when the horse went down. But he didn't have to wait long for it to show itself.

Rising from behind a boulder was the tall lizard man. It roared joyously, then began to bound toward the wounded officer. Macklin aimed with pain-blurred vision, fired, and missed. He fired again, at close range. The bullet hit the left arm of the lizard man, but it didn't slow the creature. If anything, the beast seemed to relish the pain.

"If you like it, monster, I've got more where that came from," Macklin cursed through clenched teeth.

Already his reflexes were slowed, and the biting pain

Storm Knights

Alan Jude Summa

threw off his concentration, so the next two shots were wide of their mark. Then the lizard man was upon him. Its claws ripped at his stomach, and its teeth tore at his face. It pushed downward on the arm holding the pistol, and Macklin's last shot thudded dully into the ground. While the lizard man amused itself with Macklin's body, the now-riderless flyer landed atop the broken-legged, screaming horse, and calmly tore out its throat.

The exodus over the bridge into what had been Fort Providence continued while Macklin's blood flowed onto the ground, and over the next few days. Five tribes of edeinos spread sixty miles to the northwest, along the north bank of the Mackenzie and fifty-five miles to the northeast, along the north shore of Great Slave Lake. Using the Yellowknife Highway, they managed to travel nearly eighty miles toward the provincial capital at the town of Yellowknife. They had not yet found a ford that would allow them to cross to the south bank of the Mackenzie. They would, though, and the edeinos would continue to spread, following the waterways and valleys of the north.

When the optants connected with the trees and other living things of nature, all the beliefs of the Jakatts flowed into the land, making it their land and the land of Lanala. What few Indians were left in the territory quickly succumbed to the spirits of the newcomers, and in their minds, life was as it always had been and always should be. If one of the locals ever dreamed some vague dream that the gods had changed names and shapes, he would shrug, on awakening, and know that the gods were the gods and could do as gods chose.

And, as they settled, the edeinos and their new tribe members prepared the land for the planting of the gospog. For this was the will of their Saar, Baruk Kaah.

40

At Trenton, Father Bryce and his companions caught up with the refugees. They were fleeing the madness that had claimed New York as its own, running from the marauding lizards. There were other working vehicles on the roads now, so the van did not stand out as it had in Manhattan and Newark. But the group decided to keep Tal Tu out of sight, just in case the refugees turned ugly.

In Bristol, Alder turned the van into a gas station/convenience store. It appeared closed, abandoned. Still, Alder parked near the pumps and shut off the engine.

"We're running low," he said, "and who knows, maybe there's still some in the lines. We won't know unless we try."

As Alder prepared to work the pump, Coyote eyed the convenience store. Its windows were smashed, and much of the merchandise appeared to be missing.

Coyote shrugged. "We won't know unless we try."

Alder smiled, and Coyote, Rat, and Tal Tu ran over to take a look.

But something more important caught the priest's eye. Across the road was a liquor store. It looked to be in worse shape than the convenience mart, but it was possible that something was left inside. He started toward it.

"Where are you going, Father?" asked Alder as he examined the pumps and hoses.

"I'm out of wine," he called back, "without wine or hosts, how will I comfort the dying?"

The liquor store was a mess of smashed glass and powerful smells. Not only had the display window and door been smashed in, but every shelf and rack had been overturned, every case emptied. Bryce carefully stepped into the gutted building, making his way around the interior.

Sip by sip, he thought, the blessed wine he carried in his mass kit had moistened parched, moaning lips, and finally run out. If he could find something — anything — to replace it with, he would feel much better. As he shoved the glass around the floor with his foot, he happened upon an unbroken bottle. He reached down and clutched the fifth in his hands. Reverently, he lifted it to examine. It was a bottle of Mogen David.

"I'll take that."

The voice startled the priest, and he nearly dropped the precious bottle. But, though he fumbled with it, he managed to hold it tight as he turned to see who spoke.

Standing in the broken doorway was a large, blonde-haired man dressed in dirty work clothes and heavy, metal-tipped work boots. On his right forearm was the tatoo of a cobra, poised as if to strike. Bryce's gaze drifted to the man's hand, which clutched a large, serrated hunting knife.

"Come on," the man said, "unless you want me to cut you?"

Bryce stammered, trying to explain that he needed the contents of the bottle for the dying souls he was sure to still encounter. But what came out was an incoherent mumble that was part fright and part gibberish.

"Maybe I'll cut you anyway," the man said as he shuffled forward, brandishing the blade.

Bryce looked into the man's eyes and saw bottomless pools of madness that frightened him more than any weapon ever could. He handed him the bottle without being asked again, letting his overcoat fall open.

The man studied the bottle label for a time, then looked at Bryce's soiled, white collar that peeked out of his open coat.

"You're the priest," the man exclaimed.

Bryce only nodded, as he was still unable to find the words to say, and he had no idea where this man knew him from.

"I've never killed a priest," the man said, and Bryce swore that in that instant the man's eyes lit up. "But I don't want to deal with all your friends, too."

He shoved the bottle back at Bryce. "Take it and get out of here, Father."

As the priest cradled the bottle and pushed his way carefully past the tatooed man, the man said, "We're a lot alike, Father. We both send people on their way." The man looked again at the bottle Bryce carried and added, "I hope it does somebody some good."

Me, too, thought Bryce as he looked at the label on the bottle. Maybe sending people on their way with a taste of sweetness was not such a bad idea.

"Maybe next time we'll try it the other way, Father," the man called as Bryce left the building. The priest ignored the remark and continued to walk, hoping that the tatooed man could not see how badly he was shaking.

When Bryce returned everyone else was back in the van and the motor was idling. Bryce climbed in and took his seat, not certain if he should mention his encounter.

"Father," Rat said, "Tal Tu has something for you."

The priest, in surprise, took the small carton the lizard man presented. It was a box of Saltine crackers.

"Hosts," said Tal Tu, and the priest smiled, forgetting all about the incident in the liquor store.

41

Captain Ondarev drove the truck through the fields and forests outside Gor'kij. His concentration was split between the road and the young woman seated beside him. On a particularly straight portion of the road, he risked a longer glance at the woman.

Katrina Tovarish sat straight backed, her sightless eyes staring out at the horizon. Her head was tilted slightly to one side, as though she was listening to something. Ondarev could not help but notice how beautiful she was, especially now that she was in real clothing and not hospital garb. Still, the blouse and pants were simple, plain, but on Katrina they outshined any ball gown he had ever seen.

They had not spoken since earlier that day, when Katrina directed him north toward Kirov. Now he simply followed the roads, winding the truck through empty fields in search of something Katrina knew was out here. What it was or where, that was still a mystery. He only hoped she could locate it in time.

"Stop, Captain Ondarev," Katrina said in her haunting voice.

Ondarev, caught by the surprise of her sudden outburst, slammed on the brakes. He turned to ask her what was the matter, but she was already stepping from the truck. He joined her outside.

He walked around the front of the vehicle, moving to lend his arm and eyes to Katrina. But she didn't need them. She rested the long, slender fingers of her hands on the hood of the car, feeling the warmth and vibrations of the engine, as she slowly scanned the horizon to the left of the road. He imagined he felt her mind reaching out, searching with senses that Ondarev hoped were as real as the reports he had read indicated.

"I know you doubt that I can really help you, captain," Katrina said, "but if it makes you feel any better, I am not actually helping you."

"Then who are you helping, Katrina Tovarish?"

The young woman hesitated, for the first time since he met her she showed a sign of uncertainty. "I am not sure, but I hear its pain and fear calling to me. It is so afraid of these invaders. That is who I am helping, captain, a voice that is not a voice, a cry for help that only I can hear."

Ondarev did not understand what the young woman was saying, but the way she said it convinced him that she was not a charlatan or a faker. She was sincere, and as dedicated to fighting her prophetic storm as he was to defending the Soviet people. At least in that regard he could agree with her — stop the storm, and the voice that Katrina alone could hear and the country that Ondarev was sworn to protect would both be saved.

"Out there, captain," Katrina said, pointing toward the open field that stretched before them. "That is where we will find it."

"Find what?"

Katrina hesitated, searching for words to describe what her mind was seeing. "The ... alien thing. It is out there, waiting to guide the storm here. It is ... a marker of a sort, or perhaps an idol. It resists my efforts to examine it closely. It tries to hide."

"Then, my young friend, it is time to bring in searchers," Ondarev said as he reached for the radio in the truck.

He made the call, noticing that the horizon had filled with dark clouds.

42

Father Christopher Bryce watched the mass of people that filled the streets and sidewalks as Alder navigated the van through Philadelphia. Watching people, he decided, was much better than watching the falling rain, even if the people were drenched to the bone.

Philadelphia was a city of refugees, Bryce thought, and we have come to join them in this crowded, dirty, beautiful bastion of civilization. The trip down had been a slow one, as the priest forced them to stop time and again along the way to help other travelers on I-95. Bryce was dressed in black, still wearing the uniform of his station as Jesuit priest. With everything that had happened in recent days, he wondered why he still wore his cassock. Then he smiled wryly. It was because of everything that had happened that he still wore his collar.

Everything. That had happened.

He had witnessed the destruction of New York, had escaped dinosaurs and madmen, and now traveled with a New York cop, two street kids, and a renegade edeinos lizard man. What else could possibly be more natural?

Bryce reached down to his mass kit on the floor near his feet. As he bent, fatigue from lack of sleep and praying at the sides of too many deathbeds made his vision dim. It had been seven days since the beginning of the invasion of New York City. Seven days since the storm clouds opened and the rain began to fall. He and his companions had spent much of those days tending to the wounded and the dying as they fled south into New Jersey and Pennsylvania. Precious few hours of those days were spent in rest.

"Even God rested on the seventh day," Bryce jokingly muttered.

"Did you say something, Father?" Alder asked.

Bryce did not respond. After all, they were tired and wet and unsure of their next step, and humor suddenly didn't seem appropriate.

God rested on the seventh day.

The words swam up in his mind and Bryce studied them for some meaning. God had only created the world, so time to rest was available, he mused. Bryce, on the other hand, was trying to save it. After God had allowed it to come tumbling down, Bryce was trying to fit the pieces back together, the way they were supposed to be, even if all he could touch and help were small bits of it here and there. Just like all the king's horses and all the king's men, he imagined. But like them, he didn't think he could put Humpty Dumpty — or the world, for that matter — back together again.

"What does Christopher mean, Father?" Tal Tu asked from the back of the van. His command of the English language was remarkable after so short a time, but the edeinos had explained that he owed it more to conditioning by his former High Lord than to any natural ability.

"Christ bearer," Bryce said, and the words conjured images of days past.

In the midst of refugees fleeing the madness of New York, he had carried Christ down the New Jersey Turnpike, through Trenton, and into Philadelphia. He knew that his trip was not quite like the trip Joseph and Mary made as they bore Christ to Bethlehem. There was no star to follow, and he doubted if there were any wise men waiting for him at the end of the road.

Christ bearer.

He had already carried Christ to more dying souls than he would have thought possible in his entire life as a Jesuit. And here he was, in Philadelphia, on his way to who knew where to send who knew who to whatever waited on the other side of this fragile veil called life.

His thoughts continued to jumble on, but his mind registered the actions outside the van. Bryce saw a blue Ford jump out of the intersection at a speed that was more suited for a highway than a city street. He heard the van's brakes squeal, heard Alder's call to hang on. He watched the Ford fly past them, barely missing the front grill and throwing up great flumes of water as it cut through deep puddles. He heard screams and a sickening thud, and then he heard the Ford peel out, its engine's roar fading as it moved farther away.

Neither Bryce nor Alder moved, too stunned as they were by the sudden happening. But Rat and Coyote had the side door opened almost instantly. Both leaped to the sidewalk and ran over to see what damage the car had caused. It was their action that roused the two older men.

Alder moved to restrain Tal Tu, as he was certain that exposing the lizard man to a crowd would result in panic, violence or death for someone involved. Bryce simply grabbed his mass kit and followed the boys.

The three pushed through the circle of people that had gathered. The object of attention was a woman lying on the cold, wet pavement. Her body was bent in unnatural ways, and blood matted her long, dark hair.

"It was a hit and run, Father," Rat said sadly.

"It might be a D.O.A. if we don't do something," Coyote shouted, moving to examine the victim.

Bryce prayed to God that this wasn't another person he would have to send on her way with a taste of salt and sweetness, the substitute ingredients for his own brand of last rites, and the staples of his much-used mass kit.

43

Andrew Decker waited for the lights to dim in the House Chamber. Today they would see footage from California that could provide Congress with facts to work with instead of speculation. The Congressman watched as Jonathan Wells entered the hall and took his spot behind the podium. The podium was the traditional platform from which the President addressed the House and Senate on such occasions as the State of the Union. Decker hoped the union was in better shape than it appeared to be.

"Members of Congress," Wells began strongly, but it was still strange to see the Speaker of the House at the podium instead of in the seat behind it. "The United States is under attack. Earlier today, the area around Sacramento, California was invaded by the same creatures that have been reported in the Northeast. The footage you are about to see was taken by Captain Eugene Johnson of the Air Force from the reconnaissance camera mounted on his A-10 close air support aircraft. Captain Johnson will provide some narration as the film progresses. Please watch the monitors."

The lights dimmed and television monitors that had been placed throughout the chamber snapped on. The first scene to appear on the screens was a dark, cloud-filled sky. The clouds exploded with bursts of silver as jagged lightning bolts jumped among them.

"I was on my approach to McClellan Air Force Base when I noticed the storm building on the horizon," explained Captain Johnson. "It was intense, powerful, and I figured the boys in the lab would be thrilled with some actual footage, so I flipped on my camera."

Huge crackling bolts struck the ground over and over. The wind picked up, shaking the plane and blur-

Jeff Menges

ring the action for a few seconds. Then the camera showed the clouds roll back. And from that break in the clouds, a swirling wave of energy fell to the Earth, followed by an expanse of mutated jungle.

"At this point, I became confused and, I have to admit, more than a little frightened. This wasn't an ordinary storm anymore. But I didn't have time to stay scared, because this was when I lost power."

The image on the monitors dissolved to static, then to black. The black image was frozen momentarily while the pilot spoke.

"I fought with the controls for about twenty seconds, trying to get the engines and instrumentation to respond. The aircraft was falling, and all the while the storm raged outside my cockpit. I knew this because of the booming thunder that shook the craft, and the flashing lightning that provided me with light to see by. Otherwise, my attention was riveted to trying every trick I knew for jump starting a jet engine."

The image on the monitors began moving again, changing from black to a field of static to a close up of the mutated jungle. The image showed that the plane was very close to the jungle, and flying at a weird angle.

"I regained power after dropping some two thousand feet. Now, with working engines, I could concentrate on what was happening around me. The image you are seeing is an extreme close-up of what I have come to term the "jungle bridge." It dropped out of the opening in the clouds to strike the Earth just outside McClellan. It was over a half a mile at the base, and the vines and plants grew to form a pathway down to the ground."

The camera spun around as the plane leveled off, then it panned around the bottom of the bridge before swinging over the top for a better view. What it showed was a mass of giant lizards, what Decker identified as dinosaurs, parading down the topside of the jungle bridge. One of the lizards of the flying variety launched itself from the bridge and headed directly for the camera. On its back sat a smaller, humanoid lizard that appeared to be directing its flight. Before it got closer, the aircraft's nose-mounted Gatling gun fired a series of bursts that chopped the lizards to pieces. Then the monitors went dark and the house lights were turned back up.

"We had been briefed on what was known about the New York incident, and I decided that this manifestation was of a related nature," Johnson continued. "I released my payload of bombs over the bridge and proceeded to fly south. I eventually exited the zone of silence and made my initial report to officials at the Lemoore Naval Air Station."

The crowd began to talk at once, asking questions, demanding action. Wells called for order, then said, "Now you've seen what we are up against. Like on the east coast, all communications within a three hundred mile area of California have ceased. We must assume that the footage and eyewitness testimony of Captain Johnson reflects what occurred in New York seven days ago. I have already ordered the armed forces to mobilize."

Wells paused to let the new information sink in, then he said, "Ladies and gentlemen, I'm open to other suggestions."

44

Swinging doors slammed open. A doctor and nurse administered to the young woman on the gurney while Alder rolled the wheeled table through the halls of the

Hospital of the University of Pennsylvania. Bryce kept up as best he could, trying to match the police officer's quick strides but failing miserably.

They had left Coyote, Rat and Tal Tu with the van, parked behind the medical facility and out of sight of casual observers. Alder had ordered them all to stay with the vehicle while he and Bryce rushed the victim into the hospital. Both had known that moving a patient with possible back and head injuries was dangerous, but they decided she had little chance lying in the street. Now they were wheeling her into an operating room and praying that their actions would not prove to be wasted.

Once in the operating room, Bryce moved to the side so that the doctor could work unhindered. He noticed his reflection in a stainless steel pitcher that rested on a counter. The reflection showed what the priest felt. He looked awful. Not enough sleep, not enough food, and too much exercise were taking their toll on Father Bryce. His weight had dropped since this began. Not that he was totally svelt yet, oh no. What remained of his hair (which had disappeared long before this ordeal had started) was full and frizzy, a lighter shade of red than his beard as premature gray crept in. And, of course, there was his nose. It could honestly be called bulbous, remaining shiny no matter how much dust and grime covered the rest of his face.

Shouts from the operating table pulled Bryce back to attention.

"Severe head and spinal damage," the doctor said. "Her autonomic system is shutting down."

The words made Bryce's heart skip. Monitors attached to the woman registered her vital signs, but the irregularity of the beeps indicated that she was getting weaker.

The priest, needing to do something — anything — opened the young woman's wallet. Her driver's license identified her as Wendy Miller, age twenty-six. He looked at the smiling face in the picture, then looked at the dying woman on the table. Wendy Miller should be running and laughing and making the most of her life, not fighting to hang on to it in a crowded hospital.

She had glossy chestnut hair that looked long enough to fall past her shoulders if she were standing. But she wasn't standing. She was lying on a table, her hair matted with blood and fallen back around her head.

"We're losing her," the doctor cursed, vehemently trying every trick he knew to stabilize her condition.

Bryce studied the woman closely, noting a dusky creaminess to her skin that hinted at a Mediterranean heritage despite her name. Her eyebrows were straight and dark, over a high-bridged nose. She had a strong, square chin under a wide, full-lipped mouth. She had the figure and muscle tone of someone who worked to keep themself in good physical shape.

But all the exercise in the world couldn't stop a speeding car from crushing the life out of her.

"Father," the doctor called softly, "we need you."

Bryce moved closer. The monitors buzzed, wailing their death cries for all to hear. Wendy Miller was dead.

"We lost her, Father. The damage was just too great."

The priest looked down at the young woman, trying to swallow his remorse. He had to complete the last rites before he could grieve.

He opened his mass kit, paused.

"No," he whispered, then louder, "no."

Bryce snapped the case shut. "No more deaths!" He threw it across the room, then turned back to the woman on the table.

"Live!" he shouted, grabbing her arms and shaking her as if to wake her from sleep. "Don't die! Please, don't die."

45

"Tolwyn. My name is Tolwyn."

She felt such joy, remembering something as simple as her name. She was still floating near the light, and the darkness still waited for her nearby. But nothing else had changed since the pulling sensation had stopped.

Until now.

Now she had a name that identified her, made her more real. And, as she watched the warm, glowing light, something else appeared. There, floating in the light, was a small object. As she watched, enraptured, the object unfolded. It became a flower, its petals blossoming before her eyes. It was one of the rare crys flowers from the place behind her.

From her home.

She reached out and took the fragile bloom. She admired its overlapping petals of turquoise run through with veins of deep crimson. She brought it toward her face and inhaled the aroma of open fields and bright sunshine. It was the smell of a summer day, so full of promise that her heart ached. The scent cleared her head, and she remembered her unfinished work. Not clearly, not completely, but enough to know why she could not enter the dark space yet.

"They need me," she whispered, "they sent me away so that I could return to help them. Help them …"

The tunnel stretched out then, and she was moving back the way she came, speeding through the darkness. She cupped the flower protectively in her hands. It was a gift that she did not want to lose.

Back, back, back she flew, faster and faster until the tunnel was nothing but a blur. Risking a glance over her shoulder, she could see a light far ahead. Was it *the* light? Was she returning to the brilliance that had reminded her of her mission, that had given her the bloom?

The blur of darkness took shape, and she was running bare-legged with long skirts hiked up above her knees; running through fields of crys flowers and through the greenswards of the courtyards of a castle; running through the halls, corridors, and up and down the foot-worn stone stairways enclosed in the walls of the castle itself; running through ponderously moving, pontificating herds of older people who jammed the corridors and clogged the paths, swirling their brightly colored robes and gowns with the wind of her quick passage, unseating their stately hats and veils and bringing soft smiles to their somberly adult faces. The light was closer now, and her ascent much steeper.

It was like she had never known a time that wasn't filled with movement. From moment to moment she was flying, running, falling, sliding, back and back, faster than ever before. The blur shifted again and she was in the dark tunnel, but now the featureless walls were closer, pushing in at her. She was suffocating, choking on the fear that welled up from her forgotten depths. And the pain returned, fierce and hot. It would not be ignored. The light was directly above her now, and she was hurtling quickly toward it. Below her, the dark space shifted angrily, its buzzing sound swarming up to batter her senses and add to the pain.

The light appeared to shimmer and ripple as though it were beyond a veil of water, as though she were simply a swimmer beneath the surface of a clear pool.

Suddenly there was another swimmer beside her, a brown-eyed young woman who reminded her very much of herself. The young woman smiled and gently touched her cheek.

"Help them," the young woman said, and then she was gone, moving in the opposite direction from Tolwyn's own flight.

The light was closer now, beckoning Tolwyn forward, rushing her back from the dark space. Its brightness filled the space with color, blinding her. As she sped toward the rippling veil, as she prepared to explode into the light, she heard a voice call to her. Softly, beseechingly, lovingly, the strange, unfamiliar words eased the last moments of her journey out of the depths, accompanying her as she hurtled upward.

Besides the voice and the pain and the speed and the light, the last thing she remembered was her hands, still cupped protectively around the crys flower.

46

Alder and the doctor tried to pull Father Bryce away from the table. The young woman was dead, and it appeared that recent events had finally gotten to the priest.

"Father Bryce, that's enough," Alder said, hoping to get through to the priest. "This isn't going to help you or her."

The priest ignored them, continuing to gently shake the young woman. "Please," he intoned, "don't die."

"Father," the doctor pleaded, "let her go."

But then the monitors resumed their regular beat pattern, and Wendy Miller moved.

"Dear sweet Jesus!" Bryce exclaimed as the woman on the table snapped open her green eyes and sat up quickly, as though waking from a bad dream. Something dropped onto the table as she grabbed the priest with her strengthening hands.

The nurse backed away, a shrill breath escaping her pursed lips. She was staring at the young woman, trying to understand how she could be sitting up — how she could be alive.

But Bryce was not looking at the woman who grasped him tightly. He was not looking at the monitors, or at Alder, or at the doctor. No, he was looking at the table. For there, where it could not possibly be, showing clearly against the white surface, was a beautiful turquoise and crimson flower.

47

Ondarev handed the soldier beside him the map he had been examing, then turned to meet the car that was coming up the road. It was a long, black vehicle that screamed politician or high-ranking Party official. Whichever, it meant they had come to check up on him.

The car parked, and the Premier himself emerged, along with a Japanese man. Ondarev tried not to show any surprise as he stepped forward to greet them.

"Captain Ondarev, I presume the operation is proceeding successfully," the Premier said, continuing to speak before the captain could respond. "This is Ambassador Nagoya from Japan. He has come to help us deal with the problem you are working on. I will leave him here to discuss matters with you."

The Premier got back into the car, and the vehicle pulled away. Nagoya, who was shorter than Ondarev, wore dark sunglasses and was of an indeterminate age. He carried a leather briefcase.

"You have a lot of soldiers in this field, captain,"

Nagoya said in passable Russian.

"Why are you here, Mr. Ambassador?" Ondarev asked, deciding to dispense with social pleasantries.

"As your Premier explained, I am here to help you. Like yourselves, our government discovered that our country was in immediate danger from forces unknown. Through the use of technology, we were able to develop a method for dealing with the danger before it came to a head — as it did in the United States."

"Go on."

Nagoya bent down and placed his case on the ground. He flipped the lid open, revealing a compact computer, monitor, and pop up sensor array. A simple logo was stamped on the computer; a chrome "K" on a red circle. It was so like the Japanese to use English letters on their high-tech machinery. Still, it was an impressive looking piece of equipment.

"We have determined that the threat comes from outside our reality, captain, from what we might refer to as alternate dimensions. It takes the form of invaders that have decided to attack our planet for some as yet unknown purpose. We were able to identify the energy patterns of their advance forces, use those patterns to find their locations, and then remove the devices that provide them with access to our world. We found three such devices in Japan."

"These devices, Mr. Ambassador, can you tell me something about them?"

"We have termed them "stelae," and they are physical manifestations of the invading dimensions. By studying the ones that we uncovered, we determined that when placed in a triangular pattern the stelae formed an area that could then be filled with an alternate reality. We believe that this is what happened in the United

States."

"Why are you here, Mr. Ambassador?" Ondarev asked, "and how can you know so much about these things?"

The Japanese adjusted his sunglasses before answering. "I am here to help you, captain, because it is too late to help the United States. Others like me are on their way to other countries that may also be in danger. We are trying to save the world. And I know these things because our science has told us of them."

Something about this man bothered Ondarev, but he couldn't put his finger on it. Before he could ask any more questions, however, a shout of triumph erupted from the field. He raised a pair of binoculars to his eyes and searched for the origin of the jubilation. There, beside a crane and bulldozer, a dozen soldiers were shouting happily as they helped pull something from the ground. With them, directing their activity, was Katrina Tovarish. She was an amazing young woman, he decided, blind yet so full of vision.

The captain lowered the binoculars and turned to Nagoya. "Mr. Ambassador, I thank you for your concern and offer of assistance. But, as you can hear, we do not require it. Besides, we cannot afford to pay the price that I am sure comes with your machine."

Nagoya turned darker at these words, and Ondarev could see his brow furrow behind the dark glasses. But the Japanese did not say a word.

"If you'll excuse me, I am sure that one of my soldiers will be happy to return you to the Premier."

Ondarev walked away from the ambassador, anxious to see what a stelae looked like up close. He had already put the Japanese behind him, but the Japanese had one more thing to say.

"You seem quite capable of handling this yourself, captain," Nagoya called. "But heed my words. Destroy the stelae quickly. Do that, and I will consider the bill for this discussion paid in full."

48

Dr. Michael Forkner of the Kitt Peak Observatory finished his third check of the computers and instrumentation. He rubbed his weary eyes and sat back for a moment to gather his thoughts. He would have to confirm his readings with Dr. Eisner, then see if the other observatories had experienced the same observations. But even before he did all of that, he knew that his own tests were enough.

All of the instrumentation was computer controlled to observe specific portions of the sky at different times of the day and night. But for the last twenty-four hours, the telescope had been pointed at the wrong areas. By running various check programs, Dr. Forkner had come to his conclusion. The Earth's spin was slowing down. And over that period of time, it was getting increasingly slower.

Dr. Forkner did his calculations another time. If the current pace of deceleration continued unabated, the planet would come to a complete stop in eighty-three days. But over those eighty-three days, weather patterns would be radically altered, and temperatures would disperse toward their two extremes.

Death and destruction would be on a scale not experienced since the dinosaurs were wiped out sixty-five million years ago. And, like the dinosaurs before them, Forkner had no idea what humanity could do to save itself.

49

Bryce stared at the turquoise and crimson flower, totally absorbed by the incongruity of its presence. He remembered Wendy Miller when her ferocity carried Bryce backward, tumbling him, Alder and the doctor to the floor. Beeps and buzzers began sounding as the wires connecting Miller to the machines that had been monitoring her were pulled loose. Glass crashed and fluids flooded across the tiled floor as the stainless steel standards holding glucose bottles toppled and fell. As he was hurled to the floor, face to face with the crazed woman, a small part of his mind wrestled with the fact that the doctor had declared her dead, that the monitors had flatlined, and then she had opened her eyes. A larger part of his mind, the part that had always acted as his personal Devil's Advocate and caused him to question his faith, began to squirm and gather arguments against Bryce's beginning thoughts of the woman's return from death.

As Bryce struggled with Miller, trying to restrain her without hurting her, the doctor and Alder grabbed her from behind and tried to pull her off the priest. Ignoring them, the woman flung one leg over Bryce's body and straddled his waist as he lay with his back pressed to the floor. Her thumbs sought his windpipe, pushing his head backward. His spine arched as Miller's arms straightened with the force of her effort. The cross that Bryce wore on a chain around his neck slid upward toward the hollow of his throat, between the hands of the woman. Her eyes opened wide as she saw the cross. Suddenly, she let go of Bryce. As she did, Alder and the doctor were able to pull her away.

Bryce rolled to his knees and stood up. Wendy Miller no longer struggled. She looked at Bryce and the now dangling cross, and said, "Dunad. Sintra vas Dunad?"

Her words were spoken slowly, and her mouth struggled in trying to sound out the syllables.

"What language is that?" Alder asked.

Bryce shrugged and shook his head. Then he turned his attention fully to the woman. She held her face and her body calmly now, but he saw confusion in her eyes. He spoke to her, slowly, trying to make her understand. "Miss Miller, do you speak English?"

The woman raised her head and looked up at Bryce, and at his cross. Without struggling, so as to indicate that her intentions were peaceful, she tried to free one of her arms from Alder's grip. Bryce nodded to the police officer to let the woman go.

When her arm was free, she slowly reached up to take Bryce's cross in her hand and carefully, as if speaking an alien tongue, said, "Dunad. I have been sent to Dunad."

Then, as if weakened from her struggles, the woman collapsed into Alder's arms.

"Let's get her back onto the table so that I can examine her," the doctor said. "Nurse, clean up this mess and help me get the monitors and fluids hooked back up." Gently, Bryce pried Miller's fingers loose from their grip on his cross. Then he stepped back as Alder and the doctor lifted her onto the table. While they had her in a standing position, Bryce realized that the woman was taller than he was, by at least three inches. And from their brief struggle, he knew she was stronger than he. The doctor knocked the flower off the table as he rested Wendy Miller upon it. Bryce bent and picked up the flower, carefully examining its strange coloration. He had never seen anything like it before. It had a strong aroma that reminded the priest of a clear spring day.

As the doctor and nurse worked, Alder came to stand

next to the priest. He saw the flower, and his eyes met Bryce's. "What happened here, Father?" Alder asked.

"I don't know, Rick. I wish I did, but I just don't know."

The doctor walked over to the pair. He looked haggard, confused. "Her pulse is strong and steady, her respiration is regular, and her eyes seem normal and reactive," the doctor explained. "But she was dead, for a few brief seconds, that young woman was gone. And now most of the major damage she had sustained has disappeared, and what remains is healing rapidly. I honestly don't know what to make of it, except …"

And here the doctor paused, seemingly embarrassed by his own thoughts.

"Except what, doctor?" Bryce asked.

"Except that maybe she heard you calling her, Father. Maybe your prayers were answered."

Alder retrieved the young woman's wallet from where it fell when Bryce dropped it. He opened it to examine her license, just as Bryce had done earlier. "You know something? They made a mistake on her driver's license," Alder said. "It lists Wendy Miller as having brown eyes, and this young lady has the most intense green eyes I've ever seen."

Bryce was suddenly very afraid. He needed to know if his prayers had had anything to do with Wendy Miller's miraculous return to life, or with anything at all. He needed to know if he did truly bear Christ, not only in the wafers he handed out but also in himself. He pushed past Alder and the doctor to stand beside the operating table. The young woman was awake, her green eyes moving to meet his own.

"Wendy, Miss Miller, how are you feeling?" he asked. He needed to touch her, to feel the life in her veins, in the warmth of her skin. He placed his hand on her right forearm. As he did, he felt ridged scars beneath the palm of his hand. He didn't remember seeing those scars earlier, but he could have missed them in the confusion.

"Dunad," she said. Her voice had an accent that the priest couldn't place. "The words are a war in my head. For everything I hear and for everything I want to say, two words rush to do battle. Great gaps have been torn in the walls of my memory. I remember very little. Darkness clawing at me, a brilliant light, a beautiful crys flower …"

Bryce handed her the flower.

"Thank you, Dunad," she said, "for returning one of my memories. Will you return the others?"

"Miss Miller," Bryce said, pulling his hand away from her arm. As she spoke, he had been leaning forward, feeling himself drawn into her oddly green eyes, eyes that were like the color of dark green grass after a rainstorm. He needed to pull back, to distance himself from this woman who had died and come back to life in front of his eyes. "My name is not Dunad," he said, but part of him wished it were. She spoke the name in a familiar, loving manner, as if she were speaking to someone who had known her all her life, someone who knew her as she knew him, closely, intimately. "My name is Christopher Bryce."

"Oh," she said. Her eyes glanced at his cross where it lay silver against the blackness of his shirt. "But then you are a follower of Dunad."

"No," he said, "I am a Jesuit priest, of the Society of Jesus." He held up his cross. "This is the symbol of the cross upon which Our Lord Jesus Christ was crucified. I'm sorry, Miss Miller, but I have never heard of Dunad."

"Why, Christopher Bryce of the Society of Jesus, do

you call me Miss Miller?"

Startled, Bryce stammered for a moment and said, "But that's your name. Your driver's license was found with you."

"It also says she has brown eyes, Father," Alder added.

"No. I do not have many memories left, but of this I am certain — my name is Tolwyn, Tolwyn of House Tancred."

Bryce stared at her, felt himself pressed hard against the wall of her conviction. He thought of the buzzing of the monitors as she had died, of the flower he had never seen before, of the scars on her arm that had not been there, of her green eyes. And he knew she spoke the truth.

She looked him in the eyes and asked, "Can you, Christopher Bryce who is not Dunad, give me back my memories?"

"No. I'm sorry."

"But you gave me my crys flower."

He remembered the flower falling from her hands as she had sat up.

"You brought that with you," he said.

Her eyes bore steadily into him as she asked, "From where, Christopher Bryce?"

50

Andrew Jackson Decker stood under the rotunda, listening to the heavy rain beat against the dome. He nervously tapped the fingers of his left hand against his leg in time with the rain drops. It was a habit he developed back in his days of high school baseball and perfected through college and pro ball. It calmed him down, helped him focus. It had become a ritual over the last nine days, and he was surprised he hadn't tapped little craters in his leg.

He had been in the White House before, of course, but never under such dire circumstances. How often was the United States invaded, after all. But something had happened in New York and was now spreading. If it wasn't contained, he had no idea what would be the final outcome. And so far, most containment methods had failed.

The door opened and a marine entered. He marched into the room, his polished black boots echoing loudly under the dome. "Congressman Decker, the President will see you now," he said.

Decker nodded and followed the young man. Presi-dent, the congressman thought. That was the first time since the crisis began that Wells had let the staff use that title. That could mean anything, but Decker assumed it meant the Speaker of the House had received the confir-mation he had been waiting for — and praying against. It also confirmed what most of the rest of Capitol Hill had been whispering about these past few days, and Decker dreaded. Rumor was that Jonathan Wells, previ-ously Speaker of the House and now apparently Presi-dent of the United States, was going to recommend Congressman Andrew Jackson Decker to be his Vice President. Why else call him up to the White House without notice?

The marine halted before a door. Decker paused as well, his fingers unconsciously tapping faster. What-ever the situation, he would find out in the next couple of minutes.

"You may go right in, sir," explained the marine.

Decker took a deep breath. He glanced sideways and caught the marine watching him. The congressman flashed his best smile, the one the press called boyishly innocent, noting the name tag sewn on the marine's uniform. "Thank you, Private Rider," he said in as friendly a tone as he could manage. "It's not everyday you get called to talk to the President."

"No, sir," the marine agreed, smiling himself. Then his expression went neutral again, and he resumed his watchful stance.

Decker reached out and opened the door.

"Listen, John, we need to do something. My proposal cannot just be ignored, and unless you can convince me of something better, than I must insist you give me your support."

Decker knew the voice before he saw the speaker. It was Senator Ellen Conners, affectionately referred to as Old Lady Medusa. It was said that her look could turn a reporter to stone, but Decker knew from experience that her words were even worse.

The senator stopped when Decker entered, turning to glare at him with her patented look. Decker swallowed, he hoped not too noticeably, and tried to shake off the feeling that his flesh was hardening.

Conners was standing beside a large, cluttered desk. Behind the desk, leaning back in a heavily-cushioned chair, sat John Wells. He looked older than the last time Decker spoke with him, older even than his sixty years warranted. How could he have aged so much in just a few days, Decker wondered. Finally, seated to Wells' left, was Dennis Quartermain, Secretary of Defense. Decker didn't like that man, but he respected his ability in a crisis. And this was a crisis.

"Ellen, Dennis, you both know Congressman Decker," said Wells as he leaned forward. His smile wiped away some of the added years from his face, but it could not bring back all of the youthful vigor. Decker was afraid that was gone forever. "How're you doing, Ace?"

Ace. That wasn't a name that many people called Decker anymore. It was a remnant of his baseball days, not dignified enough for a member of the United States Congress. But John Wells was never one for formalities.

"Mr. President, please ..." began Conners, but Wells shook her off.

"I've heard your proposal and I'll consider it," he said in a stern tone that surprised Decker. "For now, I've got something to discuss with Ace. Leave us now, Ellen, Dennis. And close the door on your way out."

The two left and Wells motioned for Decker to sit down. "I suppose you're wondering why I called you here, Ace," Wells began. He stood up and reached for the Mr. Coffee on the cabinet behind him. "Would you like a cup," he asked as he filled his own mug with dark brown liquid. "The Boss? Me? If You Say So" was printed on the mug, and Decker smiled at the message as he declined the offer.

"I've finally gotten confirmation, New York is lost," Wells said, his tone heavy and forlorn. "President Kent and Vice President Farrel were in the city to attend the United Nations conference on terrorism, along with other world leaders. They were to ratify and sign a history-making treaty, Ace. It was going to usher in a new age of peace and cooperation. Now I don't know what's going to happen. Some countries are offering us aid, others are claiming the entire invasion is some sort of trick and they are demanding the return of their countrymen. I wish to God it was a trick of some sort."

Wells paused to gulp some coffee before continuing. "The invaders have completely taken over New York and the surrounding area. Reports are that they have killed a large number of citizens. I … I have no reason to believe that the President is still alive. Reluctantly, I am assuming the office of President for the remainder of Kent's term. I've asked Quartermain to serve as my Vice President. He has the skills and experience I need to salvage this situation, Ace, even if I can't stand the bastard."

Decker tried to grasp what Wells was telling him. Kent, Farrel, an entire city, all written off? He couldn't accept that. "John, what are you saying?" he demanded, rising to tower over the man sitting behind the desk. "How can you simply decide that all those people, the President, are beyond our help? How?"

Wells stood as well, falling short of Decker's six-foot-two frame. "Simply? Nothing has been simple these past nine days, Ace. You should know that better than anyone! There are dinosaurs walking in Manhattan, Ace, pouring down a bridge that fell from the sky. This is a nightmare, man, but there's nothing simple about it! There are no television signals, no phone calls, no news wires — there's nothing coming out of New York! Nothing but refugees! And do you know what's behind the refugees? The dinosaurs, that's what! Pushing the survivors before them as they take more and more of our country. They've already taken land as far west as Ohio and as far north as parts of Canada, plus you've seen the footage from California. There doesn't seem to be any way to stop them. As their front advances, our weapons tend to malfunction and break down. We haven't determined why that is yet, but until we do we will continue to lose ground and lives to these invaders. My God, we're at war and we haven't figured it out yet."

The President collapsed back into his chair, the weariness of the situation pressing him down and making him look smaller.

The President.

That's who he was now, and he needed Decker's help and support. Decker realized that, and was sorry that he had exploded. But he felt so helpless. He, too, sat back down, trying to focus, to make sense of the situation.

"You asked Quartermain to be your VP," Decker said, "so what do you want from me?"

"Disappointed, Ace? Don't be. I have something else in mind for you. But first, let me finish the rest of my news, bad as it may be. Prior to the invasion of New York, the world lost contact with Indonesia. As no communications have come out of or have gotten through to the island nations, we must assume that what befell New York has also befallen Indonesia. The northeast, the west coast, the south Pacific — all contact with the areas immediately around the invasion sites has been lost."

"What do you want from me, Mr. President."

"Don't get formal on me now, Ace. And please, bear with me."

The President drained his cup and placed it on the desk. He paused for a second to gather his thoughts.

"Have you ever had a dream that kept repeating itself night after night?" he asked, his voice gaining a strange, far away tone. "I've had one ever since this all started. It comes to me every time my eyes close. Did you know that I'm part Indian. American Indian, that is. Crow, to be specific. Well, this dream has to do with Indians — at least with one of the legends. Have you ever heard of Coyote? He was a trickster, but he was also a hero that helped mankind. The stories reveal that he transformed aspects of the world for man's benefit. But in my dream Coyote encountered Death. Death was a terrible being, dressed in a short cape and old-fashioned hat, sort of like a Puritan. And he stood in a whirlwind, drawing power from the swirling column of air. Death was searching for a large stone in my dream, a stone that was important. Using his normal pranks, Coyote found the stone first. He stole it before Death could reach it and placed it out west somewhere."

President Wells leaned forward, staring directly into Decker's eyes. "Then, before I wake up, Coyote turns to me and says the damnedest thing. He says, 'What is given is given.'"

"And what does that all mean, John?"

"Ace, I have absolutely no idea. But I know that I need you to find out for me, because I certainly can't go."

"Go? Go where?"

"West, young man. You have to go west."

Decker felt beads of sweat form on his forehead and his throat got dry. "The stone, John, tell me about the stone."

"An amazing sight, actually. It's a blue stone, like a piece of the sky made solid, and ..."

But before he could finish, Decker said it for him. "... and it's run through with veins of red."

51

Dar Ess was a gotak of great authority and great sadness. The title, which meant "being who feels no passion," was a new addition to the religion of the edeinos. It was created by Baruk Kaah prior to the edeinos' first raid into the cosmverse, and it went against everything the edeinos believed. But the Saar gave the position meaning and merit, and few dared to oppose his authority over the tribes.

Unlike the optants, the priests of life, gotaks were the

keepers of all things dead. It was not a title that drew respect. Instead, other edeinos looked upon gotaks with pity, for they were relegated to handling those things that were not of Lanala, the edeinos goddess. Still, Dar Ess did not require respect to lead her acolytes into the world of the dead. She required only her power, which the younger ones feared.

She traveled with Beca and Tred, who carried the stelae; with the stalenger Two Taps, who found the digging spots; and with the benthe Geebo, the small amoeba-like being with the ability to manipulate emotion-controlling pheromones. Dar Ess was the leader, and it was her duty to perform the ceremony at the digging spot that would activate the stelae.

They had left the boundary of their own reality, the Living Land, and were now walking in the Dead Land that was the reality of Earth. None of the acolytes were comfortable here, but they had all done this before. That was their duty as gotaks. That was their shame.

Two Taps spun through the air ahead of them, his star shape a beautiful beacon for them to follow. Dar Ess noticed that Two Taps had changed color, switching from a neutral tan to a reflective rainbow pattern that indicated joy or excitement. The gotak indicated rapid movement by clacking her claws together three times fast, then ran ahead to converse with the stalenger.

Not bothering to see if the other acolytes were following her, for they knew that to disobey her command meant their deaths, Dar Ess stopped beneath the spinner. Two Taps uncoiled long tendrils from beneath his body and snaked them out to touch the gotak. Once in contact, the two could converse freely — one through speech, the other through a series of taps and vibrations.

"What have you found, Two Tapsss?" Dar Ess demanded, as was her practice when dealing with acolytes-who-were-not-yet-gotaks.

"I have found the digging spot, the place where the boundaries must meet," Two Taps answered, using his most humble vibrations.

"Mark it," the gotak ordered, turning away and breaking contact with the stalenger's tendrils before he could reply. She expected Beca to be behind her, waiting, and she was not disappointed.

The young edeinos, who was the newest member of Dar Ess' team, stood shaking in place, obviously nervous yet anxiously waiting to experience the pleasures of the dig.

"Beca, find the ssspot that Two Tapsss marksss. There you will honor our Sssaar by digging the hole of placement. Geebo, sssupervise the young one. Go."

Beca bowed respectfully to the benthe, then waited for the older being to make the sign that signaled he could be picked up. Geebo extended a pseudopod straight up from his hemispherical body. The sign given, Beca gently lifted the benthe and placed Geebo on his shoulder. Then he ran to find Two Taps.

"Bring your sssstelae, Tred, and come with me," Dar Ess commanded the remaining acolyte. The gotak hefted her hrockt shoot, its roots dangling from one end, and led the way.

When Dar Ess and Tred arrived at the digging spot, Beca was already hard at work. He used his claws to scope out large handfuls of dirt, nodding frequently which indicated acknowledgement of Geebo's instructions. Two Taps rested on the ground nearby, offering his own advice through the almost-invisible tendrils that gently rested on Beca's ridged head. While Beca continued to dig, Tred examined one of the stelae he carried, making sure it was still intact. Dar Ess examined

Jeff Menges

it herself as well, for if a damaged stelae was placed Baruk Kaah would punish them all.

The stelae was about four feet long. On the outside it looked like an oval of vines and leaves and thorns. But within the oval-shaped wrapping were bones and carcasses of creatures from the Living Land. When three stelae were laid in a triangle, the area within the bounded points would be ready to contain the reality of the cosm that created the stelae — in this case, the Living Land. Dar Ess observed the rituals, noting that they were good. Already she could feel the excitement building, and the sensations reminded her that even those who worked among the dead could know life.

She watched in anticipation for her own part in the ceremony, when Two Taps leaped into the air. Dar Ess came to attention immediately, hefting her hrockt shoot and looking for whatever danger the stalenger had sensed.

Coming over a nearby rise were two of the soft-skinned beings of the Dead Land. They wore dead coverings and carried dead items that Dar Ess could not fathom. But they had not yet seen the gotak and her acolytes, and that meant the ceremony did not have to be interrupted.

The gotak clacked her claws together once, signaling that the others should continue their work. Then she moved away from the digging spot, quietly praying to Lanala as she did so. Almost immediately she felt her god's presence, manifesting throughout her scaled body as a pleasant tingling sensation. She focused her prayer, asking that her hrockt shoot change to serve her better.

With that, the top end of the shoot reformed, growing to a sharp point that could pierce even the hide of an udatok. When the spear had finished forming, Dar Ess yelled a challenge to the soft-skinned beings. Both looked up, startled by the terrible sound. The smaller one tried to run, but Two Taps caught her in his tendrils and held her fast. The larger one, confused, simply stood there.

Dar Ess listened to the babbling the soft-skinned male made. If she concentrated, she could understand the primitive language that used nothing more complicated than words. But she did not want to concentrate. There was no need to use the gift that Baruk Kaah had given them, no need to hear the death pleas of a dead thing.

The gotak shouted in honor of Lanala, then tossed the hrockt spear at the soft skin. It pierced his chest and knocked him onto its back. Dar Ess shook excitedly at the spray of blood that erupted as the spear hit. She had added a prayer that caused the pointed head of the shoot to grow thorns once it struck its target. The thorns would do even more damage to the frail being.

She bounced over to the male. When she reached him, Dar Ess saw that he was already dead. The thorns had done their job. Too bad, she mused, that she was unable to give the soft-skinned one more sensations before death had claimed him. She grasped the hrockt shoot and pulled it easily from its victim, the point reformed to its original shape.

Then Dar Ess remembered the smaller one.

Two Taps still held her, and the soft-skinned woman reminded Dar Ess of a fly in a spider's web.

"To you, woman of the Dead Land," Dar Ess proclaimed in the hissing language of the edeinos, "I give the reward of sensation. Cherish this last pleasure of life."

The stalenger felt every bit of the young woman's pain through his tendrils that wrapped about her. The sensations were so intense, he knew that the gotak had seen fit to truly grant the soft-skinned one life at the moment of her death. The sensations lasted almost ten minutes, and then the soft skin died.

Dar Ess, a wild gleem in her yellow eyes, returned to the dig spot. Only her shaking body, still ripe with excitement, and the single splash of blood on her left arm showed that anything had occurred.

Without a word to the others, the gotak hefted the prepared stelae and offered a prayer to Lanala. Then she produced a stone dagger — truly a tool of the dead — and offered a second prayer to Baruk Kaah. Beca, the youngest, turned his head from the sight of the dagger. Yes, Dar Ess had once been repulsed by the dead tool, but she had learned to work with it. That was the duty of a gotak. Beca would learn as well.

The gotak cut a slit in the stelae with the stone dagger. If the prayers had been accepted, then the wound would bleed, giving Dar Ess the sign of life.

Blood welled from the slit as the dagger cut, dripping down the sides of the stelae, forming rivers of red through the tangle of vines. With a yell of triumph, Dar Ess placed the bleeding stelae in the prepared hole. Then she backed away so that the acolytes could scoop dirt atop the stelae. They chanted as they worked, and soon the hole was filled. Dar Ess prayed once more, and Lanala caused grass and plants to sprout from the replaced soil. Within moments, the digging spot looked as though it had never been disturbed by claw or talon.

Dar Ess, pleased with their success, ordered Two Taps again into the sky. It would be a long march to the next digging spot, and the sooner they started the sooner they could return to the Living Land.

52

During the first week of Wendy Miller's recovery, except when his duties called him to the bedsides of others or when the doctors chased him out of the room to examine their patient, Father Christopher Bryce was constantly at her side. He joyed in the rapid growth of her strength when his world was filled with ministering to the dying. He joyed in merely being with her, feeling a connection to her, as a father would who had been present at the birth of his child. Yet, his fondness for her slid in and out of the realm of the paternal to those feelings that were of a man for a woman. Feelings a priest could have, but feelings that a priest must never act upon.

She believed she was Tolwyn of House Tancred, and she honestly had no remembrance of the name Wendy Miller. The doctors, in their infinite fear of anything that would not fit into their orderly system, insisted upon referring to the young woman as "Miss Miller, the woman with the remarkable recuperative powers." Except for Dr. Monroe, the doctor who was on hand when Bryce and Alder brought the young woman in, for he had witnessed the events as they transpired and was leaning toward believing her. And, he had to admit to himself, so was Bryce.

Rick Alder spent some time with Tolwyn, as he called her, and Coyote and Rat paid visits as well. Only Tal Tu stayed away, and that was because Alder insisted he remain hidden in the van.

On the eleventh day after the destruction of Shea Stadium and the beginning of the invasion, Father Bryce entered Wendy Miller's room. He carried a tray of food, lunch for the two of them. It was good to see that the young woman had been removed from the monitors.

Soon, Dr. Monroe had told him, she would be released. But before that happened, Bryce had to know the truth.

She was sleeping when he entered. So Bryce placed the tray on the table beside the bed, next to the vase that held the blue and red flower, and sat down. He watched her for a time, noting the strong, even rise and fall of her chest, the curves hidden beneath a thin hospital sheet. Eventually, he noticed that she was watching him with a similar scrutiny.

"Hello, Miss Miller," he stammered. "How are you feeling today?"

"I do not know how Miss Miller feels," the young woman replied in her unfamiliar accent, "but I am well."

"Of course," Bryce said, fumbling with an apple he picked off the lunch tray. He handed it to the woman.

"If you are really Tolwyn of House Tancred …"

"I am."

"… if you are really Tolwyn," Bryce continued, trying not to sound nervous, "then what happened to the brown-eyed person who knew herself as Wendy Miller?"

The woman started to say something, but then she stopped and a pained expression crossed her face. She looked at her hand, flexing her fingers and turning it from side to side, as though she were examining it for the first time.

"I am Tolwyn of House Tancred," she finally said with conviction.

"But who is Tolwyn of House Tancred?" he asked.

Sinewy muscles played in her forearms as the anger of frustration rose in her eyes. "I do not remember."

"Who is Dunad?"

"I do not remember."

"Where are you from?"

"I do not know!" she screamed, overturning the tray

of food and leaping from the bed.

He did not ask her any more questions after that. Instead, he sat at her side over the next two days. Sometimes Alder or the boys sat with them, sometimes it was just the two of them. He called her Tolwyn, so as not to disturb her, told himself. He spoke to her, telling her things she could not understand, answering questions she could not ask. And it didn't matter that, most of the time, she lay with her head turned to the side and looked at the crys flower. He told her about New York City and the start of the invasion, of his meeting with Coyote and Rat, of Rick Alder, and of his parents.

Bryce stopped talking whenever he mentioned his parents. But Tolwyn refused to let him mourn alone.

"Tell me what you are thinking about, Christopher Bryce," she asked, but even her questions were delivered in a tone that demanded immediate compliance.

"I never got around to telling my parents any of the important things," he explained. "They weren't supposed to die so soon."

"Death never comes when it is expected," Tolwyn said. "That is why we must be ready for it at all times."

"I was in New York not just to visit them, you know. I was there waiting for a new assignment from the Church, but I was also taking some time to think about my vocation. I had ... doubts. I still have them, I guess."

"Everyone has doubts from time to time, Christopher Bryce. Even about a calling." When she mentioned that, she frowned. Bryce could tell that she wanted to remember something about a calling, but it was still beyond her grasp.

"There is something I cannot remember, Christopher who wears the sign of Dunad. The things you tell me about your world cause stirrings of uneasiness deep within me. The invasion of your world evokes ... vague feelings of memories. But those memories stay in the shadows of my mind, refusing to emerge into the light of recollection. This has happened before."

"Where?"

"I do not know," she said, clenching her fist and beating at the mattress in frustration.

"Try to remember ..."

"Father," Coyote said from the doorway, interrupting the conversation. "You're needed in room 128."

"Another death?" he asked.

Coyote nodded.

"On my way," he said as he picked up his bag and started out of the room.

Briefly, as he passed through the doorway, Bryce paused to say that he would be back as soon as possible. But Tolwyn was again looking at her flower, so he left without speaking.

53

Deep within Illmound Keep, in the realm of Orrorsh, the Gaunt Man sat upon his throne of bones. He was alone in his chamber, with only the song of his Darkness Device to soothe his tired thoughts. It sang to him of conquest and immortality, of darkness and dominion. And it sang of the Gaunt Man's greatness as first among High Lords, as the personage of prophecy, as the Torg.

After listening for a time, the Gaunt Man rose from the throne feeling almost refreshed. He stepped over to the Device. It was an obsidian heart, carved from the blackest night and hardest stone. Measuring over four feet in all directions, the heart's surface was smooth as though polished. The Gaunt Man could see his own image reflected in the black surface. He gently ran the tips of his fingers over the stone, feeling the heart's heat rising from within, feeling the beat of its eternal existence.

The Gaunt Man reached for his silver goblet from its place on the mantle. He placed the goblet beneath one of the heart's open arteries, then spoke softly to the great artifact.

"Heketon the Obsidian Heart, the Darkness Device that found me and revealed my grand destiny to me, I ask you to provide sustenance to refresh me."

The heart glowed with an internal fire, and its song grew stronger, louder. From the artery, bright red liquid dripped into the goblet. Each drop was as liquid fire, and the Gaunt Man heard them sizzle as they fell into his drinking vessel.

"Thank you, Heketon, for the blood of eternity." He raised the goblet to his lips and drank deeply. Within the heart's black surface, he saw his own reflection once again. But now the reflection also showed a shattered landscape, a planet stripped clean of its power in order to elevate the Gaunt Man to the next level of existence. Upon that shattered surface, the Gaunt Man stood triumphantly.

"Yes, together that shall be our destiny," and with that said, he gulped the last of the blood.

Replacing the silver goblet upon the mantle, the Gaunt Man stepped across the room to stand before a large, ornate mirror. "I shall need assistants from this world, Heketon, pawns to serve as insurance should the game take any unexpected turns. Show me, through the mirror I have name Wicked, those whose souls hunger for darkness and thirst for power. For those are the souls that shall be ours!"

54

The tatooed man walked west, his metal-tipped work boots pounding upon the blacktopped highway. So far, none of the passing traffic had stopped for him. But he wasn't worried. He liked to walk, and eventually someone would stop.

He continued at an even pace, but he had to pause when a sharp pain stabbed through his head. He clutched his blonde hair and dropped to his knees. The pain was intense, shattering his thoughts and blurring his vision.

Then, through the pain, he heard a voice.

"Malcolm Kane, behold your new master!"

Through tear-filled eyes, the tatooed man saw a skeletal face before him. Later, he would not remember any of its features, just its sunken, piercing eyes. It spoke again, and this time he recognized his own name.

"How do you know me?" Kane asked. "Who are you?"

"You shall know me as the Gaunt Man," the voice said, "and if you serve me well, then I shall reward you with a portion of this planet as your own."

At this promise, Kane pushed the pain away. It was still there, but he ignored it. He did not want something so trivial to interfere with this conversation.

"What do you want me to do?" Kane asked. Then he added, "Master."

55

On the twelfth day since New York became a zone of silence, Andrew Decker watched marines load up jeeps for his trip west. He had selected the squad of soldiers personally, working with Sergeant Lewis to weed through dossiers and service records. When they were done, they had a squad of eleven specialists ready to accompany him on his mission. The marines had orders to protect the congressman on his fact-finding mission. What they did not know was that Decker had a secret mission, from President Wells himself, to find a stone that both men had seen in a dream. It was crazy, but so was everything else that was happening in the world.

Sergeant Lewis approached Decker, saluted, and said, "The squad is ready to move out whenever you give the order, sir."

Decker, while theoretically in command of this mission, had been given Lewis to handle the soldiers. "Then I guess we should ..."

"Congressman Decker, might I have a word with you?" Decker recognized the voice without having to turn to see the speaker. It was Dennis Quartermain, previously the Secretary of Defense but now serving as Vice President.

"If you'll excuse me, sergeant," Decker said. Lewis nodded, then left to rejoin the squad.

"What can I do for you, Dennis?" Decker asked rather informally.

"You may not like me, congressman, but I am the Vice President now."

"What's your point, Dennis? I'm in kind of a hurry here."

"My point is this, Decker. I don't like you either. You're nothing but a glorified sports hero going out on a public relations tour so Wells doesn't have to do it himself. I would like nothing better than to hear that you were lost somewhere in the zone of silence, but that would mean we would be losing eleven good soldiers as well."

Quartermain stared into Decker's eyes, scrutinizing

them for some hidden meaning. "Why did he give you eleven specialists, Decker? What are you really going out there to do?"

"It's like you said, Dennis," answered Decker, "I'm going out to smile and shake hands and kiss babies. Maybe I'll even give a few speeches and tell everyone that the government is still here."

"I don't believe you. And as Vice President I deserve — no, I demand — to know what is going on."

"I don't care who you are or what you demand. I have a job to do, and you're keeping me from that job."

Decker turned his back on Quartermain and walked away, heading across the huge garage to where the marines were waiting by their vehicles.

"Don't you turn your back on me, Decker," Quartermain raged, "I'm not through with you yet!"

The congressman ignored the Vice President, but he could feel angry eyes follow him to his jeep.

"Sergeant," Decker said, "let's get out of here."

56

Uncovered, the stelae was disturbing to look at. But Captain Nicolai Ondarev nevertheless forced his eyes to roam over its surface. It was a cylindrical piece of metal, silver in color, about three feet long. Streaks of black circuitry ran just beneath the surface, forming complicated pathways that resembled the workings of a mind gone mad.

If Ondarev examined one spot for any length of time, it appeared as though the silver surface rippled, like the surface of a pond. And beneath the shifting layer of silver, the captain thought he could see tortured, agonized faces swimming up to stare back at him. That was when he had to look away.

"It bothers you, Nicolai," said Katrina Tovarish. It was not a question.

"It disturbs me, yet it fascinates me," Ondarev explained. "Have you ever eaten something that was much too hot, Katrina? It burns the roof of your mouth because you could not wait to taste it. Afterward, the flesh is sore and tender, and it hurts to touch it, but you cannot keep your tongue from probing the wound over and over. It causes pain, but your tongue acts of its own volition. That is what the stelae is like."

"We should destroy it, Nicolai. If it solicits such attention, then it is more dangerous than I thought."

"The scientists have not finished their tests yet," Ondarev said. "There is still so much to learn about this object. Where is it from, what is it for?"

Katrina grabbed his hand and held it tight. He looked into her sightless eyes as she spoke. "There is nothing to learn! It is not from this Earth, Nicolai, and all it is good for is destruction. Can't you feel the evil of the thing? Can't you hear the pain it causes? Look at the ground beneath it, Nicolai. Tell me what you see."

Ondarev examined the dirt upon which the stelae rested. He lifted a handful. It was brittle to the touch, dry. There was no life in it, no color. It was not rich and dark and full of aroma like the soil throughout the rest of the field.

"It's dead, Katrina."

"You must order your men to tear the stelae apart, Nicolai. You must do this before the storm begins."

Overhead, the clouds were thick and black. Indeed, the storm would start very soon.

"The Japanese suggested the same course of action, Katrina."

The young woman's face fell. "The Japanese?"

"Yes. His name was Nagoya. He was sent by the Japanese government to help us find the stelae. That's what he called it, a stelae. But you had already found it, so I sent him on his way."

"Beware Nagoya, Nicolai. The image of him I see in your mind frightens me."

She looked like a little girl then, small and vulnerable. Ondarev wanted to reach out and take her in his arms to comfort her. To wipe away her fear as easily as he wiped away her tears. But he could not make his arms respond. Not yet, not now. Not in the shadow of the stelae.

He heard someone approaching. It was one of the soldiers who had been in on the discovery of the object. Ondarev tried to remember his name, but it refused to come to him.

The soldier stopped a few feet away, cautiously keeping distance between himself and the stelae. Behind him, Ondarev saw a sea of wheat, the stalks rippling in the evening breeze.

"What can I do for you, soldier?" Ondarev asked, cursing himself for forgetting the soldier's name. He had always prided himself on being able to recall the names of the men under his command. Why was this one eluding him?

The soldier saluted. "Captain, the science team has ..."

As Ondarev watched, four metal blades exploded from the soldier's chest. Blood spurted, and the soldier's sentence was cut off. His eyes widened with surprise, and then they closed. Ondarev thought there should have been a scream of pain or terror. The relative silence made the scene worse somehow.

The soldier collapsed to the ground. Standing in his place was a terrible figure. It was man sized, wearing black leather and chains. Metal wings burst from its back, and metal blades extended from its fingers. Parts of its body were metallic, full of circuitry and dancing electrical pulses. The other parts were gray, ashen. Its skin was rough and resembled dried leather of a quality much below the crisp material it wore.

Ondarev shoved Katrina behind him, while at the same time he drew his pistol from its holster. The creature smiled, and the captain saw that its mouth was filled with sharp teeth. He also noticed, quite objectively, that it had some kind of metal studs protruding from its neck and temples.

In apparent slow motion, Ondarev raised his pistol to fire. But the creature moved faster, slashing out with metal claws still stained by the soldier's blood. The claws caught the pistol on the edge of the barrel. There was a clang of metal on metal, and then the pistol flew from Ondarev's hand.

But the captain refused to wait for the claws to slash again. He leaped forward, smashing into the creature's stomach with as much force as he could muster. The creature staggered, but would not fall back. It grabbed Ondarev by the back of the neck and pulled him down.

Raising his claws to strike, the creature spoke. "You almost won, stormer. If I hadn't decided to check on the stelae, you would have caused a major system crash. That's too bad, isn't it?"

Then Ondarev heard the discharge of a pistol. And another. And another. Three spots of blood appeared on the creature's chest. It looked up in surprise to see who had shot it, then it collapsed in a heap beside the dead soldier.

Ondarev drew in a great gulp of breath. Katrina was standing there, holding his pistol in her hands.

"I fired at its voice, Nicolai," she sobbed. "Can we destroy the stelae now?"

"Yes, Katrina, yes."

He held her then, letting her cry into his shoulder. He looked down at the two dead bodies, and the soldier's name came back to him.

"Rest in peace, Private Dvorak," he whispered, "rest in peace."

57

"Repent!" yelled the robed monk. "Dark days are upon us and a new prophet shall arise to lead us into the light! But you must repent!"

"Earth peasants," muttered Yukira as he pushed through the crowded Paris street. His leather briefcase bounced off a number of the men and women listening to the monk, but most dismissed him with a harsh look or a mumbled word. He didn't care.

Finally he was past the crowd, but he was still blocks from his destination. Yukira hated to be late, but with the primitive modes of transportation available in this cosm, he didn't have any choice. He checked his watch, then double tapped the band. This caused the face of the watch to opaque, then, when it cleared, the digital readout was replaced by a grid with two blinking lights. The yellow light represented Yukira, the red light his destination.

He could cut across the alley up ahead. That would cut blocks off his walk and get him to Elysée Palace slightly faster than his original route. He stopped briefly at a sidewalk cafe to make use of an empty table. He rested his briefcase atop it and snapped the lid open. The machinery did not appear damaged, but he noticed a streak on the chrome logo. With his finger, he wiped the streak from the chrome "K", so that no mark would hinder it from standing out against the red circle it sat upon.

The alley was nothing more than a deserted passage between the back doors of small shops and cafes. Yukira hurried along, letting some of his natural caution lapse. Perhaps that was why he was unprepared when the kitchen boy stepped out of a doorway with a tray of food scraps. Yukira plowed into the boy, and the two, the briefcase, the tray, and the food scraps all landed in a heap on the ground.

Yukira, brushing fruit rinds from his lapel, grabbed the boy roughly and hauled him against the wall. "Ord!" he screamed at the boy. But, in his anger, he spoke the words in Japanese, so the boy only got the tone of Yukira's vehemence, not the actual meaning. "You dare interfere with a servant of Kanawa? I should let the Inquisitors arrive so that you can learn true fear! But that would not serve my master's purpose."

The boy, confused and frightened, struggled vainly to get free. Yukira, however, had no intention of letting him leave until he learned proper respect for his betters.

"Speak, ord! Beg for your worthless life!"

"You serve your master well, heathen," said a voice from behind Yukira, speaking fluent Japanese. "Bullying an ord in a language he does not understand no doubt accomplishes some great sacrilegious task that is beyond my sensibilities."

The Japanese started to move, but a sharp metal object placed in the small of his back gave him pause.

"You have come to this land to interfere with *my master's* work," the voice continued. "Perhaps you meant to warn the government? Maybe give them the secrets to discovering stelae? No matter. I have found you and I shall save your heathen soul. Tell me, do you repent of your sins?"

"I repent nothing!" Yukira shouted. "I defy you and your master! As an agent of a High Lord, I demand you release me!"

"Very well, I release you," the voice said, burying the sharp metal object into Yukira's spine. Yukira fell forward, sliding off the object and spinning with his last ounce of strength to face his adversary. He spun far enough to see that it was the monk that had inspired the street crowd standing over him, holding a bloody knife. Then he fell into darkness.

"Go, my son," he heard the monk's words follow him into the dark. " Go and sin no more."

58

In another cosm, on another world, Lady Pella Ardinay stood upon the battlement of her castle, overlooking the assembled masses of the world of Aysle.

"They are ready, my Lady," said the elven wizard who bowed before her.

"Are they, Delyndun?" Ardinay asked. Her mood was dark, distant, on this, her day of glory. "When we are out of earshot of the masses, do not call me 'Lady'. I am still Lord Angar Uthorion underneath this feminine flesh."

"Of course, Lord Uthorion, forgive my error," Delyndun said.

"Enough," Ardinay who was Uthorion ordered, "get to the front of the line and drop the maelstrom bridge."

"As you wish, Lord Uthorion."

Uthorion, who wore the body of Ardinay, looked down at the assemblage. All the beings of Aysle under his command were represented. Humans, dwarves, dragons, the demons of the Wild Hunt. Only the giants remained beyond his grasp, and the majority of the elves, who held Ardinay in contempt.

Before the elf mage disappeared down the tower steps, Ardinay who was Uthorion called out one final order.

"Remember, Delyndun," he said through soft, red female lips, "you are to descend the bridge first. I shall not follow until you assure me that *she* is not on this world called Earth."

"But, Lord," Delyndun asked, "does not the Gaunt Man expect you …?"

"Damn the Gaunt Man! He does not have a prophecy haunting him through eternity!" Uthorion, who wore the body of Ardinay, buried his smooth, beautiful face into his smooth, beautiful hands.

"She has not appeared on any of the worlds we have taken since that day, my master," the elf said, trying to provide comfort with his words.

"Which only means that it might be the next one, or the one after that. In some ways, I hope she is on this world. Then, at least, we can finally be done with prophecies."

"I shall make sure, my Lord."

"Then," Uthorion said, letting his own darkness fill Ardinay's sparkling eyes, "drop the bridge."

Twelve days after the jungle bridge fell to Earth in New York City, thirteen days after a bridge of tormented souls dropped into Borneo, a third bridge descended out of the storm. This was a stonework bridge, formed from colossal blocks of fitted stone. It crashed upon the British Isles, and quickly the reality of Aysle washed down the bridge to fill the area bounded by previously-placed stelae. Suddenly magic was the pre-dominant law of nature, and a wave of bizarre creatures crossed over from the cosm to the newly-created realm of Aysle.

59

Tolwyn paced restlessly back and forth in the small hospital room. The doctors handling Tolwyn's case were reluctant to discharge her from their observation, even though she seemed to be in perfect health, if a bit fatigued. They refused to admit openly that something which they could not explain medically had happened to their patient.

Father Bryce stood in the doorway, watching her short, revealing hospital gown flap as she paced about the room. Her body moved fluidly in the small space available for walking, between bed and wall, between window and closet. She looked to Bryce like a caged lioness who had not yet resigned herself to the fact of her imprisonment, like a lioness waiting for the door of her cage to spring open so that she could batter her keeper and leap over his body to freedom.

When he looked at her eyes, as she turned in his direction after pacing the short length of the room, he knew she was not yet ready to escape this cage. There was confusion in her eyes, and frustration, and anger. She knew she was trapped and caged, but she did not know her keeper or in which direction to leap. Her deeply tanned legs flashed beneath the short, pale-blue material of the hospital gown. His eyes kept looking somewhere else in the room, then returning, almost but not quite involuntarily, to watch the well-defined muscles in Tolwyn's legs bunch, stretch and release as the weight of her body moved from the heel to the ball of each of her feet. His breath caught in his throat when she turned and the untied, full-length opening down the back of her gown fluttered and exposed her strong, tapering back and the swaying, firmly muscled half-globes of her nethermost cheeks.

His maleness rose within him. He struggled with himself and the way of life he had chosen. The vows he had taken never required him to deny his sexual nature. But they did require that he not act upon it. Since he had not yet renounced those vows, and, perhaps, never would, he used the mental techniques of self-control he had learned in the seminary. Then, slowly, deliberately, he took off the black cloak of his desire and placed it on a sturdy wooden hanger. He straightened its draping folds, brushed a few flakes of dandruff from its richly velvet collar, hung it on the rack in the closet of his weaknesses, and firmly shut the door on that closet.

Still, he looked at Tolwyn's legs, but now with questioning and wonderment. There were scars upon her legs, scars that had not been there yesterday, scars that were old and white and long healed.

"Good morning," he finally said, catching her attention and causing her to stop pacing and stand before the uncurtained window of the room. Through the hospital gown, the morning light backlit and outlined the curves of her body. Bryce moved farther into the room, sitting lightly on the foot of the unmade bed to deliberately change the angle of his vision.

For a moment, she looked as if she didn't know who Bryce was. Then her eyes cleared and she said, "Good morning to you, Christopher Bryce."

"Where are you going in such a hurry, and with such fierce determination?" he joked.

Tolwyn looked lost for an answer to his question, and

Bryce, regretting his need to know more about this woman, wished he had not asked it.

"I do not know," she finally answered. While she spoke, her left hand drifted to the night stand and the vase holding the blue and red flower.

Bryce's eyes widened when he saw that the flower was just as crisp and fresh-looking as the first time he had seen it.

"Well, anyway, how are you today?" he asked, avoiding asking about the unwilted flower and the scars on her legs. He had spent the better part of his adult life questioning and seeking answers to his questions. Once again, in return for his questions, life had not supplied answers to him, only more questions.

Her mouth split in a grin, showing white, evenly spaced teeth. "Hungry," she said.

Bryce laughed at her robust appetite. "Coyote and Rat are bringing breakfast. They should be here soon."

As they waited, he gently led her to the only chair in the room, got her to sit it it, and arranged the bed table to the correct height for her. As he did all this he spoke of small things, the weather and the heavy traffic in the city. He knew little of what he said made any sense to her, but his aimless chatter seemed to ease her tension.

When the boys arrived with the food, they sat with Bryce and Tolwyn. They joked about the quality, or the lack of quality, of hospital food. Tolwyn never noticed or laughed at their jokes, and she ate as if she hadn't had a meal in a lifetime.

The taste of the food never mattered to her. What mattered was that it was food. Tolwyn used the last half slice of toast to mop up the last bit of yolk on her plate and shoved the yellowed toast into her mouth. She popped the last bit of bacon into a mouth still busy chewing toast, leaned back in her chair, swallowed and burped contentedly.

Rat and Coyote laughed at the fine eating display, and at the look of shock on Bryce's face. Slowly, he began to giggle, joining the boys. Mystified, Tolwyn watched them roll with laughter. Then, without really knowing why, she laughed, too.

When they finally settled down, Tolwyn grew very quiet. Rat and Coyote looked at each other. It was evident that they were still trying to figure Tolwyn out. So am I, thought Bryce.

"Christopher Bryce," Tolwyn began hesitantly, "there is a deep gorge in my dreams lately. I have never been to this place before, never seen its like. What does it mean, Christopher Bryce? Why can I not remember?"

60

Claudine Guerault, French correspondant for the international wire services, examined the murder site with professional care. Chalk marks on the ground traced where the two bodies were found, a young French boy and a Japanese diplomat. Both had been stabbed to death. The international ramifications were yet to be determined, but with the events transpiring in America and Great Britain, Guerault did not believe it would make much of an impact. Still, she had a job to do.

Clicking on her tape recorder, Guerault began to verbally take notes. So far, the police had no suspects, no motives.

"Inspector, is it true that the Japanese diplomat was on his way to a meeting at Elysée Palace when he was murdered? That he was going to meet with the Prime Minister?" Guerault asked the officer in charge of the investigation.

"No comment, Ms. Guerault," the inspector said, waving her off. "I refuse to speculate about a case still under investigation."

"Inspector, come here please," said one of the other officers. Behar followed behind him.

"Look at this sir," said the officer, "we found it in the trash bin."

It was a leather briefcase of fine craftsmanship and make. Obviously an expensive accouterment, very much like something a diplomat might carry.

Using his gloved hand, the inspector snapped the latch and opened the case. Inside was a portable computer of some sort. Claudine Guerault noted the impressive logo on the machine, a chrome "K" on a red circle. It was not from a company she recognized.

"Ms. Guerault, if you don't mind," the inspector said, an annoyed tone in his voice.

"Excuse me, inspector, but I have everything I need for the moment. I will call you later today to see if there have been any breakthroughs." With that, Guerault turned and left the alley, her dark hair bouncing as she walked.

When she reached the main street, she had to push her way through a crowd of people listening to a preacher. The preacher caught her eye, and she noticed that he was staring at her as he spoke. He was dressed in monk's robes, reminding her of something out of the Middle Ages. She looked back at the man, but he had already turned away to address the crowd.

"The True Church is coming, and when it arrives it will drive the heathens and blasphemers before it as a strong wind drives a storm," the preacher spoke powerfully, inspiringly. But he was not an isolated case these days. Similar preachers had appeared all through Paris and the rest of France, proclaiming that the world was about to change.

"Repent!" the preacher yelled out, his gaze was again fixed on the reporter. "Admit your sins and seek the True Church!"

Guerault shivered, though the day was unusually warm. A side effect of the longer days and nights, she assumed. The world was changing, she realized. Maybe the preacher was right, maybe she should repent.

She almost laughed aloud at the thought, then dismissed the preacher and his crowd as she went to file her story.

61

Tolwyn dreamed. She dreamed of confusion and alarm on a bright, rolling plain. She dreamed of battle in a field where the wind-rippled waves of crys flowers were crushed and stained red with the blood of warriors, where a once-beautiful land was churned under foot and claw and cloven hoof. There were other memories associated with the battle, but they refused to surface yet, so her mind traveled further into the tunnel of time.

Now her dream was of the day she ran out of childhood and directly, unheedingly, into the back of Duke Tancred himself. He walked through the narrow, flagstone-paved lanes of the castle gardens, with his hands clasped at the small of his back and his head bent in thought. Tolwyn's lithe, running form caromed off the solid, warrior's body of the Duke, and she spun to a standing halt in a bed of fragrant mint. The Duke, caught completely off guard, went sprawling from the path, his hands digging up the soft earth, crushing the leaves and releasing the strong aromas of basil and chicory as he tried to halt his fall. With her hands covering her mouth and her eyes wide with apprehension over the consequences of her action, Tolwyn silently watched the Duke roll quickly onto his back, gather his legs under him, and reach for the gold-hilted dagger he wore at his belt.

"Tolwyn!" the Duke roared laughingly, his eyes losing their feral, battle-ready hardness as he recognized the girl standing knee deep in a bed of mint. "Never," he grunted while hauling himself to his feet and brushing dirt and leaves from his clothing, "Never in all my campaigns have I been dealt such a blow. Do you realize, child, that you have succeeded in doing what the assembled hosts of continental chivalry have never done? You, Tolwyn of House Tancred, have 'unhorsed' the mighty, undefeated Duke Tancred."

He chuckled and added, "I suppose I shall have to change that last epithet. I may still be mighty, but I am certainly not undefeated."

"Oh, how the mighty have fallen," said Tolwyn softly, forced by her quick humor to speak the words aloud to the Duke.

The Duke's soft laughter subsided as his thoughts returned to the troubles beginning to plague his country. Soon it would be called the War of Crowns, but for now it was just "the troubles". Quietly he observed Tolwyn where she stood watching him, her smile of relief brought about by the Duke's good humor faltering as somberness overtook him. She feared she had pushed the Duke too far with that last spoken jest.

Abruptly, he asked, "How old are you now, girl?"

"Twelve, father," Tolwyn answered, quietly at first, then gaining animation as she continued. "But I shall be counted thirteen at the summer solstice and gain the right to wear the maiden's twin braids as I wait to be taken to wife."

"Your mother was the best warrior who ever fought at my left hand side," Duke Tancred said, studying Tolwyn, almost as if he had not heard her answer to his question.

"I do not remember her, father."

"We are both more aware of that than we would ever want to be, daughter." The Duke shrugged his shoulders as if trying to shed the weight of a heavy, water-soaked mantle. "Well, conquering maiden of House Tancred, what is it you would wish to do?" he asked lightly, attempting to force the river of his thoughts into other, shallower channels.

"Was it truly a mighty blow that I struck?"

"The mightiest," he answered with mock serious-ness.

"Perhaps, then, father," Tolwyn said musingly, "I should be a soldier and a warrior as was my mother."

The Duke reached out his hand to his daughter. As Tolwyn began to reach out to her father, she saw his palm turn to cinnamon brown, and the skin of his wrist and arm become black. She looked up and her father was gone, replaced by an old black man clad in a loincloth. She looked about for her father and saw that the gardens were gone, and the castle. She and the black man stood high on a wind-swept shore overlooking a turbulent ocean.

The black man was lean and wiry and held a knotted rope in his right hand. When his broad face broke into a grin, she saw that he was missing one tooth, and she saw the hole in his tongue. "G'day, luv, where's the blokes that are supposed to be with you?" the black man asked.

When Tolwyn had no answer for him, the aborigine

studied her, shook his head from side to side, making his mound of white hair jiggle. He lost his grin, and said comfortingly, "No worries, it's too soon for you to be out here in the never never. Best you go back, now."

The aborigine pointed into the eastern distance, and Tolwyn felt herself hurtling through the air. She flew over desert lands; blue, white-capped waves; a rocky, shore; large cities full of tall buildings and milling people; and landed, on her hands and knees, in orange sand sparsely dotted with scrub brush. From somewhere in the long shadows of late afternoon, she heard a hunting howl. The horizon and the nearer distances were pierced with craggy, vertical formations of rock that rose starkly from the orange sands into the gathering blackness of the sky. Nearer still, illuminated by the sinking sun at Tolwyn's back were two monumental, weather-carved formations that looked like two mittened hands, with clumped fingers and separate thumbs, raised in salute to the coming of night.

"I am in the gorge," Tolwyn realized. Deeper still, down in the great crack in the ground, she saw a subtle blue-red glow emerging from a cave. The light spoke to her, but she couldn't hear the words. She only felt the pain and fear, the unfathomable call for help.

"I am coming," she whispered, "I vow that I will finish my mission."

Then she fell into a deeper, dreamless sleep.

62

Tolwyn awoke to sunlight and the smell of bacon. She blinked away the sleep and saw that Christopher Bryce was at the window, opening the curtains to let in the light.

"So, at last you're awake," said Bryce in a glad voice.

"You've slept away the whole morning and most of the afternoon." He seemed pleased that she had awakened.

"I remember my father, Christopher Bryce," Tolwyn said. "I dreamed about him last night."

"That's good, that shows progress," Bryce said. "What was Mr. Miller like?"

Tolwyn looked at him strangely, but ignored his question. "What manner of beast is calling?" she asked.

"Beast?" asked Bryce, startled at her question.

"Aye, that howling I hear. Do not tell me you cannot hear it screaming madly just outside the walls of this castle."

"Oh, that's the wind. There have been incredible storms since everything began. And now I hear that they think the planet is slowing down. I honestly don't understand what the world is coming to."

Tolwyn looked questioningly at Bryce. "You mean it is taking longer for the light to make its journey through the world?"

Now it was Bryce's turn to be confused. "Come over here. Take a look out the window."

She threw the sheet back and started to slide out of the bed. She swung her legs over the side and placed her feet on the floor. Her hospital gown began to rise up her thighs.

"Wait," said Bryce, "let me get a robe for you."

Wrapped in a blue, antiseptic-smelling hospital robe, Tolwyn stood next to the short figure of Bryce and looked out the window. Winds of hurricane force hurled litter, debris, leaves, and unidentifiable flotsam through paved streets lined with tall brick buildings. Hard-driven rain rattled against the glass of the window. Huge clouds scudded visibly across the sky and over the towering rooftops, looming ominously. In the streets below, a few military and police vehicles fought to make headway against the wind, uselessly trying to enforce martial law in a city whose citizens had locked themselves up in whatever safe place they could find, trying to survive the storms.

Tolwyn looked from the sky to the buildings and then to the vehicles moving slowly through the streets. "Christopher Bryce," she said, "this is not the world in which I was born and in which I died."

"What …?" But before he could ask more, the young woman spoke again.

"I must find the gorge in my dreams, Christopher Bryce. It is my mission, the purpose for which I came here."

"Tolwyn, I don't understand."

"I am Tolwyn. My father is Duke Bordal of House Tancred. Those are the sum of my memories right now, but I know that something calls to me from the bottom of the gorge. I must go to it, I must answer its call."

"That's crazy," exclaimed Bryce, "I won't let you go anywhere. You're not well, and …"

"I am not a child to be ordered, Christopher Bryce!" Tolwyn shouted. Her voice was strong, full of authority. It made Bryce pause.

"I want to help you, Tolwyn, don't you see that?"

"Then help me find the gorge, Christopher," Tolwyn pleaded, suddenly all the power was gone from her voice. "Please."

63

That afternoon, after a quiet lunch with Rick Alder, Coyote and Rat in the hospital's cafeteria, Father Christopher Bryce walked Tolwyn back to her room. She did not speak to him, and the silence was disturbing. But he still had questions, so he sat down in the chair beside her bed to gather his thoughts.

"Were you really dead, Tolwyn?" Bryce asked.

"Yes," she said, not bothering to adjust her blue hospital robe as she sat upon the bed.

"And you're not a woman named Wendy Miller?"

"No."

"You were never her, were you?"

"I have always been who I am now, Tolwyn of House Tancred."

"Do you know what happened to the woman whose body you wear?"

Tolwyn looked down at her arms and hands. She glanced at her image in the mirror over the small chest of drawers. "This is my body," she said. She pointed to the scars on her arms. "These are my scars. That much I know. And that is my face in the glass."

She ran one hand through her hair. "But someone has cut my hair."

"Where have you come from, Tolwyn of House Tancred ... and why?" he asked slowly, hesitantly, concerned that his questioning would alarm her or send her back into herself. He saw the tension ripple the muscles along the lines of her jaw and feared the worst, that he had driven her away again with his questions to which she seemed to have no answers. But she sighed and the hard planes of clenched muscles softened in her face as she shook her head from side to side, apparently indicating that she did not have the answers he sought.

"What land is this, Christopher Bryce?" Tolwyn asked as she looked out the window at the storm-beaten city. He told her.

"It is difficult to know what you know and what you don't know," he said.

"For me also," she said. She reached to the night stand beside the bed and picked up the vase that held the blue and red flower. "Do you know what this is?"

"I don't think I've ever seen its like. But, then, I'm not very knowledgeable about flowers. You called it a crys, didn't you? A strange name ..."

"Not to me, Christopher. I ran through fields of them when I was a child. They were trampled into the ground in the battle in which I died."

"Where was this battle, Tolwyn?"

He watched anger and frustration at her own lack of recollection chase each other across the windows of her eyes. "I do not ... wait ... Aysle ..." At first, the word was forced from Tolwyn's stiffened lips. But as she said it, rolled it around in her mouth, it calmed her. "My home is Aysle."

However, no other memories would surface, nothing but a name and a feeling of terrible homesickness. "My mind is a war, and I am tired." And then she turned to Father Bryce. "This bed is narrow, but I've loved on narrower. Would you lie with me, Christopher Bryce?"

Bryce felt the blood rush to his face and cause it to redden. He watched Tolwyn as she looked oddly at him where he sat red-faced and speechless as he searched for the words to explain his vocation and his vows to her.

"How odd," she said wonderingly after he had found the words and gotten them out. "Vows I understand, but to deny one's nature ..."

"That is the way it is," he said softly.

She shrugged. "I would have enjoyed it, Christopher Bryce."

"My friends call me Chris. It's short for Christopher." She looked puzzled, then grinned at him and asked, "Does that mean you have to call me Tol?"

Bryce laughed and inwardly thanked her for lightening the tone of their situation. "I'll see you later, Tolwyn," he said, rose from the chair, and walked toward the door of the room.

"Until later ... Chris," she said and lay back on the bed, closing her eyes as her head rested on the pillow.

64

Lambent energies flickered, coruscated, and Dr. Hachi Mara-Two appeared in the center of the flowing, dimension-spanning beams. Then the lambency died, the coruscation faded, and Mara found herself standing in a downpour. Mara absently wiped rain from her black jumpsuit, as she looked up at the brick building in front of her. She pulled her language logic enhancement chip from a pocket and plugged it into one of the slots behind her ear. The chip did its job immediately, and the metal letters embedded in the wall of the building, moments ago unreadable, now clearly proclaimed it the Hospital of the University of Pennsylvania.

"Giga-rad," Mara exclaimed to the empty street. "It worked. I'm here."

Suddenly, the thrill of success slipped from her mind, and she remembered the incident in the transference chamber that had occurred not more than thirty seconds ago, her time. Quickly, she looked around to see if the one who had introduced himself as Thratchen had followed her. The streets were empty of people. She had not been followed. Off in the distance, some sort of wheeled vehicle passed by, its spotlights burning holes in the darkness of the storm. Mara rolled her leather gauntlet up, uncovering the inside of her left wrist. The wrist, like the rest of the arm, was sleeved in metal flesh that protected metal sinews and veins of circuitry. She squeezed her fist and a panel slid open, revealing a keypad and display line. The code running across the display told her the program was still operating, controlling the sensor unit built into her left eye.

Mara had developed the sensor unit during the early days of the Sim War. It was apparent that select individuals on her world had undergone a change in response to the invading reality. These individuals — herself included — had started storing a form of energy that Mara could measure but not identify. Even the Sims registered on the sensor, or at least some of them. In fact, the sensor identified the energy in everything, but most things had it in such minute quantities that it was never noticed before. She theorized that the energy buildup was a natural defense mechanism that kicked into effect in the wake of reality storms, but she hadn't had time to prove it.

"I don't like this storm," Mara muttered, remembering the storms that rocked Kadandra prior to the coming of the Sims. "Okay, let's see what the energy level looks like on Earth." A few taps on the keypad shifted the sensor lense into place over her pupil. Then the world exploded into a blinding burst of blue and red light.

Mara shut her eye, but the vivid colors were burned into her retina. Even with the lid closed, she still saw the after image in her mind. "By the Net! This entire world glows like the selects! The energy is in such abundance here," she said to herself. She recalibrated the program, adjusting for the heavier concentration, and opened her eye again.

Now the scenery was as normal, without the blue-red cast. To test the sensor, she held her hand before her. It was surrounded by the blue and red glow. "Because of the abundant energy here, I seem to be absorbing more of it. Giga-rad."

Scanning the building before her, Mara saw a faint glow pulsating from an upper window. Okay, she thought. In and up. Mara found the entrance and pushed open the glass doors of the hospital. No one in the busy lobby took much notice of the young woman in the black jumpsuit as she made her way through the corridors and up the staircases of the building, following the displays in her eye. On the fourth floor of the hospital, she found a high concentration of energy coming from an open doorway. Whoever the select is, she thought, he must be positively crackling with the stuff. Quietly, she approached the portal and looked in.

65

"Put on this robe, Tolwyn," Father Bryce pleaded for the hundredth time.

Tolwyn turned, leaned close so that her nose almost touched his, and said, "If you tell me what to do one more time, Christopher Bryce, I shall personally demonstrate twenty-seven ways to disable a man without using a weapon."

Coyote and Rat giggled at the thought, but Bryce could hear the seriousness in Tolwyn's voice. It scared him, but not for his own sake. For her's. He dropped the garment onto the bed, then dropped himself into a chair.

"Tolwyn, tell me again where you want to go," said Rick Alder.

"There is a wide, deep gorge. At the bottom, a rushing river winds its way through the gorge. There is a cave in the gorge, and in that cave is the entity that called me to this world. It is in pain. It is afraid. And I must go to help it," Tolwyn finished.

"That isn't a lot to go on, I'm afraid," Alder said. "We

don't even know which direction to go."

Tolwyn jumped up excitedly, grabbing the police officer with powerful hands. "But we do, Rick Alder! We do! In my dreams I am always moving west. We have to go west."

"It was a dream, Tolwyn," Bryce said, trying to calm the excited woman.

"I must find this gorge, Chris. I must!"

"Why, Tolwyn?" Coyote asked.

Before Tolwyn could answer, Rat exclaimed, "Cool hair!"

Bryce, Tolwyn, Alder and Coyote looked up inquiringly at the young woman with the mane of silver hair who stood in the doorway. She was dressed in an oddly-tailored black jumpsuit that bristled with pockets. She looked directly at Tolwyn.

"She must find the place in her dreams," the young woman said. Her voice was tinged with an accent as strange as Tolwyn's, but definitely not of the same origin. Bryce noticed that she wore a mask of makeup that reminded him of a raccoon.

The young woman looked from Tolwyn to examine each of the others in turn. Then she spoke again. "She must go, and I am going with her."

66

Djil rose from his position overlooking the sea. He had sat there long enough, listening to the Earth and walking among the dreams. He checked the rope he had been working, examing the six knots he had tied.

"We shall be the knots which tie reality back together," he told the rope, but it was evident he was talking to those the knots represented. "But the path of the rope will be hard to walk. So very hard."

He marched into his village, ignoring the questioning stares that followed him to his dwelling. There, he gathered his few possessions into a small sack which he slung across his back. Then he started to leave the village.

"Where are you going without a word, old man," asked a village woman finally, gaining the courage to address the shaman.

"It's time to go on walkabout, m'luv."

And, as if that explained everything, the aborigine left the village without another word.

67

The elven wizard Delyndun stepped onto the ground of a new world. At his back were the forces of Aysle, jammed upon a bridge that reached into the sky and then spanned the cosmverse to connect to his home. Before him were the strange sights of this world's reality, but already he could see signs that Aysle's reality was pure throughout the area around the bridge.

He could see the dragons and their riders clearing away any opposition with blasts of fire and other energies. Warriors of the many houses spread out to secure the realm, and the creatures of Aysle were pouring forth to fill the land.

"To me, assistants," Delyndun called. Quickly, the young human mages that were his students appeared about him. "Prepare the circle," he ordered, then stepped away to watch them work.

They used their arcane powers to create the wards of knowledge and the circle of searching. When Delyndun was satisfied with their spells, he stepped into the circle and traced a shell over his head. His own spell caused the circle to fill with a blue sphere of glowing magic.

From inside, he could view most anything he wished upon the curve of the sphere — provided he had the proper artifact to power the spell.

He removed a metal gauntlet from a pouch that hung on his belt. It was an aged glove, yet finely detailed and of superior workmanship. Obviously, it once belonged to a knight of great station. Delyndun spoke words from a language only mages knew, and the glove reflected light onto the walls of the sphere.

"If the knight of prophecy, the knight that haunts my master's thoughts, is upon this world, reveal her to me!"

The face of a woman with glossy chestnut hair and green eyes appeared before the elf. Others could be seen beside her — a man in black, a woman in black, another man, and two boys — but the elf was too absorbed by Tolwyn's image to pay the others much heed.

"It worked," he whispered in awe. "After all the times I have been forced to perform this ritual on all those different worlds, this time it worked." He marked her location in his mind, then let the spell drop.

One of the students steadied the elf, who appeared ready to faint. "What is wrong, master?" the student asked. "What did you see?"

"She is here, Conkin," the mage replied, trying to keep the fear he felt out of his voice. "I must inform Lady Ardinay that Tolwyn of House Tancred has finally returned."

68

Thratchen sat amid the computers in the main chamber of the Transference Facility. He finished tearing out the throat of the last living volunteer who was plugged into the cybernet. The thought that he should not have killed them all flicked across the surface of his mind. But he knew it would not have made any difference. He could not have trusted any of them to send him after Dr. Hachi. They would have pretended to accede to his wishes, but once they had him in the transference cylinder, they would have scattered his atoms across the cosms. He and his High Lord and their armies had just fought a war with Hachi's people. But it should not have been a war. The raiders never fought wars. They conquered, quickly, completely. War was unheard of, and losing could not be tolerated. But now the armies were captured or had fled, the maelstrom bridges crumbled. For all Thratchen knew, he was the last of his people left alive on the world of Kadandra. Thratchen observed his tantrum with grim satisfaction. Dead bodies were sprawled in reclining chairs. Control panels were splattered with blood. The facility was a mess, courtesy of a Sim. But he had to get moving. Kadandra's soldiers would arrive soon. He had to be gone long before that. Thratchen pulled a small black cube from one of his pockets. The cube was given to Thratchen by his High Lord, and all he had to do was invoke its power to return to his master's side. He was about to do just that when he noticed a flashing light on the cyberdrive console.

Thratchen plugged into the console, using one of his built-in finger jacks. He studied the cybernet, discovering that the transference cylinder had syphoned enough energy from the stormers to complete a second leap into the cosmverse. It was probably a safety feature, Thratchen decided, so that they could pull Dr. Hachi back after a time. But it would not serve that purpose. Instead, it would send Thratchen to wherever she went.

"I don't know where you disappeared to in such a hurry, Mara," Thratchen said aloud. "I couldn't drag that data from Dr. Kendal's mind before he crashed. But

I am coming after you. I want to discuss some things with you. I want you to tell me how you discovered we were coming here. And then I want to find out about this use for stormers you have discovered." Thratchen fondled a cable that connected a dead stormer into the cyberdrive.

He could return to his own cosm. There was power waiting for him at the side of his High Lord. They might have failed here, but there was a major raid going on elsewhere in the cosmverse. In a few days the Sims were to join that raid as partners of the Gaunt Man. All Thratchen had to do was invoke the black cube and a bridge thread would arrive from his High Lord.

But there were other ways for him to gain power. Hachi was one of those ways. Thratchen set the automatic controls and allowed the cyberdrive to power up. Without a second look, the Sim stepped into the transference cylinder as cascading energy filled the hollow space. Then, like Dr. Hachi Mara-Two before him, Thratchen was gone.

69

"Who are you?" Father Bryce asked the young woman in the black jumpsuit.

"Dr. Hachi Mara-Two," said the woman.

"Are you handling Tolwyn's — Miss Miller's — case, Dr. Maratu?" asked Bryce.

"Dr. Hachi," the woman corrected, then added, "Yes, I've just taken over."

"Pardon me, Dr. Hachi," Bryce apologized, acknowledging the young woman's correction of his use of her name. She nodded and passed over the matter as Bryce tried to identify the slight but puzzling accent in her voice. He examined her facial features. She was striking, but he wasn't sure if it was because of her wild mane of hair, the makeup, or something deeper that showed in the way she held herself. The barely noticeable epicanthic fold of her eyes hinted at Asian ancestry, thus explaining the fact that her family name preceded her given name. And she was young, very young in Bryce's thirty-four-year-old eyes.

"You're very young to be a doctor," he said to Mara.

"Prodigy," she explained shortly, her attention focused on Tolwyn.

"Are you ready to go, Tolwyn?" Mara asked, using the name she had heard the men use when they had spoken to the woman.

"Yes."

"Wait!" said Bryce as Tolwyn picked up the vase with the crys flower. "You don't know how to get there. You have no way to get there."

"Yes they do, Father," said Rick Alder, finally speaking up. But the words were not ones Bryce wanted to hear.

"What are you saying, Rick? Certainly you aren't going to join these two in this crazy business?"

"Who's to say what's crazy anymore, Chris? But I believe Tolwyn's dream means something, and I want to know what that something is. Because if it means there's a way to get at those monsters that destroyed New York, then I want to be a part of that. I promised myself and a poor young woman that I would be a part of that."

"Us, too, Father," said Coyote. Rat, standing beside him, nodded.

"We will find out where it is, Christopher Bryce," Tolwyn said. She turned to leave.

"Wait! You need some clothes," Bryce said.

Tolwyn looked down at herself. "Yes. If my dreams are any indication, the gorge is in very rugged country. Do not worry, I will find clothes."

"Wait," said Bryce again.

"Now what?" asked Mara, the impatience of youth evident in her voice and posture.

"Wait … for me," said Bryce finally. "That is, if I'm invited …"

Tolwyn smiled and threw her right arm around Bryce's shoulders, hugging him to her chest. "Good," she said, "Now we are almost complete."

Bryce didn't really want to go on what he thought was a foolish, dream-inspired quest sanctioned by some oddly dressed teenager who claimed to be a doctor. But he didn't want Tolwyn to go without him. She might have some of the answers he needed. He believed Tolwyn had come from life, through death, and to life again. He needed to know what came after life or, maybe, what came between lives. He needed to know from someone who had been there, not from unproven dogma. He needed something to believe in. More than that, he needed to know there was something he could believe in, something true that he could trust, something in which he could have faith. And so Bryce once again faced his great question, a question that had driven him into Holy Orders and then most of his adult life in an attempt to find its answer.

But this time there was someone who might have his answers. She didn't know them herself yet, but she would — if and when she remembered who she was, where she had come from, and how she had gotten here. And that someone, possibly with the answers he sought, was about to walk out the door and chase after a dream. Bryce had to be with her when her memories came back, for in those memories he knew he would find some, maybe all, of the quest that was his life. He knew Tolwyn would not stay here with him. So, he must go with her.

"Stay here," he said, then added as Mara glared at him, "Just for a little while. We'll get some clothes for Tolwyn, some supplies."

He paused and looked at Tolwyn. "Will you wait?"

Tolwyn nodded. "I can use your help, Christopher Bryce. I will wait."

"Coyote, Rat, let's go see what we can dig up."

"I'll go prepare the van," Alder said. Then he and the other men exited the room, leaving Tolwyn and Mara alone.

70

"Stop the vehicles."

The order came from Congressman Andrew Jackson Decker, but it wasn't necessary. The drivers of the truck and two jeeps stopped of their own accord when they saw what lay before them.

"What is that?" asked Private Rider, Decker's driver. The congressman stood up in his jeep and raised binoculars to his eyes.

Ahead was a storm front that spread out across the horizon from sky to ground. Crackling bolts of lightning played throughout the rolling clouds and falling rain. And more, the landscape within the storm seemed to constantly shift and change, but Decker assumed the effect was an optical illusion caused by the fierce weather pattern.

"Sergeant, what do you make of this?" Decker asked, speaking to the soldier in the jeep that pulled up beside his.

"According to our last intelligence, that's the border

of the zone of silence," said Sergeant Lewis. "Do you think that storm has anything to do with the invaders?"

"Your guess is as good as mine, sergeant," Decker said, "but it's a good bet. Storms seem to be the common element in all this."

Decker and the soldiers watched in silence for a few moments, each thinking his own thoughts. Then Decker said, "We won't find out anything just sitting here, that's for certain. I had a coach once who told me the only way to do something was to just do it. Sergeant, let's do it."

"You're the boss, congressman," Lewis replied. Then he gave the order. "Let's move out!"

The procession moved forward, rolling slowly toward the edge of the storm. Decker looked back once, but the Harrisburg skyline was lost in thick clouds. So he focused his attention forward, trying not to let the raging wind or the lightning disturb him.

"Are you sure about this, congressman?" asked Rider, yelling over the roar of the wind.

"Not even a little," Decker called back. "But sometimes you've got to go with the long shot."

The edge of the storm loomed closer, and Decker saw that it was a virtual wall of swirling cloud. It reminded him of a tornado, except that it was stationary, in so far as only the clouds within the wall moved, not the wall itself.

"It's like the Wizard of Oz, congressman."

"What a wonderful thought, Rider."

Then they were through the cloud wall and into the heart of the storm. The road beneath them bucked and twisted, becoming ribbon thin and then billowing out like a sheet. Rider kept the jeep steady and moving straight ahead, even as the road spun around. At times they found themselves upsidedown, at others driving on their side. But Rider simply drove, maneuvering only when a bolt of lightning got too close or a fissure opened in the ground ahead.

Decker tried to keep his eyes forward. He wanted to ignore the unrealistic vista around the jeep. But they darted this way and that of their own accord, trying to catch the land in the act of its changing dance. To one side, he saw whole mountain ranges rise up and fall in the blink of an eye. To the other, he watched as lightning smashed into the ground, spewing forth unnatural shapes that scuttled away from the vehicles.

"What is happening here?" Decker screamed, but if Rider heard him he gave no indication. More likely, Decker's words were pulled away by the wind. The congressman saw that Rider's knuckles had gone white from the tight grip he had on the wheel. He wondered if they would be able to stay sane in this place. He prayed they would be out of it soon.

Rain began to fall. Large, ugly drops of water splashed across the windshield and hood of the jeep, leaving vulgar stains. Then, as Decker watched, the drops shifted into small humanoid forms. The forms were shaped like the letter "x", with two upraised arms and two shuffling legs. They soon covered the hood and began climbing over the windshield.

The congressman grabbed a machinegun from the rear of the jeep. He stood up, ready to bash the forms as they entered the vehicle. The small shapes were silent, plodding, and that made Decker more nervous than if they had been screaming madly.

"Just keep driving, private," Decker ordered.

The first of the water forms reached over the windshield. Its headless body was a storm in miniature, full of swirling rain and muck. It worked one wet arm and leg over the top of the glass.

"Get off my jeep!" Decker shouted, swinging the machinegun like a baseball bat. The stock passed through the form with a splat, scattering the rain and muck in all directions.

Then the raindrop forms advanced en masse, splashing over the windshield faster than Decker could batter them apart. They clung to the congressman and the soldier, pounding on them with a hundred tiny fists. No single punch hurt, but Decker knew that in great numbers the forms could kill them.

"We're going to drown, Decker!" Private Rider shouted. Decker could hear fear creeping into his voice.

"Just drive, soldier! We must be reaching the edge of this storm!"

The raindrop forms almost completely covered Decker now, crawling wetly up his body toward his head. One wet fist touched the skin of his cheek, and he tried to recoil from it. It felt slimy, dirty, deathly cold. They were trying to drown them! Now panic shot through his body, and Decker had to hold himself in check or he was certain to leap from the jeep. And if he left the jeep, his island of reality in the madness of the storm, then he would be lost.

Water arms and legs smacked his face. He could feel the cold of their inner storms. They covered his mouth and nose, and suddenly Decker was fighting for breath. He slipped back into his seat, letting the weight of the creatures pull him down.

Then the jeep burst through the wall of clouds. As soon as it did so, Decker could feel a change. The shifting landscape was gone, replaced by a steady horizon. The water forms held their grip for a moment, then they collapsed into a puddle underneath Decker's seat. He was soaked, but he could breathe again, and he sucked in great gulps of air.

"Good driving, Rider," Decker gasped, "But how you were able to keep going I'll never figure ..."

Decker stopped. The soldier beside him was slumped over the steering wheel. His uniform was dripping wet, but he wasn't moving. Decker felt for a pulse. There was none.

"Oh, Rider, why'd you go and die on me?" Decker moaned, noticing that Rider's leg had locked down on the gas pedal in death, explaining why the jeep had continued forward even though the soldier had died. He realized rather detachedly that the jeep should still be moving, but for some reason the engine had given out.

He sat back in his seat, weary from the trip through the storm. But he looked around, trying to see where he was. The landscape was familiar enough. It looked like the Pennsylvania he knew. But something wasn't right.

The congressman turned when he heard the other vehicles behind him. The truck and other jeep leaped out of the storm. But there was no roar of power from their engines either. There was only the sound of their wheels rolling to a halt. "I guess we made it into the zone of silence," he thought.

Then another sound caught Decker's attention. Emerging from the forest ahead of them was a huge lizard with spines along its back and a long tail. It crashed out of the trees with no regard for the damage it was causing. But it wasn't walking toward the vehicles, so Decker only sat and watched it.

"Well, Rider," he said to the dead man, "I guess we're not in Pennsylvania any more."

71

Traveling without a bridge thread! The sensation both exhilirated and disturbed Thratchen at the same time. He remembered early experiments of the Gaunt Man, back in the days when he and his High Lord both served the powerful lord of Orrorsh. The Gaunt Man tried repeatedly to hurl his advance agents to other cosms by using dimension-spanning portals. Only a handful of the poor beings survived, returning to Orrorsh as bent, twisted parodies of what they once were. It was as though they had been ripped apart, and then put back together by a child who had never seen what the undamaged whole looked like. Arms were on the same side of the body, legs were spaced further up the waist, internal organs were hung on the outside.

These thoughts flashed through Thratchen's mind, for the trip — from his perspective — lasted no more than a few seconds. Then he was standing on solid ground. It was raining. Thratchen hated the rain. That was the worst part of raiding other cosms — it always rained as a result of your arrival.

He looked around, immediately bringing his senses — natural and enhanced — to bear on his surroundings. But a quick scan told him that Mara was not within a dozen kilometers of his location. He should have foreseen that, Thratchen realized. The transference cylinder and cyberdrive had been calibrated for someone much smaller and lighter than he was. He could have been thrown thousands of miles off course.

"The price of rash actions," he muttered as he checked his body for damage. All his parts seemed to be in the right place.

The Sim examined the area he found himself in. He was in an antiquated technological culture, at least from the type of ground and buildings he saw. But his sensors told him he was in an even less advanced axiom zone. It was primitive, and in most circumstances he would not be able to use his equipment here. But Thratchen was no ord who would easily flip to the dominant axioms. No, he could retain his own reality, and he intended to do just that.

Two creatures approached him. Before he could determine what they were, the creatures raised sharp spears and rushed toward him. Without any regard, Thratchen mentally activated his built-in leg holster. It snapped open, giving him instant access to his smartgun. The weapon flew into his clawed hand and fired once, twice, three times. The creatures fell.

"Edeinos," Thratchen said, finally identifying the lizard men. He saw a maelstrom bridge in the distance, rising out of the ruins of some kind of arena and disappearing into the clouds.

"I'm on Earth. And the invasion has started. But how could I ..." Thratchen stopped. He knew how. Mara. The wretched whelp had not only determined a raid was coming to her world, she had discovered the major plot to take this possibility-rich planet as well.

"That's why she's here. She's come to help them."

At first Thratchen's rage was terrible, but then an idea began to form. He left the rage where it was, saving it for another time, for the idea had to take precedence.

"I'll never find her without help, though. And since my master hasn't arrived yet, I'll have to go to a higher authority."

Thratchen headed toward the bridge.

72

Kurst hurried through Illmound Keep. He had been

summoned by the Gaunt Man, and he knew that to keep the master waiting was to invite punishment. Shoving past servants, Kurst entered the great hall of the keep.

The Gaunt Man stood on one side of a huge banquet table that occupied the center of the hall. With arms spread, he leaned on the table and studied the maps before him. Scythak lounged indolently catlike and aloof in one of the carved, oak chairs that had been pushed away from the table. On the other side of the table from the Gaunt Man stood a demon from Tharkold. The skin of the demon shone blue-black in the light that came through the many-paned windows of the hall. He wore a black leather tunic. Chains completed his ensemble. Kurst also noted the many mechanical implants that covered the demon's body.

"Ah, Kurst," said the Gaunt Man when he noticed the hunter waiting midway between the door to the great hall and the banquet table. "Come in."

The Gaunt Man waved a hand in the general direction of the demon, and said, "Meet Thratchen. He served the High Lord of Tharkold as a chief lieutenant, but was stranded on Kadandra when that world actually managed to destroy the maelstrom bridges."

Without speaking, but with heightened attention at this new development, Kurst moved to stand near the table. He heard Scythak give a faint, mocking snort. Thratchen merely parted his lips, displaying pointed, yellowed teeth. Kurst wondered if the demon was smiling at him in greeting or threatening him. He assumed it was a threat and that Thratchen was establishing himself in the pecking order of the Gaunt Man's cadre. Kurst didn't care. As one of the Gaunt Man's hunters, he stood outside the chain of command. The threat was wasted on him.

"Tell us what happened on Kadandra, Thratchen," the Gaunt Man said.

"I can tell you about that. They lost," laughed Scythak deprecatingly.

The Gaunt Man eyed the demon, watching for any reaction that would expose him as weak or foolish. Kurst did so, too, but saw no sign of anything other than confidence and power.

"My master planned well," Thratchen said. "Everything was done as it was done so many times before. It was done as you taught us, High Lord, when we served in your cosm. But we could not anticipate that the Kadandrans would be ready for our arrival."

Kurst saw Scythak sit up at that, but the Gaunt Man remained impassive.

"The blame for our failure can be traced to one stormer, and I was sent to find and destroy this stormer before she could do more harm."

"Explain yourself, demon," demanded the Gaunt Man.

"Among the Kadandrans was a young woman — a prodigy, if you will — who proposed a theory that explained the cosmverse. She took her theory to its next step and designed an instrument for looking into other cosms. The one she chose to examine was a cosm very similiar to her own. It had similar axiom and tech levels, a similar history. But where her world had gone on to become a peaceful place, the cosm she found was the exact opposite. It was Tharkold."

The demon went on to explain how the young genius was able to tell that Tharkold was looking back. Hoping that the other cosm was friendly, but prepared for the worst if it wasn't, the Kadandrans waited for the appearance of the first maelstrom bridge. And when the

Storm Knights

Alan Jude Summa

Tharkolds proved hostile, the Kadandrans defended themselves.

"... and so we were beaten back, defeated because they were waiting for us and we weren't prepared for that occurrence," Thratchen finished.

The Gaunt Man studied the demon as he sat back in his chair. He absently twirled his dragon-headed cane while he did so, letting the light reflect off the blue and red gem lodged in the dragon's mouth.

"Why are you here, Thratchen?" the High Lord finally asked.

"Because my cosm has not arrived as of yet, and because I need help. The young genius that I seek fled Kadandra before I could reach her."

"Fled?" Now the Gaunt Man was sitting forward, a rare look of confusion etched into his taut brow. "How? And to where?"

Kurst sensed triumph in Thratchen's posture. The demon paused, tapping sharp claws on the hardwood table. Then he spoke.

"This stormer found another cosm. And she found a use for stormers that we never thought of."

The Gaunt Man smashed his cane atop the table, causing a loud echo to reverberate throughout the hall. "Enough of these games, demon! What did she find? Where did she go! Tell me or I will destroy you where you sit!"

"She discovered a gate, High Lord," Thratchen said quickly, perhaps sensing that he took his game too far. "With stormers to power it, she opened a portal between cosms. She has come to Earth, High Lord, and I fear it is to accomplish the same work she performed on Kadandra. She has come to help this cosm retain its own reality."

The Gaunt Man stood up and paced around the table. Kurst could see the thought processes playing across his face and shoulders. He almost pitied the stormer who could cause such anger in his master.

"And you, Thratchen? How did you come to this world?"

"Through the same portal, High Lord. Then across Baruk Kaah's cosm to the maelstrom bridge connecting Takta Ker to Orrorsh, and here I am."

Kurst traced Thratchen's path in his mind, acknowledging to himself that the demon took the fastest route to the Gaunt Man's realm on the other side of Earth from where he arrived.

"Gibberfat!" the Gaunt Man called, and a small, bloated demon appeared on the table in a cloud of brimstone. Gibberfat stood about a foot tall, with red, smouldering skin, and webbed hands and feet. There was even a hint of gills around his flabby neck. He bowed nonchalantly, then started to dig into the bowls and platters of food that filled the table. He paused when the dragon cane pushed into his round stomach.

"Go prepare a flight of ravagons, Gibberfat," the Gaunt Man said, ignoring the demon as he downed a handful of nuts. "Have them ready to fly when I give the word."

"Of course, master," Gibberfat mumbled around a mouth full of food and sharp teeth. "Whatever you say." He dove into a platter of meats, cutting through the thick slices like a shark through water.

"Go!"

"Oh, very well," the demon called from underneath the pile of meat. A burst of foul vapor punctuated Gibberfat's departure.

"High Lord," Thratchen said, "I don't think you

should destroy this stormer yet."

Scythak leaped across the table and grabbed Thratchen by his leather shirt. He lifted him out of his chair. "You dare question the Gaunt Man's judgment?"

Kurst sat back to watch the spectacle. He imagined he would enjoy it.

The huge hunter towered over Thratchen, but the demon seemed unimpressed. Steel claws extended from the fingers of his right hand, and with one motion he sliced the flesh of Scythak's arm from shoulder to elbow. Scythak screamed in pain, releasing Thratchen and clutching at his arm to stop the flow of blood.

Scythak shifted then, smoothly changing from man to giant man-tiger as everyone watched. He stood on two legs, with his fur-covered arms and claws spread threateningly, looking like some gold and black striped cat in man's clothing. The weretiger prepared to pounce, but the Gaunt Man's cane slapped across his chest to bar his way.

"Shift back, Scythak. Now." The giant tiger shrank back into a large man, and Scythak backed off. But Kurst could tell that it wasn't over between the two. Maybe he had gained an ally against the weretiger.

"Speak, Thratchen, and make your explanation very good," the Gaunt Man said, letting the implied warning speak for itself.

"Of course, High Lord, I meant no disrespect. It is just that I believe someone with as much scientific interest as yourself would be curious about this new power. I suggest you capture this stormer and bring her here for further testing."

The Gaunt Man dropped his cane to his side and resumed his pacing. He circled the table once, turning dozens of plans over in his mind as he walked. He stopped when he reached Kurst's chair.

"Go prepare yourself, hunter," the Gaunt Man said, resting his hand on Kurst's shoulder. "I believe I have a mission for you."

Thratchen turned to Kurst and asked, "And what tricks do you do, little one?"

Scythak laughed aloud at this mention of Kurst's size, as the hunter was smaller than any of the other three people present. Kurst merely fixed Thratchen with an evil glare. Perhaps his ally wasn't as true as he hoped.

"Go, Kurst," the Gaunt Man said again. "I will send for you as soon as I determine the stormer's general location."

"No! I am your greatest hunter! Send me," Scythak said defensively, finally comprehending the Gaunt Man's intentions.

"If that is true, Scythak, then it makes sense that I keep you here at my side," the High Lord soothed. Scythak puffed up his broad chest with pride at the words.

As he rose to leave, Kurst heard the Gaunt Man speak to Thratchen a final time. "Come, demon, let us go and find your stormer. Then we can send the wolf out to hunt."

73

In a small Australian airfield, Tom O'Malley was giving his plane the final once over before takeoff. He liked to do this himself, as he trusted his own eyes better than any mechanic's. So far so good, he thought, checking off boxes on his pre-flight clipboard.

"Where are you off to this time, O'Malley?" asked Jimmy Hogan. He was on his way to his own plane when he stopped to say a few words to the other pilot.

"Britain," Tom said cheerfully, inspecting the right

engine one last time.

"I hope you got cargo going in both directions this time," Hogan laughed, "'cause it sure did cost you on that last run."

"Don't worry about me, Jimmy. Just watch behind you, because O'Malley's Transport Company is going to pass your dinky operation any day now."

"Dream on, Tom. You've got this one cargo jet. I've got a fleet of six aircraft."

As the two pilots talked, an aborigine appeared on the airstrip. He was dressed scantily, as was the manner of those from the Outback, and he looked to be very old. But he walked straight and there was a strength to him that belied his white hair and wrinkled features. He stepped up to Tom's plane, looked it over carefully, then walked around it a second time.

"Yes, this will do nicely," the aborigine said, running his hand across the plane's belly. "Please have it back in a timely fashion, Mr. O'Malley." Then the old man turned and walked back the way he came.

"That was damn weird, Tom," Hogan declared. "What are you going to do about it?"

O'Malley shrugged. "Make my run and get back quickly, I guess."

74

Toolpin walked behind his fellows, in his usual spot as rear guard. He was of average size, as far as dwarves go, but he spun a wicked pickax. He and his companions marched to spread the enlightenment of Lady Pella Ardinay and Aysle to a new world. But Toolpin felt little jubilation over the event.

"Why does she call it enlightenment," he once asked, "if the land has gotten so dark?" His only answer was a sharp rap on the head from Pluppa, and she told him to mind his tongue before the Huntsman took it for a souvenir.

The bridge was up ahead. It was a physical connection to another world, and it frightened Toolpin to walk upon it. The way to cross a maelstrom bridge was to keep your eyes straight ahead and your feet in constant motion. But Toolpin hated the feel of the stones beneath his boots. He once asked if any of the others felt the stone moving of its own accord, as though it were breathing, or perhaps, writhing in agony. They all looked away when he asked the question, and even Pluppa only sighed. She didn't even rap him on the head. Legends spoke of the mortar that Lady Ardinay used to construct the bridges, that if you stared at the stones you would see faces looking back at you — the faces of the souls that held the bridge together, trapped within the writhing stones. If your eyes locked with theirs, the legends continued, then you would join them within the bridge.

Toolpin never stared.

But he did look back over his shoulder. Lady Ardinay's tower was there, rising over the fields of warriors marching to attack. He could see her at the battlement, watching the progression intently.

"Pluppa?" Toolpin asked, tapping the dwarf in front of him on the shoulder. "Why does Lady Ardinay watch us all the time?"

"Because that's her way," Pluppa whispered.

Then she rapped Toolpin on the head.

"Now turn around and watch where you're going. And stop asking foolish questions," she said sternly.

"What is more foolish," Toolpin thought, but he did not say it, "to question or to follow blindly as our world grows darker and darker?"

He knew the answer, but he didn't know how to make use of it. So he marched on with his companions, making sure to keep his eyes forward, fixed on Pluppa's back, and not look at the stones.

75

Baruk Kaah, Saar of the Edeinos and High Lord of the Living Land, basked in the power of the newly-planted stelae. He could feel the caress of Lanala in its waves of energy, the presence of Rec Pakken in its silent call.

"You do not yet feel Lanala, Eddie Paragon," the High Lord said to the human beside him. "You have not yet found life."

"I'm sorry, but other than a slight tug now and then, I have little desire to go romping into the woods on all fours," Paragon said.

"That is good singer, because I want you to tell me all about this cosm. With information, I can conquer more territory and gain more power."

Baruk Kaah stopped talking when he heard the powerful flapping that signaled the approach of the ravagons. The three representatives of the Gaunt Man landed a short distance from the High Lord, then moved closer on foot.

"Greetings, High Lord," the first ravagon said. "Your realm grows by leaps and bounds. The Torg is pleased."

Baruk Kaah gave only a slight nod at the compliment. He noted, from the corner of his eye, that Paragon had moved behind him. The human was frightened of the ravagons, and he did little to hide that fact.

"Have you brought me the information I requested?" the High Lord asked.

"Of course," the ravagon sneered, folding his wings tightly about his body. "Twelve stelae areas have been bounded, spreading the reality of the Living Land over a great portion of this continent, and more shall be in place over the next few days. The eastern land has fallen quickly, and your tribes have multiplied."

The High Lord rocked back on his tail and roared his approval. "Then it is time to turn my attention to the western land."

Baruk Kaah spoke through the stelae to Rec Pakken, his darkness device, which still resided in the Takta Ker cosm. He asked for it to open a path for him, so that he might return to its side. Then, out of the sky, a thin bridge of living jungle descended to the Earth.

"Come, singer Paragon," Baruk Kaah ordered, "you are about to see what no one from this world has ever seen before."

He grabbed Paragon firmly about the waist with one scaled arm. The other he wrapped around the dimthread. Then the miniature bridge receded into the sky, taking the High Lord and the singer with it.

The ravagons, without being asked, grabbed onto the dimthread as well. Together, the group was pulled back to where the darkness device rested in Takta Ker.

76

Lord Angar Uthorion, who wore the body of Lady Pella Ardinay, waited atop his tower in trepidation. He always felt like this before a raid, ever since the final battle in his conquest of Aysle some three hundred years ago. On that day, before the Carredon delivered its killing blow, Tolwyn of House Tancred vowed to return and slay Uthorion. Then her comrades sent her spirit flying into the cosmverse as the Carredon's claws struck home. Uthorion has watched for her return ever since.

He watched the warriors continue to stream down

the maelstrom bridge, eagerly marching to another world because their beloved Ardinay ordered it. If only the fools knew! He saw the ring of spectral knights that circled his tower, and his thoughts returned to Tolwyn. He wished the Gaunt Man had not called the Carredon back to Orrorsh when Aysle had been secured, but Uthorion could not think of a way to hold on to the beast. It was, after all, the Gaunt Man's most favored pet.

A disturbance in the crowd below brought Uthorion out of his memories. He scanned the bridgehead for signs of trouble, but the masses appeared more excited than worried. Then Uthorion saw, through Ardinay's lovely eyes, the flying form that swooped above the crowd and made its way toward his tower. It drew closer, and the High Lord recognized the elf mage Delyndun. The mage was using a spell to reach Uthorion as quickly as possible.

Lord Uthorion allowed Delyndun to land atop the battlement. He looked weary from his flight, but Uthorion had neither time nor inclination to let him rest.

"Speak, wizard," Uthorion growled through Ardinay's full, red lips. "What have you learned."

Delyndun did not look at Uthorion. Instead, he rested his hands upon the battlement and stared out at the dark, twisted countryside. Once the land had been rich and pure, and light filled even the deepest forest. Now, after centuries of Uthorion's ministrations, the land was tainted and full of shadows. Reaching into one of the pouches that hung on his belt, the elf produced the aged gauntlet and dropped it at Uthorion's richly-clad feet — feet that actually belonged to Pella Ardinay.

"The time has come, Lord Uthorion," Delyndun said sadly. He spoke the words of magic and gestured with one hand. An image leaped from the gauntlet and hovered before Ardinay's eyes so that Uthorion could see it. The image was that of six people, but only one made Uthorion gasp. It was the face of a woman with glossy chestnut hair and piercing emerald eyes.

"Tolwyn," Uthorion gasped.

"No! This means nothing!" Uthorion raged. "It simply signifies the end of Ardinay's hope!"

He spun the female form around, marching toward the entrance into the tower.

"Lord?" Delyndun asked tentatively, hoping not to direct the High Lord's anger to himself.

"Come with me, wizard," Uthorion called without looking back. "We must speak to my old master. For he holds the chains that bind the power that destroyed Tolwyn once before. The Gaunt Man shall provide me with that power, or Aysle will pull out of his grand scheme."

77

Thratchen followed the Gaunt Man through the winding corridors of Illmound Keep. It had been a long time since the demon had last walked these foul halls, but he was still impressed by the macabre architecture. He especially liked the Gaunt Man's special touch that masked the true nature of the cosm from those without the ability to see through its charade.

They finally reached a door that was made of heavy wood — at least to untrained eyes — and carved with obscene images of death and torture. At the Gaunt Man's approach, the door swung wide and revealed a demented throne room. A chair of skulls filled the center of the chamber, and a large, ornate mirror covered much of one wall. Beside the throne of bones rested the legendary darkness device, Heketon, black as night and shaped like a human heart.

The Gaunt Man ushered Thratchen in, shutting the door behind them. "Before we begin to search, Thratchen, you must do one thing for me."

"Whatever you ask, Lord Salisbury," the demon replied, using the Gaunt Man's proper name — or at least the name the general populace of Orrorsh knew him by.

Ignoring the demon's familiarity, the Gaunt Man led him over to the black heart. It seemed to grow warmer at their approach, glowing brighter from somewhere deep within its obsidian interior.

"Swear fealty to me, the Gaunt Man," the High Lord ordered. "Denounce your ties to Tharkold and promise to serve the Torg as a trusted lieutenant."

Thratchen's senses reeled at the Gaunt Man's demand. And did he hear right? Did the Gaunt Man claim the title of Torg? That was unheard of — impossible.

"I know what you must be thinking, Thratchen. You must feel that after all these eons, the Gaunt Man has finally gone mad. But on the contrary, I am as sane as I ever was. And now, on this world, my ages old plan will finally come to fruition. Gaze into Heketon's black surface and you will see the truth."

The demon did as the Gaunt Man asked. For a moment, he saw nothing but his own reflection in the shiny blackness. Then a blasted landscape came into view. It was this planet, sucked dry of its energy and submerged beneath a constant storm. The Gaunt Man stood over the land, bursting with the power that once belonged to this rich cosm. Truly, one with such power must be the Torg.

Thratchen turned away from the scene and fell at the Gaunt Man's feet. "Master, forgive my arrogance and doubt. I wish to serve you, to bask in the dark light that shines from you." Then he looked up, meeting the Gaunt Man's gaze. "I wish to serve the Torg."

Lord Salisbury smiled. "Rise, Thratchen, and welcome back into the Gaunt Man's fold. You shall be my second, running this realm in my stead should I need to be elsewhere. Like Uthorion before you, like your master before him, you shall be my chief administrator. Now, let us find this stormer you chased across the cosmverse."

The ornate mirror clouded as the two worked their powers upon it. Then it reached out to find Dr. Hachi Mara-Two. After a time, the clouds parted to reveal a stark white room. Within the room were a group of people. One had a mane of silver hair, and the mirror focused upon her.

"That is the stormer," Thratchen exclaimed.

"Of course," the Gaunt Man said. "With her location marked, we can now send Kurst to retrieve her."

"Where is she?"

"Just beyond the realm of Baruk Kaah, in a place that still holds the axioms of this world. I have ravagons working with the edeinos. Perhaps I should send them ahead to hold her, for it could take Kurst time to reach her. Yes, I shall send the ravagons."

The Gaunt Man paused then, tilting his head as though listening to a distant call. He passed his hand before the mirror and the scene shifted. Looking back through the glass was a striking woman dressed in regal clothing. Beside her was an elf mage, which placed them as being from the Aysle cosm. But there was something familiar about the woman's dark eyes.

"Angar Uthorion!" Thratchen laughed. "My! You are looking beautiful this evening. The look suits you and is a big improvement over your last form."

"I am in no mood for your jokes, Tharkold scum," Uthorion flared through Ardinay's mouth. "High Lord, I must ask for a favor in order to complete my part of our bargain."

"Speak, Uthorion," said the Gaunt Man impatiently.

"I need the Carredon, High Lord, for the prophecy has been fulfilled."

Thratchen kept quiet now, intrigued as he was by this new development.

"Tolwyn of House Tancred has returned from death as she promised, and she walks this planet called Earth."

The Gaunt Man was silent for a moment, contemplating the request. "I shall deal with your prophecy, Uthorion. Just get your realm established according to our schedule."

The Gaunt Man waved his hand and the mirror returned to the scene with Mara. The view expanded to show the others with her. The Gaunt Man stared for a time at the other woman, the one with the green eyes.

"That is Tolwyn Tancred, Thratchen, and she is with your stormer. I do not like the way this is developing."

Thratchen was confused, but it had been a long time since he or his master had involved themselves in the Gaunt Man's or Uthorion's affairs.

"It is time to send out my hunters," the Gaunt Man decided. He left Thratchen in the throne room to puzzle out the situation for himself while he went to take action.

78

Eddie Paragon held tight to the huge lizard man, fearful of falling as the jungle dimthread carried them to another world. The one-time rock'n'roll singer wasn't sure what scared him more — Baruk Kaah, the strange form of flight, or the three ravagons that also clung to the intertwined roots and vines.

"Open your eyes, singer," shouted Baruk Kaah joyously, "and look upon the world of Takta Ker!"

Paragon did as the High Lord bid, forcing his closed lids to open just a crack. They were descending toward a mist-shrouded, primeval land. Huge plants sprang out of the deep mist, and already the humidity had soaked Paragon's clothes with sweat. Before he could see much more, they were dropping through the mist and his visibility was blocked by the thick clouds of warm, moist vapor. Then their feet touched the ground.

"Welcome to Vandast, the continent that houses Rec Pakken," Baruk Kaah boasted proudly.

Eddie noticed that the ravagons had dropped to their knees. They were bowed before something that was hidden by the mist. He moved closer, forgetting his fear of the demons. He had to see what was powerful enough to humble the vile, winged monsters.

Baruk Kaah stepped in front of him. "Prepare yourself, singer. You are about to meet Rec Pakken, the darkness device that serves me."

The mists parted, and before them stood a gnarled forest of thick trees and twisted, impossibly large roots.

"The trees," Paragon gasped, "they're black as night."

"Only one tree, singer," Baruk Kaah explained, "a single tree grown from a single seed. Behold the origin of my power. Behold Rec Pakken!"

Now Eddie saw it, the twisting branches all grew out of a common trunk. They wrapped around, over and under each other, forming a thick canopy high above the tangled roots. The branches, trunk, and roots were made of a reflective black stone, and the leaves were like the night sky, filled with fiery stars.

The ravagons had completed their silent prayers and came to stand with the High Lord and the singer. "Rec Pakken sings of power and conquest," the first ravagon declared.

"It joins Heketon, the Gaunt Man's darkness device, in a grand song of destruction," the second ravagon said.

The third ravagon, as was his practice, said nothing.

Mist swirled and a dimthread descended to the ground. It was made of writhing souls, which marked it as coming from Orrorsh. Then a burst of brimstone exploded upon the miniature bridge, and Gibberfat appeared.

"He has made me, Gibberfat, a common messenger," the bloated red demon brooded. "I might as well get this over with. Hail, Baruk Kaah! Greetings from the Gaunt Man, he who is now the Torg!"

Baruk Kaah examined the demon curiously. "What can I do for yet another of the Gaunt Man's many servants?"

"Absolutely nothing, High Lord," the demon quiped. "I'm here with orders for the ravagons."

Gibberfat weaved a spell, forming an image from the deep mist. It was a woman with a mane of silver hair. "The Gaunt Man wants this stormer captured alive. No harm is to befall her."

He paused to let the ravagons focus on the stormer's image. Then Gibberfat continued. "She was last marked in the Core Earth city called Philadelphia, housed in a structure called the Hospital of the University of Pennsylvania."

Another spell, and the mist took the shape of another woman. This one had chestnut hair and emerald eyes. "This stormer is to be captured as well. The Gaunt Man has questions for them both. They are traveling together."

"What of the other scents?" the first ravagon asked. "There are others with these stormers. What should we do with them?"

"Anything you want," Gibberfat giggled evilly, showing rows of pointed teeth. "Now fly, ravagons, fly."

Two of the winged demons took to the air, disappearing into the mist. The third remained.

Gibberfat strode over to the ravagon, tapping a clawed finger into its folded wings. "And what are you doing? Didn't you hear what I said?"

The ravagon just stood in place, silently eyeing the red demon.

"Hmmph! If that's the way it's to be." Gibberfat vanished in a cloud of brimstone, and the soul bridge retracted into the mist.

Eddie Paragon had no idea what was going on, and from the confused twitching, Baruk Kaah was as mystified as he was. But the edeinos was still a High Lord, and he had his own agenda to follow.

"Come, singer," the High Lord said, "come meet Rec Pakken."

The High Lord led Eddie Paragon into the black stone forest. After a few seconds, the remaining ravagon followed them in.

79

Father Christopher Bryce led Tolwyn and Mara to the rear of the hospital where the van was waiting. Rick Alder opened the sliding side door and ushered the ladies into the vehicle. Both women appeared curious, but Tolwyn in particular paused to run her hand over the smooth metal exterior.

"Hop in, Tolwyn," Alder said. "It might be a bit crowded in there, but it sure as hell beats walking. Sorry, Father."

Tolwyn, who now wore blue jeans, a pair of Puma sneakers and a sweat shirt that bore the emblem "Penn State," asked, "What is this thing, Christopher?"

"It's a van, Tolwyn, a vehicle," the priest said, trying to find the words to describe something that was so familiar to him that it was just what it was. He could see that the words made little sense to the young woman.

"It's a chariot, Tolwyn," Coyote called from within the van, "a carriage. But it doesn't need any horses to make it go."

Tolwyn laughed out loud at the thought. "Is it indeed, young Coyote? And which of you is wizard enough to make such magic work?"

Alder dangled a set of keys before her. "Me," he said with a large smile.

But Bryce snatched the keys from Alder's hand. "I think not, Rick. You worked all through the night to get the van ready. So I'll drive the first leg of this trip while you grab some sleep."

"Whatever you say, Father."

Bryce hopped into the driver's seat and inserted the key. But before he started the engine, he heard Tolwyn gasp. In the rearview mirror he saw Alder and Rat holding her back as Tal Tu, obviously the source of her agitation, watched curiously.

"Tolwyn, calm down! It's just Tal Tu! We told you about him," Alder tried to explain as he struggled to restrain her.

"He's a friend, Tolwyn, he won't hurt you," Rat said.

Tal Tu, the edeinos who aided Rick Alder back in New York and had traveled with him ever since, held the gray cat in one hand. He extended the other toward Tolwyn in a gesture of greeting.

"I am pleased to meet you, Tolwyn of House Tancred," the edeinos said. Bryce noted that his English was getting better every day. Coyote and Rat were teaching him well, and it didn't hurt that he was given the ability to pick it up by the High Lord he once called master.

Tolwyn calmed visibly at Tal Tu's words, but Bryce could see that her body was shaking. She sat down against the wall of the van, resting her head back and closing her eyes.

"I am sorry, Rick Alder, Tal Tu," she managed to say, "but your form brings to mind violent memories that are just out of my grasp. Perhaps they will become clearer as we get nearer the gorge."

She looked across at the young woman named Mara, who was sitting opposite her, watching with obvious concern. Tolwyn shook off the bad images and smiled.

"Let us see how this magical carriage works, Christopher Bryce."

Bryce returned her smile, and turned the key. The engine roared to life and Tolwyn jerked forward. "Relax, Tolwyn," he told her, "that's just the magic working. Hang on everyone."

Within an hour, Bryce was driving west on the Pennsylvania Turnpike. The fury of the storm had lessened, but the sky was still gray and overcast. Jokingly, the priest asked aloud, "Where to, everybody?"

"To the gorge, Christopher Bryce," Tolwyn answered. There was no humor in her tone, and her eyes were wide and serious.

80

Andrew Decker checked his gear for the third time.

Then he scanned the remainder of his group. Of the eleven soldiers he started with, only seven had made it with him out of the storm. They stayed with the vehicles through the long night, but were not ready to move further into the zone of silence.

"Sergeant, what's the diagnosis?" Decker asked Sergeant Lewis.

"There's absolutely nothing mechanically wrong with the truck or the two jeeps," the sergeant replied, "but we can't get the engines to turn over or anything. If we're going to go on, it'll have to be on foot."

He hated to leave the vehicles, but whatever was blocking radio and television signals was apparently affecting their transportation as well.

"We either sit here, walk back into the storm, or continue north, sergeant," Decker said. "I'm for going forward."

The sergeant nodded. "Sounds good to me."

So the group left the dead soldiers in the shallow graves they had dug for them, and proceeded to march along Highway 15. The Susquehanna was on their right, and some thirty-five miles north was I-80. Decker planned to turn west there and keep the soldiers moving until they passed out of the zone of silence.

But before they had walked two miles, the group encountered a band of refugees. They were dirty and disheveled, and they carried with them whatever possessions they could. Decker halted the soldiers, then stepped forward to speak to the refugees.

"Where are you heading?" he asked, turning on his best politician charm.

"Get out of our way," one of the men said, placing himself between Decker's group and the women and children that traveled with him.

"I'm Congressman Andrew Decker, and I'm here to help you."

"Bah," the man spat, "look around you, 'congressman.' America doesn't exist anymore. At least not here, not up north. The land's been claimed by dinosaurs and savages. That's why we're heading south, to get away from the monsters."

"What's up the highway?" Decker asked. "What will we find?"

"Death," a woman answered from the back of the group. And then the refugees walked past, leaving Decker and the soldiers alone to contemplate their own course.

81

Thratchen ran the fingers of his natural hand across the smooth stone surface of the obsidian heart. He looked deeply into its reflective blackness, fascinated by the images it showed him. The shattered planet, with its energy drained, was particularly appealing. Especially when it showed him his own reflection standing upon the ruined landscape.

"Why be a servant, when I can be a master?" he asked himself. He heard footsteps then, and moved away from the heart before the Gaunt Man entered the room.

"The ravagons have moved to detain the stormers, and Kurst is on his way to bring them back to us," the Gaunt Man explained. "With that taken care of, I can concentrate on my work."

"Tell me of Heketon, master," Thratchen asked suddenly. For a moment, he thought he had said the wrong thing. But the Gaunt Man did not seem angry. He stood beside the obsidian heart and spoke in a far away voice.

"The heart came to me on a world very far from here,

its distance measured in both space and time. From the moment I first heard its song of power, I knew that that world would be mine."

"What of the legend, master?" Thratchen pressed, eager to hear the tale again.

"The darkness device claimed to come from a nameless god who thrived on destruction. It told me that untold power would be mine if I used it to destroy. But every act of destruction provided me with strength, and when I destroyed my homeworld I received power on a grand scale. I never encountered a nameless god, not through all my travels through the cosmverse. If this being ever existed, it must have died a long time ago."

"Do you really believe that, master? Is the Nameless One nothing more than a myth?"

"If the Nameless One were anything more, would it not have contacted me? Have I not been the greatest of the cosm raiders? Have I not spread its religion of destruction across a hundred worlds? No, the Nameless One is gone, Thratchen, and in its place will rise the Torg — as the legends also say. And I shall be the Torg."

The look in the Gaunt Man's eyes frightened the demon. This High Lord was power incarnate, and the game Thratchen played was virtually suicidal. But the questions that he yearned to answer were never closer, and he would play the game to the last move, no matter its outcome.

"Now leave me, Thratchen," the Gaunt Man ordered. "I have much work to complete before the other High Lords arrive on Earth."

82

The van traveled west on I-76, making decent time despite the falling rain. Father Bryce was at the wheel, talking quietly with Coyote. In the rearview mirror, he could see the rest of their band. Rick Alder and Tal Tu were asleep, resting after working throughout the night to tune up the van. Mara was fidgeting with a small object, and had remained quiet since they left Philadelphia. Rat was reading a comic book and cracking gum. Tolwyn, who Bryce hardly thought of as Wendy Miller anymore, was watching the passing scenery in fascination. He smiled at her wide-eyed expressions and soft sounds of wonder, then he went back to concentrating on the drive.

Most of the traffic was going east, cars and trucks filled to overflowing with personal possessions and families. Many of the refugees were on foot, moving along in groups huddled together for safety. If they were fleeing from the same creatures that drove Bryce and others like him out of New York, then the problem was of an even larger scale than the priest had imagined.

On the northern horizon, a massive storm front loomed threateningly. It had been with them since they passed Harrisburg, always on the edge of their vision, always out the corner of their eyes. Bryce glanced to his right every so often to track its progress, but it didn't seem to be advancing. Still, the lightning that danced along its edge frightened him like no storm had ever done before, and that made him uncomfortable.

Bryce checked the rearview mirror, and Tolwyn again caught his attention. He was amazed at the vitality and the strength in Tolwyn's body. She had gotten visibly stronger each day at the hospital. Somehow, he knew that this young woman named Tolwyn was already physically stronger than Wendy Miller had ever been.

A road sign showed golden arches, and words beneath them proclaimed "food." Both Bryce and Coyote turned to each other simultaneously, smiles of anticipation spreading across their faces.

"Why not?" Bryce asked no one in particular as he slowed to exit the highway.

Storm clouds scudded through the gathering darkness in the eastern sky as Bryce pulled the van into the parking lot of the McDonald's.

"Come on, everybody, let's go grab some hamburgers," he said as he parked the vehicle and turned off the engine.

Mara looked up from the object she had been working on. "What's a hamburger?" she asked groggily, rubbing her eyes with her knuckles.

"And why would we want to grab them?" asked Tolwyn puzzledly.

"A hamburger is something to eat," Bryce answered, his attention focused on Mara. He wondered where she could have grown up without ever hearing of a hamburger. Because of her memory loss, he could understand Tolwyn's ignorance, but the golden arches had conquered the world — he knew that from his travels. He also knew the doctor wasn't joking. But even a child prodigy attending college and medical school would have heard of, and probably eaten, hamburgers.

But he was even more fascinated by the sight of Mara's left hand as she used it to rub at the corners of her eyes. The hand was clawlike; the fingers were banded and tipped with gleaming metal; the thumb was flattened, looking almost as if it were meant to have something placed upon it and held there. In the hospital she had been wearing leather gloves. Now one glove was resting across her lap.

"What happened to your hand?" Coyote asked before the priest could get the words out.

"Surgical enhancement," Mara answered nonchalantly, as though it was a most natural thing.

"For what reason?" asked Bryce.

"To help me do what I do," Mara said, looking Bryce directly in the eyes. Her eyes told him she was not going to lie to him. For whatever reason, she was here to help Tolwyn, just like the rest of them.

"What is it you do?" The question came from Rick Alder, ever the police officer, who was sitting up now, obviously wakened by all the talking.

"I design and build microchips."

Bryce was taken aback for a moment, having thought of Mara as a physician. "What kind of a doctor are you, Dr. Hachi?"

"Physics and microengineering."

"Two doctorates! How old are you?"

"Sixteen."

"I don't understand," said Bryce, ignoring for now the apparent conflict between her age and her stated abilities. "Why did the hospital put you in charge of Tolwyn's case?"

"Yes," said Tolwyn. She was facing Mara. "Who are you?"

Mara took a deep breath and sighed. "It's a long story," she said and held up her right hand to stop Bryce as he opened his mouth to object. "Get me one of these hamburgers, and I'll tell you while we eat."

"I'll buy you a dozen hamburgers if you answer our questions," promised Alder.

"Be careful. I'm liable to take you up on that offer," Mara said and grinned impishly.

"I don't think we have anything to worry about, Rick. She's too little to eat that much," Bryce said and chuckled. His suspicions were allayed as he got caught up in

Mara's infectiously good humor.

"Yeah, but I'm giga-hungry!" exclaimed Mara as she slid open the side door of the van and jumped down to the gravel of the parking lot.

The others piled out, too, except for Tal Tu. They still felt it would be better if he remained out of sight in public places. The edeinos nodded reservedly, agreeing to their logic. But as the others started to shut the door, Tal Tu reminded them, "Bring Tal Tu and Cat something to eat."

"What do you eat?" Rat asked innocently.

"Meat," Tal Tu answered. "But I will try this food Father Bryce called hamburger."

"Enough of this Father Bryce nonsense," the priest shouted. "Will everyone please just call me Chris?"

As they walked toward the glass door at the front of the restaurant, Mara took Bryce by the arm and pulled him to a stop. "I cannot answer all your questions, Chris. I can only tell you what I know."

"Fair enough, Dr. Hachi," Bryce said.

"Enough of this Dr. Hachi nonsense," she smiled. "Call me Mara."

"Not Maratu?"

Mara sighed. "This may take longer to explain than I thought."

83

The two ravagons stood in the alley behind the Hospital of the University of Pennsylvania. They had traveled from Takta Ker to the Living Land realm via maelstrom bridge, then had flown from New York to Philadelphia under their own power. The hospital staff had not been helpful, running and screaming at the sight of the powerful beings. But the ravagons found the room where the two stormers met with little trouble. Finding it empty angered them, however, and they vented much of that anger on patients and hospital staff.

"Let the bloody mess serve as a warning," the first ravagon declared.

"Yes, but there is no challenge in ripping apart ords," the second ravagon noted.

The first ravagon examined the alley closely, touching the ground and extending his supernatural senses. Finally, he spread his black wings.

"I have the trail," he informed his partner. "Follow me."

The ravagons took to the sky, flying west to intercept the female stormers and their traveling companions.

84

Bryce was beginning to doubt the wisdom of Alder's offer as he sat and watched Mara bite into her fourth hamburger, pick at her second order of fries, and drink her second milk shake. Tolwyn was eating even more than the kid, but Bryce could understand that. Tolwyn was a tall, athletic woman, and her metabolism probably needed large amounts of fuel to burn. But he couldn't figure out where Mara was putting it all. Even Rat and Coyote had slowed after their second burgers.

Bryce himself had only eaten one hamburger, some fries and a cup of coffee; he was content with that. Youth must be able to eat more, he figured, growing bodies and other nonsense. With bellies full and hot coffee steaming in white styrofoam cups in front of them, Bryce, Alder, Mara and Tolwyn leaned back in the booth and relaxed. Rat and Coyote had gone to the counter to order "something for the road — and for Tal Tu and Cat."

The priest watched as Tolwyn picked up her cup of

coffee, sipped tentatively at the hot, black liquid, and made a face. She sipped again. Mara had tasted the coffee and immediately put the cup back on the table and pushed it away, her decision made.

"The milk shakes were better," said Tolwyn.

"Yeah," said Mara, "and the hamburgers weren't bad."

"So, tell us about yourself," Alder suggested to Mara. Mara sat quietly for a moment or two, then said, "Let me show you something first."

With the back of her head positioned where Bryce, Alder and Tolwyn could see it, she moved her silver hair aside and uncovered her right ear. Bryce was startled as Mara revealed two metal slots beneath the lobe. There were small chips in the slots, reminding Bryce of miniature computer disks in drive units. Mara pulled one chip out, showed it to the three, and replaced it to demonstrate more precisely what the slots were. She turned in her seat to again face them, letting her hair fall back into place.

"Enhancement chips," she explained. Then she began her story.

Mara told them about her own social and career advancement thanks to personal ability and wonder drugs. She told them about Kadandra and her discovery of the cosmverse. Then she told them about the coming of the Sims and the terrible battle that followed. Finally, she told them about her discovery of Earth and her trip to make amends for the terrible events she had caused.

"But you defeated the invaders," Tolwyn stated after Mara had finished speaking, grasping at one of the few facts of the narrative to which she could relate and understand.

"Yes, with our technology, our science. We pulled

down their bridges and cut off their connections to their home cosm. Then we mopped them up. But millions of my people died."

"But you won," persisted Tolwyn.

"Yes, but at what cost?"

"What is the cost of losing?" asked Tolwyn.

"The war wouldn't have happened if it were not for me, and there would have been no price to pay."

"I can't believe that," said Alder. "Just because you discovered something doesn't mean you caused it to come into existence. Did you ever think that these invaders were already on their way to your world, and you saw them just in time to do something about them?"

"But I also led them here!"

Bryce watched as the young woman who called herself Dr. Hachi Mara-Two lowered her head and sobbed. He wasn't sure just what he believed yet, but he knew that there was no reason someone so young should be carrying around the guilt of the world — make that worlds.

"Mara," Bryce said softly, "none of this is your fault. I won't let you beat yourself up over something you had no control over."

The young woman looked up at the priest, and he saw the weight of a dozen lifetimes reflected in her eyes. Then she spoke. "You may be right, Chris. But then again, you may be wrong. And until I know for sure, the responsibility remains mine."

85

In Sacramento, California, Kerr Naru sat in contented contemplation, watching the warriors rock triumphantly after the long battle to secure the pure zone. Lanala had truly blessed the edeinos! he thought happily. And he,

Storm Knights

Alan Jude Summa

as an optant, was doubly blessed.

He leaned back on his tail, letting the wind and rain wash over his scaled body. The sensations were wonderful! And his warriors had brought such experiences to the people of this world! Maybe now they would reject their dead existences and join the edeinos in life.

A udatok roared nearby, and many of the warriors came out of their reverie to glance up at the maelstrom bridge that arched above them. Kerr Naru followed their gazes. Something was shambling down the bridge, pushing its way through the overgrowth at a rapid pace.

"Baruk Kaah!" one of the warriors called out.

"And Rec Pakken!" another yelled, and a shudder passed through the crowd.

"Rec Pakken," Kerr Naru thought. "The Saar brings his darkness device to the realm, and the edeinos back away like frightened trekids."

But he supposed they had a right to be afraid, because the shudder affected him as well. After all, Rec Pakken was a dead thing, and edeinos could not abide items devoid of the spark of life. Except for the gotaks, of course, those edeinos who Baruk Kaah had appointed as priests of the dead.

Now Kerr Naru could see it, crawling down the bridge like some giant black spider. Rec Pakken was a third of a mile across, a mobile forest formed from a single black, stone tree. Roots sprung from the bottom and sides of the moving forest, acting as legs to propel the darkness device across the jungle expanse. It was terrible to behold, and an abomination to Lanala besides.

Perhaps he should speak out against Baruk Kaah and his habit of using dead things, Kerr Naru considered. He knew that Lanala was not pleased with the actions of her

First Lover, that many of the edeinos were upset by the new ways Baruk Kaah had introduced. If they joined together ...

Rec Pakken scuttled closer, and Kerr Naru could see its branches of night as they swayed. What could they do against the power of the dead? he wondered to himself.

One of the gotaks stepped beside him. The priest of the dead raised a clawed fist into the sky, praising, "Hail Baruk Kaah, Saar of the edeinos, High Lord of Takta Ker! Hail Rec Pakken, who has shown the people experiences we never dreamed of!"

Others picked up the chant, and soon the crowd was singing to the High Lord and to his darkness device, with only cursory nods to Lanala. The scene sickened the optant. Still, one voice would not change anything. Kerr Naru looked away from the approaching forest, but his voice raised to join the chant.

"Hail Baruk Kaah," he sang. "Hail Rec Pakken!"

86

Kurst adjusted the denim jacket he wore, trying to fit into the grooves its prior owner had acheived after long months of wear. He didn't succeed. It was too large for his frame, and it had an air of comfortableness that the clothes of his world did not. In short, its very comfort made him uncomfortable. Still, he would keep the jacket, he decided. He had gone to some small degree of trouble to acquire it, and its prior owner would have no further use for it, anyway.

He hated entering a new cosm without preparation. The Gaunt Man provided him with the language of the world — actually, of the dialect prevalent in the area he was going — but had no time to provide him with the social conventions. Kurst would make do, however. He always did.

So this was Philadelphia, Kurst mused. He could sense the tradition of the place, the spirit. The very essence of the world was prevalent in the city. It reeked of concepts that were alien to the hunter; freedom, liberty, the pursuit of happiness. Yes, these ideals were spoken of in Orrorsh, and some of the cattle even believed they were living them. But it was all an illusion, propagated and controlled by his master, the Gaunt Man. Here it was different, though. What were cold, empty words in his cosm were living, vibrant truths here. For some reason, that disturbed the hunter. He didn't know why it should make a difference, but it did.

He let his internal discussion lapse when he found the hospital. It was where the Gaunt Man had placed it, and the scent of stormers was strong in the air. He stood before the building, looking up at the letters that identified it. Yes, he thought, this was where the one named Dr. Hachi arrived. He took a deep breath, letting her smell fill his senses. She smelled of technology and youth, almost a sweeter version of Thratchen, and her scent tingled with power and possibilities. The image the Gaunt Man had given him was good, but now he had her true scent, and there was nowhere she could hide from him.

He entered the building, easily moving through the confused corridors. Something violent had taken place here recently, he noted, but he had no time to investigate further. He let the doctors and other hospital staff work undisturbed as he proceeded toward the room the Gaunt Man had shown him.

The floor was a jumble of activity. It seemed that whatever had occurred was focused around the stormers. That worried Kurst. He didn't want his mission jeopardized by events he had no control over. He sniffed the air, following Dr. Hachi's own trail through the hospital. In the hall outside the room, orderlies were cleaning blood from the walls and floor. The door to the room was demolished, exploded by something too impatient to use the doorknob.

Kurst sniffed again. "Ravagons," he muttered. He had hoped to beat them here, but he should have realized they would arrive before he did. After all, they were already in Baruk Kaah's nearby realm, while he had to travel upbridge to Orrorsh, across a second bridge to Takta Ker, and then down a third bridge to New York before he could travel on to Philadelphia. By the look of the blood, though, the ravagons weren't that far ahead of him. But what about the stormers?

He slid into the room, silently moving with stealthy grace. But his caution was unnecessary. The room was empty, except for the furniture that had been ripped apart. The ravagons must have arrived too late, he decided, or else they never would have slashed out with such rage.

"Good," he said, "there's still a chance for me to reach them first."

The hunter moved around the room, separating and cataloging each scent in turn. Dr. Hachi had been here, and the two ravagons. The next strongest scent belonged to the other woman, the one named Tolwyn. She was a fighter, he decided, and she smelled of honor and nobility. The others, while not as distinct as the women, each had their own odors that would identify them when Kurst finally reached them.

There was a man of thought and learning, a religious man. But he was battling doubt and confusion these days. Good. That meant he wasn't focused. As his beliefs went in different directions, so too would his senses. He would not pose a problem.

The second man was more wary, more street tough. He smelled of authority and regimentation, but there was an underlying anger that spoke of a need for revenge. This was a fighter, Kurst decided, probably a soldier or guard of some sort. He could prove dangerous.

The third and fourth smells went together. They belonged to young men, boys perhaps. They were hardened by the streets, like the wary man, but lacked experience or the strength that would come with age. They would bear watching, but little else.

So these were their protectors — a troubled priest, an angry guard, and two untried youths. Kurst almost laughed. Where was the challenge that this world had promised? Where was the test he so desperately sought?

He took another breath, and this time another smell assaulted him. It was crisp, clear, powerful. It was the smell of possibilities, and he noticed that each of the people who had been in this room had it. For a moment, Kurst's confidence trembled. Never before had he encountered so many possibility-filled beings in the same location. What could it mean?

The hunter ended his speculation. He would discover a meaning — if there was one — when he reached his prey. That was the rule he lived by, and it would serve him now. He headed off, continuing after the stormers' trail.

87

Bryce briefly studied the road map and decided that the best way to make westerly progress was to stay on I-76 until they reached I-70. As he drove, Bryce gave what little driving instruction he could to Mara as she intently studied his every motion, asking why he moved his foot like that or why he changed the postion of the lever on the steering column. Rat laughed at her questions, but Coyote only stared at her. Of course, thought Bryce. The young man was beginning to take notice of the wild haired young woman. But so far, she had shown little interest in him. Ah, the idiosyncrasies of youth, he mused.

He glanced into the rearview mirror and caught sight of Tolwyn. She was watching out the back window. Bryce could see that her shoulders were bunched tightly, and she was trembling. He adjusted the mirror so that he could see better. For a moment the view was as it had been from the start, an empty road behind them and a traffic jam of refugees moving in the opposite direction on the other side of the highway. Then a fluttering movement in the line of traffic far behind the van caught his attention.

"They are coming, Christopher Bryce," Tolwyn said, fear filling her voice, clogging her throat. "I remember the pain they caused, the fear they inspired."

Bryce continued to drive, unconsciously pressing the accelerator to gain speed and distance. The others tried to see what Tolwyn was talking about.

"Who is coming, Tolwyn?"

"Just keep the van moving, Chris," Rick Alder ordered as he pulled his revolver out. The priest shuddered.

"They are clearing a path through the refugees," Tolwyn said. "They are on our trail, but they haven't located us just yet. But all those people are dying. By Dunad's sword! I wish I had my own blade!"

Rat asked her what she was talking about. Tolwyn

then turned to the boy.

"There was a sword fashioned from a solid chunk of nickel-iron. The metal had been a gift from below, from the dwarves of Aysle. It was a special piece of ore, and it was believed to be part of the land itself. Battlestar was its name, and it had been beaten into being on the anvil of Tanglan, a dwarven smith who used fire and ice and endless beating of his heavy hammer to shape the magical blade. After the smith had formed the heated metal in to rods of steel and braided those rods, he hammered them flat and folded the steel back upon itself over and over. He presented the finished blade to Solgal, the founder of House Tancred. The sword itself was broad-bladed and heavy enough to be used as a hacking weapon, yet it tapered to a point that allowed it to be used for thrusting. It was light enough to be swung one-handed, but the hilt was long enough to be held in two hands when additional force was needed. The sword was cross-hilted with a heavy pommel weight that perfectly balanced the weight of the gleaming blade. The pommel weight was made of iron and shaped into a nine-pointed star heavy enough to be used in battle as a mace or morningstar — hence, the name of the sword, Battlestar."

Tolwyn was quiet for a moment. Then she said, "I do not know why I remember that, but I do."

"Here they come," said Coyote.

Bryce risked another look back, and this time he saw them. They were two winged shadows streaking through the sky. If they hadn't known what they were after before, they did now. They were heading straight toward the van. The priest jammed his foot to the floor, trying to coax more speed out of the tired vehicle.

"This van hasn't reached these speeds in years," he

shouted back.

"I'm pretty sure it can take it, Chris," Alder responded. "Just don't make any violent maneuvers."

Alder and Mara moved to the back doors. Each had a weapon in hand, which both relieved and terrified Bryce.

The first winged monster swooped onto the top of the van, landing with a loud thump. The second one dove straight at the rear door. Alder aimed through the window and fired two quick shots. The glass shattered and the discharges were very loud inside the vehicle. If he hit the creature, it wasn't evident. It continued its flight, smashing into the doors hard enough to buckle them inward. Bryce could see its talons sticking through the metal, allowing the monster to hang on. But he had his hands full trying to stay on the road. The monster had hit them like a truck, and the van was spinning wildly.

"Stay with it, Father," Coyote said, "you can do it."

The priest hoped the kid's faith was not misplaced as he straightened the vehicle.

Then two things happened simultaneously. One of the rear doors fell in and the roof peeled back. Both events were accompanied by terrible shrieks of tearing metal, and the sudden rush of wind.

The creature in the open doorway was too tall to stand up straight in the van. It had a small head set atop a long neck. Its powerful chest hinted at strength beyond any human's, and its wings folded about it like a living cloak. It swiped Alder with its claws, smashing him into the wall of the van. He slid down the wall, deathly still. Then the creature grabbed Mara.

"Come, stormers," it rasped, "can't you do better than this?"

The other winged demon reached down through the tear in the roof. It grasped Bryce by the shoulder, its sharp claws cutting into his skin and drawing blood. The priest glanced into the demon's face. All he saw was sharp teeth and humorless, dead black eyes. It would have hauled him out of the driver's seat if Tal Tu didn't strike at that moment. The edeinos slashed with his own claws, forcing the demon to let the priest go. Then they locked in fierce battle, one on each side of the torn metal.

Bryce hit the brakes, causing the van to jerk to a sudden stop. Everyone was thrown off balance, but he hoped they could use his maneuver to good advantage.

As the van's wheels screeched in protest, the ravagon holding Mara loosened its grip momentarily. That was all the young woman needed. She spun around, burying her laser pistol in the beast's gut. Then she fired four times, changing the angle of the barrel with each shot. The monster's black eyes rolled in its head, and it fell from the van into the road behind them.

Tolwyn, meanwhile, had acquired a tire iron from its compartment with the other tools. She rushed forward, brandishing it as though it were the sword she had spoken of. Using all of her strength, she drove the metal tool into the creature that struggled with Tal Tu. It let go of the edeinos, a sound of pain escaping its toothed maw. It rolled off the roof and disappeared from sight.

"My God, what were those things?" Bryce asked Tolwyn.

"Ravagons, I think they call themselves," she said. It seemed the thrill of battle agreed with her. "I remember they were involved in the battle for Aysle, but the rest of the details are still vague, unformed."

"Tolwyn, look out!" Rat screamed. The ravagon from the roof raised itself up behind Tolwyn, on the other side of the van's side window. Before she could spin to defend herself, it thrust its powerful claws through the glass.

Bryce fought with the ignition, trying to start up the van. It had stalled after he made his desperate maneuver, and now it didn't want to cooperate with his new demand.

"Let ... go!" Tolwyn shouted, smashing the tire iron over her shoulder and into the ravagon's face. It released her, and she spilled forward into Tal Tu and Rat.

But her action gave Mara and Alder the opening they needed. Together, they pumped bullets and laser bolts into the horrible creature. It fell away from the van.

"I've got it!" Bryce exclaimed as the engine finally turned over.

"Then get us out of here, Father," Alder suggested, then he collapsed back into unconsciousness.

88

"This is ridiculous, Henri!" Claudine Guerault shouted over the noise of the crowd. Her assignments as a journalist had taken her to many strange places, but she never expected what she was witnessing in her own country.

"I think you are right," said Henri Dupuy, her photographer. "The crowds are too thick to drive through. I suggest we walk."

They were in southeast France, in the city of Avignon on the Rhone River. Guerault had not wanted to leave the Japanese diplomat's murder to another reporter, but her editor insisted she handle the story unfolding in Avignon. It appeared that the religious fervor affecting her country had reached some sort of high point in Avignon, as thousands upon thousands of faithful were gathering in the city. Now Guerault and her photographer were there as well to find out what was happening.

"Stay close, Claudine," Dupuy warned as he led the way through the crowd.

The people were excited, full of anticipation. Most of the noise that came from the crowd was just that, noise. But every so often Guerault picked up a phrase or two. The words intrigued her.

"The sign," she heard most often, whispered or shouted in awe or jubilation. "The sign is coming, the sign."

Guerault had no idea what the masses were babbling about, but the intensity in the air was palpable. "Faster, Henri," she yelled to her companion, "I want to see what's in the center of this crowd."

Pushing, pulling, but always moving, the two finally emerged in front of the old Papal Palace, once used by the Avignon popes during the time of the Great Schism. In those long ago days during the Middle Ages, two popes actually claimed to be the spiritual leader of the Catholic Church — one in Rome and one in Avignon. Guerault wondered if the location held any significance to the sign everyone was talking about.

She took out her notebook and began scribbling notes concerning the mob and the feeling that ran through the packed streets. The sky overhead was dark, and a storm was about to explode above them. Dupuy was beside her, snapping photo after photo of the scene. Then a monk emerged from the church and silence spread through the crowd. He was dressed in simple robes, much like the men that had been preaching through much of the country over the past few weeks. He looked out upon the multitude for many long seconds, then he spoke.

"This world is troubled, full of sin and sinners. The heathens have had their day, but now the Time of Judgment is upon us!" The monk's words were powerful, captivating. The crowd ate it up. Even Guerault was swayed by the emotions he evoked. "We have been looking for a sign, and I tell you that the signs are rampant these days. In heathen America, in Great Britain, the sins of the people have called their own judgment upon them! But before such disaster befalls the French people, I have good news!"

The crowd edged forward, anxiously awaiting the next words to issue forth from the monk. He let them wait for a long moment, letting their anticipation build. Guerault saw that Dupuy was still snapping away.

The monk spoke again. "Like Lot and his family, like the Jews in Egypt, we shall be spared the terrible events of the Last Days! For someone is coming who will save us from our sins, who will lead us into the New Earth that is to rise from the ashes of the old world."

Guerault had stopped writing. What was the monk saying? Who was he talking about? She pulled her jacket closed, trying to keep warm as the wind blew harder and the sky grew darker. The clouds were rolling, boiling, and she was suddenly very frightened.

"He shall banish the darkness!" the monk exclaimed. "He shall dispose of the evils of this world, the technology that is the devil's work, and he shall restore the simpler times that have been forgotten. And lo, this shall be the sign of his coming!"

With that, the clouds parted and an arch of golden light fell from the sky. It struck the church, bathing it in an otherworldly glow. A wave of energy rolled off the arch and rippled through the crowd. Streetlights went off in its wake. Even Henri Dupuy's camera stopped working. The crowd fell to its knees before the golden arch. It took every ounce of willpower that Guerault possessed for her not to follow their example.

"Look upon the sign of our shepherd, my brethren!" the monk called out. "Prepare yourselves, for soon our Holy Father shall come!"

Guerault worked her way over to the photographer. "Come on, Henri," she said. "We have to get out of here. Don't you feel it? This crowd will do anything the monk says."

"Isn't it wonderful, Claudine?" Dupuy asked. He dropped his camera, letting it smash upon the concrete sidewalk. "He is coming!"

"No, not you too, Henri?" Guerault pushed the photographer away and rushed through the crowd. She didn't understand what was happening, but she knew she had to get away while there was still time. She had to tell someone about the miracle she witnessed — and she had to decide if it was heavenly in origin, or something worse.

89

Kurst, after examining the map he had acquired, decided his best option was to travel through the Living Land. He could borrow a flying lizard to use as a mount, then catch the stormers somewhere around the city named Columbus, where the road they were traveling through Core Earth met with the road he would take through the realm. His station demanded respect in Baruk Kaah's realm, and his claws were proof of his identity. He only needed to shred two of the edeinos to obtain the lakten. Now he was atop the winged lizard, following the road marked as "80" on the map.

The remaining edeinos had been helpful enough to

provide him with a benthe as well. The small, globular being rested on the lakten's neck, commanding it by manipulating its body chemistry. That left Kurst free to examine the countryside they were flying over.

This world was more advanced than his own, Kurst noted, more technologically dependent. It was true that Orrorsh had a level of industry and mechanical aptitude, but that was a relatively new development in his society. The great cities below him gave way to fields and forests that stretched across the great continent. Everything was so much bigger, more spread out, than he was used to.

But the Living Land was already making its presence felt. The fields and forests were wilder, more primitive looking than Kurst imagined they normally were. And new lifeforms, larger than what the land normally supported, were moving everywhere. In fact, the movement of two particular groups of creatures caught the hunter's interest.

"Circle here, then land in front of those creatures," Kurst ordered the benthe. It extended a pseudopod to acknowledge the command, then relayed directions to the lakten.

The winged lizard made a wide sweep, giving Kurst plenty of opportunity to examine the two converging groups. The first group consisted of Living Land natives. A half-dozen edeinos warriors, accompanied by a huge tresir, waited to ambush the second group. The second group appeared to be Core Earthers, wearing military garb, and walking along the road in the same direction as Kurst was flying. Their walk, however, would take them right into the ambush.

"This could be interesting," Kurst noted, as the lakten came to a landing near the group of edeinos.

The hunter dismounted and strode into the group of lizard men. They eyed him curiously, unsure of what to make of the inconsistencies of his appearance. It was definite that he was not of the Living Land, but he rode a lakten. The younger hunters were already twitching nervously, but their leader — an edeinos of many years — stepped in front of the small, soft-skinned one. He jabbed his hrockt shoot spear into Kurst's chest, just touching the hunter's skin with the sharp point. Then he spoke the language of the Land.

"Who are you, dead one, and what gives you the right to command a lakten?" the old warrior demanded harshly.

Kurst smiled, and answered back in the lizard man's own language. "I am Kurst, hunter for the Gaunt Man, and Baruk Kaah himself gives me passage through this realm."

The younger warriors shuddered at the mention of the Gaunt Man, and their eyes widened to hear this soft-skin speak of their Saar in such a familiar manner.

"He lies," spat the young edeinos standing beside the tresir. The great beast roared to emphasize the young warrior's statement.

Faster than any of them could act, Kurst sprang. He leaped at the young warrior, his body changing as he quickly crossed the distance separating the two. Hair grew over his body, covering his skin with fur. He grew taller, wider. Claws extended from powerful fingers, and his nose elongated, becoming a tooth-filled snout. When his sharp claws struck the lizard man, slicing through scales and flesh, he had transformed completely into a demonic werewolf.

The young warrior fell, hitting the ground with a thud. Kurst stood over him, watching the light of life quickly fade from the warrior's eyes. Then he turned to the old lizard, holding the young warrior's still pumping heart in one clawed fist.

Impressed, the old one said, "Join us, honored hunter, in the attack we are about to engage in."

The werewolf nodded, then gulped down the beating heart before all the blood drained out.

90

Andrew Jackson Decker concentrated on putting one foot in front of the other, willing his legs to walk. The seven marines with him were doing a little better, but it had been a long time since Decker had had to do a sustained march. He wished they could stop and rest, but he didn't want to show the soldiers that he wasn't up to the task at hand. He didn't even want to admit it to himself. Still, while he was in decent shape, his days of professional baseball and his own stint in the armed forces were far behind him.

"Congressman," Sergeant Lewis said, "with your permission, I'd like to call a five minute break."

"Is all this excerise starting to get to you, sergeant?" Decker huffed.

"No, sir," the sergeant replied. "We can keep going if you want to."

"That's all right, sergeant," Decker said quickly. "I think a short break is in order."

Decker collapsed on the side of the highway, trying not to let his fatigue show too much. He grabbed his canteen, unscrewed the top, and drank deeply. Lewis and the marines, he noted with some satisfaction, did likewise.

"You used to play ball, didn't you, sir?" the marine named Sanders asked.

"That was a long time ago, soldier. You and President Wells are probably the only people who remember that. I wasn't very good."

"Nonsense!" Sergeant Lewis said. "You were one of the most promising pitchers of your day. If memory serves, Ace Decker had a three point two ERA, a thirty-four and fourteen record, and three hundred and fifty-two strikeouts in two seasons. Then you left the game. Why, congressman?"

Decker returned his canteen to his belt strap. "You've done your homework, sergeant."

"I like to know who I'm serving with, sir."

"Commendable. So I might as well fill you in on the rest of the story. I went right from high school into Triple A ball, spent one season in the minors, then was called up to play in the major leagues. It was a dream come true for me, and I wanted to show everyone that I could do it. But after the first season, it started to seem trivial to me. There had to be a better way to use my life. So I enlisted in the marines, finished college, and later entered political life."

"Don't you miss the cheers?" Sanders asked.

Before Decker could answer, a violent noise interrupted him. The congressman rose, turning to see what was crashing through the bushes beside the road. He saw movement, something large and fast, then it burst from the foliage. It was as long as a station wagon and twice as tall, running on all fours. It reminded Decker of a cat, but only its grace and speed were feline in nature. While it was sleek and sinewy, instead of fur it was covered in shiny black scales. Talons sprang from its four feet, and its head was reptilian. It had the teeth of a meat eater, and a mane of black fur fell from the top of its head to its powerful shoulders.

It smashed into Decker, hitting him with its leg. Had he remained sitting, its talons would have raked him as it passed. As it was, the scales along its leg sliced through his fatigues and ripped away skin from his chest and left arm. He fell hard, and the world went black.

Sergeant Lewis and his men leaped up at the same time Decker did. But Sanders and Dallas never had a chance. The huge beast — which Lewis took to be a cross between a crocodile and a lion — tore into the two men with its clawed paws.

Teagle and Burton swung their M-16s off their shoulders and leveled them at the creature. They pulled the triggers, expecting the familiar recall and feeling of power associated with firing the weapons. But nothing happened. Like the vehicles they had to abandon, the weapons refused to function. The creature continued its frenzied attack, grasping Burton in its huge jaws. It fastened its teeth around his mid-section, and blood spurted as it bit into him. The soldier screamed.

Teagle went to his friend's aid, using his otherwise-useless rifle to batter the monster. Lewis heard the butt clang off of the creature's scaled hide. Then he watched in horror as Burton's body fell away, savagely bitten in half.

"Teagle, get away from that thing!" the sergeant ordered. But the creature was fast. It plowed into the soldier and landed on top of him. Then it began to feast.

Lewis looked around. Jones was beside him, staring in shock at the events that were happening so quickly. Miller, the last of his remaining men, was running back down the road in the direction they had come from. Before he could clear his head and issue orders, other creatures emerged from the brush. There were five lizard men, each carrying a spear, and a giant wolf that stood on two legs. The wolf exploded after Miller, running like a streak of fur and fangs. The lizard men stepped toward Lewis and Jones.

"Come on, Jones," the sergeant cajoled, "give me some help here."

"We're dead, sarge," Jones blubbered. "Oh God, look at what it did to Burton!"

Sergeant Lewis raised his weapon and fired. Nothing!

"I'll be damned if I'll just stand here and let them kill me!" Lewis shouted, running forward. He smashed the butt of his rifle into the skull of one of the lizard men. He smiled at the satisfying sound of shattering bone, and the lizard dropped.

One of the lizards roared something that almost sounded like speech, then it tossed its spear at Jones. The marine staggered back as the heavy shaft burst through his chest. "I'm sorry, sergeant," Jones said. Thorns sprouted along the shaft. Jones tried to say something else, but all that came out of his mouth was a fountain of red. Then he collapsed.

The sergeant swung his rifle like a club, and the remaining lizard men kept their distance. Five men killed in less than five minutes, Lewis counted. And they had only been able to take out one of the enemy. Not a good showing of ourselves, he decided, not for marines. He hoped Miller had escaped from that wolf.

That slim hope faded when Miller's scream sounded. My men, Lewis thought, they killed my men. Then he steeled himself, and leaped at the lizards. One more of the monsters fell under the sergeant's barrage of blows, then three spears pierced him at the same time, skewering him where he stood. At least, he thought as his vision faded, *I took a few of them with me.*

Decker opened his eyes and found himself looking at the sky. It was a dark, cloud-filled sky, but at least the rain had stopped falling. That seemed to be important to him, but he didn't know why. His body ached, and he could feel a warm, sticky wetness across his chest and arm. He decided that it would be best if he just stayed where he was. He wanted to rest. Maybe that would make the pain go away.

But the sky was behaving strangely. The clouds were spinning, twirling faster and faster. They were forming into a shape that Decker had seen a lot lately. It filled his dreams almost every night. Now it was hanging in the sky over his head. The blue stone with the red streaks imbedded inside it.

"What do you want from me?" Decker asked.

The stone hung silently before him.

Then the image shifted, becoming the face of a woman. He couldn't make out her features, but she had the most penetrating emerald eyes he had ever seen.

"I tried. Now it's over."

Then his old manager's voice rang in his ears. *It isn't over til it's over, Ace. Get back in there and win the game for us!*

Decker sighed. Then he sat up. His rifle was beside him. He grasped it, clicked it to automatic, and slowly rose.

He didn't like what he saw.

Sanders, Dallas, Teagle, Burton, Jones, and Sergeant Lewis were all dead. He didn't see Miller, but something told him that he was dead, too. Three lizard men were standing over the marines' bodies, and the black cat-lizard was some feet away. Decker dropped back to the ground, trying to stay hidden until he had a better chance of taking them all out.

As he watched, a man walked into sight on the road. He was of average height, but of powerful build. He wore a denim jacket that looked to be a little big on him. Judging by that and the rest of his ill-fitting clothes, Decker took him to be a refugee. The cat-lizard perked its reptile head at the man's approach. Then it started toward him.

"You killed all of those marines, you bastards, but I won't let you kill anyone else!" Decker swore as he jumped up. He leveled his M-16, pointed it at the four-legged monster, and squeezed the trigger. Automatic fire exploded from the barrel, cutting through the monster's scales and ripping away its life. Then he swung around and mowed down the lizard men before they could bring their spears to bear.

"Are you all right?" Decker called to the man.

The man looked confused for a moment, and Decker couldn't blame him. "Don't worry, I'm not going to hurt you. My name's Andrew Decker. I'm a congressman."

The man nodded, then smiled faintly, showing his teeth. When he spoke, Decker detected a definite British accent.

"My name is Kurst, Congressman Decker."

"Well, Mr. Kurst, let's bury these soldiers and get out of here before it gets too dark." Then Decker moved to do just that, not looking back to see if the man named Kurst was coming or not.

91

"How is he, Doctor Hachi?" Father Bryce asked.

Mara, her face clean of makeup, shook her head.

"He's lost a lot of blood, but I've cleaned the wounds and bandaged them. He should be all right, as long as he doesn't move around too much. Those cuts will open up and start bleeding if he doesn't take it easy."

"I'll do my best, Doc," Alder said, grimacing with pain. "It's a good thing we're taking this nice relaxing vacation. It'll do me a world of good."

Bryce smiled. "Get some rest, Rick. Stay with him, Mara."

The young woman nodded.

It was getting dark. Bryce wasn't sure he wanted to face the night after meeting the ravagons, but he knew he had no choice in the matter. Even if the world were slowing down, day and night were still inevitable — at least as far as he knew. He stepped out of the van and looked it over from the outside. Much of the metal was ripped or missing. The windows were smashed. The rear door was gone. He stepped to the front of the vehicle, to where Tal Tu, Coyote, and Rat were working on the engine.

"Any luck?" the priest asked.

Coyote shrugged. "Maybe a few more miles, maybe not. It's an old van, Father, and it sure did take a beating today. I just don't know what to tell you. None of us are really very good at this."

Tal Tu, who had Cat rubbing against his leg, agreed. "I know what Rick Alder showed me, but that will not keep this machine going forever. We will have to find new transportation if we are to go much further."

Bryce spent a few more minutes with the trio, then went looking for Tolwyn. He was concerned about her reaction to the ravagons' attack. Unlike the others, she actually seemed to enjoy the combat. That scared him. He found her sitting in the dark, some distance away from the van. She was staring at a billboard across the highway, studying it with fierce intensity.

"We're looking for a few good men," he quoted from the sign. "The slogan of the United States Marines."

"Hello, Christopher," she said, not taking her eyes from the billboard. It showed a marine in dress uniform, holding a sword before him. She pointed at the sword. "I want one of those."

"Well let's see. Tal Tu and the boys want a new van. You want a sword. While I'm taking orders I might as well see what Rick and Mara want."

"There will be more of them coming," she said, his attempt at sarcasm going over her head. "We might not stop them next time."

Bryce sat beside her. They sat quietly for a time, letting the darkness build around them. Then Bryce spoke softly. "Some of your memories returned today, didn't they?"

"I remember a little more. Fighting the ravagons, my family's sword. But I still don't know why I am here, or why these creatures would be after me."

"You enjoyed it, didn't you?" he asked.

"Enjoyed what, Christopher?"

"The fighting, the rush of adrenalin, the blood, all of it."

She looked him straight in the eyes. "I was very good at warfare and combat, that much I remember. Today, the battle brought back memories and movements that were familiar, comfortable. Do I enjoy it? Yes, in a way. Something tells me that it is what I do best. Does that bother you?"

"Yes," he said, but did not press the issue. And neither did she.

Bryce looked up. Mara was approaching.

"I hope I'm not disturbing you," Mara said, "but dinner is ready. Rat cooked it."

"Mara, why did the ravagon call us stormers?" Tolwyn asked.

The young woman sighed. "You've noticed the storms all around us? When the raiders' reality sweeps across a world, it comes into conflict with the reality already in place. The two realities clash, and this battle is manifested by violent weather and other natural disturbances."

"Sort of like the world is fighting back, trying to defend itself?" Bryce asked.

"Exactly," Mara answered. "When the storms pass over and the raiders' reality takes hold, many of the features of the land — even the people — succumb to the new reality. They conform."

The priest remembered the savages he had encountered in New York, people who had given up thousands of years of civilization and reverted to cave-dwelling primitives.

"But there are those who don't conform," Mara continued. "These individuals retain their own reality after the storm has changed everything else. Hence the name, stormers."

"It fits," Bryce noted.

"Yes," said Tolwyn, "but I hate it. If it is what the evil ones call us, then it is no better than being called a peasant."

Bryce stood, stretching the kinks from his back and shoulders. "Come on, let's go try Rat's cooking."

"Aye," Tolwyn said, but she sat there in the dark, thinking, long into the night.

92

Under the same night sky, within fifty miles of where Tolwyn contemplated the events of the day, Andrew Decker and Kurst set up camp. Kurst had no supplies of his own, but Decker had salvaged as much as they could carry from the dead marines. Now they had a fire going, and food was cooking over the comfortable blaze.

Kurst studied the man while he worked with the food, never looking directly at him but taking in every detail nonetheless. Decker was tall and lean, and muscle played beneath his green outfit. It was the muscle of a civilized man, but muscle just the same. He was a stormer, of that there was no doubt. Kurst could smell it on him, the aroma as bright as the fire before him.

"Who are you, Mr. Kurst?" Decker asked finally. He had finished setting up his tent, had laid out two sleeping bags, and was now sitting beside the fire. He had a sword in his lap, its blade still sheathed within its fine leather scabbard.

"I am Kurst, a traveler far from home caught in a strange land."

"Do you have a first name Mr. Kurst?"

"Just Kurst. That's all I have ever been called for as long as I can remember."

Decker fell silent for a time, examing the weapon he held. "Teagle had this in his pack," he said at last. "I have no idea why he brought his dress sabre with him, but I felt compelled to take it with me. Who knows? Maybe it will do some good if my rifle fails on me." He paused, running his finger tips across the polished brass scabbard frame. Then he asked, "What brought you to America, Kurst?"

The hunter looked up from the food after checking on

its progress. He scanned Decker's eyes for some hint of distrust, but all he saw was honest, good-natured curiosity. "I'm looking for someone," he replied, deciding to be honest as well.

"Really? So am I, in a way." Decker poured himself a cup of coffee, then replaced the pot over the fire. "I'm actually looking for something else, an object, but more and more I'm sure that there are people involved in my quest. You may find this a little strange, come to think of it."

"After what I have seen these past few days, nothing will ever seem strange again," Kurst said, scooping food into his bowl.

"Good point. I've been having dreams lately, and in these dreams I see the object that I'm after. And then I see a woman. She has long brown hair and beautiful green eyes. I don't know what it means, but I have a feeling she's out here somewhere, looking for the same object I'm seeking."

Kurst choked on his food, spitting bits into the fire. Decker had described the woman named Tolwyn — the woman who was traveling with Thratchen's quarry. Never had he heard of stormers behaving in this manner!

Decker came around the fire and began banging Kurst on the back. "Are you all right? Did I say something wrong?" There was actual concern in the man's voice, and that disturbed Kurst.

He wiped his mouth, shifting his gaze to meet Decker's. How far should he take his ploy, he wondered. All the way, he decided, all the way.

"I am fine, Mr. Decker. It is just that you have described the person that I am seeking as well."

"What? How can that be?"

Kurst simply shrugged. "Perhaps, together, we will find this out."

Yes, Kurst thought. If this stormer is following the others, then it should be a simple task to let him lead me to them. If I can gain his trust. Then I will have them all in the same place, and my job will prove to be that much easier.

They talked until the fire dimmed and the coffee grew cold.

93

Bryce and Mara sat outside the van. The others were asleep inside, and Tolwyn was still off by herself. So the priest and the young scientist from another reality talked quietly.

"It must have taken a lot of courage to leave your world to come here," Bryce said.

Mara, who was fiddling with a small metal plate no larger than the tip of her finger, pursed her lips but offered no comment. It seemed to be a sore point. She had removed the heavy makeup, Bryce noted, revealing a pretty young face. Even with the wild hair, he found it almost impossible to believe that she was from some-place else. Almost. Then he remembered her hand.

"Tell me about Tolwyn, Chris," Mara said as she continued to work with the tiny plate.

"What's to tell? She used to be someone named Wendy Miller, but I never met that woman. I've only had the pleasure of meeting Tolwyn, a young woman who seems to have come back from the dead."

"And from another cosm," Mara added.

"But I am here now," said Tolwyn as she emerged from the darkness to stand beside Bryce and Mara. "I have done much thinking this night. First, we must get an early start. I want to reach the stone as soon as possible."

"And second?" Bryce asked lightly.

"And second, we shall not use the term 'stormers' ever again," Tolwyn said very seriously.

Bryce and Mara looked at her expectantly, waiting for her to continue. She did not disappoint them.

"We shall be called 'Storm Knights', for that is more noble a term. More valiant."

Tolwyn turned away, and Bryce knew that if he laughed, if he so much as giggled, she would pound him senseless — or worse. He did not laugh. In fact, when she said the words, they did sound noble. She leaped into the van, but turned once more to speak.

"And Christopher," she said, "I want a sword."

94

The fire had burned low. Only the cinders still glowed, softly illuminating the immediate area. Kurst sat beyond the glow, wrapping himself in the night. He watched Decker sleep, watched the rise and fall of his chest as he breathed. His rifle and the sword were resting right beside him.

"An interesting situation, I dare say," whispered Thratchen, his foul lips almost touching Kurst's ear. He heard the demon approach, but just barely. Thratchen was good. Kurst would remember that.

Kurst flexed his hand, letting it shift from soft human fingers to hair-covered claws and back with each clench of his fist. "What do you want, Thratchen?" he asked, his voice low but menacing. "You can see that I am busy?"

"I, too, have a job to do. I seek a woman tainted with the stench of Apeiros. I want you to understand exactly what you are to do when you find her."

"I know my mission, demon," Kurst warned. But his mind tried to connect the ancient name out of legend with the current situation.

"Of course," Thratchen said. "You have heard the legends of Aperios and the Nameless One?"

"Children's stories, nothing more."

"Perhaps," Thratchen said, turning to examine Decker. He reached out a clawed hand, almost as though to fondle the possibilities that virtually clung to the sleeping figure. "The stormers of this world are strong, hunter."

Kurst merely nodded. It was foolish to state the obvious.

"Keep this one alive, Kurst. He can lead you to Hachi and the Ayslish woman."

Kurst's hand shifted back to flesh and nails.

"You do understand me, don't you Kurst?" Thratchen asked.

Flex. The hand shifted to claws. "Decker will live. At least until the hunt is over and I have them all."

The demon retreated into the darkness. "Be sure that he does, hunter. Be sure that he does." Then Thratchen was gone.

"I do not know what game you are playing, Thratchen, but I will figure it out."

Another flex, and hand replaced hair and claw.

95

The Soviet army was in place, ringing the area exactly as Katrina Tovarish had instructed. The stelae they unearthed had been rigged with explosives and placed back in its hole. All appeared to be ready, noted Captain Nicolai Ondarev. Then he shuddered when a chill wind blew past.

"Are you cold, Katrina?" he asked the young woman standing beside him. Her head was tilted slightly, as though she were listening to something.

"They are coming, Nicolai," she said. She had not even heard his question.

Ondarev looked up at the sky. It was very dark now, filled with black, bloated clouds that blocked the light of day. The wind had picked up, howling across the field as though it were rushing to escape. He had to admit that he wanted to flee, too. Katrina, without saying a word, reached out and took his hand.

Overhead, the clouds began to roll violently, as though something was stirring them vigorously. Thunder sounded, and an opening appeared in the clouds. But no light fell through the crack. If anything, it was even darker within the hole in the sky.

"Something is happening," Ondarev shouted so that Katrina could hear him over the howl of the wind.

She was looking at the hole in the sky with her sightless eyes, but Ondarev knew that she saw more than he could ever hope to. "Destroy the stelae," she ordered.

Ondarev gave the signal. A moment passed, and the clouds moved even faster. Lightning began to play across the dark sky. Then a mist of glowing light rolled out of the crack in the clouds, expanding as it fell toward the ground. A metallic mass bubbled out of the hole, forming an arch that stretched from the sky and dropped into the field.

An explosion sounded behind him, barely audible over the sound of the wind and thunder, but Ondarev knew that the stelae was destroyed. As the glowing mist touched the ground, miniature storms were formed. It was like the mist was battling for admittance, but the little storms were not going to let it through. The soldiers backed away as the mini storms played themselves out, for they were violent tempests, filled with wind and lightning.

"Without the stelae, the alien reality cannot take hold," Katrina explained. "The Earth itself fights for us."

Ondarev watched as the mass of metal continued to bubble forth. It was a moving mass that seemed to drip from the sky. And within the bubbling metal, the captain saw human forms. They writhed within the metal, helping to shape it with their own bodies.

"My God," he swore, "it's alive!"

"It is an abomination, Nicolai," Katrina said. "It is a thing of evil."

She was right, he knew, and it pained him to see the dread construct touch the ground. But the moment it did touch down, the miniature storms exploded. The glowing mist rolled back upon itself, smashing into the metal arch. Another explosion shook the area, and the arch fell apart as the mist rolled back up into the sky.

For a moment Ondarev thought he saw something at the top of the arch. But then the mist hit the crack in the clouds. Lightning fell to the ground like rain, each bolt targeting a piece of the shattered metal with its searing energy. Both lightning and metal disappeared in a brilliant flash. Then light exploded throughout the dark clouds overhead, radiating out from the crack in an ever-widening circle.

"What's happening?" a soldier screamed. Others were running. Most were glued in place, watching the violent show play out.

Finally, the rolling lightning reached its limit somewhere beyond the horizon. Like a rubber band stretched too far, the lightning snapped back, vibrating through the clouds and back into the hole in the sky. This caused another explosion of thunder, and Ondarev was sure they would all be deaf when this was finished. The dark clouds followed the lightning into the crack, sucked in with a sustained peel of thunder that knocked the soldiers to their knees.

When Ondarev's senses cleared, he saw that the crack, the clouds, and the metal arch were all gone. The sun was shining, and there was no sign of the evil storm.

A cheer went up from the soldiers — almost as loud as the earlier thunder — but it was a good sound. Ondarev laughed.

"We did it, Katrina! You did it!" he shouted with glee.

The young woman collapsed into his arms and wept.

Storm Knights

They call us stormers. When I finally meet these High Lords, I will introduce myself as a Storm Knight. Then I will sheathe my blade in each of them in turn.

> — Tolwyn of
>   House Tancred

Stormers defy the natural order. But they do provide such amusing diversions.

> — The Gaunt Man

96

Thratchen reeled in pain, collapsing to the thick carpet on the floor of his room in Illmound Keep. The pain assaulted him, battering his body from all directions. It felt as though he was being torn apart. Even his cybernetic enhancements throbbed, and it was all he could do to keep from crying out. Then, as suddenly as it arrived, the pain was gone.

He rolled onto his back, resting for a moment before rising. He had experienced such excrutiating pain only once before, and that was fairly recently. It was back on Kadandra, when the stelae were destroyed and the connections to his cosm of Tharkold closed. Could something similar have occurred on Earth?

There was a knock at the door. Thratchen ignored it as he tried to gather his strength and his thoughts. The knock sounded again, and it was followed by a voice.

"Thratchen, sir? It is Picard, sir. The Gaunt Man has instructed me to summon you," said the timid voice.

"Go away," Thratchen called, hoping his voice sounded stronger to Picard than it did to his own ears.

"I'm afraid I can't do that. The Gaunt Man was quite insistent, sir."

Yes, thought Thratchen. He always is. Thratchen forced himself to rise. He would appear as ordered. To do less could jeopardize his plans.

The Gaunt Man was waiting for Thratchen in the Grand Parlor, standing at the bay window that looked out upon the maelstrom bridge to Orrorsh. When Picard announced Thratchen's presence, the Gaunt Man whirled angrily.

"Your old master is a fool!" The Gaunt Man exclaimed. "He has allowed the Earthers to push him back

Storm Knights

Alan Jude Summa

up bridge. We needed his realm established in order to secure our own hold on this world. Now the operation is in jeopardy. With only four cosms connected to Earth, there is a significant chance that the planet can produce a possibility surge of such magnitude to eradicate our realities. Tharkold was to eliminate that chance."

"Tharkold was repelled?" Thratchen asked.

"Repelled? After what happened to your old master on Kadandra, it is possible that the power of this world destroyed Tharkold completely."

Thratchen sat heavily on the long couch against the wall. He had to think about this. He had to decide what it meant to him and his own agenda. The Gaunt Man, however, would not let him alone.

"These next few days will be crucial. I will do what I can to maintain the four realms, but one of the others must make it through or we are doomed to failure. How could your High Lord be so stupid, Thratchen? Why did he try to take Kadandra on the eve of this conquest?"

"He is my High Lord no longer," Thratchen replied. "I have sworn myself to you. As for why he chose the course he did, who can say? I suspect, though, that it was the same reason that drives all the High Lords. He wanted the power that it promised, power that would place him above some of the others coming to Earth."

"But now he has nothing," the Gaunt Man spat.

A burst of fire and brimstone exploded in the center of the parlor, and when the fumes cleared Gibberfat was there. He dropped to his knees before the Gaunt Man.

"Forgive my intrusion, master, but I have news you will want to hear," the small demon said.

"Speak, Gibberfat," the Gaunt Man ordered. "And if it is not of the utmost importance I will return you to the hell I pulled you from."

The demon paled considerably at that, turning a lighter shade of red. He gulped, then spoke. "The ravagons you ordered to detain the stormers. They've been destroyed." He ducked, hoping to protect himself from a cane swipe or worse. The blow never came.

"The stormers. They did this?"

"Yes, master. They defeated two of your best ravagons."

"And Tolwyn and Hachi? What of them?"

"There were no other bodies, master. Just the ravagons."

The Gaunt Man stepped back to the window, looking out at his new domain. He was quiet for a time, and that made Thratchen very nervous. And, from the expression on Gibberfat's face, it made the demon uneasy as well.

"This disturbs me, Thratchen," the Gaunt Man said without turning. He continued to look out the window. "These stormers do not behave like stormers. Only once before have they demonstrated such abilities, and this Tolwyn was a part of that, too. I do not need this right now, not with everything else that is happening."

He spun and walked out of the parlor, leaving Thratchen and Gibberfat behind without so much as a glance.

97

President Jonathan Wells sat in conference with his advisors. Among them were Senator Ellen Conners and Dennis Quartermain, the Vice President. Wells had grown older since this had started. He was aging rapidly under the weight of the office. But he was doing everything in his power to keep the country alive. He had the armed forces mobilized. He had refugee centers set up all along the storm front that separated the zone of silence from the rest of the country. And he had sent Ace Decker to follow his dream. But there was still so much to do.

"We've analyzed the newest data, Mister President, and we think there is a definite pattern to the invaders' attack." The voice belonged to General Clayton Powell, of the Joint Chiefs of Staff. He was standing before a map of North America. A gray diamond stretched across the map from New York to Michigan, showing the zone of silence. Around the diamond was a lighter shaded zone. It covered most of the surrounding area north into Canada and as far west as the Great Lakes.

Powell continued. "The lighter area is where most of the fighting is now occurring. The invaders have pushed into these directions, and we are now learning much about them. Unlike in the zone of silence, we are able to battle the invaders within this expanding zone. But we are running into problems of frequent mechanical breakdown, lose of unit cohesion, and other strange effects that we do not understand."

"What are you trying to tell me, General Powell?" Wells asked, hoping to cut right to the point.

"In a nutshell, sir, we're losing. When our weapons work, we drive the invaders back. When they fail — which is a chronic occurrence — we must retreat or be slaughtered."

"Your suggestion?"

"Evacuate Washington, D.C."

The chamber grew quiet. Wells looked at the faces of his advisors. None of them wanted to leave the capitol to the invaders. Wells didn't either, but he had to do what was best. He stood up to address the group.

"Do you have an alternative spot to put the government, Clay?"

"Yes sir, I do. A number of cities have been recommended — Montgomery, New Orleans, Houston. I feel Houston is the best choice because of its distance and facilities."

Wells nodded. "I concur. Ladies and gentlemen, make it so."

The voices assaulted him at once, each arguing a different option. He slammed his fist on the table. "I did not ask for opinions on this matter!"

"John, if we evacuate it will look like we're admitting defeat," said Quartermain.

"If we don't, Dennis, what will we be admitting if the city falls? My decision stands. We're moving to Texas."

The chamber emptied as each of the advisors went to put the evacuation in motion. Quartermain and Conners remained, as did Powell.

"Clay," Wells began, "I want you and your boys to keep working on this. I want to contain the invaders, stop them from taking any more land. Once that's done, then we can figure out how to take the land back."

"I'll do my best, sir."

"I know you will."

Powell left then, and the chamber seemed extremely empty.

"John, we have to discuss the proposal now," said Ellen Conners.

"Ellen, you know what I think of this proposal. If the powers it grants were to be abused, it could eliminate everything this country stands for."

"Dangerous times demand dangerous measures, John," said Quartermain, leaning back in his chair.

"The Delphi Council will report directly to the Executive Branch, allowing decisions of import to be made quickly, without the delays of Congress that could cost us this war. That is what is important, especially in light of what you have done today," Conners explained.

Wells looked first at Conners, then at Quartermain. Both nodded, and Conners pushed the document in front of him.

"Sign it, John," she said.

"Sign it," Quartermain coaxed.

Wells read the first line. "By Executive Order ..." The document scared him, but the arguments that Conners and Quartermain had made to him over the last few weeks also held a ring of truth. He hoped he was doing the right thing. He reached into his coat pocket, searched for a moment, then laughed softly. "I seem to have lost my pen."

Quartermain pulled out his own and handed it to the president. "Here, John, use mine."

"Then, let the Delphi Council be formed," Wells declared as he signed his name in the space provided.

98

Thratchen slowly pushed the door wide. Within the Gaunt Man's tower room, the darkness device called Heketon was glowing brightly. Thratchen watched from the doorway, hoping to learn something before the Gaunt Man noticed him.

The Gaunt Man was kneeling before the black heart, staring into its glowing surface. He was watching a scene. The image was of a great gorge carved out of the earth. It was a breathtaking sight.

"That is where they are going, Thratchen," the Gaunt Man said, aware of Thratchen's presence. "To a hole in the ground that contains an eternity shard. But my forces will reach the spot first. I no longer care to learn from these stormers. I simply want them dead."

"Who can beat them to the canyon, master? Kurst is behind them, and to send another flight of ravagons will take …"

The Gaunt Man stood and walked to the mirror that hung upon the wall. "It is not your concern. Leave now."

"As you wish," Thratchen replied, slowly closing the door. But before it clicked shut, he heard the Gaunt Man call forth an image in the mirror.

He heard him call for Malcolm Kane.

99

Father Bryce, at the wheel of the van, could tell that the vehicle was dying. They were still a few miles from Columbus, on the edge of the storm front, but he knew that they would have to find another van. The sign ahead said that they were near the town of Flat Rock, so Bryce took the exit.

"What's up, Father?" Alder asked from his place in the back of the van. He was recovering from his wounds, but was still taking it easy.

"The engine is overheating, and there's a weird hum. I don't think we're going much further in this van, and I thought a town would be a much better place to conk out than on the highway."

Another sign proclaimed "Flat Rock, Population 436." Bryce smiled. "How quaint! A real small town in middle America."

His joviality faded as they drove closer, however. There was something wrong up ahead. It couldn't be the dinosaurs, though. Those were still behind them. But the feeling would not go away.

"Look," exclaimed Mara, who was sitting in the passenger seat.

Bryce followed her pointing finger to the edge of the small town. There were mannequins hanging from buildings, from lamp posts, from telephone poles. However, as the van crawled closer, the priest saw that they weren't mannequins.

"My God, what's happened here?"

The bodies were all hanging upsidedown. Each had a gaping hole in its chest, its heart cut away.

"It's like what we saw in Newark," Coyote said. "But the lizards didn't tie ropes around the others."

"The lizards haven't gotten this far yet, Coyote," Alder stated, "and even if they did, I don't think they would use rope."

"Rope is dead thing. Edeinos do not use dead things. Edeinos did not do this," Tal Tu explained.

Bryce stopped the van, and Rat slid open the side door.

"There are more than fifty of them," Rat counted as he and the others exited the van. Tal Tu, by habit, remained inside.

Tolwyn had a grim look upon her face. "The villains who did this deed must pay."

Suddenly a great banging sounded, and figures appeared in the doorways of the buildings. These figures were alive, and they advanced on the group, banging sticks upon the ground and making an awful racket.

Mara and Rick pulled out their guns, while Bryce, Tolwyn, Coyote and Rat gathered around them. The crowd was a ragged looking bunch of men, women and children. They appeared to be refugees that had claimed the town as their own. They stopped advancing about a dozen yards from the group, forming a semi-circle around them.

"It's just like Kane said," one of the older men called

out. "More sacrifices have come to us."

"More sacrifices!" another yelled, and the chant was picked up by the whole crowd.

"Rick, we can't shoot all of these people," Mara said.

"At least not before they were on top of us," Alder agreed. "But we can't let them take us without a fight."

The old man raised his stick into the air, and the chant died down. He looked at the group, then smiled. "We have a way to keep the lizards at bay. They cannot enter our town as long as we keep the warnings posted!"

"Post more warnings! Post more warnings!" the crowd echoed.

"Kane taught us that. He showed us how to post warnings that the lizards would understand."

Bryce felt sick. Who could have convinced these poor, scared people that murder was the way to save themselves?

"He told us to watch for a van carrying a priest," the old man continued. "That would be the next set of warnings we would have to post."

"I don't like the way this is developing, Father," Alder said, raising his revolver slightly.

The crowd started forward then, slowly moving toward the group. Coyote turned to the van and shouted, "Tal Tu, come out!"

"What are you ...?" Bryce began, but he stopped when a cry of alarm raced through the crowd.

"Kane lied!" one woman cried.

"The warnings didn't work," a man moaned.

"The lizards have come!" another shouted, and the crowd scattered back into the buildings.

Bryce turned to see Tal Tu leaning back upon his tail beside the van. He seemed to have a very satisfied look on his lizard face.

"Come on," Alder warned, "let's get back in the van before they realize we have just one lizard."

100

Andrew Decker navigated the minibus around the flock of winged lizards in the road ahead. Kurst was in the seat next to him, curiously watching every move he made.

"What's the matter, Kurst?" Decker joked, "never seen anyone drive a standard before?"

"No," Kurst replied.

They came across the minibus while they were walking along I-80, and Decker decided to give it a try. He had never actually attempted to operate the jeeps once they gave out, but he had made the M-16 work when none of the other marines had been able. So he opened the door, found the key in the ignition, and turned it. On the second try the engine coughed. On the third try it turned over, and they were on their way.

They drove in silence for awhile. Kurst did not seem to be much of a conversationalist, although they did talk the night before. He was a strange fellow, but not overly so. In fact, with all that was going on around them, Kurst was behaving rather well.

Without knowing why, Decker turned off the highway and took a smaller road south. He was cutting down much earlier than he had planned to, but he had a hunch that this was the road to take. Decker, ever since his baseball days, had always followed his hunches.

"Follow your feelings, Decker," Kurst said, somehow picking up on the congressman's thoughts.

The road twisted and curved through the countryside, refusing to follow a straight path. Decker maintained his speed though. He felt that time was important all of a sudden, that it was imperative he reach the end of this road. When he saw the sign for Flat Rock, it was like a bolt of energy shot through him.

"We have to go to Flat Rock," he explained.

"So it would seem," replied Kurst.

They saw the mutilated bodies hanging from the poles and buildings first, then they saw the crowd. Dozens of refugees were converging on a battered and torn van. But an occasional gun shot or flash of light drove them back into the few buildings that made up the town.

Decker gunned the minibus, screeching to a halt alongside the van. He looked into the open window and saw the woman with the emerald eyes looking back at him. "I've come a long way to find you, miss," he was finally able to say.

"And I," Kurst echoed.

"Then make room in your magic chariot, because we do not want to share the same fate as those hanging above us," the emerald-eyed woman said, indicating the mutilated bodies with a nod of her head.

Then her and her companions — a priest, a wounded man, two boys, a young woman with wild silver hair, and a lizard man with a cat — piled into the minibus. Without asking any questions, Decker pressed down on the gas pedal and drove off, leaving the angry crowd of Flat Rock behind them.

101

Once he had put twenty miles of road between themselves and Flat Rock, Decker pulled off the road and stopped the minibus. He gave the disheveled group the once over, then introduced himself and Kurst.

"I am Tolwyn of House Tancred," the emerald-eyed

woman said. "And these are my companions, Christopher Bryce, Rick Alder, Dr. Hachi Mara-Two, Tal Tu, Coyote and Rat."

Decker examined each in turn, trying to get a handle on the people and why they were together. He gave up after the lizard was given a name. He paused to think for a second, then decided to be honest with them.

"I've seen you in dream, Miss Tolwyn," he started, hoping he didn't sound as crazy to her and it did to his own ears. "I knew I had to find you, to help you."

"What?" exclaimed the priest. Decker ignored him for the moment.

"But I have to tell you the truth, you're not the main part of this recurring dream." Decker saw that Tolwyn's eyes were wide, and the others were looking at them both, weird expressions on their faces. "I'm looking for a stone. It is blue — turquoise actually — and it …"

"… is full of swirls of crimson," Tolwyn finished. The group was quiet for a time, trying to fathom the implications of this meeting. Then Tolwyn said, "I have been waiting for you as well, Decker. The knots … you are one of the black man's knots …"

"That isn't part of my dream, I'm afraid," Decker confessed.

"Do you know where the stone is, Decker?" Tolwyn asked hopefully.

Decker shook his head. "Somewhere out west is all I know."

"Yes, in a great canyon."

"That's more than I knew."

"If we're done comparing dreams, I suggest we get moving," the priest said. "I for one would like to get out of this area before nightfall."

The others agreed. Decker started the minibus and

drove back onto the highway heading west.

102

The Gaunt Man leaned against a great well that stood behind his manor. It was thirty feet across, a huge hole that fell into darkness. The hole was rimmed by huge stone blocks, carved with scenes of battles between men and monsters. Standing some distance away was Scythak, the huge hunter. He held a prisoner, one of the natives from the island. Beside them was Thratchen.

"Bring the stormer forward," the Gaunt Man ordered, never taking his eyes from the dark hole.

Scythak shoved the native toward the Gaunt Man, using but a fraction of his great strength. The High Lord of horror gently positioned the man before the well.

"I must prepare for the worst," the Gaunt Man explained, pulling a large dagger from the folds of his black outfit. The native's eyes grew wide, but he did not run. The Gaunt Man admired that.

He grabbed the prisoner by the arm and lifted him over the well. With a casual swipe of the blade, blood flowed from the man and dripped into the well. Somewhere deep below the ground, a great roar sounded. The Gaunt Man dropped the prisoner into the well and called out, "Come forth, Carredon! Come forth, my destroyer!"

Dark water splashed over the sides of the well, and a nightmare creature rose out of its depths. It was a dragon-like monster with wings as black as night and scales of armor. Blood covered its terrible, tooth-filled maw — the remains of the prisoner. It stepped out of the well, dwarfing even Scythak with its size and power.

"You have summoned me, my master?" the Carredon roared, its voice projecting waves of fear that even

Alan Jude Summa

Thratchen felt.

"I have a mission for you, Carredon," the Gaunt Man said. "Listen well to what I say."

As the Gaunt Man spoke, Scythak stepped forward and handed a pair of rune staves to the dragon. Carredon took them carefully, repeated its orders, then spread its black wings.

"As you command, my master, so shall it be." And then the Carredon flew.

103

Tom O'Malley waited beside his airplane on a small airstrip north and west of London. He had delivered his cargo as promised, and was now awaiting the goods he was to transport back to Australia. He looked again at the sky to the south, in the general direction of London, and was disturbed by the dark clouds. The man he delivered the cargo to had been nervous, frightened even, rambling on about the terrors that were assaulting London. O'Malley had heard as much on his radio. He had even been warned off by air traffic controllers on the continent when he wasn't able to raise the London tower.

He checked his watch again. He could only give his client a few more minutes, then, cargo or not, Mrs. O'Malley's little boy was taking to the sky and flying home. There was too much weirdness happening in the world right about now, he decided. America, England, France, and even the Indonesian islands closer to home were under attack or worse depending on the reports you heard. It was crazy — but it was also very scary.

Just as Tom O'Malley was about to call it a trip, he noticed an automobile racing onto the airstrip. It zigged and zagged as though out of control, and it was moving much too fast when it wasn't jerking to a stop, but it seemed to have a definite destination in mind. It seemed to be heading right for Tom's plane!

O'Malley, nervous now that his beloved airplane was being threatened, leaped in front of the swerving vehicle and yelled for it to stop.

It kept on coming.

Tom swallowed hard, put his hands out more for protection than as a signal to the car, and closed his eyes. He heard the car's engine race, heard the tires squeal, heard the brakes catch. He opened his left eye a crack, and saw that the car had finally stopped — right in front of him.

It was a powder blue four-door that didn't look too old. But it had more dents and scratches than Tom had ever seen on one vehicle before. He tried to see who was driving, and Tom did a double take. The car was empty!

"What in the world is going on here?" he shouted out loud as he ran around to the driver's door. Before he could grab the handle, however, the door flew open and a small, stocky woman leaped out. She was about three and a half feet tall, had braided black hair, and wore a combination of leather and armor that made her look very formidable. So did the array of weapons she carried on her person — an ax, a mace, a number of daggers, and a large pistol.

"Who? What?" O'Malley stammered.

Then more of the small people filed out of the car. Tom counted as they emerged — one, two, three, four, five, six. Plus the woman. There were seven of them! And they were driving a car! Tom felt as though a cruel joke were being played on him.

The woman fell to one knee before him, and the others did likewise. She held her ax before her, offering it to Tom.

"We ask for asylum in your cosm," the woman said. She had a thick accent that was almost German, but had a hint of somewhere even farther away than that. "We have decided we have had enough of conquering, and ask that you take us to your High Lord."

She lowered her head again, and the other dwarves followed her lead. All that is except one, who stared at Tom's plane with something akin to awe. The woman rapped him atop his metal helmet, and he obediently dropped his gaze to the floor.

"I don't know what you're talking about," Tom said calmly. "What's the punchline?"

One of the older-looking dwarves leaped up. "I knew it! The folk of this cosm make trolls look smart! How many times are we going to make the same speech, Pluppa? How many times?"

The woman named Pluppa turned to Tom. "Please, good sir. The forces of Aysle could be right behind us. They will only kill you. What Lady Ardinay does to traitors is not something I wish to burden you with. But we cannot control the magic chariot very well, and we really do need to get away from this place."

Tom thought for a moment, looking over each of the dwarves in turn. They certainly didn't look like they were joking. And he did need cargo.

"Can you pay your way?" he asked.

"Oh sir, we are able warriors, and we are engineers and craftsmen of exceptional ability," Pluppa boasted. "And we have gold." She tossed him a small sack. He hefted it, feeling the weight. Then he opened it and poured seven large nuggets into his palm.

"Come on, then," he said, still not positive about the whole deal, "you've just bought yourself passage to Australia."

104

Decker was driving the minibus west, with no destination in mind. He trusted that the woman named Tolwyn would know where to go when the time came. But he would need to get gas soon, and he needed to check in with President Wells.

"We're going to stop in Indianapolis," he explained. "I have to make a call and we could use some new supplies. Just keep the lizard out of sight."

The gas station had a small snack shop attached to it, and while Decker went to use a phone the others headed into the shop. He deposited a handful of coins and dialed the private number Wells had given him. He listened to the phone ring two times, then the ring was replaced by a buzzing that didn't sound good to him. He hung up and tried again. This time there was no ring, just the buzzing. He would have to try later.

He entered the snack shop and saw that it was decorated with giant prints of American landscapes. There was Old Faithful. Over there was Mount Rushmore. Tolwyn was standing before one of the prints. She wasn't moving, just staring at it. Decker walked over to her.

"Tolwyn? Are you all right?"

"That is the place," she said. "That is where we must go."

She pointed at the picture. It showed the rugged, beautiful scenery of the Grand Canyon.

105

Baruk Kaah sat among the black roots of Rec Pakken, basking in its evil aura. Eddie Paragon was with him, explaining everything he could about Earth. Baruk Kaah did not understand much of what the singer said, but

Rec Pakken did. And, the High Lord decided, that was good enough.

An edeinos entered the dark forest, making the signs of apology as he approached.

"Why do you disturb us, gotak?" the High Lord demanded.

"The expansion has been halted, Saar."

"What?" Baruk Kaah raged, rising to his feet.

"In the middle of our realm is a place of the dead. We cannot defeat the warriors there."

"Leave. I shall deal with this soon."

The gotak scrambled out of the forest.

Baruk Kaah opened his senses to Rec Pakken, asking for guidance. The darkness device showed him a Core Earth hardpoint, an area within their stelae bounds that refused to give up its reality. The darkness device suggested that he ignore it and continue to expand around it.

"No!" the High Lord raged. "I will destroy this hardpoint by personally imposing my reality upon it! Come with me, Paragon. You shall see the power of a High Lord. You shall sing of the power of Baruk Kaah!"

The tribes were poised within their own reality, just beyond the pocket of Core Earth that had formed around Silicon Valley. Baruk Kaah could feel the dead land. It was like a festering wound within his healthy, living realm. He would heal the wound.

The High Lord stepped forward, cloaking himself in a swirling storm of his own reality. The storm moved with him into the hardpoint.

"Be with me, Lanala," Baruk Kaah prayed. "Stand beside me, Rec Pakken."

The reality of Takta Ker entered the reality of Earth,

and a fierce storm formed around Baruk Kaah. Staggered by the surge of Earth energy, the High Lord fell back a step. Then he spread his arms wide and expanded his own storm. He pushed it wider, trying to overwhelm the Earth storm. Lightning swirled around him in a wide arc as the two realities battled for dominance. Thunder filled the area for miles around with noise. Then the storm collapsed back upon Baruk Kaah.

One tribe rushed forward, surrounding the High Lord. Gun fire sounded, and many of the edeinos fell. But enough made it back into the realm, carrying the body of Baruk Kaah.

Eddie Paragon rushed to the Saar's side. He saw that the silent ravagon was with him, too. The High Lord appeared to be dead, but then his yellow eyes opened.

"Rec Pakken," he whispered. "Get me to Rec Pakken."

The gotaks came forward, hefted the Saar, and headed back to where the darkness device waited.

Paragon stood watching for a moment, then looked back toward Silicon Valley.

"Your reality is strong, singer," the ravagon said, speaking for the first time ever in Paragon's presence. "And Baruk Kaah is a fool. He shall cost my master much before this is done."

Then the ravagon spread his wings and followed after the gotaks.

106

Thratchen went from room to room, searching for the Gaunt Man. He checked the tower room, the Grand Parlor, the banquet hall. He looked in the gardens, the hedge maze, the kitchens. Finally he descended into the basement levels and entered the laboratory. The Gaunt Man's machine hummed evilly. He could see the energy

Storm Knights

Alan Jude Summa

of this planet's possibilities playing across its gridwork surface.

"Intriguing device, don't you think?" Gibberfat spoke from atop one bank of levers and knobs. The tiny demon was reclining, hands behind his head and one knee dangling over the other.

"Have you seen the Gaunt Man?" Thratchen asked.

"He's gone. Took off. Should be back soon. Or not. That's the way he is, you know."

Thratchen cursed and turned to leave. But Gibberfat called him back.

"Why have you returned, Thratchen? You left so long ago. What brings you back now?"

The Tharkold shrugged. "I want to be where the power is."

"More likely, you want the power for yourself," the demon laughed. "I've seen the way you look at Heketon. I've heard you ask about the old legends. But you haven't asked me, and I've been around for a long time."

Thratchen hadn't thought of that. The demon had been around even before he had appeared on the scene.

"Very well, demon. What can you tell me about the legends?"

Gibberfat laughed. "Just that. They are legends, nothing more. But I do know the story, if you want to hear it."

Thratchen nodded, folding his metallic wings about himself.

"Legends," Gibberfat began, reciting the words from an ancient memory. "They speak of The Place, in the Time of Nothing. The Void was alone in The Place, possessed by an unending hunger but unable to sate it. Then Eternity entered The Place, full of dreams and possibilities locked within its infinite instant with no method of release. Void and Eternity met, and The

Maelstrom was formed.

"The Void tasted the essence of Eternity, and it became aware of what it craved. Eternity boiled away into the Void and billions of possibilities were destroyed. Whole galaxies came and went as the Void fed. The Maelstrom endlessly tossed out possibilities that were destroyed in the whirling currents of creation. But, eventually, two possibilities survived.

"The Nameless One, a being that took after the Void, was destruction personified. Apeiros, created from realized possibilities, was of Eternity's image. The two waged a war of creation and destruction — Apeiros setting possibilities free, the Nameless One feeding on their power. But as fast as the Nameless One could feed, Apeiros could create. There could be no victor. Then the Nameless One invoked the Void.

"With no other course available, Apeiros left The Place. It appealed to Eternity and saw an infinite number of possibilities opened before it. Apeiros took them all, diffusing the possibilities throughout the new place — throughout the cosmverse.

"The Nameless One, now alone in The Place with the Void, vowed to hunt down Apeiros and Eternity, no matter how long it took. It used what limited creative powers it had learned during its war against Apeiros to create the darkness devices. Then it sent these items of evil into the cosmverse to perpetuate acts of destruction and capture the dispersed shards of Eternity."

Thratchen moved closer. "Speak the rest, demon. Finish the tale."

"Legends," Gibberfat continued. "They tell of the discovery of the first darkness device, and how it elevated its possessor to High Lord and then led him to other cosms to destroy and drain possibilities. Thus was born the first of the Possibility Raiders; thus was spoken The Prophecy — there would arise a High Lord with the knowledge and power to absorb so much energy as to become immortal, all-powerful, a god. And this High Lord would be called the Torg!"

"But," Gibberfat finished, "they are only legends."

107

On the world of Terra, in a cosm far removed from Earth, the Gaunt Man walked the shadowy streets. This reality was ridiculous, the Gaunt Man thought, the design of a madman. And, in truth, that was what Terra's High Lord was. Mad.

The Gaunt Man entered a run-down tenement in a rather shabby section of the Terran city. Why did the High Lord keep up these shams, he wondered. Why does he play these games with the stormers of this world? The Gaunt Man shoved the thoughts aside. How the High Lord handled his cosm was no concern to him. But how he handled his part in the Gaunt Man's plans, that was his concern.

Deep beneath the tenement, the setting changed. The Gaunt Man was now walking through stone passages decorated with Egyptian hieroglyphics. Men garbed in traditional Egyptian dress tried to bar his way. But the Gaunt Man walks where he pleases, and they suffered for their duty.

He entered a large chamber. A massive black idol rose above seven sarcophagi. The Gaunt Man bowed before the idol, acknowledging the darkness device, then moved further into the chamber. He noted that the sarcophagi, their tops open, were filled with the mummified remains of past pharoahs of this world's Egypt — except for the seventh, which was empty.

"Welcome, Gaunt Man, to my domain," a muffled voice called out.

The Gaunt Man turned to see a tall man approach. The man wore Egyptian clothing, reminiscent of the Old Empire, but he had a pistol at his side and a mask covered his head.

"Greetings, Mobius, High Lord of Terra and the Nine Empires," the Gaunt Man said.

"What brings you here unannounced, Lord of Or-rorsh?"

"I have come to see what delays you. Have you forgotten our appointment on Earth?"

"No," Mobius said, indicating another figure sitting in the shadows, "we were just discussing that venture."

The small Japanese businessman stood, bowed, and returned to his seat. He never said a word.

"My regards to your master," the Gaunt Man said. "I hope Kanawa is well."

Then he turned again to Mobius. "I demand that you open the maelstrom bridges and establish your realm. Tharkold has experienced a few problems, and the time table demands another realm before Earth's energy compensates for the four currently connected."

"Tharkold didn't make it?" Mobius laughed insanely. "Then that means more energy for me."

"Of course, my friend," the Gaunt Man promised. "But if you are not in place by the proper time, I shall personally destroy you and award your darkness device to one of my lieutenants."

The Gaunt Man stepped back, and a tendril of his soul bridge fell from the air. "Remember that, Mobius." Then he stepped upon the bridge thread and was gone.

108

Fourteen hours after Tolwyn saw the picture of the Grand Canyon in an Indianapolis snack shop, the group arrived at Fort Riley, Kansas. Fort Riley, Decker explained, was where he was to report in. As he still had to do that, and the officials there would be able to provide them with transportation to Arizona, he figured that was the logical location for them to head to.

While the others rested and cleaned up, Decker met with General Edward Talbot. He told the general about the trip through Pennsylvania, about the deaths of the marines, and about the meeting with Kurst and the others. The general listened, scribbling a note here and there, but he did not interrupt Decker's narrative. When the congressman finished, the general spoke.

"President Wells asked me to cooperate with you in any way I could. I have to inform you that the capital has been moved to Houston, Texas for the remainder of this crisis."

Decker was shocked by the news. However, for Wells to make such a decision, the zone of silence must have been spreading south.

"General," Decker said, "I need transportation to Arizona. A cargo plane perhaps, or maybe a helicopter."

"That's a big request, congressman. But I do have orders. I'll have a chopper and pilot ready for you first thing tomorrow morning. Until then, I suggest you get some rest. You look like you can use it."

Decker nodded. "Yes sir. And thank you." He went to find the others and tell them what was happening.

109

Mara sat in the base cafeteria, watching Kurst eat. She ran her scans of him through her internal computer three times. Then she went over and sat across from him.

"You carry your own axioms with you, Kurst," she said.

Alder and Bryce looked up from their own meals. "What are you talking about, Mara?" Bryce asked.

"Kurst is a stormer ... excuse me, a storm knight. Like myself, like Tolwyn, like Alder and Decker. He carries his own reality with him, but it is not a reality that I have ever seen before," she finished.

Kurst watched the group for reactions. There were only the four of them in the mess. The others were off sleeping or bathing. For a moment he contemplated striking quickly, but then he decided to keep on his mask.

"I am like you, Mara," he said carefully. "I am from another cosm. But that cosm has arrived on Earth. It is called Orrorsh. It is a terrible place, full of evil things you would call monsters. It is also the most powerful of the realities attacking Earth, at least that is what our High Lord claims."

"High Lord? You work for these invaders?" Alder raged, rising over Kurst violently.

It took every ounce of control he could muster for Kurst to keep his own instincts in check. That was why Alder still lived. Instead of striking out, he said simply, "I have left the realm of Orrorsh. Like Mara, I am here to help. Like Decker and Tolwyn, I follow a dream."

"Do you, Mr. Kurst?" Bryce asked. He did not require an answer.

"Let's get some rest," Mara suggested. "We can discuss this more fully in the morning."

The three left the room, but Alder glanced back at Kurst before he exited. "I hope you're telling us everything, Kurst." Then he disappeared through the door.

If I told you everything, Mr. Alder, Kurst thought, then nightmares would haunt what few hours of life you have left.

110

Tolwyn came across Decker in the corridor of the building they were being housed in. He was carrying a scabbard. Her eyes grew wide at the sight of a familiar weapon.

"Andrew Decker, may I see that?" she asked.

"Of course," he said. He handed her the leather scabbard. It had a brass frame, and the polished hilt of the saber fit snuggly against the top of the scabbard.

Tolwyn turned the sheathed weapon over in her hands, examining the workmanship of the casing. Then she slowly pulled the sword from its sheath, watching as the light gleamed off its polished surface.

"What a fine weapon," she said admiringly. "It is not as great a sword as my own, but it will do. Where did you get it?"

"It belonged to a young soldier that was with me when my quest started. He died in the battle I spoke of. I was just taking it to the general so that it could be forwarded to his family."

Tolwyn nodded, replacing the blade into its covering. "May I have it?" she asked. "A warrior's blade should be used by a warrior. I will honor your soldier's memory by using it well."

Decker was taken aback by her request. But something inside him said that this was why he had carried it out of Pennsylvania in the first place.

"Use it well, Tolwyn," he said. "I think Teagle would be pleased that his sword was going to do some good. But remember, it isn't meant for battles. It's just a dress sword."

Tolwyn ran her hand over the fine leather. "It will do, Decker. It will do."

111

Malcolm Kane walked along the south rim of the Grand Canyon, letting the wind blow his blonde hair. His work boots were ideal for this terrain, he decided. And when the sun hit the jutting rock formations just right, it looked to him like they were covered in blood.

He had come to this place at the Gaunt Man's command. He had with him a number of followers, those who were learning the art of death at his feet. They would serve him well when the priest and his group arrived. That's when the test would begin, to see which of them served death better. The priest had his way, Kane had his own. The Gaunt Man said to kill them all, and Kane would make each death a masterpiece. Each would be an offering to the Gaunt Man, a human shrine to the destruction that he had shown to Kane in a vision.

"The end of the long road is coming, priest. You give your sacraments," Kane whispered to the canyon, drawing his serrated hunting knife from its sheath. "And I have mine."

112

Tom O'Malley had his plane in the air, heading east toward Australia. He was carrying the most unusal cargo he had ever hauled, seven dwarves decked out in armor and wielding melee weapons. What's more, these dwarves were terribly interested in anything mechanical. They were sitting on the floor in the cargo hold examining his tool kit, reading his manuals. Every so often he heard an "ohhh" or an "ahhh", but mostly they talked quietly about the possible uses for each tool, the relative merit of design, and the ways they could improve the airplane.

"How can you people read English?" Tom called back. "I thought you said you came from someplace else?"

"We do come from a different land," the female named Pluppa said. "We come from Aysle. But the High Lord always prepares us with the language of the land we are to bring enlightenment to."

"Is that what your High Lord calls it, enlightenment? I call it tyranny."

"Aye, Tom O'Malley, that's what it is," Pluppa sighed. "But it wasn't always so. Once the dwarves ruled Aysle, and in those days the sky was bright and the land was alive."

"Tell us the story, Pluppa!" Toolpin exclaimed. "Tell us about the gods!"

"The gods?" Tom asked.

"We should tell Tom O'Malley the story, for that will let him know where we come from, our heritage. But I am not a storyteller. Gutterby should tell it."

"Yes, Gutterby tells it so well!" Toolpin agreed.

The old dwarf looked up from the engine manual and sighed. "Oh very well. I'll tell the story. Now listen carefully, 'cause I'm not gonna tell it again for at least ten years."

And the story that Gutterby told went like this …

In the beginning there was Nothing. Nothing had been here always, timeless, unchanging, infinite, eternal.

Then the Creators came. Mighty builders, they had labored long and hard and well for others. But their masters had spit upon them and called them bad names, so they fled.

Enduring much hardship and misery during their journey, chased always by the creatures of their vengeful masters, the Creators sought a place where they could be free. A place where they could build for themselves, and not for others.

Finally, after many long years of travel, they arrived at this place. They knew that their masters would never look for them in the midst of Nothing. They knew they were safe. They decided to create something of their own.

Building Something from Nothing is a difficult job, even for the Creators. But they were not dismayed, for weren't they the greatest craftsmen of all? Stopping only for a quick bite of lunch and a puff on their pipes, they rolled up their sleeves and began.

Fordex, the Eldest, looked about him. "This Nothingness offends me!" he cried. Reaching into his sack, he brought out a single grain of dust. He placed it in the Nothingness before him. "I banish you!" he cried.

Now that it contained a thing — yea, even but a grain of dust — the Nothingness was no more. For the Law says, "if a thing be one thing, it cannot also be another." A thing cannot be both Nothing and have Something in it. The Nothingness was banished forever.

Exhausted by his labor, Fordex rested.

Mighty Errog worked next. "Yes, this is Something, but it goes on Forever! Even We cannot work our will on Forever! I shall create a Limit!" Reaching into his sack, he pulled out a handful of sand. Placing it in his pipe, he puffed mightily, heating the sand until it melted and became glass. He shaped the glass into a mighty ball and placed it around the grain of dust, saying, "This shall be the Limit and Extent of our Creation!"

Exhausted by his labor, Errog rested.

Terrin was next. Reaching into his sack, he brought forth a round, flat grindstone. Using his smallest finger, he carefully poked a hole in its center. He placed the stone in the glass ball, surrounding the mote of dust. "Is that not fine?" he cried.

Exhausted by his labor, Terrin rested.

Movin and Weeble, the Brothers, worked next. Reaching into their sacks, they brought forth chisels and carved the stone, sculpting deep pits, high mountains, oceans and riverbeds.

They, too, rested.

Ghanthor brought forth a flask of water and poured it on the stone. Charon brought forth a twig, and planted it by the water. Mhyrron brought forth an egg, and set it next to the twig. Plantir brought forth a knife and cut off the tip of his finger. Carving it into the likeness of the Creators, he placed it next to the egg and the twig.

They rested.

Then it was the turn of Harp, the last Creator. He looked in his sack, but it was empty! "Alas! I have nothing to give to our Creation," he cried sadly. Then he brightened. "Ah, I know! I shall give Life!"

Saying thus, he breathed upon the twig, and lo! it grew into a mighty oak!

He breathed upon the egg, and lo! it hatched forth a beautiful bird!

He breathed upon the image of the Creators, and lo! it became a Dwarf!

Giving Life, Harp died.

When the other Creators awoke, they were dismayed. "Alas! Harp is dead! He died to give our Creation Life! But look! The oak withers; the bird huddles upon its branches; the Dwarf is afraid! Our creation is flawed!"

Fordex, the Eldest, spoke. "Fools! Living creatures cannot be in the Dark! We need to give our creation Light!" Saying thus, he reached out and picked up the single mote of dust in the center of the creation. He placed it in his pipe, and puffed mightily. It began to glow in the hot embers of his fire.

When it was burning, he placed it back in the creation. He tapped it with his finger, causing it to move within the globe, giving the creation Day and Night.

The oak thrived in the Light, giving birth to all manner of trees, and grass, and flowers.

The bird thrived in the Light, giving birth to all manner of beasts and fish.

The dwarf thrived in the Light, giving birth to many sons and daughters.

Well content with their creation, the Creators rested.

Soon, however, they became dissatisfied. "It's fine," said Errog, "but I'm not really happy with the limits. Perhaps something could be done with infinity …"

"You know," added Terrin, "I don't quite like the flatness. Maybe a round world …"

Movin and Weeble began excitedly discussing the possibilities of continental drift. "Let us try again!" they demanded.

The others agreed. Their creation was very nice and all, but they were sure they could do better next time. Shouldering their packs, they cheerfully set off to try again elsewhere.

"… and since then," Gutterby exclaimed, "the dwarves have survived on their own, without the help of any gods!"

"Except for the spark of Life that Harp gave us,"

Toolpin corrected.

"Who's telling this story?"

"Sorry."

"Where was I? Oh yes, we have survived without the help of any gods — and that's the way we like it!"

Tom O'Malley smiled. "What a wonderful story."

Toolpin jumped up. "Now teach us how this magic flying machine works!"

"Teach us! Teach us!"

It was going to be a long flight, Tom decided.

113

Aboard Air Force One, President Jonathan Wells was en route to Houston. He was resting, trying to catch up on some much needed sleep when his aide entered.

"Sir, I have a call from General Powell."

Wells opened his eyes and returned the chair to its upright position. He checked his watch. We should be in Texas soon, he noted.

"Very well, Carter," the president said. "Put the call through."

The light on the phone in front of him started blinking. Wells cleared his throat and lifted the receiver. "Yes, Clay?"

The voice on the other side sounded far away, but Wells could hear it. "John, I've just received reports from a number of refugees. New York isn't as dead as we thought."

"What are you saying, Clay? What have you found out?"

"There are still people alive in there, John. From reports, they've set up a small government in lower Manhattan."

Wells was completely awake now. A dozen possibilities raged through his mind.

"What does this mean, Clay?"

"I'm not sure, John. But it does mean that there are people alive. It could be just wishful thinking, but if some form of government can exist in the zone of silence, then maybe Douglas Kent survived as well."

"Let's keep this between ourselves for the time being, Clay. I'll talk with you soon."

The president hung up the receiver. He needed to find someone to take another trip for him, someone he could trust. Decker was already off on one mission. Wells thought for a moment, then remembered an agent from his days as head of the CIA. If he was still available, he would be perfect for the job. If he would even talk to Wells. If, too many ifs.

Wells called for his aide.

"Carter, I have to place a call," he said. "Find out how we can reach Quin Sebastian."

114

The Chinook helicopter approached the Grand Canyon from the north as the sun was setting. As usual, a number of delays had postponed the group's departure from Fort Riley, and now as the day was drawing to a close they were at last reaching their destination.

Tolwyn sat at a window, watching for the first sign of the image from her dreams. Perhaps with the sign would come the rest of her memories. They were flying over flat country of familiar-looking fields and forests. Occasionally a picturesque gully broke the land, but nothing that resembled the canyon in her dreams.

Father Bryce sat beside her, watching her reactions at the sights. "This is truly new to you, isn't it?"

"Yes, Christopher," she replied. "Never have I seen a

world from such a vantage point. The magic of your world is remarkable. And the sun works differently than I remember. Are you sure it does not move through the center of the world?"

"I'm sure."

She turned her attention to the sights below, trying to see everything before darkness covered the land. Then, suddenly, the canyon was there. The size of it astonished her, and the sunset painted the canyon walls with bright reds and oranges. The stark formations, silhouetted against the sky, were breathtaking.

"Christopher ...?" she stammered, trying to find the words she wanted to say.

"Yes, Tolwyn. That's the Grand Canyon."

A park ranger met the army helicopter when it landed. He had been advised of the group's arrival by General Talbot in Fort Riley, and he arranged accommodations for the party.

As he spoke to Decker and the pilot, Tolwyn slowly stepped to the edge of the canyon. It was dark now, and the few lamps that provided light along the paths did not even dent the night beyond the canyon's brink. She could feel the open space beyond the edge, even if she could not see it. The air was different, something. It was like looking into a star-filled sky and realizing your insignificant size as compared to the majesty. She wanted to step back, to get away from the maw.

Maw ... suddenly memories overwhelmed her. She saw a raging battle. She saw the terrible beast cutting through the other warriors on a course to reach her. She heard the chant her comrades sang, heard the words that sent her out of her body just before the claws struck. But she still felt a burst of pain. But the image passed. She would dwell on what it meant later. For now, she let the scope of the canyon overtake her. It was truly grand. She could not wait to see it in the light.

Then she heard the song from her dreams. It called to her from far below. "I am coming," she whispered.

115

Morning came late because of the planet's slower spin, but finally the sun rose and the canyon was drenched in wonderful light. Tolwyn was out to greet the dawn, and the others soon followed. She watched her companions approach, feeling good about their company. She knew there was tension between Kurst and some of the others, but she believed that that would work itself out. He followed the dream, and he had even been spoken of in her own. He belonged, she decided. Let any of them try to tell her otherwise.

She tested the weight of the saber, then sheathed it as the ranger appeared with mules for the entire party.

"The cave you're looking for, it could be anywhere," the ranger explained. "The canyon is two hundred and seventy-seven miles long. It's four to ten miles wide in places, and five to six thousand feet deep. The cave could be natural, or it could be an Anasazi granary. Those chambers are all over the canyon. You could look forever and never find what you seek."

"I will find it," she said, swinging herself onto a mule.

Decker smiled at the ranger. "You heard the lady."

"Well, I'm going along for the ride," the ranger said as the others mounted up.

The mules — and the ranger — were nervous around Tal Tu, but both seemed to get used to him relatively quickly. Then they started down into the canyon.

Some hours later the group had made it past the mid way point to the bottom of the canyon. Tolwyn still seemed to know where she was going, and she was content to stay on the provided trail for a little further into the canyon.

"Are you sure about this, congressman?" the ranger asked.

Before Decker could answer, a loud crack echoed through the canyon. Red began to soak the front of the ranger's shirt. He stared at it, then looked at Decker. "I think I've been shot …"

The ranger fell from the mule. Decker leaped down to examine him while the others sought cover. Bryce appeared next to Decker. "How is he?" the priest asked.

"He's dead," Decker said with finality. "Stay down everyone."

They waited for almost an hour, hiding behind rocks or trees, or lying flat against the ground. But no further shots were fired. Tolwyn, tired of waiting, flung herself back atop the mule.

"I am going," she stated. "I am going now." And she rode off down the trail.

The others, with nothing else to do, followed her example, each hoping that another shot would not claim them as well.

116

The sun grew hotter as the day advanced. Tolwyn had turned off the main path and was now leading the group along a ridge that overlooked the Colorado River below. The water raged through the canyon, filling it with a constant noise. It was beautiful, but none of the party could enjoy it.

Sweat poured down Father Bryce's face, and he

wished they could stop to rest. But he knew that Tolwyn would not wait for them, and he wanted to be with her when she reached her goal.

"We are being watched," Kurst said. He offered no further details.

The nine rode in silence for a time, letting the sway of the mules provide their rhythm. There was little shade along the trail once the sun reached its zenith, and the pounding rays were wearing on the priest. He knew the others weren't faring much better.

Then another shot sounded.

The party leaped to the ground, seeking cover. Bryce quickly spotted everyone visually, checking that no one was hit. Everyone appeared to be all right.

"Welcome to my canyon," echoed a voice from somewhere nearby. But the way the sound bounced, it could be coming from any direction. "I am Malcolm Kane, and you are about to become shrines to my art."

Father Bryce recognized the voice, but he couldn't place it. The name, however, was the one the refugees in Flat Rock had used. This was the man who had taught them to murder people like the edeinos did.

"I told you we would meet again, priest," the voice called. "Now is the time when we see which of us serves death better. Did you like the message I left you in Flat Rock, Father? What did you think of my work?"

"Show yourself, villain!" Tolwyn called.

A long, evil laugh was the only response she received.

"I have a group, too, Father," the voice called again. "They are my disciples, learning my art so that they can carry it throughout the world."

As though on cue, a lizard man leaped down from a ledge above them. He wielded a long spear that he drove through Tal Tu's stomach and into the tree behind him. Then it whirled to attack Rat.

Mara, however, was there to defend the boy. She stepped in front of Rat, brandishing her laser pistol. She did not even wait to see what the lizard was going to do. Three quick bursts exploded from the gun and the edeinos fell.

"There are more of us, priest," the voice called one final time, "and now there is one less of you."

Then the voice was gone.

117

The group continued cautiously ahead after making Tal Tu comfortable. He was not dead, but he was badly wounded. He demanded that the others go on though. It was important for Tolwyn to find the stone. Reluctantly, the others agreed.

As they continued the trek, Father Bryce told them of his brief meeting with the man he assumed was Malcolm Kane. It had occurred beyond Newark, in a demolished liquor store. "I knew he was mad then, now I believe he is insane," the priest declared.

Up ahead, Tolwyn brought her mule to a halt. She pointed to a ridge just above them.

"There. That is the cave that holds the blue and red stone."

Decker dismounted. "We can't take the mules up there. We're going to have to walk."

The group started climbing the narrow trail. Tolwyn was in the lead, followed by Kurst, Decker, Bryce, Mara, Alder, Rat and Coyote. After they had gone a few dozen feet, Kurst tensed. Then he leaped forward, slamming into Tolwyn and knocking her to the ground. Bryce moved to help her when suddenly the world shifted.

A net rose up from its hiding place beneath dirt and stones, capturing the group and lifting them into the air. Suspended, with no means of leverage or escape, Bryce and the others could only watch as a man in a soldier's uniform emerged onto the path ahead.

The soldier held a rifle. Beside him was a large blonde man in work boots. He had a tattoo of a cobra on his arm, and a wicked smile played across his lips.

"Be careful, Tolwyn," Bryce called from out of the net. "That's Kane."

Faster than the soldier could react, Kurst was upon him. They wrestled for the gun that the soldier carried. Kane turned to assist his minion, pulling a large knife from a hidden sheathe. He raised the blade to strike at Kurst's exposed back when another blade knocked the knife from his hand.

Tolwyn stood before him, her saber ready to skewer the madman. "This is for the people you had killed, villain," she swore. But before she could deliver her blow, strong tentacles dropped from above and pinned her limbs. She glanced up to see a starfish-shaped creature, but she looked away so that she could watch Kane. But in the split second, he had vanished.

118

Alder watched as the stalenger tightened its tentacles around Tolwyn. She was strong, but the creature was choking the life out of her. Kurst and the soldier were out of his line of sight, but he could hear the sounds of their struggle. He tested the net, but he had no leverage and didn't think he could break it if he did.

"Mara, can you reach me?" he asked.

The young woman was able to get her hand within inches of his face. "I think I know what you want," she said as sharp-edged nails sprang from her finger tips. She sliced the net, and Alder fell to the ground.

Tolwyn continued to struggle, but her movements were becoming weaker. The stalenger was killing her. Alder pulled his pistol, aimed at the body of the beast, and fired two shots. It crashed to the ground beside Tolwyn, the life spilling from it. He ran to her, helping her remove the tentacles from around her throat and limbs.

"The beast was strong, Rick Alder," Tolwyn gasped.

"Not as strong as you, Tolwyn," he said.

They heard a noise on the trail before them. Alder raised his gun, but then lowered it when Kurst emerged. He was carrying the soldier's rifle.

"Kane is gone," Kurst informed them. "He has retreated up the trail toward the cave."

The others, with Mara's help, were freeing themselves from the net. Alder helped Tolwyn to her feet and returned her sword.

"It's going to be a long climb with that madman out there." He mentally counted their weapons — his pistol, Kurst's rifle, Decker's pistol, Mara's pistol, and Tolwyn's sword. The others were not armed. "All right, let's regroup before we do this."

119

Mobius examined his troops one last time. The shock-troopers, the tanks, the super-powered agents, the mummies — all were ready. He turned to his attending priest.

"Open the bridges, Ahmed," he ordered. "It is time for the Nile Empire to extend to Earth. Let us send forth the Tenth Empire!"

And with that, the reality of Pharaoh Mobius connected to Earth, turning the land around Egypt and the Middle East into a new realm. The fifth reality had arrived, and the Gaunt Man's plan was back on schedule.

120

The group climbed the trail up to an overhang. Beneath the massive rock was an opening. It was dark and uninviting.

"That is where the stone is," Tolwyn said.

"It might also be where Kane is," warned Bryce.

"No matter, the villain is a coward who I will easily dispatch."

Bryce wasn't so sure, but Tolwyn, once on a course, could not be swayed.

Decker stepped forward. "Kurst, you stand guard out here with Rat and Coyote. The rest of us will see what's in the cave."

Bryce watched for some negative reaction from Kurst, but he merely nodded.

"Then what are we waiting for?" Tolwyn asked. "Let us proceed."

Decker followed her, and Mara, Alder, and Bryce were right behind.

121

Kurst waited outside the cave with the two boys. He stretched his senses in all directions, watching for any signs of danger. He looked at the rifle in his hands, and knew that it was not something he wanted to use. He handed it to Coyote.

"Coyote, huh?" Kurst asked.

The boy nodded.

"That is what Decker calls the stone they seek," the

hunter told them. "He says that it is a legend from this world, a legend called the Heart of the Coyote."

"You aren't from here, are you?" Coyote asked.

"No. I am from a place called Orrorsh. There I am a hunter for the High Lord, a common servant who is treated well because of his skills."

"What were you before that?" Rat inquired.

A puzzled look crossed Kurst's face. "I do not remember."

"Do all of you people from other worlds have bad memories? First Tolwyn and now you," Coyote said.

"My memories were taken from me, boy," Kurst responded. "I do not know what happened to Tolwyn's."

Coyote cradled the rifle carefully. "Are you sure you want me to have this?"

"You will need it more than I. Now watch for signs of Kane or his followers."

"Mr. Kurst," Rat whispered, "is that one of them?"

Kurst turned to see a figure standing in the shadows some distance away. It was Thratchen. "Stay here, and guard the cave," Kurst ordered as he stepped to meet Thratchen.

"Are they still alive, Kurst?" Thratchen asked.

"What do you want here? You will ruin everything."

"The Gaunt Man has sent others to do your job," Thratchen explained. "He grows fearful of these stormers and has decided to eliminate them. There is one called Kane that I have not met."

The hunter nodded. "We have met him and his band. They have been hounding us all through this canyon."

"There is also another. The Gaunt Man has called forth the Carredon."

Kurst paled at the mention of the terrible dragon. It was the monster of Orrorsh, the scourge of every world the Gaunt Man ever conquered.

"You must not let them die, Kurst. If we do not learn why these stormers are different, then we will never learn how to defeat them."

"If the Gaunt Man has ordered their deaths …"

"The Gaunt Man fears his plans are collapsing! My master failed to arrive on schedule, and now this planet threatens to throw us from it. Because of this the Gaunt Man is not thinking, he is simply reacting. We must do what is best for him in the long run."

Or is it what is best for you, Kurst thought. But he said, "I will do what I can."

Thratchen smiled wickedly. "I know you will, hunter."

122

Tolwyn yielded the lead to Decker, who had a flashlight that cut through the darkness of the cave. He trained the beam along the narrow passage. It stretched back as far as the beam reached, neither widening nor narrowing as it went. They followed the passage for many long minutes, and then it opened into a larger chamber. The chamber was full of Indian relics, all preserved through some quirk of the cave, or weather, or something none of them understood.

"Decker, dim your light," Bryce called.

The congressman did so, but the group was still able to see. The room was bathed in a soft blue glow.

Tolwyn stepped around Decker and walked over to the far wall. "This is a holy place, Christopher," she said with conviction.

The priest moved beside her. In a cavity in the wall rested a turquoise stone. Crimson bands swirled within it. It was shaped like a human heart, and about the same size as one, only it was made of the strangely-colored stone. It glowed softly, illuminating the chamber with its own light.

"It sings to me, Christopher. It greets us. But it is in pain, as well. The invaders have hurt this world, and the stone feels the pain," Tolwyn told them.

"That's the Heart of Coyote," Decker explained. "Coyote was a hero of Indian legend, who helped mankind by bringing us things from the gods. I guess he stole them, actually. The legend concerning this relic is that when Coyote was preparing to leave man on his own, he left a piece of himself behind in case we ever needed it."

Mara moved forward to view the stone, letting her sensor lense drop into place. The stone shined even more brightly on her sensor than the world itself did, and even after she had adjusted the intensity. The stone was literally a piece of the energy she and the other stormers contained.

"Hey," Alder said. "Do you feel anything?"

"You mean that vibration?" Bryce asked.

Then the wall behind them exploded, filling the chamber with shards of stone.

123

Minutes before the wall exploded into a thousand pieces, Kurst was rushing through the narrow passage. His own eyes were better accustomed to the darkness, but even he had to feel his way along because of the lack of light beyond the few feet provided by the entrance. He had to reach the group before the Carredon did. He refused to yield a catch to the monster, and more, he agreed with Thratchen that these stormers should be studied. There was something about them that went against every experience he ever had on other worlds.

A few feet more, and he could smell the oldness of the cave. More, he could smell the "stench of Apeiros" as Thratchen called it. This place literally reeked with the scent, if you were familiar with its smell.

Ahead he could see a soft blue light now, and he could tell by the way his foot falls echoed that a larger chamber opened further up the passage. The lack of violent sounds encouraged Kurst. Perhaps, Thratchen was wrong. Perhaps the Carredon was not on the stormers' trail.

Then an explosion knocked him to the ground. Something was happening in the chamber, and Kurst knew he had to get there before it was over.

124

Malcolm Kane watched the small man rush past his hiding spot. He was wedged within a fissure in the passage wall, trying to decide how to proceed. He had not yet completed the task the Gaunt Man had given him, and that bothered him. He did not like to fail.

But he knew that to attack so many people by himself was foolish. Some of them had guns, while all he had was his knife. The bitch named Tolwyn had cut him, and he wanted to make her pay for that. He just had to figure out the best course open to him.

He should have recruited more help, he realized. He didn't know how large the priest's party had grown on its trek across the country. He figured that a lizard man, one of the flying starfish, and the soldier who deserted his unit would be more than enough to take out a cop, a priest, and two kids. And it would have been, too, he was certain. But the priest changed the rules. He added more players to his team. That was unfair.

Kane hated unfairness.

And, the more Kane thought about, he hated the priest and the bitch, too.

125

The cloud of dust and flying rock cleared, and Tolwyn could see again. She wiped dirt from her eyes and looked to see what had caused such destruction. What she saw made her heart skip a beat.

In the shattered opening where the rear wall had been stood the Carredon. It barely fit within the tall chamber, even with its black wings folded behind it. But there it was, just like in the fragments of her memory.

There was the monster that killed her.

And now it was here to kill her again.

The stone cried in her mind, pleading for her help.

But Tolwyn could not even help herself. She saw the beast's huge dagger-like claws, and she remembered the pain those claws had brought to her a lifetime ago. She saw its tooth-filled maw, and she remembered it tearing through her fellow warriors. And she saw its armored hide, and she remembered how sword and spear and arrow bounced away without harming the creature.

And, for the first time in her memory, Tolwyn was afraid.

126

Alder watched as the dragon pushed into the chamber. It didn't have a lot of room to maneuver, but it looked very formidable. The police officer thought back to how this had begun for him. It seemed like decades had passed since the events at Shea Stadium, not weeks. He felt older, worn out. The only hope his promise of revenge had was if Tolwyn and the others escaped this

chamber with the stone. Otherwise the entire trek out of
New York and across the country was meaningless. He
refused to let everything they had fought for end here.

He checked his pistol. It had three slugs chambered.
He decided that three would have to do. He raised the
pistol. Then he halted, amazed.

The dragon spoke.

"Remember me, Tolwyn of House Tancred?" the
dragon asked. Its voice was hollow, like a bottomless
pit. "I killed you once. I have come to kill you again."

Alder watched as Tolwyn curled up in the corner. She
was frightened past the point of sanity. He guessed that
if the monster that killed him had returned, he might go
over the edge too. But Tolwyn had the power to fight the
thing, if she could be made to realize that. If he could
show her that the beast wasn't invincible.

The police officer rolled forward, coming up on one
knee with his gun extended. He knew that the move had
opened the wounds made by the ravagon, but he could
live with that. He aimed at the dragon's head and
emptied his revolver.

The first shot ricocheted off its armored snout, causing it to turn his way. The second shot went wide of his
mark, bouncing off the wall behind it. The third shot hit
soft flesh, burying itself in the dragon's left eye. Dark
fluid ran down its cheek, and its roar rocked the chamber.

"The stormer draws blood!" the dragon bellowed.
"Now the Carredon has a turn!"

One taloned paw flashed opened, and the three clawed
nails pierced Alder's body and lifted him from the floor.
The officer never knew such pain or fear, but he had
accomplished his goal — he had shown them that the
monster could be hurt.

Though it hurt him, Alder twisted on the claws so that he could look at Tolwyn. Blood welled from his mouth, and his vision was starting to fade, but he forced his vocal chords to work.

"It can be hurt, Tolwyn," he gasped. "It can be hurt."

The Carredon flexed his claws and Alder slid off of them, landing in a puddle of his own fluids. His last sight was of Kurst entering the chamber. Good, he thought, now they're all together.

For Rick Alder, the war was over.

127

Kurst entered the chamber as Alder fell from the Carredon's claws. The others were still standing around in shock, and it appeared that Alder's sacrifice hadn't roused them as he had hoped it would.

The hunter wracked his brain, trying to figure out a strategy to employ. Everything he thought of kept coming back to the original problem — the Carredon was designed to kill and kill well. It had no weaknesses that Kurst knew of. He could remember no battle where it had received a wound. But here was a situation that looked hopeless, but Alder had wounded it. It had one less eye now, and that could be the way to defeat it.

But a voice in the back of Kurst's mind gave him pause. What, the voice asked, would be the price for countering an order of the Gaunt Man? Before he answered that for himself, the Carredon spoke again.

"You, the one called Decker," the dragon intoned, waving the claw covered with Alder's blood at the congressman. "No unnecessary deaths need occur. My master is impressed with you, stormer. I bring you an offer from the Gaunt Man, High Lord of Orrorsh and Torg of the cosmverse."

Decker stepped forward, but stayed beyond the Carredon's reach. "What is this offer?"

The dragon seemed to smile. "The Gaunt Man has the power to grant your greatest wish."

"And how does this High Lord know what I wish for?"

"Because he has looked into your heart."

Decker seemed taken aback by that. The Gaunt Man had actually used his powers to find out what he could about these stormers! Remarkable, he thought. Kurst decided to let this gambit be played out before he made his own move.

"What did he see, dragon?"

"He saw your love for this country, and he saw your sorrow at its wounds from Baruk Kaah's invaders. He has authorized me to offer you this."

The Carredon clacked its claws together and an image appeared within the chamber for all to see. It was the image of a black stone, as dark as night and shapeless. Still, it radiated power, not unlike the blue stone the group had come to find. Kurst knew it for what it was. It was a darkness device, like the Gaunt Man's Heketon.

"With this object of power, you could become the High Lord of this world and join the Gaunt Man as an equal being. Instead of destroying this world, you could save it. You could impose the laws and doctrines you hold so dear not only in this country, but in every country. You can be president, and then you would have the power to reshape this world into the image that burns so fiercely in your heart. And more, with the power of reality, you could bring back the woman named Vicky."

Decker lowered his head for a moment, then looked into the Carredon's remaining eye. "That's a very tempting offer. But if I were to impose my will onto this country, then it wouldn't be America. It would be something less, no matter how strong it was. It would be a sham."

The Carredon was losing patience. "What is your answer, stormer?"

"My answer? Go to hell!" Decker raised his pistol, a Beretta, and fired at the dragon's other eye.

128

Kane watched from the shadows of the narrow passage, letting anger and disappointment fill his hollow spaces. The Gaunt Man had promised him power! Now he was offering it to one of the priest's companions. That wasn't right!

He would show them that Malcolm Kane deserved the power and the glory. He would find this black stone of power and claim it for his own. Then he would make the priest and his group pay. And he would make the Gaunt Man pay as well.

With those thoughts firmly running through his mind, Kane went back down the passage toward the opening to the canyon. He had no interest in the outcome of the events unfolding in the chamber. He had only his own vision, and that was enough.

129

Father Christopher Bryce backed against the wall of the chamber, not heeding what Indian relics he was crushing beneath his feet. He was trembling with fear at the sight of the monster, sickened by the death of Rick Alder. And now the beast was tempting Decker, showing its true demonic nature. But Decker was not swayed by the offer. Instead he fired shot after shot into the beast until the sound in the enclosed area was deafening. And then his pistol clicked, indicating that it was empty.

Mara took up the battle then, firing blasts of high-intensity light from her laser pistol. These caused burn marks to appear across the dragon's chest, and it roared in anger. It prepared to launch itself at the girl, but she resumed firing.

"She will run out of energy soon," Kurst said. "Pray to your god, Bryce. I do not think we will defeat the Carredon."

"You speak as though you know the creature."

"I do."

Then Kurst's body began to shift, flowing from flesh to fur. He grew to over six feet tall, and widened as his body grew muscle. His features elongated, stretched, and formed into a muzzle full of sharp teeth. As the priest watched, Kurst had become a man-shaped wolf of gigantic size. The wolf looked at the priest, then charged toward the Carredon.

With a mighty leap, the wolf was upon the dragon, raking it with his powerful claws. The wolf slashed at the burns Mara's laser made, adding to the beast's injuries. Deep cuts sliced across the dragon's scales, staggering it. But it was stronger than Kurst. The wolf was no match for the terrible engine of destruction. It grasped the giant wolf in one powerful claw and dug its talons into his flesh.

"You should never have challenged me, Kurst," the Carredon boomed. "I am not some stormer for you to dispatch, and my claws can harm you." The Carredon squeezed its talons together to prove its point, and the life began to slip out of Kurst, splattering the ground with bright drops of red.

Storm Knights

Decker, his gun reloaded, resumed firing at the monster. He picked up on the wolf's strategy and aimed for the wounds already inflicted upon the creature. The wolf was dropped when the bullets hit, forgotten in the haze of pain that Decker brought to it.

"Never have I been so wounded, stormer!" the Carredon screamed. "But the pain I feel is nothing compared to the pain I will bring you."

The congressman stood his ground, firing bullet after bullet until his clip emptied. And still the Carredon advanced. It raised its talons high into the air, prepared to bring it down on Decker. But Mara leaped between them, driving her own metallic claws deep into the dragon's chest. In pain-driven rage, it struck out blindly and caught Mara with the back of its paw. That saved her from being decapitated, but it still sent her flying across the chamber. She landed in a heap and was still.

"Go ahead, monster," Decker declared. "Go ahead and strike me down."

"No, Decker," the Carredon said. "The rage has left me, and I have a more lasting pain to inflict upon you."

The Carredon raised one talon and brought it to rest upon a scale near its shoulder. It carved a symbol into the scale, scratching it through the top layer of its metallic hide.

Bryce saw Kurst, again in man form, try to rise. But his wounds were too great and he fell to the chamber floor. But he read the rune that the Carredon carved. "Never life."

Then the beast moved to a second scale. It repeated the carving ritual, forming another rune upon its own body.

"Never death," Kurst read weakly.

The Carredon gripped the scales and tore them from

its flesh, ripping away meat with the pieces of armor. It spoke words that Bryce did not understand, and it blew upon the twin scales, pointing them toward Decker. With the words of magic completed and the breath to move them, the scales flew from the monster's claws. They spun in the air, forming into pointed staves of metal each about a foot long. The carved runes could be clearly seen upon the shaft of each staff, glowing brightly with magical energy.

Faster than either Bryce or Decker could move, the staves struck the congressman, burying themselves in his chest. Decker screamed in agony as lambent energy played across his body, flowed into the jutting staves, and shot out into the darkness beyond the chamber. Decker collapsed, but the energy continued to dance along the metal rods formed from the Carredon's own body.

"Now, priest," the monster laughed, "perhaps I'll let you watch as I flay the skin from Tolwyn's bones.

130

Coyote and Rat watched the cave entrance nervously. They felt the earthquake-like tremor that rocked the area moments ago, unaware that it was caused by the Carredon crashing into the chamber of the blue and red stone. But both knew something terrible was happening within the cave, and they struggled with themselves over whether they should stand their ground as Kurst had ordered or rush after him into the cave.

As they watched and waited, they saw movement at the entrance. "Look," Rat shouted, running toward the cave to meet the group.

"No, Rat, wait!" shouted Coyote, but his warning was too late.

Rat ran to the opening, trying to see which of his friends was emerging. When he saw the blonde hair, he knew that it wasn't any of his friends. It was Kane.

The big man grabbed Rat and lifted him to his chest, using the boy as a living shield against Coyote's rifle. He had his large, serrated knife in his hand, holding it just beneath Rat's chin.

"Drop the gun, boy," Kane commanded. "Do it!"

Coyote hesitated, knowing that whatever he did in the next few seconds would be wrong.

He lifted the rifle to his shoulder and aimed along the barrel. "Let go of Rat," he said in his toughest voice, hoping the fear he felt wasn't too noticeable. "If you hurt him, so help me I'll kill you."

Instead of screaming in rage or tossing Rat aside or any of the other things Coyote imagined he would do, Kane simply smiled. "All right, boy, let's see who handles death better."

131

"No, spawn of hell, I'll not let you hurt her!" Father Bryce screamed across the chamber.

The Carredon chuckled. "And what will you do to stop me, stormer?"

As the dragon and Bryce glared at each other, Tolwyn stood up. The fear was still with her, but she was fighting it, pushing it away.

"I am tired of hearing the word 'stormer', Carredon," she said. Her voice began weak, but grew in strength as she spoke. "Would you like me to call you worm?"

"But that is what you are, Tolwyn," the Carredon said. "You are worms. You are stormers."

"We are storm knights!" she shouted, drawing her saber from its sheath.

"You are dead, little woman. Look around you. Your companions have fallen, like that last time we battled so many centuries ago. History repeats itself, and I see that you have failed to learn from it."

"I have learned enough, worm!"

Tolwyn launched herself at the dragon, slashing away with the saber. Her intensity drove the dragon backwards, but it would soon realize she was unable to truly hurt it. Then it would strike back.

Father Bryce desperately sought a solution to the problem of the Carredon when he heard the gentle song. He looked around and realized that the sound was coming from the blue and red stone.

"I hear you," he said. "I actually hear you."

132

Malcolm Kane held the young boy named Rat as a shield, daring the other boy to fire his rifle. Kane was impressed with the older youth so far, for he had not thrown the weapon away like Kane demanded, but instead made his own demand. But the game was still in the opening moves, and Kane would get his way. When he first saw the boys in front of the cave blocking his path of escape, he thought only to get past them and away as quickly as possible. But now that he was wrapped up in matters of death, he wanted to enjoy the experience.

"Very well, boy," Kane called, watching with satisfaction as the rifle shook in the youth's unsteady hands. "I'll tell you again. Drop the gun."

"Drop Rat," was the youth's response.

Kane merely smiled. Then he calmly jabbed the point of his knife into Rat's shoulder. The younger boy screamed.

"You bastard!" Coyote cried, aiming down the length

of the rifle's barrel.

"Are you good enough to pick me off, child?" Kane taunted. "I don't think you've ever even fired one of those. You could hit your friend. Or you could miss completely. Now drop the gun or I'll keeping cutting him until you do."

Kane smiled as the youth began to lower the rifle. As soon as the gun was out of his hands, Kane would kill the brat he held and go after the one called Coyote. He would leave both of them as evidence that this wasn't over yet. The priest still had to face him. He wanted the priest to remember that.

A noise on the ridge above them made Kane jerk his head. Something was crashing through the underbrush. He looked up to see a lizard man leap toward him. Instinctively, he dropped Rat and raised his knife. The lizard man smashed into him, and the two of them went sprawling. They landed dangerously close to the edge overlooking the river.

"Tal Tu!" Coyote yelled in relief. Then he saw that Tal Tu was still nursing his own wounds.

Kane struggled with the edeinos, trying to get his knife in position to stab. He noticed that the lizard had a wound that had been bandaged, but the dressing was soaked with the creature's blood.

"You should have stayed where they left you, lizard," Kane said, finally freeing his knife hand. He plunged the blade into Tal Tu's side, burying it as far as the hilt. The lizard was weak, and a few more stabs would bring it down. Kane slid the blade from the lizard, than plunged it in again.

"Die, lizard!" he screamed joyously, reveling in the blood and pain he inflicted.

He pulled the blade free again, and prepared to stab

at the lizard's chest. But before he could deliver the killing blow, Kane heard a loud crack. Pain shot through his body, starting in his shoulder and radiating outward. He realized that he had been shot, and the power of the impact was carrying him over the edge and into the air. He was falling, and his vision was fading. But he saw the smoking barrel of the rifle as Coyote lowered it from his eye.

Then he saw nothing but blackness as the raging river reached up to claim him.

133

Tolwyn never knew such fear. She was actually battling the creature that had killed her once before, and she knew she had no hope of defeating it now. That other time she had her sword and armor, and even those magical items were not enough to stay the Carredon's claws. Now all she had was a dress saber and the images of her friends falling; Alder, Kurst, Mara, Decker. Only Christopher remained standing, and he would fall quickly once she had spent herself.

But she could not stand by and simply let the dragon kill her. Alder had shown her that it could be hurt. She just had to figure out how to inflict that hurt in turn.

"Enough of these games, Tolwyn!" the Carredon yelled. It swung back at her, driving her away step by step with mighty swipes of its claws. "Lay down your weapon and I will make this death quick."

"Like you have for Decker?" she said, referring to the glowing rune staves jutting from his chest. But while it looked as though Decker should be dead, his chest continued to rise and fall with breath. "Never shall I simply surrender, monster!"

She fought on, intensifying her attack. She used every

move she could think of, every half-remembered skill that her body could call upon, searching for an opening. But no matter her skill and daring, she knew she could only last as long as her strength held out.

And the strength of the Carredon was far greater.

134

Christopher Bryce stood before the stone that Decker called the Heart of Coyote and listened to its song. There were no words to the song, and he could not hum the melody, but he knew it as a song nonetheless. It was a song of life, like the song of nature you could hear in a breeze, in the babble of a running brook, in a peaceful forest. But this song, while akin to those others, was louder, more intense. It sang of possibilities, for that was what life was. As long as there was life, there were endless possibilities.

And suddenly the stone filled his mind with one possible outcome to the battle that raged behind him. He reached out and grasped the stone.

135

Tolwyn was covered with cuts and scratches. Blood ran down her body, mingling with her perspiration. None were serious yet, but the total effect was painful. She blocked out the pain and continued to hack and stab at the Carredon, slicing deep cuts into its armor but unable to get to the soft flesh beneath.

Then Tolwyn slipped on a splash of blood, hitting the chamber floor hard.

The Carredon rose over her, victory shining in its evil eyes. "And now this ends, Tolwyn," it sneered.

"Yes, demon, it does!" yelled a powerful voice from elsewhere in the chamber.

The Carredon looked up to see Bryce. The priest held the blue and red stone firmly in his hands, pointing it at the dragon.

"Please, God," Father Bryce called out, "make the image I was shown come true!"

A beam of pure light burst from the stone and struck the Carredon in the chest. The energy danced across the dragon's armor, bathing the creature in lightning. The Carredon screamed in pain, but the energy seemed unable to penetrate the beast's scales. However, a portion of the light had been deflected by the armor. It bounced clear and wrapped itself around Tolwyn's saber, drawn to it like lightning to the highest tree.

As the dragon writhed in the pain caused by the light, Tolwyn watched as her saber blade glowed with the same power. She did not know what it meant, or why she wasn't being assaulted by the lighning as well. But she knew an opening when she saw one. The Carredon had dropped its defensive stance and forgotten about her as it vainly tried to brush away the crackling light.

With all the strength she had remaining, Tolwyn aimed her glowing blade at the Carredon's shoulder, at the spot where the creature had removed two of its scales. She screamed a war cry that rocked the chamber. Then she drove the blade home.

136

Quin Sebastian was on a plane heading for Houston, Texas. He wasn't sure why he had agreed to meet with the man he swore never to deal with again, but here he was. It had been a long time since Sebastian had last seen John Wells. It was when Quin had resigned from the agency, and Wells had accepted that resignation. Since then, Quin had been a freelancer, a soldier of fortune, using the skills the United States had taught him to help whoever could pay his fee. So why was he rushing to meet with newly-appointed President Wells?

"Because he asked you," Quin told himself.

He adjusted the airplane seat all the way back, closed his eyes, and tried to get some sleep before the plane touched down in Houston. That was a ritual with Sebastian — find sleep wherever you could, because it could be a long time before another opportunity presented itself.

When the stewardess came by with the complimentary dinner, Quin Sebastian was fast asleep.

137

Thratchen watched as the group boarded the helicopter. He saw that the man named Rick Alder was dead, for they sealed him in a black body bag. The others were in various states of pain, except for the priest and the boy named Coyote. Father Bryce was not hurt at all. But he did carry an eternity shard which he thought was safely hidden in his pack. Fool, Thratchen thought. You cannot hide an exposed shard from those who have come to rob them.

Of the others, Kurst, Mara, and Tal Tu had the worst wounds, but each would heal in time. The child named Rat had his arm in a sling and a bandage over the wound Kane had inflicted. Tolwyn was cut in a dozen places, but she had faced worse wounds over her career. Amazing that she had been able to take down the Carredon. The Gaunt Man would be very upset about that. Very upset.

Then Thratchen turned his attention to the still form of Andrew Decker. The magical rune staves were buried within his chest, their tops jutting out. Energy danced across the tops, jumping from one stave to the other and then into the air. Those were the runes of never life and never death, and that was the state they would leave Decker in until every possibility was drained from his body. Even now, the energy was flying to feed the Gaunt Man's machine in Orrorsh realm. It was too bad he had been removed from the experiment that Thratchen was conducting, for he appeared to be as powerful as Tolwyn and Mara.

The helicopter door was shut, and it lifted into the sky. Now the next phase of the experiment can begin, Thratchen thought. He only wished he had been able to find the body of Malcolm Kane, but the fast-moving river had claimed it. He wanted to make sure the youth's shot had done its job so that the Gaunt Man's agent could not interfere again. Ah well, the demon thought, I have other work to do and chances were Kane was dead. If he wasn't, then the stormers would have to deal with him themselves. As they had shown, they seemed quite capable of handling whatever was thrown at them.

With that thought, Thratchen spread his metal wings and flew out of the canyon.

138

Uthorion sat in his throne room, waiting for word from the Gaunt Man. He had to know if Tolwyn was dead yet, for he refused to set foot on Earth until that deed was accomplished. With him was Pope Jean Malraux, High Lord of Magna Verita. The false pope's realm had been established, as had Uthorion's, but neither had taken a personal hand in the conquest as yet. The false pope was waiting to make a grand entrance to play up the trappings of his theocratic reality. If it worked, many of the Earthers would flip over to his reality without the need for war.

And so the High Lords waited.

After a time, the wizard Delyndun entered the chamber. He was accompanied by a ravagon.

"My lord," Delyndun said, "this ravagon has brought a request from Baruk Kaah."

Uthorion rose to face the ravagon, moving Ardinay's body in a very male manner. "Speak, demon," he commanded with Ardinay's lips.

The ravagon looked from Uthorion to Malraux and back again. "The High Lord of Takta Ker has suffered a temporary setback. While he regains the strength he was forced to expend, he asks the powerful Uthorion to provide the assistance he once offered."

"What does the lizard want?" Uthorion demanded, hoping to cut through the protocol.

"He requests the Wild Hunt."

Uthorion smiled, twisting Ardinay's lips into an evil grin. "Tell the High Lord of Takta Ker that the Wild Hunt is his to use. It is on its way."

The ravagon bowed slightly, then left the throne room.

"Is that wise, Uthorion?" Malraux asked. "Do you really wish to put such destructive power in that savage's hands?"

"Of course, my friend," Uthorion laughed. "With this invitation I can send my greatest weapon into the land where Tolwyn roams. Let the Wild Hunt do Baruk Kaah's bidding. But when it finds Tolwyn, it will have special orders directly from me. Delyndun, call out the Hunt."

Epilogue

The storm has a name…
       — Katrina Tovarish

The Gaunt Man stood on the deck of his ship, staring out at the sea off the coast of Christmas Island, above the Java Trench. Rising out of the churning water was a great spinning vortex that disappeared into the dark clouds overhead. The vortex was the key to the Gaunt Man's plans. It was his greatest creation. For the vortex was the physical evidence that his infernal machine that rested on the ocean floor was working. It was sucking in the Earth's own energy, slowing its spin. The energy was being stored for the Gaunt Man's use when he set the final stages of his plan to gain the power of Torg in motion. Until then, Earth would continue to slow down until its energy was completely tapped.

"A remarkable sight," Scythak said, looking out at the vortex. "Only the Gaunt Man would think to tap a world's own energy to use in its destruction."

The demon Gibberfat, standing upon the railing, was also subdued by the tremendous display. "Your plans go well, master."

"Yes, Gibberfat, and I have another job for you," the Gaunt Man said.

The demon turned to face his master. "As per our agreement, I am yours to command."

"Then listen well. The infernal machine below us must be protected at all costs. It is the key to my plans, and even the other High Lords are ignorant of its purpose. It has minor guards now, but they need someone to lead them. That is the job I place before you, Gibberfat."

The demon stammered. "But … but, master. You want me to stay out here, in the ocean …?"

"Yes." There was no further discussion necessary, so the Gaunt Man walked away.

Scythak, however, remained. His hearty laugh carried across the ship. "Well, little demon, have fun with the fishes! Be careful they don't mistake you for a guppy and swallow you whole!"

The little demon glared at the hunter, then began to change. He grew larger, becoming so big that he dwarfed Scythak with his size. He leaned close, and the hunter could smell the brimstone on the demon's breath.

"You have a problem with size, Scythak," he said in a low, threatening voice. "Remember, no matter the size of the fish, there is always something larger. And it usually has teeth."

Then, before Scythak could respond, Gibberfat dived into the ocean, disappearing beneath the churning waves.

Here ends
Storm Knights,
Book One of the Possibility Wars.

The story of Tolwyn, Bryce and
the Storm Knights continues in
The Dark Realm,
Book Two of the Possibility Wars.

The
Saga
Continues ...

TORG™

The Dark Realm

Created by Greg Gorden and Bill Slavicsek

*Book Two
of the
Possibility Wars*

*Book Three
of the
Possibility Wars*

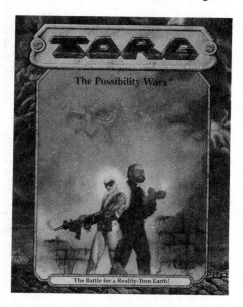